**In a world surrounded
by the fires of war,
they fought and loved as if
every day would be their last .**

GEOFFRY HIGGINS: The well-bred son
wealthy family commanded a gun turret o
battleship *Lion*. His death would plunge his
family into grief—and conflict.

RANDOLPH HIGGINS: A man of restless,
magnetic power, he went to Europe with a
squadron of Nieuport fighter planes—and
played in a reckless and deadly contest with the
greatest German ace.

BRENDA HIGGINS: The American wife of
Geoffry Higgins knew the effect she had on
men. Now she was a widow, and her passions
would take her where she dared not go.

LLOYD HIGGINS: Wounded on the French
front as a captain of England's most elite infantry unit, the Coldstreams, he had the right to
sit out the rest of the war. But the horror of the
front would keep coming back to him—until he
went back to it . . .

REGINALD HARGREAVES: His piercing eyes
caught the attention of Brenda Higgins the first
time they met. But his extraordinary naval
record catapulted him into the most dangerous
sea mission of the war—against the German
U-boats.

Y0-AGJ-608

ATTENTION: SCHOOLS AND CORPORATIONS

POPULAR LIBRARY books are available at quantity discounts with bulk purchase for educational, business, or sales promotional use. For information, please write to SPECIAL SALES DEPARTMENT, POPULAR LIBRARY, 666 FIFTH AVENUE, NEW YORK, N Y 10103

**ARE THERE POPULAR LIBRARY BOOKS
YOU WANT BUT CANNOT FIND IN YOUR LOCAL STORES?**

You can get any POPULAR LIBRARY title in print. Simply send title and retail price, plus 50¢ per order and 50¢ per copy to cover mailing and handling costs for each book desired. New York State and California residents add applicable sales tax. Enclose check or money order only, no cash please, to POPULAR LIBRARY, P. O. BOX 690, NEW YORK, N Y 10019

WAVES OF GLORY

PETER ALBANO

POPULAR LIBRARY

An Imprint of Warner Books, Inc.

A Warner Communications Company

POPULAR LIBRARY EDITION

Copyright © 1989 by Peter Albano
All rights reserved.

Popular Library® and the fanciful P design are registered trade-
marks of Warner Books, Inc.

Cover design by Jackie Merri Meyer
Cover illustration by Ron Lessor

Popular Library books are published by
Warner Books, Inc.
666 Fifth Avenue
New York, N.Y. 10103

 A Warner Communications Company

Printed in the United States of America

First Printing: October, 1989

10 9 8 7 6 5 4 3 2 1

11-7-89

Sandy —
Best wishes to a lovely
lady —

Peter Albano

To Kurt Warner and Dennis Ogren
for the inspiration and encouragement
they provided.

ACKNOWLEDGMENTS

I am indebted to Master Mariner Donald Brandmeyer who advised on problems confronting warships at sea. For solving problems encountered by pilots of antique pursuit planes, my grateful thanks to airline pilots William D. Wilkerson and Dennis D. Silver.

Finally, my gratitude to librarians Robin Swallow and Ann Rumery who helped lighten the heavy burden of research.

WAVES OF GLORY

Prologue

The North Sea, May 31, 1916

Turret captain Lieutenant Geoffry Higgins, R.N.R., despised the cold, windswept North Sea, particularly the Skagerrak where perennial banks of fog smothered the sea, deadening sounds and muting all colors to the putrescent gray of a day-old corpse. High on the compass platform of battle cruiser, "big cat" *Lion*, the turret captain shuddered as he stood between two lookouts and brought his glasses to his eyes and scanned directly over the bow to the southeast where the sky was low and twisting squalls of rain slanted from it like lead dust. If Admiral Hipper's battle cruiser force of *Lützow*, *Derfflinger*, *Seydlitz*, *Moltke*, and *Von der Tann* were over that horizon as reported by scouting destroyers and a single seaplane from seaplane carrier *Engadine*, they would be hard to see. Swinging his glasses with the short, jerky movements of a trained lookout, he glassed the horizon to the east and north where he found a buildup of thunderheads, tall ramparts, and buttresses turned purple and sullen leaden blue by the weak rays of the sun that filtered through the thin cirrus over the ship. And astern the five other ships of the first battle cruiser squadron steamed hard through *Lion*'s spreading white wake—*Princess Royal*, *Queen Mary*, *Tiger*, *New Zealand*, and *Indefatigable*—while all around a screen of twelve torpedo-boat destroyers charged, crashing through the seas recklessly like wolves scenting game, torpedoes ready, depth charges armed.

A severe shock staggered Geoffry and he brought both hands to the windscreen. The many moods and faces of the North Sea were changing. Since early morning freshening northeasterlies—Force 5 on the Beaufort scale—had

1

whipped the tops from the chop in ostrich plumes of spray. But now from the south row after row of combers advanced on *Lion* like legions of an implacable enemy, taking her hard on the starboard bow and sending reverberating shock waves through her plates and frames. But *Lion* fought back with her 29,680 tons of steel, her knifelike bow smashing and slashing through the combers, flinging spray and dun-colored water over her bows sometimes as high as the bridge.

Sighing, Higgins gave thanks for his lined greatcoat—the best fashionable Swan and Edgar had to offer—leather gloves and silk scarf. Yet, he was still cold—chilled to the bone. But it was not just the North Sea. They were there. Yes, indeed. The Hun was over the horizon. He was sure of it.

Thirty-six years of age, tall and slender with thinning brown hair and gray-green eyes, Geoffry's pale complexion had faded to a pasty hue of vanilla pudding, revealing to all the empty, sick feeling gripping his stomach this afternoon of May 31, 1916. *Lion*, the flagship of the grand fleet's first battle cruiser squadron with the bellicose Admiral Beatty on board, had left Rosyth the day before when Whitehall radio operators deciphered German signals ordering the entire German high seas fleet to sea. Now trailed by her five consorts, *Lion* prowled east, fulfilling her battle cruiser destiny —scouting and acting as a lure, hoping to bait the German High Seas Fleet into an imprudent charge into range of the Grand Fleet.

But Higgins felt none of the exhilaration that seemed to possess the other men in this horrifying hunt for like creatures of like intelligence. Instead, timorous spasms flowed from his viscera like electric waves, trembling his fingers and slackening his jaw despite efforts to clench his teeth and jut his chin like that bulldog first lord of the admiralty, Winston Churchill. Geoffry braced his feet and gripped the windscreen with new strength as the great warship took a particularly vicious roll. He could see most of the weather decks from the compass platform—actually the armored roof of the bridge and the highest point of the conning tower. Forward he could see the forecastle with its skylight over the wardroom and his own cabin in "officer country." Then turrets "A" and "B"—flat, squat vaults ironically armored with Krupp-cemented ten-inch plate, each with a pair of Vickers Mark V 13.5-inch guns jutting over the bow like gray tree trunks. Behind him was the control top with its range finder and fire control plot all hooked up to that unreliable new system of electric telegraphy called telephones that sometimes slipped without warning from one circuit to another, confusing everyone. Fortunately, the old reliable voice tubes were still in place, connecting the bridge to all turrets and battle stations. Just aft were two of the ship's three funnels; too close and capable of spewing coal smoke in his face when *Lion* was whipped by a quartering wind. Abaft the second funnel was his own "Q" turret stupidly mounted amidships on the forecastle deck forward of the third stack and limited to 120-degree arcs of fire on each beam.

"Reduces the bending moment to which the hull would have been subjected by locating all four turrets fore and aft," gunnery officer Anthony Saxon, R.N., had explained one evening in the wardroom when queried by Higgins.

"But I'm limited—one hundred twenty degrees," Geoffry had protested.

"We'll confine the Boche to our beams," Saxon had said with a smirk.

Laughter had rippled around the table. But there was no laughter in *Lion* now. No indeed. Not with reports of a German scouting force of five or six battle cruisers under that clever tormentor of the fleet, Admiral Franz von Hipper, just over the horizon.

Beneath his feet on the bridge he knew Vice Admiral Sir David Beatty and the ship's captain, A.E.M. Chatfield, strained at binoculars while ratings read engine revolutions from counters and the helmsman stood to the big spoked wheel, following his southeasterly course from the hooded light of the brass binnacle. But he didn't feel confident. A sudden fierce blast of Arctic-cold wind struck like a block of ice, whipping the breath from his lungs, singed his eyes until they watered, and brought a sudden longing for his wife and home at his family's estate, Fenwyck. Brenda. Brenda, his American wife; their warm bed, her soft body.

He preferred American women to Englishwomen who had grown up with Queen Victoria, armoring their souls with her preposterous morals and their bodies with layers of petticoats and undergarments. Bedding one was more difficult than breaking through the Turkish batteries in the Dardanelles. But Brenda was a different breed. She loved sex; responded to him with fire. Closing his eyes he could see her auburn hair spread on the pillow, eyes slitted, full lips twisted by waves of ecstasy as he drove into her. And she was his—only his. All men lusted after her: his brother Randolph, so randy semen seeped through his eardrums and who jig-a-jigged one of the maids regularly like a stable hand, caught Brenda's scent the moment he brought her home to Fenwyck. And his father, Walter: the old lecher pointed his ears and arched his back whenever she passed him. But she belonged to him, Geoffry Higgins, and to no other.

Suddenly, as so often happens to lonely men at sea, the memory became real, she was on the platform, and he could feel her against him, the soft malleable body shaping itself to his own so that he could feel her from knees to firm young bosom, the heat of her soaking through his heavy foul-weather clothing, igniting a long-dormant fire deep in his groin.

"They've laid out tea in the wardroom, old boy," a casual voice mumbled suddenly, jarring him from his thoughts. "Better have a spot before we have a go at the Hun. They're out there somewhere."

Without turning, Higgins knew Commander Anthony Saxon, *Lion*'s range-taking officer, was standing at his left elbow. He disliked the brusque, low-class son of a Newcastle miner who had risen from the ranks. Poorly educated in public schools, Saxon slurred syllables together through the thick red lips of a sensualist, speaking in short bursts with his head canted birdlike to one side, eyelids heavy and drooping like the hooded eyes of a falcon. However, the most galling aspect of the man was the superior bearing of one of inferior breeding looking down on Geoffry with the usual disdain "regulars" reserved for "temporaries." Built as wide as a door, the gunnery officer worked hard at acquiring the "salty" look: light brown hair bleached in silver white streaks from sun with darker splashes beneath; face driven and weathered to honey gold leather so that the intense blue of his eyes paled in contrast. Geoffry did not belong here with men like this. He was a civilian playing at war while Saxon wallowed in it.

A cough into a cupped hand cleared Higgins's throat but not his mind. Forcing his wife's memory back into the recesses with a physical effort, he spoke in a high nasal twang. "Thank you, sir. But if 'Kaiser Willy's' ships are out there," —he waved with exaggerated bravado—"we'll be at battle stations soon and I may be battened down in Q turret for hours."

"Give them a full one hundred twenty degrees of fire power, Lieutenant."

"That wasn't necessary, sir," Higgins said, bristling.

Saxon dropped his glasses. "Sorry, old boy . . ."

He was halted by an excited shout from the foretop. "Smoke! Ships, fine off the starboard bow!"

Higgins, Saxon, and the two lookouts raised their glasses as one to the starboard bow. Cursing the fog and muttering "Green forty" to the lookouts, Geoffry moved his focusing knob. Suddenly, the fog broke and the sun poured down in a cold golden shaft of light between gashes in the clouds and he saw them under a black cloud of coal smoke hulled down on the horizon—fighting tops; either battleships, battle cruisers, or both. And torpedo-boat destroyers.

"Enemy in sight!" came from the voice tube. Then the blare of a bugle. "Action stations!"

Saxon whirled toward the door to the main director station while a trembling Geoffry dropped his glasses from numb fingers and stepped to the ladder.

Commander Anthony Saxon could never adjust his big bulk to the close quarters of the director room. An eight-by-twelve-foot box plated with two-inch steel, it was placed between the compass platform and number one stack. From this position one hundred twenty-four feet above the waterline, the fire control crew had a horizon of almost fifteen thousand yards. But the room was jammed with range finders, communications equipment, calculators, and twelve men sweating the subtle odors of fear.

Dominating the steel box was the new Dreyer fire control table. Bewilderingly complicated, the eight-foot table was manned by Sublieutenant Joseph Booth and three P.O.s who faced a jungle of dials and machinery, which included a clock range screw, clock range scale, rate grid, deflection master transmitter, bearing plot, own course plot, range clock, gun range counter, spotting plot, a complete Dumaresq calculator, and even a typewriter. Its banks of dials could be set with the target's estimated speed, bearing, and range, and the known course and speed of *Lion.* Also weighed in were data for wind force, direction, wear of guns, drift of shells imparted by rifling twist, and air temperature, which affected the propelling powers of cordite. In theory it was a highly sophisticated and efficient system that juggled all these factors in its spindles, springs, and wires for a moment and then produced a set of instructions that gave gunlayers the degree of barrel elevation, told the gun trainers the angle of deflection the barrels must be turned from the ship's center line, and even produced a rate of change of range to keep the fall of shot on target as *Lion*'s relative position to her target changed. The machine was a real marvel on paper but produced nothing except distrust in Commander Saxon. In his mind F.C. Dreyer, Henry Ford, and Tommy Sopwith were all lunatics who belonged in the same asylum. He was a nineteenth-century man who preferred to find his target in his cross hairs, try a few ranging shots, correct and salvo fire. These newfangled machines were too complex, consumed time that could never be bought back, and tended to fire long with maddening regularity.

Grunting, Saxon slipped on his headset as he seated himself in front of the eight-light panel of the gun-ready board of the Scott-Vickers gun-director system and pulled down the fifteen-power lens of his periscope so that the rubber-molded eyepiece was just above his forehead. Then the flick of a switch opened his earphones to the gunnery circuit, connecting him to the bridge, turrets "A," "B," "Q," and "Y," the after director and spotters atop the mainmast and stern mast.

Already, leading seaman Ian Edwards and C.P.O. Archie Strutt were seated next to him in their pointer's and trainer's seats, testing handwheels as they stared into the lenses of their periscopes, which led to the telescopes projecting above the director room.

"Manned and ready, sir," they chorused.

"Very well." Saxon turned to his left where midshipman Bertram Ramsey pressed his face to the rubber-padded eyepiece of the main range finder—a sixteen-foot Barr and Stroud optical range finder that towered above the director room like the ears of a giant rabbit. He was flanked by his two assistants seated in high steel chairs attached to the postlike shaft of the Barr and Stroud: Sean Henderson, a skinny range taker from Sussex, and a young ox of a farm boy from Nottinghamshire named Ethan Blakemore who read bearings. But every man and all this equipment worth thousands of pounds were useless until young Ramsey brought the split images of the target together in his lenses.

"Manned and ready, sir," Ramsey piped in a high, taut voice and a rolling of Rs that spoke unmistakably of Scottish heritage.

A voice crackled tinnily in Saxon's earphones. "All stations muster."

"Manned and ready," Sublieutenant Booth said from deep in his throat, turning from the Dreyer apparatus.

"Main director manned and ready," the commander shouted into the phones just after the captain of "Y" turret made his report.

Captain Chatfield's voice, not quite masking a timbre of anxiety, was in his earphones: "Five battle cruisers in a column, steaming one-three-zero, speed twenty-four, eight torpedo-boat destroyers screening." He was halted by a cough; returned with a stronger voice of command, "All ahead flank, come right to one-four-zero, fire control—all hoists filled, armor piercing, full charge powder, wind force four from zero-four-zero, temperature of cordite sixty-two degrees. We have five enemy capital ships at green forty, range seventeen thousand." And the words that chilled Anthony's soul and sent ice cold insects crawling up his spine, "Ship's main and secondary armament, load! Commence firing on our corresponding ship. Signal bridge make the hoist, engage corresponding ship. Execute!"

Now the fate of the ship and perhaps the outcome of the battle itself was in his hands, hinging on the speed and efficiency of his crew. Gripping the gun-ready board, he could feel new vibrations as *Lion*'s sweating stokers, stripped to the waist and blackened by coal dust, fed her forty-two Yarrow boilers with wide-mouthed shovels, spinning the four Parsons turbines until they shrieked their objections, delivering 73,800 horsepower to her four shafts and driving her through the sea at twenty-eight knots.

Anxiously, his eyes moved to Booth and his assistants who leaned over the Dreyer table, a pair furiously turning dials while the fingers of the third, a yeoman, flew over the typewriter. Looking up, Sublieutenant Booth's usually handsome, unexpressive visage was suddenly twisted by new ugly lines born of fear as he shouted at Commander Saxon, "Range? Bearing, Commander?"

Saxon whirled to the range finder crew. "Mister Ramsey! Confound it, man—give me a bloody range and bearing on our corresponding ship. The whole British Empire is waiting."

"It's foggy, sir, and the sun's behind them," the midshipman pleaded, turning a pair of cranks with quick, jerky movements, striving to bring the two halves of the enemy ship together in his lenses. Every man stared and fidgeted while the seconds passed like dripping oil. After an eternity, the young range finder finally shouted through tight lips, "On target! Mark!"

"Range sixteen thousand six-zero-zero," Henderson shouted, reading a scale attached to the tube.

"Bearing green forty-three," Blakemore added, reading another vernier.

"Too bloody close," Anthony Saxon muttered under his breath, knowing the fog had cost them the one-thousand-yard advantage in range their 13.5-inch guns had over the Germans' 12-inch cannons. He turned to Lieutenant Booth, who scanned the bearing plot while cranking the "own course" handle of the Dreyer machine. "Damn it, man," the gunnery officer persisted. "Can't you read it? We've got to start ranging before we take a broadside."

Booth's voice was high like a taut violin string. "Elevation two-four-zero-zero minutes, direction lead ship forty-three degrees, deflection thirty-seven left, range one hundred minus sixteen thousand five-zero-zero."

Instantly, Saxon set his deflection and elevation dials, knowing turret captains in all four turrets were at that moment reading identical dials repeating his settings. Within seconds, eight red lights glowed on his gun-ready board and he felt the Scott-Vickers control chair begin to turn as Edwards and Strutt brought their telescopes to the target. "On target," they chorused.

"Very well." Saxon shouted into the phone, "Left gun, 'A' turret—fire!" He threw a switch and a small gong much like the bell rung by an altar boy at Mass began to chime. On the third strike there was the sound of a great cathedral door slamming, a whoosh, and the director moved under the commander's hands. Pencils, dividers, parallel rules, and the Dreyer machine vibrated and rattled. "Watch for the fall of shot," he shouted at the men at the scopes.

Saxon disliked the British system of range finding: one round either short or long, observe, correct, fire another, approach target, straddle, and then main armament rapid fire. Everyone knew the Germans used the ladder system, which the commander felt was superior: main armament ladder short, main armament ladder over, down ladder, range found, main armament rapid fire.

"Over one-five-zero-zero," Ramsey said, eyes glued to the range finder.

"Damn! Damn! That bloody machine's always long," Saxon exploded. "Give me another reading, Mister Booth."

"Elevation two-three-three-zero minutes, direction zero-four-zero degrees, deflection three-four left, range one hundred minus fifteen thousand five-zero-zero yards," Booth said staring at the Dreyer, perspiration beading in glistening lines across his forehead.

Saxon bawled the corrections into his phone. Again the acknowledgment, the chimes, the concussion.

"Five hundred over," Ramsey said. Then gasping the most fearful words a man fighting at sea can hear, "They've opened up on us."

There was a sound like the Royal Scot rumbling over a bridge followed by the unmistakable thunder of twelve-inch shells ripping the sea with thousands of pounds of high explosives. Then the clatter of steel splinters striking armor plate like thrown gravel.

"Close. Close," Saxon muttered to himself. Unbelievably close for an opening salvo. Damn those Zeiss range finders. The Germans had the best in the world. The commander took a chance. Curling his hand around the pistol grip of the main firing trigger, he shouted into his phone while adjusting his dials, "Ship's main armament salvo fire, elevation two-three-two-five minutes, direction zero-four-zero, deflection three-four left, range one hundred minus fifteen thousand five-zero-zero yards."

Eight lights glowed. "Fire!" The gongs rang and he squeezed the trigger. With a shock like a collision at sea, eight 13.5-inch guns fired as one, rocking the ship from side to side. Snapping like a serpent searching for quarry, the drafting machine mounted above the Dreyer's rate grid broke its lock and swung across the plotting sheet. Cursing, Ramsey rubbed an eye, bruised by the range finder's eye pad. A yeoman of signals manning the new electric telegraphy phones staggered and fell heavily against the aft bulkhead while dust and chips of paint rained.

"Under! Under two hundred," Ramsey shouted. "And they've increased speed—direction zero-four-two."

"Deflection! Blast it, man—deflection?" Saxon bellowed angrily.

"The same, sir."

"Very well." And then to Booth, "Plot it."

Quickly, Booth and his men reset dials and marked grids on the Dreyer. With a single twist of a clawlike hand, the young lieutenant turned the clock range screw and stared at the bearing plot grid all the while chewing his lower lip until it was flecked with blood. Then with his lips skinned back, he spoke hoarsely. "Elevation two-four-three-zero minutes, direction zero-four-one degrees, deflection unchanged, range fifteen thousand six hundred yards."

"Very well." Saxon called the changes into the phone as he adjusted his dials. Lights, chimes, and the trigger. The ship staggered and rocked.

The next four minutes—the last four minutes in the life of Commander Anthony Saxon, D.S.O., M.B.E.—were a lifetime compressed into 240 seconds. A lifetime of exhilaration and terror. *Lion*, leading her squadron, was locked in a duel with battle cruiser *Lützow*, which headed the German column. The Germans had the advantage of the sun behind them to illuminate the British and a mist haze to conceal themselves from the English range takers while the British used their superior speed to block the enemy's route back to base at Wilhelmshaven and at the same time tried to maneuver the five enemy vessels into range of the Grand Fleet.

Unable to contain his curiosity and knowing at least forty seconds were required between salvos to bring the guns back to battery and reload, the commander grabbed his periscope and focused on the enemy battle line. Wide-eyed, he stared into a scene stolen from Dante Alighieri's *Inferno*, glassing five great behemoths, charging through shrouds of mist and black and brown clouds of fog, coal smoke, and burned gunpowder. And they flashed with lightning that rippled up and down their line as they salvo fired, lighting the smoke and mist with their fury while British shells crashed down among them, raising two-hundred-foot towers of water greened by the burning picric acid of exploding lyddite. Between glances, the lights, the chimes, and the trigger.

"We've 'it her—by God, we've 'it the bloody blighter," came from the cockney voice of a spotter high on the mainmast. Saxon heard cheers.

Eye pressed to the rubber-lined eyepiece, Saxon saw

flashes on *Lützow*'s bridge and more flashes on the forecastle. With the range down to 13,000 yards and with fifteen power magnification, he saw at least four 13.5-inch shells blast great chunks of plating, debris, and men high into the sky, twisting and turning, raining into the sea. But the German shells roared in, landing in evenly spaced rows, precise, regimented towers. Shocked, the gunnery officer watched as *Lützow* fired a full salvo and he actually saw eight 12-inch shells approach lazily like huge bluebottles, thundering into the sea two hundred yards short, two not exploding, richocheting and lolloping crazily over *Lion*. Her next salvo was over.

"Bracketed! The bloody bastards have bracketed us," Saxon muttered as he squeezed the trigger.

He heard the cockney's frantic report in his earphones. "Crikey! The fuckers 'ave hit *Indefatigable*!"

Focusing far aft to the last ship in their column, Saxon saw a glow and then flames leapt from the trailing battle cruiser amidships. With horror, he watched as she vanished in a giant yellow white pillar of flame that hurled "B" and "Q" turrets and most of her superstructure intact hundreds of feet into the air while strakes of plates, twisted wreckage, and men were consumed by a panorama of flames and spark-dappled smoke, raining and pockmarking the sea in a radius of at least a mile. Then there was nothing—absolutely nothing at all except the usual grave markers of the sea—casks, broken planking, shattered boats, debris, bodies, all bobbing as air escaped from the sunken, dead hull and erupted on the surface in huge green-gray geysers.

His numbed brain brought back something he heard Admiral Beatty say about the slaughter at Dogger Bank: "It was like egg shells battering each other with hammers."

The howl of an approaching coven of banshees tore him from the lens and a cold snake unwound in his stomach as he realized *Lützow* had the range. Gripping the gun-ready board with wet palms, he held his breath, hunched, and pulled his head down into his shoulders like a frightened turtle. The other eleven men in the compartment all mirrored the gunnery officer, turning pasty white faces to starboard and the approaching hell. There was the sound of ripping canvas overhead. Detonations. The clank of metal on metal. Raining gravel.

"Over! They're over," came through the earphones.

But the shells were not all long. A defective barrel liner dropped one shot short and Saxon felt a single thud, followed by a deafening report as a large-caliber shell hit the foretop. Edwards and Strutt were hurled from their seats, the Dreyer table jumped up and down, snapping its deck bolts, and its Dumaresq calculator and rate grid clattered to the deck. Despite holding desperately to the gun-ready board, the commander was lifted from the seat as if catapulted, only held back from smashing his head into the overhead by his firm grip and the powerful muscles of his arms and shoulders. Then gagging on the nitric acid stink of explosives and twisting, he managed to straddle his seat again and plant his feet on the deck. However, midshipman Ramsey screamed in pain and fell to the deck, gripping his forehead, blood oozing through his fingers from a gash ripped in his head by the crazily tilting periscope of the Barr and Stroud range finder, twisted and bent, hanging from the overhead by a single bracket.

Coughing acrid smoke from his lungs and blinking stinging moisture from his eyes, Saxon managed to say, "Henderson, Blakemore—help Mister Ramsey to the sick bay."

Dazed, Ramsey's two P.O.s pulled the midshipman to his feet and turned to the door.

The high, keening shriek of an animal in pain turned the commander to the Dreyer table. Sublieutenant Booth and his three ratings were all down. One, David Hollingsworth, a pink-faced tanner's son from Camden Town, was a hideous confusion of angles. Crumpled on his side, his head was twisted on fractured vertebrae all the way around so that he stared at the commander over his left shoulder, eyes wide open like ivory billiard balls while his right leg was broken at the hip and stretched upward in an impossible kick, foot resting on the side of his broken neck. The yeoman was sprawled on top of Sublieutenant Booth, lower jaw smashed, exposing broken teeth and a shredded tongue. Again and again the yeoman screamed, choking, spraying blood, strangling on his own gore. The third rating sat numbly, back braced against the table.

Choking back a sour gorge rising in his throat, Saxon set his jaw grimly. "Out, Mister Booth—all of you. To the sick bay. We can't fight a war with all this bloody noise."

Gripping the Dreyer table, Booth and the uninjured rating slowly came to their feet. "And him?" the sublieutenant asked, gesturing at the grotesquely twisted corpse.

"He's quiet. Leave him."

Carefully, Booth and the rating pulled the gagging yeoman upright, undogged the door, and left.

Captain Chatfield's voice in the commander's earphones turned his head. "Main director—damage report."

"Casualties. One dead, at least two wounded. Main range finder out, Dreyer table out," Saxon answered. He turned to Edwards and Strutt who had regained their seats and were staring into their lenses.

"Manned and ready," they both said doggedly.

The gunnery officer spoke into his phone. "We can resume fire control from our Scott-Vickers gun director, sir."

"Very well. The after director is out." The rumble of an approaching salvo turned his head. He heard Strutt praying. Chatfield's voice droned on, "Commander Saxon, I want . . ." There was a thud deep in the ship, a sound like an immense temple gong, and *Lion* leapt and twisted like a mortally wounded warrior. The gunnery circuit went dead.

"Blast it all!" the gunnery officer shouted, pounding his earphones with open palms. A strange voice stopped the hands in midswing and the commander sat like a Buddhist in prayer, listening—". . . starboard side between frames forty-two and forty-six, a heavy shell has penetrated the side armor and burst in the starboard dynamo room, penetrated engine room three, cut through the fresh- and saltwater mains, severed the H.P. air pressure ring main. There is saltwater in engine room three—smoke, gauges can only be read by the aid of torches . . ."

"Damage control—blast it!" Knowing the ship's electric telegraphy system had been damaged, he tore the earphones from his head and leaned over a clutch of voice tubes bolted to the left side of the gun-ready board. Opening one, he blew into it, raising a shrill whistling sound—a sound that grew and grew even after the commander stopped blowing. "These won't be over," he said grimly to himself. Both Edwards and Strutt were praying, but God had turned his back on *Lion* this day.

There was a bone-rattling shock, the clang of steel on steel, a flash, and an earsplitting roar followed by blackness, screams, Strutt crying "Mother," unbearable heat, then pain as something massive struck Saxon's chest, driving his breath from his lungs through a constricted channel that compressed his last breath into a shriek of pain and anger like the high, mindless keening of steam from a kettle. He felt himself lifted and flung skyward in a dream, turning and twisting into the cosmos. Then something darker than black engulfed him like the folds of a cloak as big as the universe.

Fifty seconds after leaving the compass platform, turret captain Lieutenant Geoffry Higgins entered "Q" turret through the single small hatch mounted in the rear of the turret above the barbette—a small opening protected by the massive steel overhang of the turret itself. Quickly, he moved to his station next to the emergency shell bin and in front of the range finder. Charged with adrenaline and churning with an amalgam of excitement and fear, he ignored his padded chair and stood facing a gun-ready board mounted on a partial bulkhead duplicating Commander Saxon's. Next to the board was the firing key that had two positions: "Director" and "Local." Below the firing key and appearing much like the ignition switch on his Rolls Royce Silver Ghost was the power supply key with two settings: "AC" and "Battery." Overhead was his periscope and to his right stood a small table with a plotting sheet, drafting machine, dividers, and parallel rules. Above the table a calculator—a small Dumaresq machine—was bolted to the partial bulkhead with settings for elevation, bearing, deflection, cordite temperature, muzzle velocity, and all of the other factors required if ever the main director were knocked

out of action and "Q" turret fired from local control. Below
the calculator the big red fire emergency switch jutted from
the panel. Connected to the magazines on a direct line, the
switch set off a gong in the magazines that were flooded
immediately by the "Chief Powder Monkey," who simply
turned a valve one counterclockwise turn, releasing tons of
water instantly and inevitably drowning some of his men
along with the explosives.

Snapping on his headset, Higgins looked down into the
gun bay where his two gun captains manned their stations.
Gunner Dennis Harwich, a burly black-haired youth from
Bournemouth, was standing next to the breech of the right
gun, hand on breech lever. The left gun captain was Gunner
Stephen Chalmers, a bright-eyed, blond musician and music
hall singer from Pembrokeshire. With an uncanny ear for
music, he could sing the lyrics of scores of popular songs
from memory: "Farewell, Leicester Square," "Little Gray
Home in the West," "Oh, You Beautiful Doll," "A Broken
Doll," "Tipperary" were just a few of the melodies he knew
by heart, apparently learning the words after just hearing a
song once. But he was not singing now. Instead, he was
hastily adjusting his gloves and pulling down the long
sleeves of the wool flash-resistant clothes every man in the
sixty-man crew of the turret and magazines wore.

Geoffry loathed the tight, hot flash clothes that even fit
down over his head and cheeks with holes for earphones.
But if ever the powder . . . He shuddered, choking back the
sour taste of vomit rising in his dry throat, mind racing with
a strange confusion of thoughts. *Why am I here? God, king,
and country? Family tradition?* It was more than that. And
then he glimpsed a truth. War was a magnet to youth that
must risk life to prove manhood while other men watched.
And there was fear of missing this great event, this enormous exclamation mark in history. But he could die. Lose
Brenda forever. Then the questions that plague all men just
before engaging other men in the game of death called war
raced through his mind: *Will I stand up? Be brave? Conduct
myself like a man?*

Captain Chatfield's voice rasped tinnily in his earphones,

shocking him from his musings: "Main armament—director fire. All turrets acknowledge."

With trembling fingers Geoffry reached up to the gun-ready board and threw the firing key to "Director" and the power supply key to "AC." Then after hearing "B" turret acknowledge, he spoke into his phone, "'Q' turret on 'Director' control and ship's current."

"Very well. All stations muster," came back through his earphones.

Anxiously, he stared down at the left gun where Chalmers finally took his station next to the vaultlike breech. The gun was fully manned, the rammerman facing the breech and seated next to a lever reminiscent of an automobile's emergency brake with two settings, "Ram" and "Withdraw." In front of the rammerman and in direct line with his hydraulic ram and the breech was the loading tray, a curved polished brass surface like a baby's bassinet wide enough for a single 1,250-pound shell or two 640-pound bags of powder. To the left of the rammerman, the powder hoist operator sat beside his powder cradle, ready to throw a switch that would dump two bags of powder into the loading tray. Behind the gun captain and in front of the rammerman stood the primerman who loaded shells into the tray by pushing a foot lever activating a hydraulic lift that tilted and rolled a shell into the loading tray.

Geoffry darted his eyes to the shell hoist. Only one shell —coded black for armor piercing—was visible. But he knew the hoist was filled all the way to the magazine and the powder hoist, too, filled with silk-bagged cordite. Dangerous. Very dangerous. A mixture of nitroglycerine and nitrocellulose. The admiralty had replaced gunpowder and guncotton with the new propellant because of its slower burning, accelerating a shell along the length of the bore of a gun instead of decelerating, which was the tendency after the massive initial ignition of gunpowder. But cordite was highly unstable. Volatile. Even the introduction of a petroleum jelly-based solvent failed to slow the threat of "flash off" in the event of accidental ignition. The Germans encased theirs in brass; however, here, in *Lion*, Geoffry stared at flammable, old-fashioned silk bags.

And there was a scuttlebutt that after magazine fires ravaged *Seydlitz* off Dogger Bank, the Germans had installed baffles in their turrets, baring flash downs to their magazines in the event of turret fires. But standing at his station staring down into the gun bay, Higgins saw loaded hoists, filled with shells and cordite, unimpeded all the way down to the magazines.

He heard the crater-deep voice of the magazine commander, Marine Major Francis J.W. Harvey, a tough veteran of Indian and South African campaigns, in his earphones: "Magazines manned and ready."

"Battery?" Geoffry shouted.

"Right gun manned and ready, sir," Harwich answered.

"Left gun manned and ready, sir," Chalmers sang out with his unmistakable Welsh burr.

And then from behind, "Range finder manned and ready, sir." Without looking, Geoffry knew that Sublieutenant George Halstead and his two P.O.s were manning their station at the rear of the turret—a Barr and Stroud range finder, a smaller version of the range finder mounted in the main director, and only to be used in the event both the main director and the aft station were disabled. Geoffry liked young Halstead. The son of a wealthy viscount who owned over twenty thousand acres near Tunbridge in his own county of Kent, the youngster showed breeding. A graduate of Oxford, he dressed impeccably, obviously shopping at stores as stylish as Swan and Edgar, Selfridge's, and Harrods.

Nodding, Geoffry barked into his phone, "'Q' turret manned and ready. All hoists filled with full charge powder and A.P. shells."

Captain Chatfield's voice came back reporting the enemy ships only seventeen thousand yards away and a cold, heavy lump of dread began to grow under the turret captain's ribs. *Too close!*

Immediately, the captain's order came that told all hands the ship was irrevocably committed and that they were all at risk to face some of the most hideous deaths contrived by man: "Ship's main and secondary armament load! Signal bridge, make the hoist, engage corresponding ship. Execute!"

Geoffry took a deep breath and then shouted, "Load!" with a steady timbre in his voice that surprised him.

Simultaneously, Harwich and Chalmers struck the breechblock locking levers with the palms of their hands and the massive, perfectly balanced breechblocks swung open. Hinged at the bottom, the great doors dropped down like foot-thick tables, convex "mushroom" faces of gleaming stainless steel surrounded by the ridges of their interrupted screw threads, exposing cavernous firing chambers. The Bank of England, Geoffry thought. Big as a vault.

Although Geoffry's earphones buzzed with sighting reports, commands, and musters, he knew he could do no more than load his weapons and wait for Saxon's commands. With turret silence in force, Harwich and Chalmers flashed their hand signals like choreographed mimes on stage at the Savoy. They were the best, bringing an old navy saying to mind: "Officers lead, P.O.s drive."

The turret captain liked to watch Harwich who moved as gracefully as Harry Lauder in one of his loose-limbed dance routines. Bending over the breechblock, the gunner extended one hand, palm down. Instantly, the primerman pressed a pedal and a 1,250-pound projectile rolled into the loading tray. A thumb forward through a short arc and the rammerman threw his lever to "Load" and the hydraulic ram—playfully painted by Harwich with the red and black head of a cobra with huge yellow eyes—leapt from its cylinder like an attacking serpent, driving the shell into the firing chamber. He flicked his thumb in the opposite direction and the cobra withdrew. Harwich turned a palm up and the powder hoist operator threw a switch and two 640-pound bags of cordite rolled into the tray. Quickly, the primerman and gun captain aligned them, then the ram drove and withdrew. Two more bags of powder were loaded before a palm on the breech-locking lever activated a hydraulic drive, sending the breechblock hissing into the breech, threads turning fifteen degrees and locking with a loud click. With a hard twist, the gun captain turned his locking lever while thumbing a button just to the right of the breech. A red light glowed on Geoffry's gun-ready board. Then Chalmers's left gun light came to life, followed by six more lights as all of the ship's 13.5-inch guns were loaded.

Geoffry spoke into his phone, "'Q' turret. Both guns loaded."

"Very well," Saxon's voice responded.

With every man staring at him, Higgins watched the deflection and elevation dials of his Dumaresq calculator. At last they moved. "Gunlayers," he shouted into his phone. "Elevation two-four-zero-zero minutes, direction forty-three degrees, deflection thirty-seven left."

There was a whine of electric motors and the turret began to move, controlled by two men Geoffry could not see: the trainer who was seated in the left front of the turret, and the pointer who bent over his crank in his tiny compartment on the starboard side. Slowly, the turret turned to the right on its rack and pinion gear as the trainer cranked his motor to life while the breeches dropped, answering the pointer's gear, elevating on polished steel trunnions like the fulcrums of perfectly balanced children's teeter-totters.

Anxiously, the turret captain watched his elevation and deflection indicators until they coincided with Saxon's. Immediately, he pushed his ready button. Now he must wait, listen to the flurries of commands on the gunnery circuit as *Lion* and her adversary probed with ranging shots, squaring off for their moment of truth. But there were no rules—no Marquis of Queensberry. It was kill—or be killed.

He felt pressure mount in his chest like an uncoiling spring and his dry throat was lined with sandpaper. Strangely, the excitement seemed sexual in intensity and Brenda was back. In his mind's eye he saw her again—the way she looked the first time they met. It was in her family's mansion on New York's fashionable Fifth Avenue. He had been seated in the study with her father, John Ashcroft, discussing a textile merger, when she glided in as if moving to music. Sheathed in a tight green silk chemise that clung to her slim body like mist to an undulating landscape, her narrow waist was spectacular, flaring into hips sculpted like the curve of a Venetian vase. Her breasts were large, perfectly formed and pressed so hard against the silk he could see her nipples.

He had known many women during his business travels as the young owner of one of England's biggest textile firms: Nicole in Paris, Nona in Birmingham, Jacqueline in Bristol stood out. And there had been dozens more, most just faces and purses. All had been beautiful—select and choice, befitting a man of his station. Yet, they were ordinary when compared with Brenda. She had a long aristocratic neck that balanced her head like an orchid on its stem. A straight chiseled nose and large azure eyes above high cheekbones gave her face a Grecian flair. Fine silky hair tumbled to her shoulders in lustrous folds like watered silk. Colored the rich hues of a tropical sunset, it flickered with glowing red evening stars each time she moved her head. Yet, he never knew, never was aware of her true beauty until their honeymoon at Cannes when he first saw her naked. Her skin was hot marble, her breasts even larger than he thought, hard round areolas growing like buttons under his lips. And his tongue found hers between the small perfect teeth, a slithering serpent dwelling in a wet, hot lair. He remembered thrusting into her, mad with desire. Her moans. Again and again . . .

"Left gun 'A' turret, fire!" came through his earphones. The chimes rang, he felt the ship tremble, and the corrections came through. Frantically, he reset his dials, relayed the commands to his gunlayers. More ranging shots, changes, and the first German salvo avalanched in, the dull thudding roar shaking the turret, vibrating up from the floor plates to meet in his middle—in his guts and genitals. With each new salvo, the hair on his forearms and at the back of his neck came erect and his bowels seemed to drop out of his body. Brenda was gone now; was only part of the past; could not exist in the future because now he knew in war there is no real future.

Suddenly, his mind was filled with the greatest horror—a dread that always lurked in the shadows of his mind, even in his dreams; the nightmare of all men who fight at sea. The ship was sinking and he was trapped in a pitch black compartment, water pressure superheating the air, tearing bulkheads from their frames, rupturing watertight doors while the cold sea roared in to claim its screaming victims.

Mercifully, he was shocked from the horrific vision by Saxon's shout of "Ship's main armament, salvo fire!" The chimes began and the gun captains stepped to the sides of the breeches. Every man was a statue. Despite his gripping the panel, the concussion of eight 13.5-inch guns firing as one staggered Geoffry.

Like twin battering rams, the two cannons recoiled a full two feet into their gun pits while a great roar filled the turret. Deck plates rattled, the ship heeled and staggered sending the parallel rules sliding off the plotting sheet. A loose rivet popped from the calculator, stinging Geoffry's cheek before ricocheting to the deck. Dust drifted down from the overhead.

"Load! Load! Continuous fire!" Geoffry shouted, pulling a reddened finger from his bleeding cheek. Blood. A glorious wound. He almost laughed thinking of his heroic return home, cheek bandaged, a Victoria Cross hanging from his neck.

Automatically, the well-drilled gunlayers brought the guns back to battery and the two gun captains opened the breechblocks. Smelling like incinerated paint thinner and paneling, the stench of burned cordite filled the turret. There was the hiss of high-pressure compressed air as both barrels were blown clean, then the gun captains wiped the "mushrooms" with damp cloths while sticking their heads into the yawning firing chambers, looking for the tiny bit of burning silk that could destroy the ship. Again, the silent palm-waving ritual, the lights, and "Q" turret was ready to deliver her load of death.

More corrections, a resetting of dials, the chimes, the concussion. Like jolts of summer thunder, the German shells kept roaring in, laddering closer. *Lion* was in trouble and every man knew it. Then Higgins's spirits soared as the cockney voice came through his earphones, "We've 'it 'er—by crikey, we've 'it the bloody blighter!"

But then came the cockney's reports of hits on *Indefatigable* and cataclysm. Higgins pulled down his periscope, saw the Vesuvian horror astern, the great mushroom-shaped column of smoke standing three thousand feet tall. More corrections. Salvo firing. He was becoming numb, like a machine.

There was a thud like someone had swatted a fly next to his ear and the dials on his calculator spun crazily. The main director. Saxon's grim casualty report came through his headset, but the commander would not relinquish fire control.

Geoffry turned to Sublieutenant Halstead who was peering through the eyepiece of his range finder. "Stand by to take over. The main director's caught one and the aft director's out."

"Ranging, sir," the sublieutenant answered, training the periscope around. Then Geoffry heard Halstead's P.O.s begin reading ranges and bearings as the range taker mumbled, "On target, on target . . ."

Lion got off two more salvos before a single 12-inch shell struck her starboard side, penetrating the starboard dynamo room and knocking out the gunnery circuit. Immediately, Higgins heard Saxon's whistle coming through the gunnery voice tube. Snapping it open, the turret commander heard a shattering blast, then Saxon's last scream—a high-pitched shriek of pain and anger that turned his blood to ice.

Captain Chatfield's voice on the tube shocked him from his terror. "All turrets, local control. The starboard dynamo room is out. Port is overloading. Switch to battery."

With Saxon's death shriek still curdling his blood, Higgins reached up to the control board with a trembling hand, turning his firing key to "Local" and the power supply switch to "Battery." He shouted into the voice tube, "'Q' turret on local control and battery power."

"Very well. Continuous fire."

"Range twelve-zero-zero-zero," came from one of Halstead's P.O.s.

"Bearing zero-three-eight," the other added.

Geoffry set the dials of the Dumaresq calculator, made a quick reading, shouted at his gun captains and gunlayers, "Elevation two-three-three-zero minutes, direction zero-three-eight, deflection three-five left, range two-zero-zero minus twelve-zero-zero-zero. Continuous fire." Within seconds, the guns were elevated, trained, pointed, and red lights glowed.

Pulling down his periscope, Geoffry focused on *Lützow*, which was clearly visible. He pushed the firing button. There was the usual concussion, stench of cordite followed by the twenty-second wait for the fall of shot. Knowing at flank speed *Lützow* could steam over two hundred yards before his shells landed, he clung to his lenses anxiously, praying his deflection was correct.

Fascinated, he watched *Lützow*'s entire length flash with flames like snakes' tongues as her eight guns fired. But there were too many explosions. The enemy's bridge and forecastle erupted, steel plates blossoming from her like petals from a storm-tossed rose and her number one turret spun crazily around to her starboard side.

"We have her taped!" Halstead cried triumphantly.

"Continuous fire. No changes!" Higgins shouted without taking his eyes from the eyepiece. Mesmerized and oddly calm, he watched as a covey of enemy shells approached. They impacted just a few yards off *Lion*'s starboard side, raising a curtain of tortured seawater two hundred feet high, dumping tons of saltwater on *Lion*'s weather decks.

"Mother of God," a lookout's voice agonized through the voice tube. "The *QM*."

Geoffry swung his periscope astern. *Queen Mary*—sister to *Lion* and the third ship in column astern of *Princess Royal*—was only fifteen hundred yards behind *Lion*. Geoffry watched with awe as the battle cruiser glowed red amidships like a furnace in a steel mill and then opened up with great balls of flame, pulsing suns that rolled skyward hurling men and chunks of steel and debris in a huge circle. With disbelief, he saw her fifty-foot steam picket boat soar three hundred feet straight up. But there was no sound;

Lion's own guns and the roar of *Lützow*'s incoming salvos drowning out everything. Then *Queen Mary* was gone, leaving only a spreading brown mushroom cloud to mark her end.

Magazines! Magazines! "First *Indefatigable* and now *QM*," Geoffry cried to himself, shuddering and staring at his own jammed hoists.

There was a clang of steel striking steel, a whiplash detonation that shattered his eardrums and hurled him to the deck like a sack of potatoes. Heat. Screams. The choking, pungent odor of trotyl explosives. Stars flashed in his head and eyes—some from the crashing impact with the floor plates, others retinal memories of the flash of the exploding shell.

Lying on his back, he wondered if he were dead. Incongruously, there was a fresh breeze blowing the smoke away and he could see the ship's after mast and more stars overhead. Not stars in his scrambled brain or overwhelmed retinas, but real stars and constellations. And his hearing was returning. Then he felt more heat. Smelled cordite. Heard a high soul-wrenching wail like an animal caught in the steel jaws of a trap.

Despite terrible pain in his chest where the Dumaresq calculator had struck him breaking ribs and tearing flesh, and spitting blood from a tongue lacerated by his jarred teeth, he pulled himself to his feet by gripping the ruined, bent control board. Looking to the rear, holding his ribs and spitting blood, he saw Halstead and his ratings where they had found death in a common heap of smashed bones and mingling blood and viscera. Screams turned him to the gun bay. Tilted skyward at maximum elevation from the weight of the breech mechanisms, the breechblocks of both guns were open, spewing smoke and bits of burning silk. Not one member of the gun crews was on his feet. Both rammermen were dead, one cut nearly in half, intestines snaked on the deck in a heap, the other almost decapitated and hurled into a corner where he oozed blood from severed veins. Gunner Dennis Harwich was draped over the breechblock of the right gun, the yellow custard contents of his skull pouring onto the deck from a head shattered like a dropped melon. Both primermen were stretched full length on the deck either dead or unconscious while the two powder cradle operators had been smashed to bloody pulp and lay side by side moaning.

Again the animal wailed. It was gun captain Stephen Chalmers, seated with his back to the breech of the left gun, holding his stomach. Blood welled between his fingers and a bit of intestines protruded like a gray snake. Two ripped powder bags were at his feet and cordite was scattered over the deck and piled in corners.

Holding his chest and choking back an atavistic urge to run, to flee this slaughterhouse, the turret captain shook his head and looked up. With his brain clearing, he realized that an enemy shell had hit the turret's front plate at its joint with the roof plate, blowing the top off the turret like peeling the top off a tin of bully beef. *Lion* was in danger of blowing up like her sisters.

A flash of flame turned him back to the gun bay. A small pile of cordite next to the left gun was flaring. Again the impulse to run. But *Lion* would die—die hideously like *Indefatigable* and *QM*. More flames. Heat. A trail of fire across the deck, snaking toward ripped bags and the loaded hoists. Praying that the circuits were still intact, he reached up to the ruined control board and threw the red switch.

Instantly, the emergency gong rang in the magazines and Higgins knew Marine Major Harvey would flood the racks of powder and shells. Just as the sound of high-pressure water reached his ears, fire crept to the broken bags of cordite. There was the flash like a thousand suns at noon and Geoffry Higgins had time only to scream "Brenda!" once before his immolation.

I

Fog-filtered sunlight crept into the room muting the color of the royal blue bedspread pulled back from the George III gilt-wood bed. It was a large room hung with Raphael tapestries, paintings by Vuillard and Renoir, and with french windows that gave on the misty Kent countryside. If the morning had been clear, one could have seen broad views of the Kentish weald as far as Canterbury, dappled with cherry and apple blossoms. A proud William and Mary cabinet stood against one wall and a massive Chippendale library table squatted in front of the windows. It was beautiful, enormous, sterile, and cold, and would have dominated any room except this one.

Brenda Higgins stood quietly, looking out at the weald. She despised southeast England in the spring. In fact, she loathed the whole damp, foggy country regardless of the season. Every day thunderheads built up all around, tall silver ranges of clouds turning purple gray and sullen leaden blues threatening rain but never making good that threat, though thunder rumbled and lightning flickered on the horizon like dueling armies. June was a time for Cannes, Greece, Monte Carlo, or Capri, yet, because of "Kaiser Willie," travel was restricted and civilized people were forced to give up their Mediterranean spring. June of 1916 was especially depressing. With the war two years old and no end in sight, she looked forward gloomily like a prisoner of old Newgate to more confinement in the rambling old house.

Her dislike for Fenwyck seemed to have its roots in the house. She hated Fenwyck. She knew its history. Lord, she couldn't avoid history. The English wallowed in it. Maybe they liked to look back centuries because the bloody history being made at Ypres, the Somme, Gallipoli, and Loos in a war to end all wars was written in casualty lists yards long.

Pridefully, Geoffry had bored her to death with tales of the old estate. Originally a castle built on a small knoll by Donald Northfield, the first Earl of Fenwyck, Castle Fenwyck's glowering battlements had dominated the surrounding countryside and its toiling serfs for centuries. Foolishly in 1645, the then Lord of Fenwyck, William Northfield, a distant cousin to Charles I, made the mistake of picking the wrong side during the civil war. William and his son did valiant battle when Oliver Cromwell led his men at arms against Fenwyck. The old earl was killed and his son, Edward, the fourth earl, wounded. Counting heavy losses, a piqued Cromwell took a thousand captives, confiscated hundreds of farm animals, uprooted two orchards, and killed every deer in the forest. Finally, to assure himself of no resurgence, the "Protector of the Commonwealth" pulled the battlements down and filled the moat, reducing Fenwyck to a manor. Then the backbreaking fine of ten thousand sovereigns was levied against Edward. Unable to raise even a hundred guineas, the wounded and impoverished aristocrat boarded up what remained of the castle's keep and vanished.

For nearly a century only wretched peasants squatted in Fenwyck, blackening the stone walls with their fires and discarding small mountains of garbage and trash. Then in 1760, a commoner, Cedric Higgins, Geoffry's great-great-grandfather, bought Fenwyck and began restoring it. Starting with the keep—the only substantial part of the original structure still remaining—the modern Fenwyck began to grow, and to Brenda, it grew like a cancer. As the decades passed and Cedric's descendants continued with the project, rooms were piled upon rooms haphazardly with halls that wandered aimlessly, and a corrugated roof line like a ploughed field grew on top of the stacked rooms. There was an absolute maze of rooms, all drafty and poorly lighted.

On the first floor there was a drawing room, dining room, library, morning room, breakfast room, smoking room, billiard room, chapel, gun room, and business room. However, only bedrooms were on the second floor, approached by a grand cedar staircase for family and guests and by back stairs for servants. Male servants' quarters were upstairs, females' downstairs with separate stairways to preclude chance meetings and the temptations of the devil. The main hall was enormous with giant, hand-hewn beams so beloved by the English and drafty enough to give an Eskimo pneumonia. It was enough to make Brenda ache for the warm comforts of her Fifth Avenue home.

Adding to her discomfort were reports of a great battle off Denmark—a place called Jutland. For days Danish papers had been filled with accounts of burning ships on the horizon and the washing ashore of scores of corpses. There had been no word from Geoffry and his silence could mean only that *Lion* was at sea. She felt a sudden chill.

She turned to a full-length pier mirror, but the chill persisted, seemed to concentrate in her spine, sending tiny frozen fingers tracing lines up her back all the way to her neck. She shook worry from her head, stared at the mirror. She liked what she saw. Draped in a green silk chiffon *robe de style* with a net-filled wide neckline and pulled in at the waist by a yellow sash—a small waistline not yet betraying a two-month pregnancy—the sculpted dress showed off her full figure subtly yet with immense style. The gown had been made for her by Lanvin. In fact, most of her dresses were made by Parisian couturiers: Lanvin, Calbot Soeurs, and Borie counted most of her business while English dressmakers, whom she considered butchers with scissors, received none. She pushed at her auburn tresses that flowed alluringly even in the dim light, framing a lovely face as white as a St. Moritz ski slope. Her neck was long, tapered, and aristocratic, breasts firm, pointed and without a hint of sag. She was glad, now, that that cow of a wet nurse, Bridie O'Conner, had suckled both Rodney and Nathan. The thought of a child clamping his jaws on her breasts turned her stomach. Her breasts were the province of her husband and when he was at sea, her lover. A sudden dizziness brought a hand to her forehead.

"Will you take breakfast here, *ma maitresse*?" came from a petite young woman with large dark eyes and alabaster skin who entered the room after a perfunctory knock.

Feeling a hollow nausea deep in her stomach that she was convinced came from her pregnancy, she answered sharply, "No, Nicole. Not yet. I'll take it in the dining room later."

"It is late, Madame Higgins."

"That's for me to decide," Brenda snapped.

"*Oui*, Madame Higgins," the maid said demurely, turning with a swish of taffeta and closing the door.

Servants. Servants had run her life. Their announcements always seemed like commands. And Fenwyck's staff was particularly galling. They seemed to look down their noses at the American. Actually acted superior when out of earshot of the rest of the family.

"Time to rise, *ma maitresse*," Nicole would say early in the morning. This announcement never changed and came at precisely the same hour. Before the war the call came when Geoffry was away on business and now, when her husband was on duty in *Lion*. "Madame is served," always announced dinner. Actually, Brenda felt the maid was saying, "Can't keep the lord waiting, you lazy colonial."

And the barely suppressed surliness was there in Pascal the chef, his assistant, the butler, Dorset, three house-keepers, Caldwell and one other chauffeur, a grounds man named Sanders, and a pair of apprentices who lived in a cottage on the edge of the estate. Fenwyck's staff differed from her father's servants only in degree. It seemed servants had always ruled her life; they had told her when to rise, when to eat, when to study, and how to dress as far back as she could remember. But her father's servants were part of her childhood memories, for the most part. As she matured into young womanhood, there were subtle changes in atti-tude; except for Gracie, the old Negress who raised her and babied her until she died. All of Fenwyck's servants had some of old Gracie in them without the softening of human-ity. Indeed, they often moved like wraithlike machines that were so silent and faceless they became unnoticed—even invisible.

The mist parted and a rare shaft of sunlight inflamed the sky with virulent reds, bleeding on the clouds like a mortally wounded warrior and pouring through the french windows in warm torrents. Piqued by the maid, Brenda lingered in front of the mirror, watching the *robe de style* twist around her hips, outlining her sculpted buttocks stylishly. Then she heard the motor car. Turning to the window, she saw a black sedan with a naval ministry logo on its side winding up the drive. A cold hand clutched her stomach and she put her hand to her mouth, gasping for breath as the long sedan stopped at the main entrance. A rating opened the door and a naval officer clutching a briefcase stepped out. Then the reverberating sound of the great iron knocker striking oak echoed through the house. Frozen like a statue, she was still staring at the motor car when Nicole's voice, ringing with a timbre of anxiety she had never heard before, came from the hall. *"Ma maitresse! Ma maitresse!* A visitor for you . . ."

When Brenda entered the drawing room she found three people waiting for her. Seated in an overstuffed leather chair was her sixty-seven-year-old father-in-law, Walter Higgins. Rheumy-eyed and with florid cheeks crosshatched with a latticework of alcohol-distended veins, the old man's flaccid muscles and paunchy waistline attested to years of inactivity, rich food, and too much liquor. Short of stature, he was crowned with a full shock of unkempt white hair that hung over his ears and down his forehead like a valance, matching the color of his mustache, which drooped over the corners of his mouth. One eyelid sagged and the other was narrow, giving a crafty yet sorrowful look to blue pinpoints that burned in a dim watery way as if he had just turned his face to a fierce rainstorm. His face revealed no emotion. He avoided Brenda's eyes.

Seated on a scroll-ended, richly upholstered black and gold Regency sofa was Brenda's mother-in-law, Rebecca Higgins. Small and frail, she wore the weight of every one of her sixty-four years on her bent, bony shoulders. Her small features were still delicate, hinting at beauty long vanished despite the sags and lines of advancing years. Her wide hazel eyes were rimmed with tears and she dabbed with a linen handkerchief nervously as if she could wipe away the officer and his news. She, too, avoided Brenda's eyes.

Standing in front of a chair in front of a huge Louis XV pedestal clock, the naval officer faced Brenda over a rosewood center table. Tall and middle-aged, he had wispy sandy hair, solemn eyes, and the large beaked nose so often found in British aristocracy. "I am Commander Roderick Harborough," he said, placing his briefcase on the rosewood table.

After Walter introduced himself and the women, Harborough seated himself while Brenda found her place next to Rebecca. The women clutched hands. Commander Harborough cleared his throat as he reached into his briefcase. "I dislike bearing this news," he said, removing a dossier.

"We know why you're here," Walter said hoarsely. "It's Geoffry. He's dead."

"Yes. I'm sorry. I bear news regarding Lieutenant Geoffry Higgins."

Stunned, Brenda caught her breath then turned her head to her mother-in-law's shoulder, biting her knuckles. Rebecca trembled, appearing paralyzed to the point of speechlessness. For a long moment only the slow ticktock of the great pedestal clock could be heard as silence poured into the room like a viscous fluid, coating everyone and everything.

Finally, Walter spoke and his question was shocking. "Did he die well?"

The commander fielded the question as if he had expected it. "Yes. Splendidly, sir. A possible D.S.O. or even the Victoria Cross. Saved the ship, he did, by throwing the emergency fire switch."

The feeling of loss, the aching emptiness came as no surprise to Brenda. True, she had never truly loved Geoffry and had married him only as a financial expedient. Nevertheless, he had fathered her sons and made her pregnant again and she knew he had loved her and respected her and she had grown genuinely fond of him. Now he was lost. Irretrievably lost. Suddenly, the cold fingers were back and she was dizzy again. She spoke through a clenched fist. "His body," she managed. "A funeral . . ."

"I'm afraid, Mrs. Higgins," the commander said softly, finding sudden new interest in the Savonnerie rug under his feet, "there was a powder fire. He threw the switch. The entire crew—ah, I understand the heat . . ."

Rebecca came to life, face tight with shock, eyes balls of glass. "No! No . . ." Brenda tightened an arm around the skeletal shoulders.

"Please, Becky," John snapped. "He died well."

Fanned by her dislike for Walter, Brenda felt a new emotion; a surging, burning visceral wave of rage rise from the grief and horror and engulf her, flushing her neck and face scarlet with its heat. Her breeding, years of training went by the boards. "Died well? Died well?" she cried. "Why is that so damned important? Must you British die elegantly, too? He's dead, isn't he? Just as dead as a dead coward. Even a *colonial* knows that." She felt Rebecca's grip loosen as the old lady turned away, shuddering.

"Important doesn't describe his conduct at the last," the old man retorted hotly, voice deep in his chest, eyes boring through the American. "No, indeed—it was everything! Everything! Can't you understand?"

"No! No! No! You bloody British with your unruffled aplomb. Is it undignified to mourn your own son—my husband?"

"Go to your room!"

"Enough!" Rebecca cried in a hard, anguished voice Brenda had never heard before. Walter looked up, eyebrows arched by surprise. Harborough shifted his weight uneasily. "My son's dead—incinerated—and you two can only fight at his wake," Rebecca hissed unevenly, glaring at her husband.

Brenda bit her lip while a scowling Walter shot back, "He's gone, brought honor . . ."

"Damn the honor. My son's dead!"

"Many sons, Mrs. Higgins . . ." Harborough began gently.

"That makes it no easier, Commander," Rebecca interrupted.

"I'm sorry."

"I'm not looking for that," the old woman shot back. She moved her eyes to her husband who had slumped back resignedly. Fascinated by a side of her mother-in-law she had never seen before, Brenda pushed her grief and anger aside, hunching forward as Rebecca pressed on, showing surprising composure. "What—what did you do with the bodies?"

"They were buried at sea."

"Thrown overboard like garbage."

"Oh, no—no, Mrs. Higgins. It's not like that—not like that at all." There was shock in the officer's voice.

"How do you know?"

"I was there. I'm *Lion*'s signals officer."

Again silence smothered the room broken only by the sounds of the swinging pendulum. Rebecca continued with a new softness. "Tell me about it. I've got to know about the place where my son . . ." She gagged and dropped her eyes.

The commander stared over Rebecca's head and seemed to lose himself in a Raphael landscape that hung gloriously in the middle of the paneled wall behind her. "Beautiful," he said to himself as if commenting on the painting. Then he was in another place, another time. "The North Sea can be beautiful. It was when Captain Chatfield said the words over them." He raised his eyes. "The clouds can do strange things at sea. It was like a cathedral that day with arches and towers. But the sun stayed with us. It was high noon . . ."

Crossing herself, the old woman began to chant, "They that go down to the sea in ships, that do business in great waters . . ."

"Yes, yes. Those are the words."

"We commend into thy hands of mercy, most merciful father . . ." She choked as if garroted. Then she spat bitterly as if she had bitten sour fruit, "Merciful! Hah!"

"Please, Mrs. Higgins . . ."

"How many? How many?"

Harborough's eyes hardened into slits, bringing to life incipient wrinkles hiding at the corners. "Seventy-six, eighty-seven miles southeast of Rosyth." He drummed the table. "But they're together—belong together."

"Coffins?"

A look of pain darkened his face like a sudden squall. "It is customary to sew the deceased in canvas bags, weigh the bags with artillery shells . . ."

"I understand," Rebecca said, sinking back, suddenly drained.

"Have you had your say?" Walter asked, eyes flashing.

His wife stared back. "Yes. No amount of words can bring him back; not yours, not mine, not God's." And then to the officer with concern, "I'm sorry, Commander. I'm a dreadful hostess." She began to rise. "Tea? A cocktail?"

"Cognac, please, Mrs. Higgins."

The old woman moved slowly to an ornately carved breakfront. "Walter? Brenda?"

"Cognac," Walter answered.

New waves of icy weakness and nausea rocked Brenda and she reeled back, hand to her forehead. "I think I'll go to my room," she mumbled. "Lie down—yes, lie down."

"You all right?" her mother-in-law asked, voice heavy with concern. "I'll send for Nicole."

"Yes, Rebecca. Send for Nicole."

Rebecca pulled a cord hanging next to the breakfront. "The doctor?"

"No. It's just my condition." Brenda palmed her stomach. Then she heard a rustle of taffeta behind her.

II

Brenda had no memory of how she managed the stairs or changed into her nightgown. As she sank back into the goose down softness of the bed, she ran a finger over her abdomen, breasts, and cheeks, finding a slippery patina and occasional rivulets. Her hair was stiff and brittle, eyes set in hot sand, aching dully in their sockets. Figures cluttered the room, floating about silently in the gloom. Geoffry loomed, smiling down at her, eyes filled with adoration. He vanished, replaced by Nicole leaning over her and then Rebecca and Walter huddled close by.

She felt a cold hand on her forehead. "Get the doctor, Nicole. Doctor Mansfield. Hurry!" she heard Rebecca say in a distant tunnel. "It's the flu—trench fever."

A penumbra of weak sunlight haloed the faces and she rolled away from it, mind out of control, flashing a feverish kaleidoscope like a new Edison moving picture machine gone mad. Fenwyck faded and the faces changed. New faces. Or were they old faces? Yes. Her father, mother, brother, and sister. Smiling. She was young again. She was home. There was no war. She was happy and warm.

Dominating the corner of Fifth Avenue and Thirty-seventh Street, the Ashcroft mansion was an immense three-story brownstone with high windows and ornate cornices. Neither palazzo nor château, as were most of the other palatial residences of "Millionaire's Row," but, instead, an eclectic blending of flat medieval lines and Tuscan arches, the huge home crowded the street, separated from gawking passersby by a high iron grillwork fence capped by a phalanx of pike-like points. The entry alone—a high-domed circular room floored with glistening gray and white marble set in a checkerboard pattern, hung with two Rembrandts, a Titian, and a pair of Holbeins, and dominated by a Garnier chandelier brilliant with clusters of bubbling glass blossoms on delicate branches of gold and silver—was worth more than a half dozen workers' combined lifetime earnings at the looms in the Ashcroft Mills. Here Brenda grew up playing in the sculpted gardens with her older brother Hugh and sister Betty, chasing through the manicured shrubs, around the pond, the carousel and its wooden horses, and over the bridge. Some afternoons the sisters would spend hours playing with their dolls in their playhouse cleverly constructed to appear as a miniature Swiss chalet while Hugh galloped over the equestrian trails in Central Park or played his roughhouse brand of rugby with his friends on the park's vast lawns.

Schools were exclusive, attended only by the children of the very rich: Mrs. Bradshaw's Academy on Twenty-third Street just off Madison Square when she was very young; the Windsor Finishing School in Connecticut came later in her teens, then Bryn Mawr. And there were men. Always men.

She met Anthony Richardson at a party in 1909; the same year Hugh graduated from West Point. She had numerous passionate flings with the muscular young Harvard football star in the dunes at Newport when they were both vacationing in the summer. But most memorable was Troy Archer. A wealthy textile importer and one of John's closest business associates, he was the best. Middle-aged and married, he had been a tireless lover and ingenious in devising ways to delight a young girl. But his wife found out—threatened exposure and disgrace for all. All parties involved retreated discreetly without a murmur of scandal.

She met Geoffry Higgins in 1910 just after her graduation summa cum laude. It was a terrible year—the year southern mills and their cheap labor sent her father's business spiraling toward the abyss of bankruptcy. John met Geoffry in England while discussing a possible merger with Geoffry's firm, Carlisle Mills, Limited, one of Europe's great textile firms, which had just landed a lucrative contract for uniforms. Panicking, John persuaded Geoffry to inspect the Ashcroft Mill and then invited the Englishman to dinner at the Fifth Avenue home.

From the first, Brenda found Geoffry unexciting. Tall, slender with a weak chin, watery gray eyes, and thinning brown hair, he was at least fourteen years her senior. In addition, he seemed to have no imagination, a dull wit, and lacked the style to match his fine clothes. Most irritating, he had the habit of chewing on the frame of his pince-nez when speaking. Notwithstanding, he was a bachelor and one of the world's great powers in textiles and Brenda knew her father sensed a merger consummated in the conjugal bed.

"Handsome young man, fine family," John would hint, fishing for his daughter's reaction.

Brenda would only nod and choke back her gorge.

"The Englishman would be a fine catch, my dear," Ellen commented one day as the women sat embroidering in the parlor. "You're almost twenty-two and unspoken for."

"I know! I know, Mother," Brenda said, tying a loose end. And then forcefully, "I hardly know him and he's not even interested, anyway." She broke a thread.

"Yes he is! Yes he is!" came the quick retort.

"He's never shown it."

"He's British. They never show anything."

"His upper lip is too stiff, Mother." Both women laughed.

Early in 1911, Carlisle Mills opened a New York office and Brenda saw Geoffry Higgins at least once a week. But Geoffry was discussing merger with the largest southern mill as well as with Ashcroft Mills. Brenda began to feel despair as she watched her father's business erode and the real possibility of bankruptcy loomed.

Then Brenda and Geoffry began to date, always dining in New York's finest restaurants and always chauffeured in Geoffry's new Rolls Royce Silver Ghost motor car by his personal chauffeur, Caldwell. And his proposal had been stiff and unemotional like a man negotiating a business venture. "We could have a strong, productive union," he said, adding a new scar to his frames. "Our interests are similar and you're from the upper classes, too," he added generously.

"I'm flattered, Geoffry," Brenda answered. "Give me time—I need to think."

John and Ellen were thrilled, urging Brenda into the marriage. She never told them the man had the appeal of a marble pillar. And, true, she was twenty-two and, despite her beauty, had no serious suitor. Finally, after watching her father's business collapse and sickened by the desperate look haunting his eyes, she consented. The Ashcrofts were ecstatic and Geoffry was so delighted he dropped his pince-nez.

Within a month, Brenda and her parents crossed the Atlantic and took up residence at Fenwyck. Two nights after her arrival and a fortnight before the wedding, they entered the great hall for a formal family dinner. After introductions to twenty-two guests, Brenda, uncomfortable in a tight-fitting satin gown her couturier called *en grand toilette*, found more discomfort with her father and Geoffry on the hard cushions and straight back of a Victorian papier-mâché settee. Forced to sit erect by the bulging balloon back, she felt her silk crepe de chine chemise tighten and bunch beneath her in maddening creases and folds. Squirming, she moved her eyes around the great hall.

The vast chamber seemed as big as the new Metropolitan Opera House. Two stories high, the ceiling was carried on a great arch hand hewn in Romanesque style from a single giant oak, spanning the chamber from wall to wall and anchored at each end on middle buttresses twenty feet thick. A cavernous fireplace big enough to drive Geoffry's Rolls through opened on one wall and tiny high windows placed in regular intervals broke the stone high overhead. Fireplace and windows were all surmounted by characteristic moldings of the Romanesque period.

Staring at the fireplace where a half dozen flaming logs roared, hissed, popped, and sparked, Brenda noted, "Big enough to roast an ox."

"That's precisely why it's that big," Geoffry answered, nursing a glass of Graves. "In the early days the family and its retainers not only ate here, they cooked and slept here as well."

"Slept here? Did everything here? In one room?"

"Everything." He grinned.

"Lord."

The furniture was eclectic, antique, and expensive. It was also overwhelming. A dozen Queen Anne, Georgian, and Regency breakfronts and sideboards of oak, mahogany, and walnut, ornately carved and inlaid with marquetry, lined the walls, and the table, which was at least forty feet long, boasted Louis XIV lineage with the usual heavy, squarish lines, elaborate carvings, and garish gilt that Brenda considered gauche. Especially distasteful were the chairs, designed for aesthetics, not the human body. All had been polished by a thousand hands, day after day, year after year. Banners, flags, bows, arrows, muskets, spears, and even shields hung from the walls, giving a strong militaristic flavor to the medieval ambience. More militarism was found in the guests; six of the twelve men present were in uniform.

"War. War," Brenda whispered to her father. "This place is a fortress—a war museum full of battle trophies. And they're getting ready for the next one. They must love it."

"Nonsense," John responded. "Technology has made war impossible. Alfred Nobel's new explosives, rapid-fire artillery, and Maxim guns have made armed conflict obsolete. There's been peace for a hundred years and you can expect it to last indefinitely," he assured her.

"Nobel," she answered. "He'll be the greatest mass murderer in history."

He looked at her incredulously. "Why, he established a peace prize and Theodore Roosevelt won it for ending the Russian-Japanese unpleasantness, didn't he?"

"Guilt, guilt," Brenda said, turning away as a swarm of liveried servants approached after the butler's call of "Ladies and gentlemen, dinner is served."

The meal was memorable and it became obvious from the start the Higginses had a French chef. There was *poulet bonne femme* served with *petitis pois a la française*, an enormous *omelette aux fines herbes*, and glasses kept filled with dry Monopole, Graves, and Otard. Then crepes suzette—named after the Prince of Wales's latest harlot—were served, flaming, squirted with brandy and lemon over sugar. Finally, coffee and cognac.

Slowly, during the meal, Brenda became acquainted with Geoffry's two brothers. The younger, Randolph, a bachelor, sat to her left and Geoffry's older brother, Lloyd, sat on her right with his wife, Bernice, at his side.

Two years older than herself, Brenda knew that Geoffry had little patience with his younger brother, Randolph, considering him a wastrel who spent money carelessly, risked his neck with Tommy Sopwith in those flimsy "avroplanes," and indulged in short flings with music hall girls like a common libertine. Dark with heavy black eyebrows that gave his handsome face a thoughtful, brooding look, Brenda found the young man taciturn yet intriguing. There was a deep glow in his eyes that seemed to threaten, but at the same time held exciting promise, too. As the evening wore on, Brenda began to suspect the tall, athletic young man could turn women's heads and stiffen men's backs by merely walking into a room.

The most interesting man in the room was Geoffry's older brother, Lloyd. Dressed in a captain's uniform of the Coldstream's First Regiment of Foot, the forty-two-year-old officer was the tallest Higgins at six feet two inches. Thin as a bamboo tree as though the flesh and fat had been burned off his bones by too much marching under the noontime sun, his splendid tailored uniform did little to hide his spindly legs and gaunt chest. Nevertheless, there was steely resolve in the gunmetal gray eyes and strength in a voice that was a rumbling basso profundo strident enough to fill Westminster. And above all, the bearing and demeanor were those of a soldier—a warrior and gentleman. Yet, he wore his hat at the table.

Noticing Brenda's curious stare at his peaked Wolsely, he explained with clear, twinkling blue eyes shaded by a burlesque of the stiff British salute, "George the Third never removed his hat at the table and he extended the privilege to all officers of the Coldstreams." A chuckle punctuated by "Hear! Hear!" rumbled around the table.

His wife, Bernice, a diminutive woman with flaxen hair, huge liquid green eyes, and delicate features like a Dresden doll, laughed into her napkin while eyeing her husband with the adoration most women reserve for a deity.

Brenda soon discovered Captain Lloyd Higgins was a storehouse of military gambits who referred to strange units as if they were chapters in an exclusive fraternity. Ignoring the civilians, he gestured around the table at the officers. "You've met these gentlemen, but we British wear a strange assortment of uniforms, don't we? Must be confusing."

Brenda acknowledged her agreement with a smile and a nod.

Lloyd inclined his head to a kilted red-faced major with

huge handlebar mustaches. "Cousin Jerry of the Royal Scots."

"Cherry Bottoms, old boy," the major retorted with a wide grin.

"Cherry Bottoms?"

"Yes, Brenda," Lloyd said. "None of those blokes wear underwear." A storm of laughter echoed from the stone walls. Holding up a hand, Lloyd nodded at a captain farther down the table. "David is of the Queen's Own Black Watch."

"Death or Glory Boys," David offered.

"Right-oh, old chap," Lloyd agreed. And then he moved to another heavyset, florid colonel who had obviously drunk too much Otard. "Cousin William of the Surreys." The colonel nodded unsteadily. Lloyd continued, "The Queen's Own Bloodhounds."

"Jolly good! Jolly good," the colonel muttered, waving a half-empty glass. "First Regiment of Horse."

In quick succession, Brenda was introduced to Cousin Thomas of the Irish Guard Cavalry, Cousin Dennis of the Welsh Fusiliers, and Cousin Kurt of the Leicesters. All were jovial, spirited, and in high good humor. But their wives were quiet, smiling, chuckling at the quips, withdrawn in the background like moons revolving about bright stars. And the five men in mufti were eclipsed, appearing as sparrows next to preening peacocks in mating season.

There was a barrage of jokes about regimental mascots: the wolfhound of the Irish Guards, the goat of the Welsh Fusiliers, the antelope of the Leicesters, the Siamese kitten of the Surreys.

By the time dessert was finished, Walter's voice—well oiled by a dozen glasses of Otard—boomed and dominated from the end of the table. Overweight, face crimson from the effects of too much liquor, mustaches dangling and speckled with bits of forgotten food and alternately waving a fork and half-empty glass for emphasis, he was a living, breathing John Bull with the dogged obduracy of George III and the manners of Henry VIII. It soon became obvious

Randolph's ambition was a bone in his throat. Shouting the length of the table in a suddenly silent room, he assaulted a stiffened, reddening Randolph. "When are you going to take hold of yourself, old boy? Shuck Tommy Sopwith and his foolishness about flying machines and come down to earth —at Carlisle Limited. There's a place for you." He turned to Geoffry. "Right, my boy?"

"Right, Father," Geoffry answered through tight lips, eyes on his brandy.

"Please Father," Randolph began. "This is not the time . . ."

"That's bloody nonsense," the old man bellowed, slamming a hammy fist on the table with so much force a forgotten drumstick leapt from the oak and fell to the Maksoud Persian under his feet where an alert servant scooped it up.

Randolph fixed his father with narrowed eyes that gleamed with an amalgam of embarrassment and anger. Obviously, the pair was involved in an old argument with the score still unsettled. "That isn't cricket, Father. You know I hate the textile business."

"Then, find something!"

There was a flurry of self-conscious coughs among the guests, but all eyes moved from father to son and back again like spectators at Wimbledon. "In my time, Father."

"Blast it, man. You're taking too much time. Must we banish you to the colonies?"

Brenda heard a gasp circle the table. Then Rebecca muttered, "Walter."

Glancing at the confused Americans, Walter mumbled an apology and pressed on. "What do you expect to accomplish with these machines?"

Randolph seemed to calm suddenly; appeared intent and determined like a man ready to plead his case before a skeptical board of directors. "The government's interested in flying scouts. A.V. Roe has joined us and we're going to start building flying machines designed for scouting." Every officer hunched forward. The two cavalry officers exchanged broad grins.

Walter picked up the gauntlet. "Airplanes as scouts? What in the world is the cavalry for, boy?"

"Earthbound, sir. Anyway, Maxim guns will cut them down like chaff." The two cavalry officers winced.

"Nonsense! What kind of position would they have for you?"

"Designer."

"Designer? You're educated in business and accounting. You know nothing about this flying business—nothing at all."

"It's not necessary, sir. It's a new science. We sketch the airframes on the wall in chalk and . . ."

"On the wall, Randolph. What about stresses? Loads?"

"Not important."

"You mean none of you know enough." He took a large gulp of cognac. "You'll work in a factory, true?"

"True, sir."

The red-rimmed eyes swept the table. "That's beneath a Higgins—fit for fishwives and Soho bummers."

The young man's face flushed and his chin hardened. "It's my choice, Father."

"Bully for you," the old man said sarcastically.

"Father," Randolph said sharply, not yielding an inch, "I have my digs in Kensington and it's time for me . . ." He rose.

"Sit down, young man," Walter commanded.

"I'm sorry, sir," Randolph said, turning toward the entry hall.

"I'm leaving, too," Lloyd said firmly, rising to his feet and followed by his wife.

"No! I forbid . . ."

"Walter!" Rebecca cried. "You're driving them out." Then to her sons, "Randolph! Lloyd! Randolph . . ."

"Lloyd! Randolph!" came through the haze. "They don't know about Geoffry." It was Rebecca's voice.

"I've contacted Colonel Courtney Covington at Whitehall

and they'll both be informed," Walter continued. "But blast it, there's security and all that rot."

"They're on the Somme. Everyone knows they're on the Somme," Rebecca choked. "Dear God. How much are we expected to give?"

The kaleidoscope had slowed and Brenda tried to turn her head back to the light and the spectral figures, but her skull had become a twenty-pound stone. She could only listen. Then the haze darkened and she drifted into a dark cloud. She saw her sons, both on biers with candles at their heads and feet. "Nathan! Rodney!" she shouted suddenly, twisting.

She heard Nicole's voice "They are fine, *ma maitresse.* They are with their governess."

"Thank God." The maid leaned close and Brenda felt breath on her cheek. Immediately, she felt her head lifted and something was pushed under her pillow. "You will be well, *ma maitresse.* I promise you," Nicole whispered hoarsely.

"Here, there," Doctor Mansfield's shrill voice broke in. "What in blazes are you doing?"

"Something to help *ma madame, monsieur docteur.*"

Brenda felt a hand under her pillow. Then the doctor's incredulous voice said, "A potato—a sliced potato."

"They say it helps. My mother . . ."

"Bloody nonsense!"

Rebecca interrupted. "Put it back, doctor."

"Back?"

"It can't hurt, can it, doctor?"

Brenda felt the potato pushed under the pillow while Mansfield muttered under his breath, "Bloody old wives' tales . . ."

Walter's voice crept in from a distance. "Randolph's squadron's based near Bailleul. Courtney Covington has assured me a telegram is on its way."

"Lloyd?"

"The fighting's heavy along the whole Somme front. It'll take a few days to find the Coldstreams."

"But Randolph will know."

"Yes, Rebecca. Randolph will know."

III

Flying in tandem—one behind and slightly higher than the other—the two Nieuport 17 scouts circled high over the Somme Valley like lazy gulls taking the wind on stiff wings. Looking down from four thousand feet, Major Randolph Higgins, commanding officer of Number Five Squadron, stared down, eyeing a tortured terrain that had been fought over for almost two years. A natural military barrier, the Somme River was the key to the defenses of Paris. To the north, Randolph could see the great bend of the river at Peronne eight miles behind the German lines, then the flow to the southwest to Amiens, and finally, like most rivers in this part of France, it curved northwesterly and flowed to the sea.

Millions of shells had churned the valley into a moonscape, obliterating villages, forests, and all signs of human existence. In fact, in one barrage, the British had fired onehalf ton of ammunition a day for ten days for every yard of German trenches until 1,850,000 shells had been expended, and then using tactics inherited from the American Civil War attacked, losing sixty thousand men in eight hours. Here and there were the pulverized ruins of smashed buildings and villages—heaps of blasted bricks and broken timbers with a few stone chimneypieces sticking up like grave markers. In all directions barbed wire entanglements crosshatched the landscape taking on the clear, sharp lines of fishnets. Entire forests had been reduced to blackened stands of lonely poles, stripped of foliage and pointing at the Nieuports with the charred fingers of cremated sentries. Occasional mean-

46

dering whitish traces indicated the remnants of roads, blasted from existence years ago; or, perhaps, a footpath braced by duckboards and used only at night by infantry scurrying in terror of the surprise barrage like frightened rats in a sewer. And, indeed, it was a sewer. Randolph knew it, had smelled it when stationed close to the front and downwind. The only thing he could see that appeared untouched, unspoiled by the havoc, was the glimmering ribbon of the river that wandered unconcerned through the carnage.

Despite a recent lull in the attacks and counterattacks, the hungry guns wanted more victims, searched with long, probing fingers that burst singly and in clusters as artillery on both sides of the front registered, ranged, and battery fired. Watching the tortured terrain erupt and heave, Randolph felt a mixture of relief and guilt—happy to be free of the horror below like a bird fleeing a forest fire, but feeling guilt over the clean air in his lungs, the hot food and Scotch he knew waited for him back at the aerodrome, and, of course, the clean sheets.

A glance at his fuel gauge told him his tank was half-empty with still an hour left in his patrol. After signaling his cover—the reliable veteran Lieutenant David A. Reed—with a palm-down wave, he carefully eased the throttle back while giving the 110 horsepower Le Rhone all the manifold pressure it could take, thinning the fuel mixture and forcing more air into the 9-cylinder heads. Just as the rev counter dropped to 850 rpms, the engine backfired its objections and Randolph knew the rotary would take no more. Another glance over his shoulder told him Reed had alertly eased his throttle and was maintaining his station as before.

Despite an embarrassing tendency to shed its wing fabric —and sometimes its entire lower wing, which was supported only by a single spar—Randolph liked the little Nieuport pursuit plane. Compared with his first scout, the Vickers Fighting Biplane, or F.B. 2, which he flew for almost a year and found as ungainly as a frightened quail, the Nieuport was a hawk. A two-seater pusher with a 100-horsepower Gnome engine, the F.B. took a full nine minutes to climb to five thousand feet where it was capable of only ninety-three miles per hour. And his gunners had been terrible—frightened young men too incompetent to be pilots who sprayed the sky with the Lewis gun at ranges that sometimes reached an impossible one thousand yards. His only victory had been over a Rumpler Taube whose terrified pilot had jerked the control stick so violently he shed his right wing, spinning into no-man's land in a heap of splintered struts, spars, twisted wire braces, and torn fabric.

But in the Nieuport he was his own master; would live or die by his own hand. After his modifications, which added delicate throttle and moisture controls, the acrobatic little aeroplane had a top speed of 112 miles per hour and could climb to five thousand feet in less than six minutes. In a dogfight it could turn, skid, and snap roll inside of any of its opponents; even the new Albatross D.1 pursuit, which was appearing in ever-increasing numbers, replacing the Fokker Eindekker, which was fodder for the Nieuport. In less than a month, Randolph had counted four kills: two Rumplers, a Fokker Eindekker, and an Albatross D.1.

Sighing, the major looked around. Nothing. The sky was empty. There had been rumors that the great German ace Oswald Boelcke and his squadron had been ordered to the Somme sector. But not one of the garishly painted Albatrosses of his famed Jagdstaffel Two had been sighted. Rumors. War was full of rumors. The lull in the slaughter below had brought a respite to the killing in the skies. In fact, Randolph had not seen a German plane for three days. Yet, that morning, Division had called with reports of a Rumpler artillery spotter that had been operating every morning for four straight days over the ridge at Thiepval, held by the Tenth Worcesters.

Moving the control stick to the right and pressuring the rudder bar slightly, Randolph banked slowly to the right. Pushing his goggles up—they obscured his peripheral vision—he leaned over the padded coaming of the cockpit and stared down over the lower wingtip. There, framed by the V strut, he could see Thiepval Ridge jutting into the German lines like a thumb. Artillery was working, the yellow brown haze from bursting seventy-sevens hanging in a poisonous lanket below the ridge. Centering his controls, he raised his eyes, cursed, and punched the instrument panel so hard the needles on his altimeter and oil gauge quivered. Clouds. Clouds that would have been beautiful at any other time; but not today—not when men hunted, sought to kill other men in the sky—had moved down rapidly from the north and had begun filling the sky. Between St. Quentin and Arras was the lowest level of filmy stratus at no higher than a thousand feet. Above this deck swirled another layer of cumulus, heavy with moisture and rising in towers and crenulated battlements to at least eighteen thousand feet. Cover; excellent cover for a snooping Rumpler. He saw nothing. No shadow. No glimmer of an airfoil. No movement. He dropped the nose of the scout and with his wires humming swooped low over the ridge: a dung brown quagmire of torn and savaged earth that seemed deserted but was peopled by legions of the living and dead rotting together in their waterlogged holes. At least the Worcesters would know the RFC was here, he thought.

Everything was brown, soaked by yesterday's rain and churned to a consistency of Yorkshire pudding. At five hundred feet strands and concertinas of barbed wire could be plainly seen and individual shell holes stood out, lip to lip and filled with stagnant water, blinking up at him like eyes of the blind. Trenches were visible; shallow depressions hastily dug between shell holes and connected by support trenches that zigzagged haphazardly up, down, and across the ridge. The men? Where were the Tommies? Then he saw them. First just white specks in the brown quagmire. But then the specks became faces and waving hands. Exhilarated at finding life in a hell of death, he banked and leaned over the coaming, waving and shouting greetings no one could hear. Then he was wiping his nose and brushing moisture from his cheeks. "They're alive. Someone's alive," he said to himself over and over again, incredulously.

Roaring over no-man's-land, he saw at least a half dozen corpses suspended on the wire and then heaps of bodies. All were clad in gray-green, all wore jackboots, and all wore coal-scuttle helmets. Germans. Dead Germans squandered in yesterday's counterattack.

Tracers arced toward him from a trench dead ahead. Maxim. Instantly, the major pulled back hard on the stick and pushed the throttle ahead. Roaring and with the rev counter needle moving toward the red, the Le Rhone rocketed the graceful pursuit upward, the horizon dropping below the cowl and the pilot's vision filling with blobs of billowing clouds interspersed with patches of aching blue sky. The tracers dropped off far below.

Bursting from behind a cloud, the sun hurled a brilliant lance of fire that forced Randolph to reset his goggles, look away, vision starred by the memory of its brilliance. "Only a fool looks at the sun," he said to himself testily. Distracted by his boredom, he was making the mistakes of a novice. Don't fix! A glance at his altimeter told him he was at nine thousand feet. After leveling off and easing the throttle, he resumed the veteran pilot's scan, the quick, flitting search that covered the sky about him, sweeping back and forth, down and over in jerky movements like an old man with palsy. A quick side glance could detect a cluster of fly specks while simply staring at the same space might reveal nothing at all. Still, the only other plane in the sky was Reed's, above and behind.

"Watch out for the Hun in the sun," his instructor had warned so long ago. And he, too, had mouthed the same warning to new chaps, too, so many, many times—too often uselessly.

"Bloody clouds! Bloody clouds," he shouted into the slipstream, suddenly blinded by a great milky dumpling that shrouded the Nieuport with the heavy moisture of yesterday's rain. Hunching over the controls, the major steered by his magnetic compass, maintaining his easterly heading. Because he had plunged into the foothills of range after range of soaring cumulo-nimbus, he banked sharply to the right, heading south and away from the clouds that moistened his windshield and goggles with an opaque coating and clung to the trailing edges of his wings with long banners of dirty white vapor.

With a suddenness that struck with physical shock, he was bathed by brilliant sun again. And Reed was off his right elevator, waving a palm up apathetically. Looking around, Randolph answered the signal, shrugging. Nothing. Nothing at all. No Rumpler. No Boelcke. The sky was still theirs. Instead of dropping back immediately, Reed clung to the leading edge of the flight leader's elevator. Again, Randolph Higgins was struck by the beauty of the deadly little Nieuport scout. Painted a glaring white, the lithe aircraft was proof that the constructors' saying, "Airplanes that look right, fly right," was a valid dictum. With a short cowl covering the Le Rhone, the plane had a stubby appearance, slab-sided fuselage emblazoned with the RFC red, white, and blue roundel tapering gently back from the cockpit to the tail. Between the cabane struts, the .303 Vickers machine gun gave the pursuit its deadly sting, firing through the wooden propeller, synchronized with a cam and push rod Vickers-Challenger interrupter gear. He could even see the stagger wires stretched and crossing from the V struts to the cabane struts and two others supporting the landing gear, which was set well forward to prevent ground looping.

Banking gently, Higgins turned to the west, staring down at the valley. His brother Lloyd and the Coldstreams were down there in that inferno, somewhere. Maybe he was dead already, rotting with tens of thousands of others in those foul shell holes. He fingered the turtleneck of the Royal Navy cable-stitched wool sweater that he wore over his fur-lined *combinaison* and under his tunic and long tan leather coat. Geoffry had given him the sweater, saying with a twinkle in his eye, "If it can keep me warm in the North Sea, it'll bloody well keep you warm ten thousand feet over Berlin." At least Geoffry was warm, well fed, and clean in battle cruiser *Lion*. But there were rumors of a great engagement in the North Sea. He shuddered.

And then, despite pangs of guilt, his mind warmed with thoughts of his sister-in-law, Brenda. Without a doubt, she was one of the most stunning and enigmatic women he had ever met. Unreadable, she had been beautiful again and a mystery forever. Although she appeared soft and delicate as bridal lace, there was steel in her, a command of herself that told one he was in the presence of unflinching, relentless strength. And, obviously, she had never loved Geoffry. Anyone could see that except, possibly, his poor brother. Had she taken lovers? Probably several. Especially her French hairdresser, Andre. Those long trips to London. There weren't nearly as many after Andre's regiment was called up.

He had had many women; some single, others married. There had been that maid, Nicole—a firebrand, a wild, thrashing, clawing animal in bed. One afternoon after a frenzied tryst with Nicole, he had met Brenda in the servants' stairwell. With the maid's body heat still lingering on his flesh, he felt arousal again as he stared down at Brenda, standing face-to-face on the landing. "You're happy here?" he had asked hoarsely, hand on her elbow.

"Of course," she answered, not pulling away.

He pressed on, unable to tear his eyes from the fathomless blue depths. "Going to London tomorrow. Pick up something for you? Going right by Lucile's." The reference to London's most fashionable French dressmaker brought a smile to her face. He knew she was a Francophile with a taste for Parisian couturiers. "You would like something?"

"Perhaps," she answered hastily. "But I was planning to have Caldwell motor me in."

"I could take you."

She hesitated, grappled for words. "No. I can ride with Caldwell," she insisted, looking up steadily.

Her nearness, her warmth, the womanly smell of *L'Heure Bleu* urged him on boldly. "You know Trafalgar Square? Lord Nelson's statue?" he asked thickly, breath short as her eyes burned all the way to his soul. Again, the enigmatic smile. He misread it. "My place is nearby. . ."

"I'm sorry," she said, pulling away. "Not this trip." She turned and holding her skirts high, mounted the stairs. As his eyes followed her, he dampened his suddenly parched lips with the tip of his tongue.

A sudden motion caught his eye. Reed was waggling his wings and stabbing a single gloved finger down and to the southwest. Cursing his inattention, Randolph repeated the signal, following the gesture with his eyes. There it was. Far below. A shadow flitting from cloud to cloud. The Rumpler. It must be the Rumpler. A quick pull on the crank handle of the Vickers and he felt the spring drive home the first round, gib of the extractor engaging the first cartridge. A second jerk sent the feed block clattering as the first round was driven smoothly into the breech. The weapon was armed and cocked. Then a finger stabbed at Reed followed by a clenched fist over his head and he knew the lieutenant would circle protectively. Pushing the throttle hard open against its stop, he pulled back on the stick, kicking left rudder and split-essing into a near vertical dive. With full throttle, the gyroscopic effect of the whirling Le Rhone torqued hard to the right, forcing Higgins to counteract by moving the stick to the left along with stiff left rudder.

Engine roaring, wires screeching like banshees, the Nieuport plunged through a layer of clouds and then Randolph could clearly see the Rumpler through a veneer of stratus, burned by the sun to a thin film. Arrogantly, the Germans had penetrated deep behind the British lines, circling not more than two thousand feet over the third line of trenches. He felt hate surge with thoughts of these German workmen hanging in the sky with eyes like vultures, calling down death with cold dispassion on the Tommies groveling in the mud, perhaps on Lloyd.

Veering but continuing the dive, the major pointed the nose of the scout at a cloud bank hanging like a giant cream Napoleon a mile behind the German plane. He preferred an attack from below—the blind spot beneath the tail was free of fire from the observer's 7.92-millimeter Parabellum machine gun. Diving into the cloud, he felt a fluttering. Horrified, he saw the right lower wing vibrate, fabric wrinkling at the root. Pulling back on the throttle, his breath exploded in a sigh as the vibrations eased and the wrinkling vanished. Although he was blinded by the cloud, he was certain he was undetected by the Rumpler; the observer had been too busy glassing the British emplacement.

Watching the white needle of his altimeter spin backward

reeling off hundred-foot marks like the second hand of a watch with a broken mainspring, Randolph grew uneasy. In addition to a highly inaccurate altimeter that could be hurtling the pursuit into the ground, a prolonged dive often forced oil into the combustion chambers, drowning the engine. When the Le Rhone backfired and the black needle passed 1,500, he could wait no longer, pulling back on the stick, one eye on the lower wing, the other focused on the two rings of his gun sight.

Bursting into sunlight, he felt himself pushed down hard in his wicker seat by a force of gravity multiplied by at least a factor of three. The wings fluttered, vibrating the airframe and twanging the wires. Praying and shaking giddiness from his head, he bottomed out and pulled the nose of the Nieuport up into a shallow climb. Prayers answered, the wings held. But high spirits turned to anger and frustration when he found the Boche still below the Nieuport and in a curving dive toward the British third line of trenches, archie erupting around it like cotton pods spilling fluffly white cotton balls of smoke.

The major cursed and struck the breechblock of the Vickers. But he was still unseen. Either the crew of the enemy aircraft were novices or fools. The observer still hung over the side, staring through his binoculars. Striking the throttle with the palm of his hand, Higgins pushed the Le Rhone to full military power, bringing the tail and left side of the German into the first ring of his gun sight. Too far. But with the range closing, every detail of the camouflaged observation plane became clear: the pilot hunched over his controls under the high top wing; observer still staring over the side and tapping commands on the pilot's back; long, slender fuselage tapering to the tail fin like a flattened ellipse; the liquid-cooled Mercedes engine, cylinder heads jutting clumsily up from its upswept blunt nose and exhaust pipe sticking straight up and over the wing like a broken mast; the huge black Maltese cross painted against a white background on wings, fuselage, tail fin, and rudder. Then Randolph felt a familiar feeling course from his groin and spread with visceral heat; the way a man feels when he stands over a beautiful, naked woman, savoring the coming moment. With trembling fingers, he opened the safety lock and fingered the red trigger button.

Suddenly, the observer turned, looked up, pounded the pilot's shoulder frantically and then swung the Parabellum around, pointing it at the death hurtling down like a lightning bolt from the storm clouds. Baring his teeth in a thin white line, Randolph felt both anger and anticipation and Brenda was very close. With the chance for a surprise attack lost, he kicked left rudder, following the Rumpler as it bounced out of his ring sight, banking into a sharp turn to the north and the German lines.

"Not so easy, Boche bastard," Randolph muttered, pulling back gently on the stick and ignoring the antiaircraft fire that was exploding far overhead. "Those buggers will never learn to cut their fuses," he growled to himself.

Immediately, glowing firebrands arced toward him and fell off beneath the fuselage. Tracers! Six hundred yards. Too far!

With the top speed of the Rumpler only ninety miles per hour and the airspeed of the diving Nieuport at least an incredible 130 miles per hour, the range closed quickly. The Englishman tingled his thumb over the red button but held his fire, the Boche growing in his sights. A hammer drummed on the scout. Canvas ripped from the upper right wing and bits and tatters streamed. The gunner was good. Very good.

The Rumpler filled both rings. Two hundred yards. Zero deflection. *Now!* Higgins jammed the red button hard. The airframe bucked and vibrated as the Vickers stuttered to life. Firing five hundred rounds of ball a minute and with every fourth round a tracer, to the major the machine gun appeared to be squirting the target like a garden hose loaded with glowing fireflies. With the button held down for a long five-second burst, the breechblock devoured cartridges like a hungry jackal, ammo-belt jerking and racing up from the ammunition tank to the right side of the block where it vanished, reappearing empty on the left side, spewing brass shells against the guards then bouncing them into the slipstream like glistening yellow confetti.

He scored. Ripped fabric streamed from the German's elevators and dust and splinters streaked and puffed from the fuselage, exposing ribs and wire stays. A hundred yards. Eighty yards. Firing short bursts, cooling his gun, which would jam if held open too long. Desperate to throw off the Boche's aim, he kicked full rudder and skidded from side to side in the flat turns that only the Nieuport 17 was capable of, feeling the wings flex at the strain and hearing the wires pop and hum with changing tension. But the Hun gunner was a good shot, Randolph's stick and rudder bar vibrating as slugs pockmarked his tail. Suddenly, the Parabellum fell silent and the observer stood straight up, frantically changing drums.

Centering his controls, the major brought the enemy back into the gun sight. Slightly above and no more than fifteen yards behind, Randolph had his killing angle. He pressed the button. Struck by a half-dozen .303 rounds, the observer jerked straight up, flinging his arms out like a crucified martyr, spurting blood from his ripped chest and throat. A fine red mist streaked in the slipstream, coating the scout's windshield and Randolph's goggles and layering his cheeks with a thin red patina. Then the observer tumbled over the side, held in only by his belt loosely like a broken rag doll.

Desperately, the German pilot dove toward the ground, but a storm of tracers from the British trenches flattened his dive. Hungrily, the pursuit plane clung to his tail as if attached by a cable, closing the range to not less than eight yards as the two planes roared over no-man's-land. Randolph fired, but the German jinked out of his gun sight, observer flopping from side to side, wind-whipped arms flailing over his head like a supplicant in a frenzy of prayer, staining the fuselage with blood and gore.

More blood splattered on Randolph, obscuring his vision. Cursing, the Englishman pushed up his goggles and wiped his windshield with the back of his glove. He had never been this close to the enemy. In fact, he was so close to the Rumpler he could feel the backwash from its propeller. With a little left rudder, he moved to the side, out of the turbulence.

The pilot turned and faced Randolph. His goggles were up showing haunted blue eyes in the smooth face of a boy not more than twenty. Thin lips were set in a slack jaw that trembled. He needed a shave, blond whiskers glistening on cheeks and chin. Randolph hated the enemy but disliked killing helpless men. Pulling even closer, he extended a palm backward, toward the British lines. The boy shook his head from side to side and then pushed the Rumpler into a dive.

"Fool! Bloody fool!" Higgins spat, half rolling in pursuit. "You have no chance!" Just as the Englishman centered the pilot's head in his ring sight, the German glanced fearfully over his shoulder. At a range of no more than twenty feet, Randolph fired only four rounds. Every ball hit, hammer blows tearing the top of the boy's head off, sending a gray red gout of blood, brains, shattered skull, and torn leather into the slipstream. Instantly, the observation plane fell off on its left wing, beginning its final twisting plunge.

Fascinated, Randolph watched as its top wing ripped off at five hundred feet and then its lower wing folded up like wet cardboard and tore away and fluttered behind, the doomed plane plummeting into the shell holes as if an alchemist had turned it to lead. There was an explosion and greasy black smoke billowed from the grave.

Tracers. Explosions. Thirty-seven millimeter and seventy-seven millimeter. He was over the German lines. Pulling back on the stick and kicking the rudder bar, the major turned for his lines, clawing for altitude. Tracers fell off below, but black and brown puffs of archie splotched the sky all around like a virulent pox. Half rolling, Randolph brought the stick back between his knees to his stomach, diving toward no-man's-land and away from the enraged gunners. Then another half roll and he leveled off, skimming a few feet over the shell holes. He sighed. Friendly trenches were ahead and he was well out of range of archie. High overhead he saw Reed, circling protectively.

Smiling, Major Randolph Higgins pulled back on the stick and turned toward home.

When Randolph arrived over Number Five Squadron's aerodrome—a French farm midway between Douve and Bailleul—it was early afternoon and a fresh northerly breeze had stiffened the T-shaped windvane flying from the peak of the barn so that the T pointed to the south. Circling counterclockwise at eight hundred feet and still feeling the exhilaration of the kill—the raptures of fighting madness in which the threat of death or hideous injury was of no consequence—Randolph Higgins chuckled as he stared down. An aerodrome, indeed? A farmhouse for headquarters and his billet and officers' mess, the barn and three canvas-covered, wooden-framed Bessonneau hangars, three long buildings also of flimsy construction serving as barracks for the fourteen pilots and fifty-seven ground crew and two crisscrossing runways in what had been a wheat field. Twelve miles behind the front, there were no trenches snaking below through leprous and pockmarked earth like loathsome reptiles. Instead, the entire green landscape was free of the pox of war—bountiful fields forming a mosaic of a dozen shades of green interspersed with the dark brown of ploughed fields and separated by long rows of poplars, oak, and hedgerows.

Although Randolph had wiped his windshield vigorously with his glove, the cold of the high altitudes had coagulated and stiffened the gore splattered on the glass and his attempts had only smeared the mess across his vision. Now in the warmth of low altitude, the hardened blood softened and sagged in rivulets like warm butter. A swipe with his glove cleared enough of the windshield to satisfy the major. Glancing at the glove, his high spirits were replaced by a sick empty feeling; the thickening blood was speckled with gray bits of brains and white splinters of bone. Frantically, he banged and rubbed the otter skin against the doped canvas of the fuselage. He had killed many men but never this close; never close enough to smear his aircraft with their bloody hash. *C'est la guerre* ran through his mind. He shrugged. Then remembering more men were shot down on their final approach on their own aerodrome than in any other situation, he made a final search of the sky. He saw nothing.

Pushing gently on the stick and balancing with left rudder, he banked to the east while Reed made his approach. Within minutes, his companion's Nieuport had cleared the row of poplars and stone wall to the south and settled down on the runway. Ground crewmen rushed to the aircraft like courtiers to a queen and pushed the little scout toward one of the hangars. A last glance at the wind sock and Higgins circled south of the field and made his approach. Reducing power, the engine's beat dwindled to a burbling murmur and the little biplane fluttered and sailed to the left as the loss in torque changed the balance of the aircraft. A little right rudder corrected and with the throttle cut to the last notch, the wind soughed and hummed through the struts and wires like the breeze off the channel whipping the great oaks of Fenwyck. Gliding over the poplars, the ground rushed up and Randolph could see the individual bent stubble of the ruined wheat beneath him. A gentle pull on the stick leveled the cowl with the horizon as he felt first his wheels and then his tail skid touch down in a perfect three-point landing. Without brakes, the Nieuport rolled freely toward the hangars but began to stop far short. Gunning his engine in short blasts, vibrating and wings rocking slightly from side to side, the exhaust ports fired blue clouds of burned petrol and castor oil into the clean air. Castor oil fumes gave a man diarrhea. He turned his head. Held his breath. Cursed as he taxied toward the hard-packed earth tarmac and the ground crewmen racing out to meet him.

Finally, only a few feet from the converted barn, Randolph turned off the ignition and the wooden propeller stopped stiffly and the fumes were whipped away. As usual, Higgins was overwhelmed by the lack of noise: the engine's roar, propeller biting into the air, slipstream, humming wires and struts, replaced by a silence so sweet it poured like nectar against his eardrums. Unsnapping his safety belt, he sagged back in the wicker seat for a moment, the same inevitable thought that flashed from his mind at the end of every patrol filling his consciousness: *The patrol's over and I'm alive*, he assured himself over and over.

As he pushed down hard on the combing, stepped out to the wing, and then lowered himself to the ground, he heard a robin. Turning quickly, he caught a glimpse of a pair of red-breasted birds racing over the strip toward the apple orchard to the east. "Not all birds kill each other," he muttered to himself.

"Good Lord, sir," a familiar voice said. "You brought part of the Boche back with you."

Randolph smiled at chief mechanic William Cochran, a short, round, white-haired, ruddy-faced Irishman with the twinkling eyes of a leprechaun. And, indeed, he was mischievous, known for his elaborate jokes and storied Saturday night drinking bouts that inevitably left the other four members of his ground crew prostrate while Cochran continued drinking and singing, his whiskey-addled baritone strident enough to fill Westminster booming through the canvas of his tent. Randolph moved to the front of the scout plane and stared at the Le Rhone with the sergeant. A half dozen ground crewmen clad in green, grease-stained overalls gathered around and stared at the engine. The propeller boss, cylinder cooling fins, front of the crankcase, cowl, and the leading edges of the wings were speckled with gore. Even the front of the fuselage and parts of the propeller were tinted scarlet as if the plane had been flown through a red fog. The rotten smell of death already hung in a heavy cloud. "No one can argue with this kill, sir. You brought the confirmation home with you." The sergeant raised an eyebrow. "Your fifth, Major. If we were Frogs, you'd be an ace."

Randolph felt his stomach knot and sour gorge rise. "Clean it up, Sergeant," he said curtly, turning to the farmhouse.

"Yes, sir." And then to the ground crew, "You heard the major, step lively, men!" Quickly, crewmen grasped wings and wheel struts and began pushing the scout plane into the barn.

As Randolph approached the farmhouse, he passed the

ready-alert room—a small tent with a wooden floor, furnished with a table made of two boxes and a pair of planks, two field cots, four stools, and an oil lamp. Four young pilots in full flight kit had interrupted their card game long enough to form a ragged line in front of the tent. Smiling as they saluted casually, they shouted, "Congratulations on your fifth, sir."

The major answered their salutes and muttered his thanks and, "Carry on, men, carry on," as he reached for the wrought-iron handle on the heavy oak door.

The farmhouse was at least two hundred years old. Built of stone and heavy oak timbers, it was large and had obviously belonged to a prosperous family. Entering the main room, which was his office, Randolph Higgins was greeted by three men: Lieutenant David A. Reed, who had already stripped off his flight clothes and was seated on a battered couch sipping a whiskey, squadron clerk Corporal Harvey Longacre, a bright young Welshman from Pembrokeshire, who was typing a report at an old sideboard that served as his desk. The third man was Randolph's batman, Sergeant Major Johnathan York, who approached Randolph with a glass in one hand and a bottle in the other.

Despite the discomfort of layered flight clothes and a desire to be free of them, Randolph dropped his helmet, goggles, and otter-skin gauntlets on a box that served as a table and moved to York, who extended him a dram of Johnnie Walker. Wordlessly, the major downed the fiery liquor with a single toss of his head and extended the glass. Quickly, York recharged the glass and Randolph sipped a mouthful, this time swirling it and working it around his teeth and gums, enjoying the sting and prickle and savoring the flavor before swallowing it. Slowly, he felt himself begin to unknot as the heat hit his empty stomach and the charge of alcohol coursed through his bloodstream.

"Congratulations on your fifth kill, sir," Sergeant Major York said in his scratchy, breathless voice. A small middle-aged man, his face was scored and riven by crags and deep lines of terrible suffering etched in 1914 on the banks of the Mons Canal when, as a member of the "Old Contemptibles," he had taken an Uhlan's lance in the shoulder—a murderous thrust that had punctured his windpipe and broken his clavicle and three ribs. A career soldier, as were all 125,000 members of the B.E.F. at the outbreak of war, and a veteran of fighting in India and Africa, he refused to die and turned his back on a discharge. Suffering a partial loss of his larynx and muscle strength in his left arm, he applied for any duty available. Eagerly, he accepted an assignment to the R.F.C. as a batman. He was conscientious, attentive, and loyal, anticipating his officer's needs and exercising the discretion and tact of a true professional. Randolph considered him irreplaceable.

Without a word, Randolph turned and he felt York's hands pull the skirtless leather coat from his shoulders. Then the fleece-lined flying jacket, the heavy Royal Navy sweater followed by the *combinaison* and two cable-stitched jerseys. Sighing with relief, Randolph flexed his arms under his tunic and loosened his collar. Even the warm afternoon air felt cool next to his skin. Seized by sudden weariness and relaxed by the alcohol, he sagged into a chair behind his desk—a battered old commode with a score of pigeon holes requisitioned from the post office at Bailleul.

Reed said, "Good show, old man. You didn't waste any ammo."

Nodding, Randolph studied Reed over his glass. The son of a wealthy importer, Lieutenant David A. Reed was a tall, slender young man with yellow hair like ripe wheat, flawless white skin, and the clear blue eyes of a poet or a killer. And indeed, he was both. A graduate of Eaton, he had acquired a taste for Chaucer, Spenser, Swift, Pope, Bacon, Shakespeare, Tennyson, and Browning. At the same time, he had become known for his violence on the playing fields. His room was jammed with books and athletic trophies. Two of the four German planes he had shot down—a Fokker Eindecker and a Halberstadt D-2—had fallen behind British lines. He had ripped the identifying numbers from the rudder of one and the Maltese cross from a wing of the other and the mementos hung from his wall, covering his bookcases.

Randolph said, "With you up there"—he gestured sky-ward—"I don't worry about a Hun sticking his Spandau up my arse."

The laughter that filled the room was interrupted by the sounds of a motor car pulling up in front of the farmhouse. Immediately, a spit-and-polish captain smelling of Kiwi polish and Brasso stepped haughtily through the door and walked to the center of the room where he clicked his heels grandly like an actor on the stage of the Old Vic. His polished boots and Sam Browne belt, glowing brass buttons and swagger stick tucked under his right arm all spoke of "staff." Randolph recognized Captain Wilfrid Freeman, a new member of General Neville Blair's staff. Gripped by the revulsion all fighting men feel toward rear echelon personnel, Randolph eyed the newcomer over his glass, not offering Freeman a drink—not even a chair. Reed and Longacre came to their feet in a mockery of attention and then slouched back in their chairs.

"I'm Captain Wilfrid Freeman," the staff officer said in a high-pitched, almost effeminate voice.

"I know. We met," Randolph said. "I'm Major Randolph Higgins.

"I'm from Division."

"I know that, too."

Freeman stared at the gore-splattered gloves, helmet, and goggles, casually thrown on the box. His face blanched and for the first time his aplomb appeared ruffled. "You're wounded," he sputtered. Randolph and Reed both chuckled humorlessly.

"No," Randolph said. "I brought a bit of a Hun back with me."

"Good Lord," Freeman said, regaining composure. "You get that close? We should issue you grappling hooks and cutlasses directly, by Jove." The captain chuckled at his own wit, but no one shared the humor.

"You should try it," Randolph said matter-of-factly. "It's jolly good fun."

"That's not necessary," the captain bristled. "I have volunteered repeatedly..."

"I'm sure you have," Randolph interrupted. "But what brings a member of Division here? There must be serious business afoot." He grinned slyly at Reed who raised his glass in response.

Uneasily, Freeman pulled a document from his pocket. Silently, he glanced at it and then looked up at Randolph, jaw working. He had the look of a man who wanted very much to be somewhere else. "It's your brother, Lieutenant Geoffry Higgins... Ah, the general wanted to—ah..."

Guessing the reason for the visit, Randolph came erect. "Out with it, man. Speak up!" He downed the remainder of the Johnnie Walker. Sergeant Major York refilled the glass.

Freeman spit it out. "Lieutenant Geoffry Higgins was killed in action on thirty-one May in battle cruiser *Lion* off Denmark. He died heroically..."

"Don't give me that tripe, Captain," Randolph said. "He's still 'gone west.'"

"'Gone west'?"

"Bought the farm," Reed explained.

"Oh," the staff officer said. And then quickly, "The general has granted you a seven-day leave beginning immediately."

Randolph stared at the glass, spoke to it. "Give my thanks to General Blair. However, I have two new flight lieutenants—Armstrong and Cartwright. They need a lot of training or they'll be two new dead pilots within a fortnight."

Reed nodded knowingly. "Major Higgins," he said. "Lieutenant Southby and I can take them in hand."

Randolph drank, shaking his head. "A week, David. I'll remain a week."

"But, sir," Freeman began. "The general..."

Randolph silenced the staff officer with a wave. "My brother will still be dead seven days from now." He came to his feet slowly, unseeing eyes like highly polished topaz staring through the captain. "Sorry, Major," he heard first from Reed, then York, and finally Longacre. Choking back the crushing sense of loss that only a brother can feel for the death of a brother, Randolph stood and turned, desperate for the solitude of his room. Walking toward the door he stopped, picked up the bottle of Johnnie Walker, and left the room.

IV

Fenwyck was sylvan tranquillity when Major Randolph Higgins returned. Standing before the great door, his eyes feasted on walks bordered with roses, violets, primroses, and bluebells. Cutting the lawn into rigid geometric patterns, a low maze of hedge crossed and recrossed the great green expanse that rolled like a peaceful emerald sea to stands of oak, beech, and elm to the distant north while nearby cherry and apple orchards bordered the lawn to the south and west. Stately and subdued and waving gently in the breeze, treetops in the forest were gilded by the afternoon sun with glimmers of silver and gold, contrasting with the rioting colors of blossoms in the fruit orchards and the colorful flowers bordering the walks. All was immutable, in harmony, and mocked the horror of the Western Front. Like all men fresh from the killing, Randolph felt a mélange of envy and resentment clutch at his guts.

Before the major could raise the heavy knocker, the door was opened by a liveried Dorset. "Welcome home, sir," the butler said, taking Randolph's bag.

"Thank you, Dorset," Randolph said, shaking the servant's hand. As he stepped into the entry, his mother and father burst from the study. Crying his name and sobbing, Rebecca clutched him, kissing his neck, his cheek, his lips.

Randolph held her close, whispering gently, "I love you, Mother."

"At last—my son, my son. You're home," she sobbed back.

He felt his father pounding his back and grasping his hand and shouting, "Welcome home, son."

Then a procession of servants trooped past, Pascal the chef, Caldwell the chauffeur, Sanders the grounds keeper, and finally a flushed Nicole who curtsied and smiled, her warm black eyes glowing like chips of black diamonds reflecting sunlight. Randolph smiled thanks back at their choruses of "Welcome home, sir."

Pulling at his tunic, Rebecca led her son to the drawing room. Quickly, she pulled him down on the black and gold Regency sofa, grasping his big hand in both of hers. Walter moved to a breakfront. "Whiskey?" he said, reaching for a bottle.

"Johnnie Walker, please."

Walter handed Randolph a glass of the amber liquid and then stood in front of the great pedestal clock, nursing a snifter of cognac filled far beyond polite levels. He looked very old, the veins of his face glaring red through cheeks rouged by too much alcohol. His stomach hung down over his belt and the overtaxed buttons of his shirt strained in their holes, pulling and wrinkling the broadcloth. Once-alert eyes were watery and dim as if he were only partially awake.

Rebecca's appearance shocked Randolph. It seemed she had aged ten years in a few months. Her skin had shrunk and faded to translucence, cheekbones protruding above deep hollows. New lines of terrible suffering sagged downward from the corners of her eyes and mouth and her eyes were fearful and filled with pain like an animal caught in a cruel steel trap, unable to free itself and tortured by its own struggles. "Geoffry's dead," she said as if she were trying to convince herself of the horrible truth.

"I know, Mother. And Brenda?"

Walter drank deeply and said, "She's upstairs—in her

room." He drank again. "She had a high fever and lost the baby last night. The fever killed it."

Rebecca turned her head to Randolph's shoulder. He sipped his Scotch and then held his mother's head. He could feel her shaking. She pulled away, turned her tear-streaked face to him. "This damned war," she gasped. "It killed Geoffry—kills everything. Even my unborn grandchild."

"Rot, Becky," Walter spat. "We must all serve. I'm too old for this one, but in 'eighty-three at Khartoum . . ."

"Please, Walter," Rebecca interrupted with a harsh timbre in her voice Randolph had never heard before. "We haven't heard from Lloyd in a fortnight . . ."

"I know," Walter said impatiently. "There's a lot happening on the Somme."

"True, Mother," Randolph said. "It's only natural mail would be slow." Randolph felt his mother shudder.

"Yes," she said. "I know. I know there's a lot happening. It took you a week to come home." And then turning away with her hand over her mouth, she said, "I've seen the casualty lists."

Silence filled the room, interrupted only by the precise ticking of the Berthoud movement of the antique clock. Walter broke it. "Geoffry was mentioned in dispatches. May be up for a DSO."

Randolph emptied his glass. His mother was crying again. The observer—the young pilot came back. The gore. The smell. They had mothers, ran through his mind. "I would like to see Brenda," he said simply.

The pain had been horrible; wrenching and spasmodic and then the life was gone. She had lost her baby. Doctor Mansfield had been there. Examining her again. "Lucky it was small, only nine weeks," she had heard him mutter to the nurse, Hilda Breckenridge. While the nurse took notes, his examination had been swift and businesslike. "Bleeding normal, temperature down to one hundred two, pulse and respiratory rates slightly elevated, skin moist." She felt fingers pushing behind her ears. "Mastoids normal." The fingers moved to her neck. Then a quick command, "Otoscope."

"Yes, doctor."

A hand turned her head and a tiny light pierced the gloom, finding her ear. "Slight inflammation has developed. Possible otitis." The hand turned her head. She felt a stick in her mouth, gagged, and tried to turn away. Firm hands turned her back and again the light. "Slight exudate on the pharynx and tonsils." The stick was removed, the light went out, and the doctor continued. "Watch for bloody sputum and chest pains. If she starts a lesion, the pain can give us its approximate site."

Brenda heard Rebecca's voice from the gloom in the corner of the room. "Does she have pneumonia?"

"Her lungs are not engorged or solidified," Mansfield said. "But the flu can very easily turn into lobar pneumonia and we've been guarding against this. She has developed some suspicious symptoms since my last examination and we will treat them."

"Will you bleed her?"

"No, Rebecca. I don't believe in venesection and, anyway, she has lost blood. We'll continue with creosote carbonate and caffeine sodium benzoate." He rummaged in his bag. "Here, Hilda, we'll start her on Dover's powder."

"Those drugs—you never told me?" Rebecca asked, a tremor in her voice.

The doctor's voice was edged with impatience. "Dover's powder is always used in cases of pneumonia or suspected pneumonia. It's a bracer—will strengthen her. Creosote carbonate helps the body fight leukopenia—loss of white blood cells—and caffeine sodium benzoate is a stimulant." Rebecca remained silent while the doctor turned to the nurse. "Give her the Dover's three times daily after meals."

"Yes, sir. Diet?"

"Continue with the diet I prescribed on my first visit— whites of eggs, plenty of milk with extra cream and sugar, gruel, eggnogs . . ."

"Continue the morphia?"

"Yes. But only in case of extreme pain. No more than one-sixth grain every six hours. I'll leave you enough for three days."

"Yes, sir. I almost ran out."

"Call me if she bleeds excessively or has severe abdominal or chest pains. And also"—he thumped his knuckles on his bag—"call me if her temperature reaches one hundred four or her respiration rate exceeds thirty-two per minute." His voice was tired and strained.

"Yes, doctor."

The case snapped shut and Brenda heard the doctor move to the door. He spoke to Rebecca. "She's not dying, Rebecca. We're giving her the latest treatment and the most modern drugs. She's a strong young woman and if she'll take her sustenance and gets plenty of bed rest, she should make a nice recovery."

There was a rustle of taffeta and Brenda sensed a new presence in the room. She heard Nicole's voice. "And we will pray, *Monsieur Docteur.*"

"I don't care if you dance around her bed with a bone through your nose and a potato in each hand." Rebecca gasped. Hilda tittered. "Just follow my instructions." He left.

Day and night blended into a pervasive twilight where the big, blond nurse who had been there for days and days either sat at her side or drifted about the room like a wraith. It had been an eternity. The heat. The aching. The damp sheets. The doctor's visits. The examinations. The pills. The needles. The dim light either from the filtered sunlight or the small lamp that burned all night while Hilda dozed in a chair. Rebecca, a praying Nicole, Walter, and her sons Rodney and Nathan appeared and faded; two-and-a-half-year-old Rodney wide-eyed and uncomprehending, standing on his toes and grasping his mother's hand while the governess, Bridie O'Conner, cuddled eleven-month-old Nathan. For them she must live, take the medication, force herself to eat. But her stomach refused food. At first, she even threw up water.

Finally, Randolph appeared with Rebecca and Walter. Loss of weight made her brother-in-law look taller, his tailored uniform creased in places where muscles had once bulged against the cloth. And there were new lines on his face, too, incipient creases of pain and cruelty that came to life when a shaft of sunlight struck his face, forcing him to squint. His once dreamy eyes had a hard glint as if he were finding it difficult to appear at ease. His big rough hands enveloped hers and she felt his lips against her forehead. "I'm sorry," he said softly. "We both loved him."

She looked up into the hard eyes rimmed with fatigue, whites veined red; eyes that had seen too much, suffered too much. They were fogged, inscrutable, beyond sorrow; perhaps, beyond feeling. "How many have you killed?" she asked in a low voice that stung like dry ice.

She heard her mother-in-law gasp. "Brenda, Randolph came home from the front to see you."

"See here," Walter flustered.

"It's all right," Randolph said, staring down, wiping his face with an open hand as if weariness was a mask he could pull off and discard. And then with the deep airy voice of a man who had seen the garden of hell, he said, "She understands—she knows."

Silence oozed through the room like heavy oil and Brenda could hear her breath laboring through the congestion in her chest. She captured his eyes with hers, blue pinpoints fixing and holding him like twin gun sights. Wordlessly, he broke away and left the room.

By the second day of Randolph's leave, Brenda had recovered enough to eat full meals and sit by her window. By the fourth day, she walked in the garden with Bridie and Nicole and laughed like a little girl, watching Rodney chase butterflies through the flowers and tumble on the lawn like a blithe spirit while Nathan crawled or tried his first uncertain steps. Even Rebecca brightened and Walter smiled over his cognac. But Randolph was restless. Especially after his daily calls to Colonel Courtney Covington at Whitehall. Oswald Boelcke and his Jasta 2 had appeared over the Somme and were on a rampage. Flying the new Albatross D-1—a sturdy machine with two synchronized Spandaus firing through the propeller—the Jagdstaffel had shot down eight B.E. bombers and six F.E.2b Bristol scout planes in four days.

Nicole's animation and barely suppressed excitement made Brenda smile inwardly. Whenever Randolph appeared in Brenda's room or joined the women in the garden, the French maid devoured him with her eyes and warm blood colored her cheeks. One afternoon, dusting paintings in the "Dutchman's Hall"—a small alcove off the hall at the head of the cedar Chippendale grand staircase hung with two Van der Weydens, three Van Dycks, a pair of Rembrandts, and a single vivid impressionistic painting by the madman, Van Gogh—Nicole, duster poised, stopped Randolph with a husky "*Bonjour,* Monsieur Higgins."

In the full bloom of her beauty, she appeared more beautiful than ever. True to her genesis in Monoesque—a small town near Toulon in the Cote d'Azur—she had huge dark eyes under thick brows set in a lovely face molded to the line of her ancestry. Black hair like silk pulled back severely in a chignon accented her high cheekbones and skin tinted by her Latin blood the color of old ivory. In the dim light, her nose appeared straight and her nostrils delicately chiseled, her mouth curved uncertainly with a slight sensual pout to the lower lip. Her breasts were large and pointed, a tight white apron nipping her black taffeta dress in at the waist, flaring to fully formed womanly hips and buttocks that flowed sinuously when she walked.

Randolph eyed her from head to toe with cold, calculating eyes. "Good afternoon, Nicole," he said simply. He made as if to pass her. A small white hand restrained him.

"Have you forgotten where my room is, monsieur?"

His gaze collided with hers like ice dropped into hot tea. "No, Nicole. I've had other things on my mind."

"*Le galant homme* no longer likes Nicole," she said, a slight tremor in her voice, eyes suddenly liquid.

"No, no," he hastened. "It isn't that, Nicole."

"Then what, monsieur?"

"I don't know. I don't know," he said huskily, tearing himself away and turning to the door of Brenda's room.

On the fifth night of Randolph's leave Brenda was awakened by the buzzing of a huge fly, the rumble of thunder and flash of lightning. Pulling on a robe, she stood at the french windows and stared toward the coast in the direction of Faversham and Chilham. The buzz was engines in the sky, the thunder was antiaircraft guns, and the flashes exploding shells and searchlights reflected by the clouds. She heard hurried footsteps in the hall and Nicole's excited shout. "Zeppelins! Zeppelins, madame! The master says you are to come downstairs."

"Nathan? Rodney?"

"Bridie is taking them downstairs now, madame."

Hurriedly, Brenda descended the dimly lighted grand staircase to the entry where Walter, Rebecca, Randolph, Dorset, Hilda, Bridie and the boys, and most of the servants were gathered. "Everyone to the wine cellar!" Walter shouted.

"Nonsense, Father," Randolph said, halting the entire group in mid-stride. "They're over Faversham, Father. Almost ten miles away. I don't think the kaiser is out to bomb Fenwyck." And then with a festive ring Brenda had not heard for years, he said, "Let's go outside and watch the show."

Walter tapped a silk slipper on the marble of the entry. "All right—women and children to the wine cellar."

Nicole and most of the female house servants turned to the cellar with Bridie and the boys in the lead, but Brenda followed Walter, Randolph, and Rebecca out onto the great Tudor porch fronting the house. Silently, the foursome stood at the corner of the stone surface and stared to the north and west. High in the sky a cigarlike shape was illuminated by searchlights, bright, probing fingers that converged on the great airship like phosphorescent sticks. All around the Zeppelin the bright flashes of archie winked like tiny stars with the lifespan of a millisecond.

"Faversham—why Faversham?" Walter asked himself. "They usually bomb London."

"The wind, Father."

"There isn't any wind, Randolph."

"There is up there, Father. They've been blown to the south and east of London by the Arctic gale and they're emptying their bomb bays before they reach the Channel. Dover may catch it, too."

"How high?"

Randolph remained silent for a moment. "Fifteen—twenty thousand feet."

"It must be cold."

"Freezing. Those Germans are brave men."

"They're vermin, Randolph, and our guns will exterminate them."

Randolph chuckled humorlessly. "Look at those bursts. Thirteen-pounders and three-inch. They don't have the range. Most are below it and the others are wild."

"Then why bother with the guns?" Walter snapped.

"It's good for civilian morale."

"But some Zeppelins have been destroyed. Sublieutenant Warneford got the VC for blowing one up with bombs over Belgium."

"True, Father. But it's hard to get above one and drop the bombs accurately enough. He was lucky. The latest thing is incendiaries. By now, most of our interceptor pursuit planes should be equipped with them."

"Ignite the hydrogen?"

"Of course, Father."

Rebecca spoke for the first time. "And they burn to death."

"All the way down," Walter said, chuckling.

A new chain of heavy explosions punctuated the cacophony of antiaircraft fire. "He's dropping his bombs," Randolph said.

"On civilians—women and children. He doesn't care who he kills," Walter barked.

Randolph remained silent. Rebecca said in a trembling voice, "Horrible. Horrible."

Walter whirled on the group, pointing at the sky dramatically. "The Hun is a bloodthirsty savage. They have taken Count Graf von Zeppelin's invention and made a fiendish killing machine of it. Never will you see the RFC—never will you see English gentlemen drop bombs on innocent people—destroy cities just for the joy of killing." He stared up at Randolph. "Right, my boy?"

"Quite right, Father. We kill like gentlemen."

Brenda was fascinated by the bright cigar. It appeared larger. "It's closer," she said. Then she saw streaks in the sky like garlands of fireflies.

"There's a pursuit up there," Randolph said. "Probably a Sopwith Pup. There are two squadrons stationed outside London."

"How can you tell?" Walter said, squinting. "I can't see an airplane."

"I saw his tracers."

"The fireflies," Brenda said.

"Right. The incendiaries glow and every fourth round is a tracer. You can see the burning phosphorus. It's very bright at night," the flyer explained like a teacher instructing a student. "Watch behind and above the Zeppelin. He'll probably attack from that quarter."

"Eighteen—twenty thousand feet," Walter said incredulously.

There was excitement in Randolph's voice. "The Pup's ceiling is nineteen thousand feet. The pilot's all bundled up and he's sucking on an oxygen bottle."

"My God, my God," Rebecca said.

Suddenly, the sky above and behind the Zeppelin was crisscrossed with tracers that appeared very bright. The antiaircraft fire had stopped, but the searchlights still held the behemoth firmly in their fingers. Turning in a futile effort to escape the lights, the giant moved south and a new battery of lights near Chilham—only three miles away—sprang to life, bathing the dirigible with even more light. The control car and four engines were visible.

"It's closer—lower," Brenda said.

"He's attacking," Randolph shouted. "And they're shooting back."

As Brenda watched hypnotized, she saw a dull red glow light up like a new Edison electric lamp inside the huge envelope of the dirigible. "He's got him!" Randolph shouted triumphantly.

There was a puff of orange flame high in the sky and all of the men cheered: Walter and Randolph on the porch, Dorset and Pascal from the doorway, Caldwell and Sanders from the drive in front of the four-car garage. But Rebecca and Brenda remained silent, staring upward, unable to break their eyes away from the tragedy flaming to life in the heavens. Quickly, flames raced the length of the great airship, as cell after cell of hydrogen puffed into flame. Dropping its nose, the great airship began to fall, burning pieces whirling off into space in the heated turbulence, other chunks of incandescent wreckage breaking away and streaming down in a fiery torrent. Great roiling areolas of flame stormed above it like luminous spheres, rising, swirling, blinking red, orange, and yellow. Its control car broke loose and dropped, a streaming meteor followed by two tumbling motors. As the dying giant accelerated its nose-first plunge, its girders, heated to incandescence, glowed through the flames and its framework buckled and broke, transforming the once majestic giant into a flaming shower of burning canvas, wood, hot metal, and blazing, screaming men.

"He'll crash in the North Downs," Randolph said.

"A new sun at two in the morning," Brenda said to herself. And indeed the cataclysm had given birth to a brilliance that reflected from the clouds in a red glow as if her men had bled on them. But the new sun set quickly, the mass of blazing wreckage plunging into the downs just a few miles east of Fenwyck. Flames leapt and curled for a few minutes, bits of burning wood and canvas swirling in thermals created by the heat of the immolated colossus like sparks in a cyclone. Silently, the spectators stared while the blanket of night closed slowly over the grave until only a dull salmon glow pulsated and faded into the darkness. A gentle breeze sprang up and suddenly they could smell it: the faint odor of burned wood, solvents, petrol, oil, vaporized metal, and a strange, sweet aroma of burned meat, much like overdone roast.

Walter broke the silence. "A victory! A victory! We showed the Boche swine." He chortled boisterously.

Without a word, Brenda turned and returned to her room.

That night Geoffry returned and stood next to Brenda's bed. His uniform had been burned off and his body was in such an advanced state of decomposition that roasted flesh putrefied in a broth of maggots. The stench was overpowering—a sweet, sticky assault of burned flesh, the reek of decay and corruption. The flames of the burning Zeppelin were in his eyes and he was smiling although he had no lips. Slowly, he raised an arm and reached for her with a hand of blackened, charred bones. "No! No!" she screamed.

Hilda was shaking her. "Mrs. Higgins!" she called in alarm. "Wake up! Please wake up."

Slowly, Brenda came erect and the nurse propped a pair of pillows under her head and turned on the lamp. "Geoffry was here," Brenda said, staring at the ceiling with eyes of glass.

"A nightmare, Mrs. Higgins. I'll get you a glass of hot milk."

"I know now."

"You know what, madam?"

"About the honor—the glory they die for. I know what it did to my husband."

"But you knew he died a week ago."

"Yes. But now I know how."

The next morning at dawn, Walter, Randolph, and several of the male servants drove to the North Downs to view the wreckage of the Zeppelin. When they returned, Walter's eyes danced with excitement and he raptured over the "Roasted Huns." Randolph was subdued and taciturn. Then early in the afternoon, Lloyd and Bernice arrived.

Rebecca's joy was unbounded and she tearfully led her son and daughter-in-law into the drawing room. Walter was in close pursuit, pounding his son on the back and shouting greetings and remarking proudly about Lloyd's promotion to colonel. Within minutes, Lloyd, his mother, and father were seated on the Regency sofa while Bernice and Brenda sat in a pair of matching stiff-back Louis XVI armchairs. Randolph bent over the elaborate marquetry breakfront and began to pour drinks. Wordlessly, the flyer handed his brother a full glass of Scotch, his father a generous charge of cognac, and each woman a polite portion of cognac in large crystal snifters.

Brenda studied Lloyd over the bowl of the short-stemmed goblet. The war had done its work. Now forty-five years old, he looked sixty. His six-feet-two-inch frame appeared emaciated, his chest sunken, fingers bony tendrils. He had lost most of his hair and the skin of his skull was pulled so tight, veins in his temples stood out in blue lines. The gunmetal gray eyes shifted nervously and had the same dull, unfeeling look she had seen in Randolph's. The shocking similarity did not end there: new creases on his face formed the same latticework of anguish and cruelty she saw on his younger brother's face. Despite nearly a twenty-year age difference, the two brothers had moved closer together and in some strange way, had begun to resemble each other.

"Geoffry," Lloyd began in a flat monotone. "I only got word two days ago."

Walter explained the circumstances of Geoffry's glorious death while his two sons emptied their glasses and Rebecca stared at hers. Lloyd nodded silently and took another drink.

"It took you so long," Rebecca said.

"Yes, Mother. We've had a bit of business on the Somme and I had the devil's own time getting away." He smiled, showing a trace of his old humor. "I'm afraid they can't keep the show going without me, Mother." Everyone chuckled.

"They've got to for a week, Lloyd," Bernice said.

"Quite so," the colonel said, taking another drink. He eyed Brenda. "You're well, sister-in-law?"

"Yes. Thank you. But I lost the baby."

"I'm sorry."

Brenda nodded her appreciation. "But I am much better. In fact, I dismissed the nurse this morning."

"The Hun, you have him on the run," Walter said after a generous pull from his glass.

"He doesn't run, Father," the colonel said.

"Your children?" Rebecca asked suddenly while Walter chafed.

Lloyd obviously welcomed the change in conversation. Smiling warmly, he talked of his fourteen-year-old son Trevor and nine-year-old-daughter Bonnie. His eyes glowed with humanity for the first time and he gestured animatedly. "They're with their governess at our place in St. James," he concluded.

"St. James?" Brenda said.

Bernice turned to Brenda. "It's our new place. You've never seen it. It's in London's West End just east of Hyde Park."

They talked of children, friends, and family, carefully avoiding mention of the war. Finally Walter rose. "Your old room is waiting for you, my boy," he said, grasping Lloyd's shoulder. "Freshen up. We have a fine dinner planned for you."

As Brenda came to her feet, Bernice took her arm. "Rodney, Nathan. I would like to see my nephews."

Brenda smiled back into the warm eyes. "The garden. It's time for their afternoon romp."

Although Pascal had prepared an elaborate meal—a vegetable consommé of leeks, potatoes, and chicken stock called *consomme julienne*; *huitres marinees*, a broth of baby oysters marinated in white wine; steaks prepared with crushed peppercorns Dorset announced as *entecotes au poivre*; exotic vegetables; and a superb crepe suzette sweetened with Grand Marnier and Graves for dessert—the meal was a disaster. Geoffry's empty chair glared back at everyone, casting a pall like a wet blanket, curbing the appetite for food and creating a thirst for liquor. The three men drank far more than customary: first the Bordeaux and the Chablis vanished before the entrée and the men switched to heavier liquors; Scotch for Randolph and Lloyd, cognac for Walter. Even Rebecca drank more than usual, gulping the Bordeaux and staring at the empty chair. Brenda sipped at her wine until her head became light and the glare from the lanterns diffused like mist-filtered sunlight in the downs.

Finally, Lloyd leaned back, pulled out a pack of Gold-flakes—a cigarette preferred by the ordinary Tommy in the trenches—and puffed a cloud of pungent smoke into the air. "My boy," Walter said, emptying his glass. "I have Turkish and Egyptian cigarettes and tobacco in my library."

"Very good, Father," the colonel said, beginning to rise.

"Turkish?" Brenda said. "We're at war with them—fighting them in the Dardanelles."

The men looked at each other. Walter cleared his throat. "There are ways to get anything you want in this world, if you are willing to pay. Daresay, I could import sauerkraut from the kaiser if I stacked the quid high enough." He laughed raucously, but the sound was lonely.

"Another cousin bought it," Lloyd said, slurring his words. Everyone turned to him expectantly while he emptied his glass and took another pull on his cigarette. "Jerry Cameron of the Royal Scots—he bought the farm at Amiens last week, the sector next to mine. He was leading a wiring party. A 'whiz bang' landed on him. Not enough left to . . ."

"Lloyd!" Rebecca said, her face a book of horror.

"Sorry, Mother." The colonel emptied his glass. Immediately, a servant filled it.

Brenda remembered the jolly, kilted major of the Royal Scots with the huge handlebar mustaches and the big laugh. "Cherry Bottoms," the Scots had been called because of their aversion to underwear. Now Jerry was gone with cousin David Gellars of the Black Watch killed at La Cateau and Cousin William Ainsworth of the Surreys lost at Mons. All three had left widows and orphans behind. Suddenly, the sharp blade of anguish twisted in Brenda's stomach and the sour taste of the gourmet meal scalded the back of her throat. But she choked it back and washed it down with wine while everyone else at the table drank and stared straight ahead, avoiding each other's eyes.

Walter thumped the table with beefy fingers and made an attempt to elevate the mood. "I have more news. Cousin Reggie's in town. His destroyer's laid up at the Royal Navy Dockyard at Chatham and he's had a bit of the flu." He nodded at Brenda. "Anyway, I got a wire from him just before dinner. Says he'll be here in two or three days."

"Cousin Reggie?" Brenda said. "I haven't met him."

"Commander Reginald Hargreaves of the Royal Navy," Walter explained. "Not really a 'cousin'—he's the son of my first partner William Hargreaves who represented Carlisle Mills in New York before—ah, before Geoffry took the position." He turned to Brenda. "William took a place on Long Island in 'eighty-eight and married an American—Eloise."

"Then Reginald is an American?"

"No. He was born in Wembley, just north of London, but has spent years in America. Speaks with an accent." Everyone chuckled. He continued with obvious pride. "Early education in America, but he was accepted by the naval college at sixteen and made sublieutenant by twenty." Walter held up his glass for a refill and downed it in one draught. Smacking his lips, he wiped his mouth with the back of his sleeve. Brenda felt revulsion.

Randolph broke his silence. "Reggie's father, William, would split his time between New York and London. He owned twenty percent of the White Star Line and he was loyal 'til the end. He always steamed White Star."

"Hear! Hear!" Walter and Lloyd shouted, holding up their glasses and then drinking. Grimacing, Rebecca and Bernice exchanged a knowing glance.

Confused, Brenda raised an eyebrow. "I don't understand."

"*Titanic* was a White Star liner. He booked the finest cabin, next to Captain Smith's." Randolph drank before continuing. "We see Eloise occasionally, but since William's death she has remained in the States with Reggie's two younger sisters. But Reggie, bless him, is an Englishman through and through. He's only twenty-eight but commands the new K Class torpedo boat destroyer, *Lancer*."

"Got knocked about a bit at Gallipoli, I hear," Lloyd said.

"That's the word," Walter agreed. "Got a letter from Eloise a couple months ago." He pushed himself to his feet and wobbled as he tried to stand erect. "Gentlemen, the library."

Blinking and walking unsteadily, Walter walked to a door at the far end of the living room. Randolph and Lloyd followed and then Rebecca stood, waved to Brenda and Bernice, and followed the men. Following her mother-in-law, Brenda moved down a long, dark hallway past the breakfast room, sewing room, gun room to the door of the library.

Brenda had only glanced in at Walter's library two or three times. A male sanctuary, the panache of the room was accented by paneled walls lined with glass-doored bookcases, hardwood floors covered with layered rugs and a half dozen sporting prints hanging from the walls or, in the Victorian tradition, resting on the shelves of the bookcases. Her eye was attracted to a corner where a magnificent eighteenth-century Carlin long-cased clock veneered with tulipwood, banded with purple-wood, and inlaid with narrow fillets of ebony and box swung its compensated pendulum, inexorably ticking off the seconds. Brenda had never seen such an elaborate timepiece. The dial was calibrated to show sidereal time by a green hand and the date within a panel below the center. Surmounting the dial was a group in gold gilt of Apollo driving his chariot. Even the signs of the zodiac were shown, painted in gold leaf around the dial. Hanging on the wall next to the clock was a wall barometer of ebony and brass, mounted on an elaborate tapering shaft veneered on oak with alternate strips of brass and tortoiseshell. Like the clock, its motif was eighteenth century and French.

Walter had sunk into the deep leather of his chair behind a huge mahogany serpentine writing desk laden with racks of carved pipes, tins of tobacco, and ash receivers. Within reach on a Sheraton sideboard were cut-crystal decanters filled with cognac, wine, and whiskey.

Randolph and Lloyd had already seated themselves in

plump chairs in postures of alcoholic fatigue, but Walter was staring up at Rebecca, his face clouded with anger. "You have your sewing room . . ." He waved. "This is my place—a man's place. Please leave."

Again, Brenda heard this hard new timbre in her mother-in-law's voice. "No," she said. "My boys are on leave—I may never . . ." She choked back the unspeakable and continued, "It may be a long time before I see them again . . ."

"All right, woman," Walter shouted impatiently. "Sit over there—all of you." He waved at a sofa in a corner.

Brenda felt anger flare and then seethed as she followed Rebecca to the richly upholstered sofa and seated herself between her mother-in-law and Bernice. Quickly, drinks were passed around to everyone; wine for the women, whiskey and cognac for the men. Then, the smoking began; Walter puffing on a pipe, Lloyd on an Egyptian cigarette, and Randolph on a huge Havana cigar. Silently, the men leaned back and the room filled with fumes. Rebecca coughed.

"You can leave," Walter said, smirking and puffing on the pipe until the bowl glowed red and blue smoke rolled in clouds.

"No!"

The men continued to smoke and drink quietly. At length, Walter said to Lloyd, "The new commander of the BEF, Sir Douglas Haig, have you met him?"

Lloyd held up his glass and stared at the contents. An acid bitterness came through the slurred words. "At the Savoy once—never at the front. None of their sort—John French, Henry Rawlinson, Haig—ever leave their châteaus. We call them 'château generals.' They don't know what it's like and don't give a toss." He drank deeply. He snickered to himself. "Do you know Haig said the Maxim gun was overrated and unimportant. He should charge one—see the results." His laugh was acerbic. He drained his glass. Walter poured him another.

For a moment only the sounds of the Carlin clock could be heard. Then Walter's next question jarred Brenda. "The front—what's that lot like?"

While everyone watched, Lloyd toyed with his glass, swirling the amber liquid around until it spilled over. Walter recharged it although it was only half-empty and looked at his son expectantly. "Muddy," Lloyd said.

"Don't," Bernice said, staring at her husband fearfully.

Walter shot a hard glance at his daughter-in-law, then turned back to Lloyd. "Muddy?" he said, leaning forward eagerly. "Is that all?"

The colonel shook his head. Blinking furiously and unable to focus his eyes, he stared at a painting of a German short-haired pointer on a shelf behind his father. He spoke in a monotone. "There are trenches, barbed wire, and we live in dugouts. The Jerries fire seven-sevens, three-nines, five-nines, whiz-bangs, crumps, woolly bears, daisy-cutters, and sometimes bigger stuff—Maxims, rifles, gas, and they throw grenades at us. We attack. They attack. The dead are everywhere—in heaps on the parapets, on the wire, in shell holes. Sometimes they choke the trenches and there are so many we can't even count them—bury them. Sometimes, the smell is so thick we've got to put on our masks . . ."

"My God," Rebecca said. "Enough! Enough!" Brenda could hear Bernice sobbing into the palm of her hand.

Lloyd looked at his mother with a sick grin creasing his face and sipped his whiskey. "Sorry, Mother."

"See here, woman," Walter began.

Randolph interrupted him. "I'm tired," he said, rising. "I think I'll retire. I've got to return to London tomorrow."

"Tomorrow? A day early?" Rebecca managed.

"I have business, Mother—RFC business." And then smiling and nodding assuredly, he said, "I still have my place in Kensington."

"Bully idea. Time for bed," Lloyd said, coming to his feet and supporting himself on a side table.

Slowly the women and Randolph stood and filed through the door, Randolph and Bernice supporting Lloyd. Walter remained at his desk, glaring.

As Brenda walked down the hall, she realized she could not remain in the same house with Walter. He was unbelievable, an unfeeling animal. Although he had lost one son, he seemed to enjoy his secondhand view of the war. He would sacrifice them all if a new honor could be added to the field of the family's escutcheon or for a chance to be presented at court.

Mounting the staircase, Brenda's mind whirled with thoughts of home, her mother, father, her sister Betty, and her strong, handsome brother Hugh. Lord, she missed them. The warmth and love of home. Holidays together. Growing up together. Playing in the garden. The theaters and restaurants of Manhattan. Shopping with her mother. She would return. Must return. Escape from Walter and his arrogant pomposity. Escape from this cold, dismal island of death that had taken her husband and was squandering the lives of hundreds of thousands of others. But when? How? She was still weak. And there were U-boats. Could she risk Rodney and Nathan? She shuddered as she reached her door. Suddenly, she envied Randolph. He was leaving tomorrow. Would be in Victoria Station by nightfall. RFC business in London, he had said.

Victoria Station was a sea of uniformed men with waves of women surging around them; mothers, wives, and lovers of departing soldiers and sailors with faces veils of anguish while others welcomed returning men with fierce embraces, tears of happiness, and little joyful sounds like starved birds. Randolph felt relief as he shouldered his way along the platform toward the taxi stand. The ride from Faversham had been interminable, the carriage crowded with officers smoking cheap cigarettes; the usual Player's and Goldflakes. Eight men had crowded into a single compartment in the first-class carriage. Three of them had worn shoulder patches emblazoned with New Zealand, South Africa, and Canada. The others were of old-line British regiments. They had all seen the front. He saw it in their old, stained trench coats, battered caps, worn leather. He saw it in their brown faces like stone Buddhas, forced half smiles. And he saw it in their dead eyes—eyes that had seen death; eyes that could only see the past, never the future.

The talk had been of Gallipoli, the Somme, Flanders,

Ypres, Jutland, and comrades—living and dead. But Randolph never joined in. Instead, he sat back puffing on a Havana his father had forced on him. He disliked the hand-rolled cigar, but it was his only defense against the clouds of fetid smoke filling the small compartment.

His mind was filled with thoughts of Fenwyck; his father, mother, brother, Bernice, Nicole, and Brenda. His mother's appearance had been shocking. She was skeleton-thin and her skin had the pallor of death. Walter had been unbearable, especially when he had bored in on poor Lloyd on conditions in the trenches. He had never seen his brother drink so much. Lloyd had seen more than he could bear. Perhaps he had used up his ration of courage. Every man was given a finite amount. Once used, all that remained was a stripped shell of a man, useless and a menace to his comrades. They were beginning to use the expression shell shock.

And why had he refused Nicole? In France he had dreamed of her a hundred hot restless nights. A hundred times he had thrashed and turned in his bed, tortured by memories of the hot wet depths of her, the way she enfolded him in the crucifix of her limbs, moaning, meeting and riding his thrusts in perfect rhythm until final convulsions left them both weak.

It had been Brenda. He was sure of it. Since Geoffry's death, there had been a change. She had seen through him all the way to his soul the very first time he saw her in her sickbed. She knew about the killing, how it was part of his life. She knew he wanted her—had hungered for her for years. She knew about Nicole.

That was it. Sleeping with Nicole would have been an obscenity. The beautiful French girl loved him while she was only a receptacle for him; a convenient vessel to receive the explosive convulsions of his frustrations and suppressions. It would have been worse than killing a helpless man. Worse than having blood and brains splattered on his plane. He had never had a whore, but war was a whore and that was what he needed.

After a frustrating ten minutes of waving, shouting, and cursing, he finally managed to catch a taxicab. His flat in

Kensington was not on his mind. "The Empire," he said, as the cabby, a huge, round old man with white handlebar mustaches, pushed the flag on the meter down.

"Right-oh, your lordship. Leicester Square," the old man said, jamming the rickety machine into first with a clash of worn gears.

Before the war Randolph had always enjoyed the Empire. The largest dance hall in London, the vast and plushly ornate ballroom operated on four levels centering around the magnificent dance floor. In addition, there was always a good show and six bars for the thirsty and those searching for romance in exchange for a fiver. The main lounge was crowded with uniformed men and attractive women—powdered, perfumed, elaborately dressed women, nocturnal creatures ready to follow the first male for a price. A true flesh market in a palace of red plush furniture, gilded decor, and soft amber lights.

Randolph elbowed his way to the bar, bought a double Scotch with a dash of seltzer, and then weaved his way through the crowd to the gallery where one could lean on an upholstered rail to watch the show below. The best in vaudeville. Better than the Palladium. Jugglers. Magicians. Dancers. Harry Tate with his worn-out jokes that still convulsed the crowd. The usual songs with the crowd joining in: "Mary," "Tipperary," "Oh, You Beautiful Doll," "Little Gray Home," "Alexander's Ragtime Band." Randolph remained silent, downed his double, and returned to the bar with a warm, happy glow spreading from the pit of his stomach. Buying a refill, he returned to the plush rail just in time for a new song that had caught on with the RFC and was sung by every man in Number Five Squadron. Waving his hands and rocking from side to side, Harry Tate led the singers in his rasping, whiskey-addled baritone. Randolph downed half his drink and basking in the heat of the spreading alcohol, joined in:

> "The young aviator went stunting,
> And as 'neath the wreckage he lay—he lay,

To the mechanics assembled around him,
. These last parting words did he say—did say.
Take the cylinders out of my kidneys,
The connecting rod out of my brain—my brain
From the small of my back take the crankshaft,
And assemble the engine again."

"You like that song, Major?" a soft, husky voice said in his ear. Turning, Randolph stared down into the smiling face of a blonde of perhaps twenty-five years. Even in the dim light, her features were too severe to be beautiful. Her forehead was deep, and she had dark thin brows over wide-set piercing blue eyes that reminded Randolph of medieval stained glass. Her cheeks were rouged and her chiseled lips drew his eyes. Painted a bright red, they were full and sensuous under the lipstick and her long neck was slender and graceful like that of a gazelle or a swan. Her full body was expensively draped for a prostitute—her sheer silk chiffon fringed with metallic lace and slashed neckline outlined with gold threaded arabesques showed the style and characteristic robin's-egg blue of the Lanvin touch. No, indeed. She was not beautiful, but very, very sexy and, no doubt, expensive.

Moving his eyes over her body with unabashed candor, he sipped his drink, and said, "I helped write it."

"You like what you see, Major?"

"I would have to be blind."

She laughed, surprisingly not the hard, forced sound of the experienced prostitute, but the music of a brook over pebbles or trickling champagne. There was a young girl somewhere under all that powder, paint, and perfume. "Buy me a tot?" the woman said.

"Of course."

"Barsac, please."

In a moment, Randolph returned with a glass filled with Barsac and another double Scotch for himself. While at the bar cursing the slow service, he had wondered if the maddeningly desirable creature would be waiting when he returned, or would some fat general wave a fist full of pound notes in her face and vanish with her. But she was there, leaning over the rail, her gown outlining her tiny waist and perfect buttocks. Randolph caught his breath. She was not the ordinary whore. No, indeed. "Your drink," he announced with barely concealed excitement.

She brought the long-stemmed wineglass to her lips and stared up at him as she drank. "Oh, sorry," she said, suddenly extending the glass. "The RFC."

"The RFC. Cheers."

They drank. "I'm Cynthia Boswell, Major," she said, refusing to release his eyes.

"Randolph Higgins," he said, touching her glass with his. They drank, never breaking their locked eyes.

"You're a flyer," she said, nodding at the wings on his tunic.

"Number Five Squadron, scout planes."

"Where?"

"Sorry. Top secret," he hissed in a burlesque of a conspiratorial voice.

Again the fresh sounds of the brook and Randolph felt an overwhelming compulsion to wrap his arms around this voluptuous child-woman. He felt strangely disturbed and nervous. "Dance?" he asked suddenly, like a young boy asking for his first date. Smiling, she nodded and after downing their drinks, they descended the wide mahogany staircase to the dance floor just as the orchestra began the "Blue Danube," which was still popular despite the war against the Central Powers.

His arms circled a cloud, a gull planing on stiff pinions, whirling and turning in sweeps that sent her skirts swirling out and as high as her knees. And they were much too close to each other for polite company. But this was not polite company. The cream of England's manhood on the brink of death and the finest of the Empire's harlots all gathered in a temple of love negotiating for one last night of frantic passion. Hot, wet kisses, round, taut breasts, soft stomachs, and firm thighs ready to part and yield their treasure for a price. It was all for sale. A Harrods of the flesh.

They were cheek to cheek and his lips were against her ear. "My place?" he said.

"Why not?"

Randolph disliked his father's passion for antiques; his flat was expensively and tastefully furnished in contemporary style. His one concession to his father's taste was an Odilon Redon landscape hanging on the wall of the large living room, which opened onto a hall leading to a study, bedroom, and bath. The kitchen was in an alcove off the livingroom.

Smiling, Cynthia sank on a plump green velvet sofa. "You're an excellent dancer," she said.

"Thank you. Would you like a drink? I have Barsac. Sorry I can't offer you a bite, but I haven't been here in months. The pantry's empty."

"A drink is fine. I'm not hungry, thank you."

Randolph moved to a small cherry-wood sideboard stacked with bottles and returned to the sofa, handing Cynthia her wine while sipping his Scotch. He sat beside her.

"You're a marvelous dancer," he said.

"Thank you." She took his hand in hers and brought it to her lap. He could feel a firm thigh through the dress.

"Dance for me, Cynthia."

The line of her mouth altered, eyes chilled to the hardness of pale sapphires. He felt she was staring right through him at another place. He squirmed uneasily, coughed into his palm, and abruptly she was back, smiling into his eyes. "You would like that, Major?"

"Very much, indeed."

She set her drink on the table and ran a single finger down his cheek. "You're very handsome," she said, searching his eyes with hers.

"We haven't talked price."

She moved closer, brushed his cheek with her lips. "You can afford me," she assured him, rising. "I'll dance for my major." Slowly, she began to sway and glide about the room provocatively while loosening her hair and shaking her head, blond tresses tumbling and flowing like sheets of gold fleece to her shoulders. She unsnapped her honeycomb quilted belt and languorously dropped it to the floor, her eyes flashing blue light as if they were backlighted. Randolph felt a familiar heat spread from his groin and screw his guts into a ball, a rush of quick blood charging his veins.

She kicked off her patent leather court slippers, then her dress fell in a heap at her feet like a crashing curtain at a music hall. It was kicked into a corner with her shoes and she stood in front of him dressed only in black—a crepe de chine chemise and black silk stockings with black ruched satin garters circling her perfect thighs.

Randolph had never been with a prostitute—had never in his wildest fantasies expected this. The power of her sexuality was a palpable force that pulled him to his feet, a million hot needles pressing against his face and neck, his heart a trip-hammer pounding his ribs. Unable to catch his breath, he watched as the garters were thumbed and pulled down her legs and the silk stockings rolled into tight bands and thrown away. Then the black lace-trimmed chemise was pulled from her shoulders and allowed to tumble down to her hips and she moved her shoulders from side to side, her large, silky white breasts tipped with ruby aureoles swaying with the movement. Only the flimsy chemise dangling at her waist remained.

"My major likes me?" she asked with the coy little girl's voice. Wordlessly, he pulled her to him, crushing his lips down on her open, wet mouth, his tongue finding hers. Then he moved down her neck, her shoulders, cupping her breasts, kissing the nipples frantically. She moaned and twisted, her body hot satin under his hands, malleable, molding itself to his so that he could feel her against him from knees to firm young bosom, the heat of her soaking through his uniform, hips pushing hard against his arousal, her hands exploring his neck, shoulders, muscles of his arms, back. Randolph's mind was almost wiped clean by desire, yet he wondered about her passion. A whore was supposed to act—feign desire and pleasure. Yet she appeared to be aflame, aching for him. Her next words closed his mind and he became an animal reacting to instinct. "Your clothes—your clothes," she hissed, pulling at the buttons of his tunic.

Randolph stepped back and with fingers of clay fumbled with his belt, tie, and buttons. Laughing, Cynthia helped him undress until he finally stood nude in the middle of the room, his fine tailored uniform scattered across the floor like discarded rags. She eyed his broad shoulders, muscular arms, narrow waist, his manhood. "You're magnificent," she said, and in one quick movement of her hands and hips she pulled off the chemise and threw it aside.

For a long moment they stood silently and eyed each other. Then, without a word, Randolph picked her up and carried her into his bedroom.

Dawn's light awakened him. For a moment he listened for the coughing bark of cold Le Rhones coming to life for the dawn patrol. Then the soft fold of silken tresses against his cheek and shoulder brought him back and he sighed happily. It had actually happened. Cynthia was next to him, her nude body against his, her arm thrown across his chest. It had been a fierce—at times savage—night. Gently, he fingered his ear where she had bitten him and three small scratches on his shoulder where fingernails had left their traces. She had been insatiable, or, at least, appeared to be insatiable. Again and again he had taken her until at last he had lain fatigued, trapped by her limbs in a position as old as man, as unchanging as the constellations. Locked together, they had slept the deep sleep of exhaustion.

He kissed her cheek, her lips. She stirred. "I love you, Sean," she said dreamily, eyes closed.

He shook her shoulder. "I'm Randolph—Randolph Higgins. Remember?" he said testily.

She blinked her eyes and came awake. "Darling Randolph," she said, running her hand through his tousled hair and kissing him gently.

Randolph was confused and angry. How could he be jealous of a whore? Lord, no doubt she could not count the men—could quite easily confuse one for another; especially when awakening from the deep sleep of lovemaking. Still, he asked the question his better judgment rejected as childish and foolish. "Who's Sean?"

She touched her pouting lips with a single finger. "You're sure you want to know?"

"Yes."

She turned her face to the diffused light of the heavily draped window. "Major Sean Boswell was my husband. Three weeks ago he was shot down over . . ."

"Don't! Don't," Randolph cried. "I don't want to know."

She turned back to him. "You owe me nothing."

He sat up and swung his legs to the floor. "You mean we paid our debts to each other."

"Yes, in a sense."

He stared at his bare feet, chewed his lips, and then skinned them back abruptly. "Last night you were making love to him, not me."

Her voice caught on the edge of tears. "At first, perhaps."

"You danced for him—the way you danced for me."

The voice was so low it was barely audible. "Yes. He loved to watch me. But later it was you, Randolph—it was you."

He seemed not to hear. "Now you'll bed every major in the RFC to show Sean how much you love him?"

"I don't know," she whispered. "I don't know."

He whirled to her, eyes flashing. "He's a corpse—that's all he is. Understand? You can't do anything for him but put a cross over his grave. Don't prostitute his memory by becoming a whore."

"Please, Randolph . . ." She began to cry.

He ran a hand through the glistening folds of her hair. The words were rough, straight from the mess at Number Five Squadron. "You poor fuckin' civilians. Some of you bloody well suffer more than we do."

"Randolph," she managed through her sobs. "Will I see you again?"

"Perhaps." He came to his feet and began to dress.

V

Time moved slowly after Randolph left. However, within a week, Brenda had recovered most of her strength. She was even able to play on the lawn with the boys and take short walks through the gardens she loved. Doctor Mansfield was delighted, boasting about the "advances in medicine and the power of the new 'miracle drugs.'"

There were disturbing rumors about Jutland. In fact, the German press trumpeted claims of an overwhelming victory for the high seas fleet. Finally, late in June, a lone communiqúe was issued by the admiralty. Listing fourteen ships lost and over six thousand men killed and with only a single reference to "serious German losses," the report did little to relieve public concerns. Nevertheless, the stories of Jutland were crowded off the pages of *The Times*, *The Illustrated London News*, and *The Daily Express* by reports of a new offensive on the Somme and great British victories. Walter blustered and muttered to himself about the end of the "filthy Boche" while Rebecca fretted and worried. There were rumors of staggering casualties.

Compounding the gloom gripping the nation was the death of the secretary of state for war, Horatio Herbert Lord Kitchener. A week after Jutland, the hero of Omdurman was aboard cruiser *Hampshire* en route to Russia on a secret mission when the ship struck a mine off the Orkney Islands and sank, killing Kitchener and all but twelve of her 655-man crew.

Mail from the front arrived sporadically. Occasionally, hastily scribbled letters were received from both Randolph and Lloyd. However, most of their correspondence was written on field service postcards, saying the sender was well and little more. Brenda wrote long letters to both, usually describing her sons and family. Write! Just write anything, she told herself. She even wrote of the weather, the view from her room, new shows in London, and the first shopping trip to Faversham she had taken since her illness. In the nearby town she and Rebecca carefully selected items to be sent to Lloyd and Randolph: lamb and ham pie, Fortnum's fruitcake, dates, Gentlemen's relish, ham paste, Hartley's jam and marmalade, pickled herring, Lazenby's sauce, Peek Frean's biscuits and, sometimes, liquor were crammed into the parcels.

She wrote her parents, but mail crossed the Atlantic slowly or not at all. Letters were rare, but the correspondence she did receive told her father, mother, brother, and sister were in good health and new contracts for uniforms, powder bags, and tents had brought lucrative profits to the business. Her sister, Betty, had a new beau and her brother, Hugh, had been promoted to captain. There was an excellent chance the army would send him to London as an attaché. "The submarines, the submarines," Brenda said to herself, shuddering. Hundreds of ships had been sunk and now, perhaps, her brother would be sent into the maelstrom.

Fortunately, Walter was forced to make frequent trips to the headquarters of Carlisle Mills, Limited. With Geoffry dead and several of his key managers called to the colors, the old man was forced to negotiate the plethora of new contracts. Grumbling and armed with two or three stiff jolts of cognac, the old man would slump in the rear of the Rolls at least twice a week. Brenda would smile as she watched the motor car wind its way out of the long drive and head for London in the morning mists.

Almost a month after Randolph's departure, Commander Reginald Hargreaves arrived at Fenwyck. Brenda was in the nursery with the boys and Bridie when the chauffeur-driven staff car charged up the long drive. By the time the car had stopped in front of the house, Brenda was entering the drawing room.

Ushered into the drawing room by a bubbling Rebecca and a blustering Walter, the young commander seated himself wearily in a large chair facing the sofa where Rebecca and Brenda sat. He was a handsome young man with strong features that appeared chiseled from stone, the bones of his jaw and cheek and forehead massive and well shaped, hair the color of freshly washed wheat. Thick eyebrows that were nearly bushy came within a hair of meeting over a pair of clear blue eyes. An expensive tailored uniform fit loosely, making it obvious the commander had suffered a recent loss of weight. Nevertheless, his shoulders were broad, waist narrow, neck full and corded.

Endless hours on the bridge of a warship had turned his skin to a burnished ocher, and when he squinted the set of the few tiny lines angling downward from the corners of his eyes gave him the appearance of a much older man. The most impressive thing about the commander was his eyes—sharp and bright as a bared blade, and when he was introduced to Brenda, they caught and fixed the American with such intensity she felt as if she had been struck by a physical force. He had the same look as Randolph and Lloyd—the look of a man who had had outward civilities and the facade of normal behavior slashed away by death and constant danger.

Walter handed Reginald a whiskey, poured a cognac for himself, but the women refused liquor. Brenda was thankful that neither man smoked. Hargreaves spoke in a deep, resonant voice honed on the forebridge of a destroyer. "Sorry about Geoffry," he said with genuine feeling. "Heard about *Lion*. Ugly show. But Geoffry did splendidly." He held up his drink and he and Walter drank silently.

"We're proud of our son," Walter said, staring at Rebecca. Rebecca turned away.

Reginald asked about Randolph and Lloyd. Walter spoke of his sons' accomplishments in glowing terms while the women stared at each other in silence. Reginald interrupted. "The Somme's been a hard slog," he said simply. "As bad as Gallipoli. A bloody foulup and I daresay, the worst is yet to come." Rebecca caught her breath. "Sorry about that," the commander said, biting his lip. "Been to sea too long, Rebecca."

Walter said, "You've been in the Med?"

"Yes. I missed that show at Jutland." He sipped his whiskey. "You know I command *Lancer*."

"Quite."

"We caught one in the straits."

"Straits?"

"The Dardanelles. A Turkish shore battery blew off our aft funnel and put X mount out of action." There was sudden pain in his voice. "Lost a dozen fine chaps."

"Winston Churchill must've been off his wick when he dreamed up that show, Reggie. Cost him his post as first lord of the admiralty. The PM made him chancellor of the duchy of Lancaster—whatever that may be. Never hear of him again, mark me." Chuckling, Walter scratched a distended vein on his nose. "I thought all our lads had been taken out by January."

Reginald squirmed uncomfortably. "Not all, Walter. A few stragglers—ah, it's all hush-hush."

"Sorry, old boy. Didn't mean to pry." Walter took a long drink. "Nasty rumors about Jutland," he said. "We got a bloody nose in that one—according to the papers." The women looked at each other and shifted uncomfortably.

Reginald tabled his drink. There was a hint of anger in his voice. "Truth was the first casualty of this war, Walter. The truth of it is the High Seas Fleet is bottled up in Wilhelmshaven and we have the run of the North Sea. The Jerries are finished as a naval power." He picked up his drink and drained half the glass. "The prisoner shook the cage but he's still in jail. That's not hush-hush, Walter."

"Then why doesn't the admiralty say as much, Reggie?"

"They have. But bad news always sells better than good news."

"You're at Chatham?" Rebecca asked abruptly, turning the conversation away from Jutland.

"Quite so. At the dockyard. We were towed to 'Gib' for temporary repairs, but *Lancer* still needs a lot of work." He finished his drink. Walter recharged it.

Brenda spoke up. "'Gib'?"

"Sorry, American cousin." Reginald smiled, shifting the midnight blue eyes to Brenda. "Gibraltar." And then staring over his glass, he said, "You're from New York?"

Brenda could not help returning the boyish stare with a smile. "Yes," she said. "Fifth Avenue. I grew up there. We lived at the corner of Fifth Avenue and Thirty-seventh Street."

He nodded knowingly. "A three-story brownstone with a charming medieval flair to it."

"Why yes." Brenda beamed. "I'm surprised you would know the place."

"Magnificent edifice," he said, eyes warm and probing. "I grew up on Long Island, you know."

"Yes." She nodded at Walter and Rebecca. "I know. Your mother and sisters still live there?"

The commander nodded, never moving his eyes from Brenda's face. "Actually on Shelter Island. It's a beautiful little island off the tip of Long Island. We had to use a ferry to reach the mainland. Got my sea legs there." He chuckled.

Rebecca entered the conversation. "You've been ill?"

"The flu. Been confined to the naval hospital at Canterbury and a piece of Turkish iron nicked me here." He patted his thigh gently.

"We didn't know," Rebecca said.

The commander smiled reassuringly. "A scratch. My ship's surgeon took care of it in our own sick bay. Daresay, deuce of a bother for a fortnight or so."

"Will you be staying?" Rebecca asked. "We have a nice room for you—the same one you used when you were a boy."

"You know I bought a place in London on Wellington Road just east of St. John's Wood. I intended to stay there and look after my ship. And it's too soon for you—not two months since—ah, since Jutland."

"Nonsense," Rebecca said. "Your company would help us over this difficult time."

Walter said, "You must be on leave. And, keep in mind, Chatham is closer to Fenwyck than to your place in London.

Stay with us for a few days." Brenda was surprised by the genuine warmth in the tone.

Hargreaves fingered the bridge of his nose. "I have a week left. Would be a delight to spend a few days with you—get away from the hustle and bustle of London." Brenda felt her spirits soar. Someone from home. Someone who knew Manhattan. What a rich find. Reginald said to Walter, "You still have Caldwell?"

"Right."

"I don't want to impose, but in a day or so I would like to see my ship."

"You're on leave—rest and recuperation. Right?"

"Quite so. But a captain is never on leave, even when he's—ah, incapacitated, and I'm feeling quite fit."

"Very well. Caldwell is at your disposal. Now join us for dinner. We'll try to make you forget about your galley."

Despite the loss of her husband, despite the aura of death that hung over the entire nation like a sheet of winter ice, Brenda began to feel the stirrings of a long-dormant warmth every time she saw Reginald. She, Rebecca, and Walter competed for the young officer's attention. The next morning at breakfast, Walter immediately commandeered Hargreaves for the short ride to the North Downs where the skeleton of the Zeppelin had begun to settle in the bog. "Be home by noon," Walter had promised over the women's protests.

However, it was one o'clock before Walter's big Austin Vitesse phaeton charged up the long drive, leaving a long brown exclamation mark of dust behind it. Immensely proud of the fast 30-horsepower machine, Walter always drove it himself with the top down and at breathtaking speeds that sometimes reached forty miles per hour. The high speeds, dust, and wind discouraged the women. Brenda knew this was deliberate.

Impatiently, the women waited while Hargreaves freshened up and then after a quick lunch, they led him out onto the lawn where Nicole and Bridie waited with Nathan and Rodney. Walter claimed he had business to complete in his library, but Brenda knew her father-in-law was undoubtedly enjoying his first cognac of the afternoon in the privacy he loved.

After seating themselves at a large round table sheltered by a colorful umbrella, Dorset served tea in fine white bone china. Rodney scampered across the lawn and hurled himself into his mother's arms while Nathan, hands held high over his head by the buxom Bridie, made a few hesitant steps.

Nuzzling his mother's neck, Rodney asked his usual impossible question. "Mummy, where is Daddy?"

Brenda bit her lip before answering. "Gone away," she said.

The boy's unusual intelligence showed through or he had been eavesdropping on adult conversations. "Gone away to the war? Forever and ever?"

Reginald placed a hand on the boy's mop of chestnut hair. "I'm Reginald Hargreaves. You can call me Reggie. Your daddy wa—is a sailor. I'm a sailor, too. Sailors take long trips, sometimes. Very long trips."

Wide-eyed, the little boy looked up. "On the ocean, Mister Reggie?"

"Yes. On the ocean."

"I saw the ocean once." He held up a single finger. "Is it fun?"

"Yes. Great fun. Like a carousel."

The boy looked at his mother in confusion. "Like a big horsey ride," Brenda explained.

"I want my daddy." He began to cry.

Brenda held him tight and stroked his head. She kissed his cheek, his forehead, his mouth. "I know, darling. I miss him, too."

Rebecca spoke suddenly. "Rodney, Grandmummy bought you a new teddy bear."

The boy whirled, great blue-green eyes wide with new interest. "All my own."

"Yes, darling. In my sewing room."

In a flash, the boy was out of Brenda's arms and scampering across the lawn. "Wait for me." Rebecca laughed as she followed him. "Be right back," she called over her shoulder.

Brenda extended her arms and Bridie handed Nathan to his mother. Holding the baby, Brenda felt a new emotion. She had been happy not to nurse Nathan and Rodney, feeling the weight of milk might destroy the beauty of her perfect breasts. Now she felt cheated. Her body had given life to the boys and her milk—not the milk of a stranger—should have sustained them. She knew she had given away something beyond price. She reflected on a hard reality that had plagued her since Jutland. Men were destroyers, killers who spent enough of their manhood to impregnate their women. Then, while they butchered each other, women produced life; sustained life for the next war. "No! Never," she cried to herself.

"Never," Reginald repeated in surprise.

Brenda clamped her teeth together, breathed rapidly, and spoke from deep in her throat. "Never will my boys go to war. Never!"

Reginald finished his tea. Nicole, leaning so close a breast brushed the commander's back, refilled his cup from a silver service. Reginald stared at his cup and spoke thoughtfully. "That's what this bloody lot's about—this will be the last one." He tapped the table with a single finger. "I've had to write a score of letters to next of kin trying to explain why and all that."

"You're trying to say Geoffry did not die in vain? That this war will end all wars?"

"Quite right. Quite right," he said, nodding at his cup.

"Geoffry died for his boys?"

"Yes. All the world's little boys."

"French boys, Russian boys, Chinese boys, Japanese boys, German boys . . ."

"Yes, Brenda. This will be a different world after this one. A safe world. You'll see."

A tugging at her blouse turned her head away from the commander. Nathan was pulling and sucking at the material of her blouse. "He's hungry, Bridie," she said, turning to the wet nurse.

"Sure and it's time, mum," Bridie said in her thick Irish burr, taking the baby.

Brenda felt a stab of resentment as the big young woman held the infant close to her breast. "How is he taking to his weaning?" Brenda asked.

"Very well, mum. An' he'd better. The little tyke's got six teeth—sharp as claymores." She rubbed a breast. "Kinda hard on poor Bridie."

Brenda and Reginald laughed as Bridie carried the baby toward the house.

"Got to go to Chatham tomorrow," Reginald said suddenly.

"Can't stay away from your ship?"

"A most demanding mistress." They exchanged a smile. "Would you like to come?"

Brenda regarded him with surprise. She was in mourning and would be for months. It would be improper regardless of how innocent the invitation might be. He was very attractive and she was lonely but, nevertheless, a day spent alone with an eligible bachelor less than two months after her husband's death was out of the question. He seemed to read her mind. "We'll take Walter and Rebecca. I know Walter would love to see my old girl." His smile was filled with understanding.

Brenda's sigh released her tension. "Of course, Reginald."

"Reggie."

She laughed wryly. "I mean quite so, Reggie. Sounds like jolly good fun."

They laughed into each other's eyes.

As the Rolls approached the Chatham dockyard, which was on a protected inlet off the south shore of the Thames estuary, Brenda saw a bustling, boisterous facility, shoreline crowded with long gray buildings, docks crammed with ships. Across the inlet she could see the nearby isle of Sheppey and the Thames estuary. Bordering the north shore of the estuary nearly eleven miles to the northeast, the soaring cliffs of Southend on Sea were visible through the haze.

Reginald tapped Caldwell's shoulder and gestured at the main gatehouse. The chauffeur nodded and wheeled the big motor car to a stop.

"Collect us here at three, Caldwell," Walter said as they stepped from the Rolls in front of the main gate.

"Right, sir," the chauffeur said, tipping the visor of his black cap in brief salute.

Quickly, Reginald ushered Brenda and Walter into the gatehouse where a very young sublieutenant—obviously awed by the presence of Commander Reginald Hargreaves—snapped to ramrod attention and then politely indicated a guest register. Brenda and Walter sighed.

"Too bad Rebecca isn't here," Reginald said.

"Feeling a bit under it. The grippe, she said." Walter muttered as he bent over the register, "Yes. I know."

A rating opened a screen door at the back of the room and Reginald helped Brenda step up into the lower level of a double-decked bus parked in a narrow alley behind the gatehouse. And Brenda needed help, hobbled by the tight fit of her frock. Disliking the somberness of the usual black worn for mourning, she had selected a mauve open-fronted frock wrapped over and fastened at the side. It was a princess cut with a tightly belted midriff that flattered her small waist and set off the flare of her hips. Mourning was indicated by a diamond broach shaped in the form of an anchor and worn on the sleeve above a thin black silk band instead of being pinned to the round neckline. The mandatory hat was a soft white cloche with a black ribbon. She had felt visceral stirrings of excitement when Reginald first saw her on the Tudor porch, his eyes running over her body, the tip of his tongue dampening his lips. There was hunger there and he had not tried to disguise it.

"Sorry we can't do better than this," Reginald said, seating himself beside Brenda. "But it's only a short ride to Pier Fourteen where my ship is docked." Walter seated himself behind the pair. Within minutes, the vehicle was filled with boisterous, talkative sailors and Brenda realized they were seated in the front of the bus in comfortable upholstered seats with a half dozen officers while the enlisted men occupied the rear on hard wooden benches. Reginald exchanged greetings with two of the officers.

As the lorry lurched ahead with a roar of its engine, a clash of gears and billowing clouds of smoke, Brenda turned to Reginald. "It was so easy."

"Easy?"

"Yes, Reggie. All we did was sign a book and we were allowed to enter his majesty's dockyard."

"You aren't spies?" he asked, raising an eyebrow in mock horror.

She laughed. "Never can tell. I could have a wireless in my room."

He smiled and held her eyes. "What goes on in Whitehall —the admiralty—is top secret." He waved at the rows of warehouses and shops lining the narrow street. "But there isn't anything here that Jerry doesn't know about. Actually, I can have any guests I choose on board my ship."

With a hiss of escaping air, the old vehicle came to a stop and Reginald said, "This is it."

Helping Brenda down the high, steel stairs, he said, "She's moored just around that warehouse." He gestured at a long gray building.

Walking as fast as the frock would permit and flanked by the two men, Brenda walked around the huge building to Pier Fourteen. She found bedlam. The long pier was lined with warships, some moored singly and perhaps a dozen nested in groups of three and four. Huge cranes like pterodactyls crouched over some, lowering pallets of supplies, guns, equipment, and in some cases, metal plating. Motor lorries, hand- and horse-pulled carts were everywhere. Men were shouting, gesticulating, and cursing. Riveters pounded their hammers incessantly and saws ground and screeched.

Reginald waved and shouted over the din as he led them toward the end of the pier. "Building, repairing, provisioning, boiler descaling—do it all here." He pointed to a low narrow ship tied up at the very end of the pier. "There she is, *HMS Lancer*." There was pride in his voice.

In the last basin, Brenda saw a low, sleek vessel painted

gray as all the others. Widely spaced, her two stacks were matched in size and height. The hull was long and graceful, the steel tower of the bridge jutting up just forward of the break in her deck line. She had two shielded guns that left their crews unprotected at the back—one on a high platform forward of the bridge and the other far aft on a raised mount. Against her dull gray paint, her pendant number, K 14, stood out in brilliant white just below the bridge. Hoses and wires snaked over her decks and a large group of workmen clustered around a jagged, blackened wound on her star-board quarter. There was much hammering and some cruelly bright lights glared.

"Those lights," Brenda said, turning away.

"Don't look," Reginald cautioned. "A new technique the Royal Navy's trying. It's called welding. If plates aren't too badly ripped, they can be joined with hot torches and flux. Saves an enormous amount of time, but it can hurt your eyes."

"Welding isn't new," Walter said. "I know a smithy who has used it for years."

"True," Reginald said. "But it's new to the Royal Navy." He waved. "On this grand scale—on heavy plates and armor."

Walter nodded. "I thought you had your aft funnel shot off," he said.

"Got this jury-rig at Gib," Reginald said. He waved to-ward the stern. "We'll get a new four-inch gun for X mount when we go into dry dock. Another week. A bit of hull patching to do below the waterline and a bent frame or two." He pointed amidships to a pair of long tubes between the funnels. "Two twenty-one-inch torpedoes." He took Brenda by the arm. "This way to the accommodation ladder."

As the trio approached the accommodation ladder, a small gangway with ropes rigged for handholds, men stepped aside and saluted as the captain passed. With Reginald lead-ing and gripping the ropes on the shaky gangway, Brenda finally stepped on the steel quarterdeck of the warship.

Reginald saluted the colors and then answered the salutes of a young officer and two ratings who snapped to attention.

One, a gnarled old chief petty officer with boatswain's badges on his lapels, put a pipe to his mouth and blew a screeching salute reminiscent of a bagpipe out of control. Everyone stood rigidly until the dissonant, ear-piercing welcome ended and the pipe was dropped to the petty officer's waist. "Captain Hargreaves," the boatswain's mate said, a broad grin spreading across his weathered and pockmarked face. "Welcome back, sir."

"Good to see you again, Withers," Reginald said, grasping the boatswain's mate's hand.

"You look well, sir," Withers said. And then gesturing, he said, "This is Sublieutenant Trevor Grenfell. 'E came aboard three days ago, Captain."

"Sorry, sir," the young officer said. "We didn't know you were coming aboard. I would've assembled a side party. The last word was you were still in the hospital at Canterbury."

"Captain's on board!" the other rating shouted. Immediately, the cry was picked up by another man and another until it was carried to every corner and compartment of the ship. Brenda began to feel a strange new force—the camaraderie men felt when they served together in war; a closeness, a male bonding women suspected but could never know.

"I'm feeling well, thank you, Mister Grenfell," Reginald said. He looked around. "Is Lieutenant Pochhammer on board?"

"He's the OOW. He's in the wardroom, sir."

"Thank you." Reginald turned to Brenda. "OOW—officer of the watch." Brenda nodded understanding.

After a quick introduction to the young officer and the two enlisted men, Reginald led Brenda and Walter forward, cautioning his visitors whenever they encountered hoses and wires. Sailors were everywhere, chipping paint with hammers and scrapers, painting, working on motors, vents, the ship's boat, guns. Reginald waved at some painters. "Rust. The cancer of the steel ship."

On the quarterdeck a cluster of torpedo men hunched over a huge dismantled torpedo, oiling and adjusting the weapons' intricate mechanisms. "Welcome aboard, Captain," crewmen shouted, beaming and snapping to attention as the commander passed. Brenda heard choruses of "Hope you're well, sir" and "Hurry back, sir." And she felt eyes; scores of hungry eyes raking her from head to toe.

Reginald saluted and smiled, thanking the men and calling them out by their first names. Finally, they reached the break in the deck and the captain led them up a short, difficult ladder to the forecastle. Pausing at the bottom of the ladder, Brenda heard the sounds of nearby work slacken and she sensed more than saw a number of heads turn and the stare of dozens of curious, hot eyes. The eyes followed her relentlessly as she carefully manipulated her way up the steel steps. The ladder drove home a lesson: women's clothes were not designed for ships; especially the princess cut, which hobbled her mercilessly. She hated cami-knickers but was happy she had had the foresight to wear a pair of the cumbersome knee-length undergarments. She smiled, thinking about the show she would be providing if she had worn a short teddy, which was her favorite choice for underwear. Suddenly, a sparkling mood of pleasure was on her and she was enjoying the sensation that the display of her figure was causing. Like most beautiful women, playing center stage did not completely repulse her. To feel attractive, to be the desired woman again brought a deep sense of contentment.

Reginald opened a door at the rear of the superstructure and held it open. Stepping over the coaming with her skirts held high, Brenda found herself in a steel passageway that spanned the superstructure from beam to beam. A half dozen doors led off both sides. After Reginald closed the door most of the pounding was mercifully closed out, replaced by ship's sounds of fans and motors turning in the bowls of the vessel—in compartments far beneath their feet. There was the smell of tobacco smoke tinged with diesel oil.

Reginald stabbed a finger aft. "Wireless room, chart house, captain's day cabin." The finger moved to the bow and overhead. "Wheelhouse, forebridge, signal bridge, navigation bridge." He gestured at a ladder in the middle of the passageway from which tobacco smoke sifted in thin strands. "Wardroom." He smiled. "Come along. Some of my officers are aboard. I'll introduce you. Fine lot." He smiled happily as he led the way to the ladder.

The ladder was narrow and descended at a severe angle. Walter and Reginald were helpless to aid Brenda. Gripping the handrails, which were wrapped with cord and varnished, Brenda turned herself slightly to the side and descended very carefully, heels clattering on steel. With Walter close behind, she stepped off the last step into a large, carpeted compartment heavy with the smell of cigarettes. There was new paint everywhere, but the furniture looked old and battered. Two couches and two large black leather chairs occupied one side of the room and on the other side there was a dining area with a long table of polished oak, a sideboard, and an open hatch through which Brenda could see the galley. A small table in front of one of the chairs held an ash receiver heaped with stubbed-out cigarettes. Overhead in a clutter of pipes and conduits two deckheads hummed as their fans whirled while four open scuttles pierced the bulkheads to port and starboard. Despite the fans and scuttles, the air was stale. The light was dim, provided by four shielded bulbs hanging from the overhead and the light streaming through the scuttles. Two smiling officers stood at attention in the middle of the room.

"You're looking fit, Captain," noted one, an extremely tall and thin lieutenant with a large, hooked nose and tilted brown eyes that gave him a hawkish aspect. He had an enormous Adam's apple that moved whenever he spoke as if his lunch had stuck in his throat.

The other, a very young lieutenant, was short and burly with a full shock of brown hair and coarse features. Surprisingly, his voice was soft and refined. "Yes, indeed, you look fit, sir," he said, with an inflection that spoke of Northumberland. "Hope you're free of the Canterbury meat locker," the young officer added, dark eyes flashing with good humor. The officers all laughed and shook hands vigorously with the arcane communion known only to men who had shared the horror of imminent death and dismemberment together.

Reginald presented his officers: "First Lieutenant Stephen

Pochhammer," he said, gesturing to the tall, thin lieutenant. Pochhammer smiled at Brenda and his Adam's apple worked as he shook Walter's hand. "My 'Number One,'" Reginald added. He answered Brenda's quizzical look. "Stephen is my number one officer—second in command to me."

"I see."

The captain turned to the young sublieutenant. "Sublieutenant Ian Carpenter. My signals officer."

"Such a young man," Walter said, unable to conceal his surprise.

"Ah—we took casualties," Reginald said. He beamed at Carpenter. "Filled in admirably—did a capital job. He's up for lieutenant."

"Thank you, sir," the young man said, reddening.

Reginald gestured to the couch and chairs. "A tot? Relax for a moment?"

"Tea for me," Brenda said, seating herself.

"Cognac," Walter said, commanding a large leather chair.

"We have Three Star," Reginald said. Walter nodded his approval.

The officers seated themselves and Reginald called out, "Fuller! Oliver Fuller!"

Immediately, a slender, balding, middle-aged chief steward in a white coat entered through swinging doors opening on the galley. He had obviously been listening. "Welcome back, sir," he said with genuine affection in his eyes.

"Thank you," the captain said. Quickly the drinks were ordered for the men and tea for Brenda.

"Do you mind if I smoke, Mrs. Higgins?" Pochhammer said, turning to Brenda.

Choking back her revulsion, Brenda forced a smile and nodded her approval. Immediately, Pochhammer and Carpenter pulled cigarettes from their tunic pockets, lighted them, and blew clouds of blue smoke into the air. Reginald did not smoke. Walter tapped a wad of tobacco into the bowl of his pipe, struck a match, and sagged back in the leather. Because he rarely smoked, Brenda knew Walter was either responding to the masculine ambience or deliberately trying to annoy her. Perhaps both.

Irritated, Brenda shifted her eyes from her father-in-law to a shiny brass plate mounted on the wall behind Pochhammer. "That shield," she said, nodding. "A decoration?"

The first lieutenant turned his head. "Oh, that," he said. "It's the ship's crest."

He was interrupted by the steward who handed each man his drink and placed a silver service on a small table in front of Brenda. Pouring steaming tea into a white cup emblazoned with *Lancer* in gold letters, he asked, "Sugar, madam?"

"One lump, please."

Reginald nodded at the shield. "Placed there by the builder."

Brenda leaned forward and read the inscription, "*HMS Lancer*, Palmers Company, Jarrow-on-Tyne, nineteen twelve." The remainder was in small, elaborate cursive lettering that she could not read. Squinting, she began to rise.

Reginald glanced at his officers and they all recited in unison, "'Plate sin with steel and the shaft of righteousness does pierce it.'"

Laughing, they raised their drinks. Then the officers and Walter touched glasses and drank.

"Mrs. Higgins," the first lieutenant said, glancing at her badge of mourning. "May I ask?"

"Of course," Brenda said. "My husband—Lieutenant Geoffry Higgins. He was in *Lion*."

"At Jutland?"

"Yes."

"I'm, sorry. I knew him. He was in gunnery. Right?"

"Why yes," Brenda said, pleasantly surprised.

Pochhammer took a long drink. "I'm Volunteer Reserve, too. I met him at the Royal Naval College in oh-eight and we took gunnery classes at Portsmouth together in nineteen twelve." He took a deep pull on his cigarette and exhaled a huge cloud of smoke. "Nice chap. I'm sorry." He glanced at Walter. "Your son was a fine officer."

"Up for the DSO," Walter said proudly. "Saved the ship." The men saluted the dead hero with a clink of glasses and drank. Walter held up his cup and Fuller recharged it.

Brenda turned to Reginald. "This ship is only four years old—built in nineteen twelve."

"Quite so, Brenda."

"Do you know, Reginald, you have told me very little about your ship?"

"Didn't want to bore you," the captain said.

"Tommy-rot," Walter said, calling on jargon popularized by the men in the trenches. He gulped his drink. Wincing, the officers stared straight ahead.

Reginald waved a hand. "*Lancer* is the third of the K class." He looked at Walter. "Nine hundred thirty-five tons, length two hundred seventy-six feet, two Parsons shaft turbines, twenty-four thousand five hundred shaft horsepower, thirty-one knots, three four-inch guns, two twenty-one-inch torpedo tubes, crew sixty-three men, nine officers." He smiled at Brenda. "That's the lot and Kaiser Willie knows it all." Laughter swept the room.

"Your next duty?" Walter asked.

The laughter halted abruptly. "That, Walter, is something known only to a few officers at the admiralty." The officers glanced at each other uncomfortably and Brenda knew Walter, in his usual boorish way, had touched a sensitive subject—a subject that was truly secret and he should have known better. Reginald turned to Stephen Pochhammer. "The condition of the ship?"

The first lieutenant's voice took on a professional timbre. "We can't be dry-docked for another four days. There were a lot of ships damaged at Jutland"—he squirmed uncomfortably—"and the dry docks are very busy. The repairs to the quarterdeck are almost completed and we should be able to replace X gun in a few days." He continued for several minutes, discussing supplies of fuel and ammunition, replacements, visits by staff officers, provisions, new guidance devices for the torpedoes, which at that moment were being installed. Brenda squirmed uneasily while Walter hunched forward, starting his third cognac. Finally, the first lieutenant leaned back, took a drink, pulled on his cigarette, and said, "That's the lot, Captain, except the new pilot has not reported aboard."

"Thank you, Number One," Reginald said.

Quietly, a slight young boy with blond hair and a pimply white complexion entered the room. He wore a white coat similar to Fuller's and carried a polished brass silent butler. Quickly and self-consciously he emptied the ash receivers and disappeared into the galley.

"Good Lord," Brenda said. "He's a child—not more than fourteen."

Reginald glanced at Pochhammer. "Boy First Class Basil Goodenough, sir. Reported aboard last week." He turned to Brenda. "He's fifteen."

"A fifteen-year-old child," Brenda said incredulously.

Ian Carpenter came to life. "I went to sea at thirteen, Mrs. Higgins."

"I can't believe it. He's a baby. He's hardly weaned."

Reginald sighed. "It's the way of the Royal Navy, Brenda. Has been since sail. Some of the boys become our most valued officers." He nodded at Carpenter, who smiled back self-consciously.

"Capital, old boy," Walter said, feeling his cognac. He waved a glass at Brenda. "You Yanks can still learn from the mother country. Right, lads?" The men stared at their drinks in embarrassment.

Brenda's voice was icy. "Learn what? To send our children to war?"

Before Walter could answer, Reginald spoke, saving the situation. "What about a short tour and then we'll leave."

"Bully idea," Walter said, eyeing his daughter-in-law with a hard glint in his eyes. Still seething, Brenda nodded her approval and finished the last of her tea.

As he came to his feet, Reginald spoke to his first lieutenant. "I'll be at Fenwyck, Kent, south of Faversham for, perhaps, two more days. I'll spend the last two days of my leave at my place in London."

"I understand, sir. Rest, sir. That flu is nasty business." Pochhammer turned to Ian Carpenter. "We can hold off the Jerries without the captain. Right, Sub?"

"Right-oh, sir," the young sublieutenant said, smiling broadly.

Following Reginald and Walter, Brenda negotiated the ladder while Pochhammer and Carpenter kept a polite distance from the base. Reentering the passageway, Reginald indicated a door. "This is my day cabin," Reginald said.

Brenda entered a large, carpeted stateroom furnished with a wide bunk with a thick mattress, two large leather chairs similar to those in the wardroom, a washbasin, mirror, desk, and a sideboard. A fan whirred overhead and the two scuttles had their deadlights opened.

"It's much larger than I expected," Walter said, moving his eyes around the room.

Reginald nodded. "Yes. It's as large as the wardroom. When these ships were built, the RN still felt one of a captain's most important functions was to entertain—to play the part of the commanding officer. Day cabins were large for that purpose."

"Day cabin?" Brenda said. "Then you must have a night cabin."

"Very astute," the commander said. "When under way, that's where I sleep. It's a small bunk in the chart house—close abaft the wheelhouse. Come along, I'll show you the wheelhouse."

He ushered them forward into the front of the superstructure. Painted a flat white, the small room was crammed with equipment. A young seaman was polishing the brass fittings on the numerous scuttles that gave excellent visibility over the bows and to both beams. He came to rigid attention. "Your name, laddie?" Reginald said.

"Able seaman Alistair Johnson, sir," the sailor said nervously.

"Carry on, Seaman Johnson." The sailor returned to his polishing. Reginald gestured around the room. "Ship's wheel, binnacle, engine room telegraph, voice pipes, telephones."

"Is this where you keep your watch?" Brenda asked.

"No, Brenda." Reginald stabbed a finger overhead. "Directly above is the forebridge. It's completely exposed with unlimited visibility. OOD watches are always stood there and that is where the captain belongs when under way." He glanced at her skirts with understanding. "I would show you, but the ladders are vertical and even more difficult than the ones you've already climbed."

Walter gripped one of the huge spokes on the wooden wheel and turned to Reginald. Brenda could smell the liquor on his breath. "The wireless must give you a big advantage."

Reginald shrugged. "You know Jerry can receive it as well as our lads. And he has direction finders—can locate a ship by listening to her transmissions. We must be very careful, and, it's no secret, when we do use wireless, we encipher the signals."

"But ciphers can be broken," Brenda noted.

"Quite so. So we do most of our signaling with pendants, lights, and semaphore." He scratched the early afternoon stubble on his chin. "And wireless isn't dependable. The tubes and wires are delicate and even the concussion from our own guns can put our set out of commission." He turned to Brenda. "Would you like to see our WT—wireless transmitter?"

"Thank you, Reginald. But I am tiring and . . ."

"Return already?" Walter said, piqued.

"I'm tired!"

"Of course, of course," Walter grumbled, not trying to hide his resentment.

Silently, Reginald led his guests back to the accommodation ladder.

The next two days were happy ones for Brenda. With Walter called to the office, the women had Reginald all to themselves and like metal drawn to a magnet, the young officer managed to work his way to Brenda's side. In fact, the last day of his stay, they spent the entire afternoon together either walking in the garden or sitting under the umbrella, watching the boys, laughing, and talking. By three in the afternoon, the boys were napping and Rebecca, Bridie, and Nicole vanished discreetly into the house.

They talked of New York incessantly. Brenda was astonished to learn Reginald had patronized her favorite restaurants: Sherry's, Delmonico's, the dining rooms in the

Waldorf-Astoria and the St. Regis and Stanford White's magnificent French Garden. Reginald had ridden in Central Park, enjoyed the menagerie, paddled a Venetian gondola on the lake, attended mass at St. Patrick's and, at sixteen, had bought his mother earrings at Tiffany's. He knew of the robber barons—Whitney, Rockefeller, Gould, Ryan, Belmont, and Morgan—and the palaces they built. He had met the Vanderbilts, the Guggenheims, the Alexanders, and many more of Brenda's neighbors. He had been charmed by the magnificent old homes surrounding Washington Square and awed by Caruso at the Metropolitan.

"Just think, Brenda," he said, fixing her with his eyes as blue as the sea. "We could have been in the same place at the same time."

"Passed in the street."

"Right. Tragic we didn't meet, Brenda."

She chuckled, trying to break the mood. "How long will you be in Chatham?" she asked. "Or is that a secret?" she added hastily.

He laughed. "That's no secret," he said. "It'll take three or four months to put the old girl right." He talked to the lawn. "I would like to see you again."

She sighed. "I'm in mourning. It's not proper. . ."

"I know. I know. But war isn't proper either. There's nothing proper about shells, torpedoes—"

She sat silent for a moment, mind spinning with thoughts of her dead husband. She had never truly loved Geoffry, but he had worshiped her, respected her, and she owed his memory respect in turn. Perhaps, now that he was dead, she was beginning to fall in love with his memory. Strange and grossly unfair to Geoffry, but the feelings were there; especially at night when she lay in her bed on the verge of sleep. "Please, Reginald," was all she could manage.

"I'm sorry, Brenda. I didn't mean to offend. I feel like a boorish cad."

"Not really, Reginald. I would like to see you, too. It's fun to talk with you."

"Will you mourn for a year?"

"I'm not sure."

"War compresses everything. Particularly life expectancies," he said bitterly.

"Live a lifetime in a few months? Is that it, Reggie?"

"Do we . . . do I have any other choice?"

"Give me a few months, Reggie."

"Is that a promise?"

"Yes."

"It's exciting when you say yes."

Their eyes locked and the stare was hard. "I don't very often and I don't know if I can ever say it again." She looked away.

"You're the most beautiful, the most exciting woman I have ever met. You would withdraw—live in your own mausoleum to honor your dead husband? Is that what Geoffry would want?" He waved boldly at her body. "Waste all that?"

Brenda flushed, fighting the conflicting emotions charging her body with both anger and desire, revulsion and attraction. She knew the turmoil within was insane, but so was the world. How else could one react? "I cannot seek out—start a serious liaison with a man now, perhaps never." She fixed him with eyes as cold and blue as frozen lapis. "Do you understand?"

"Yes." There was bitterness in his voice.

Her voice softened and she placed a hand on his arm. "But that doesn't mean we can't be friends, Reggie."

Looking up, he smiled. "Then we can see each other. You said in a month or two."

"Of course."

"You can ring me at the ship, you know."

"I didn't know."

"Chatham dockyard and ask for *Lancer*. We have a telephone on the quarterdeck."

"I will."

"We can have lunch. Agreed?"

"Quite so."

They both laughed.

They were interrupted by Rebecca, shouting and waving an open letter as she ran from the house. "Brenda, Reggie! I have a letter from Randolph. A real letter this time. Not just a field postcard." Breathlessly, she seated herself opposite Brenda. "And it's only a week old." She placed a pair of half-spectacles on the bridge of her nose and began to read, "Dear Mother and Father. I am well." Rebecca looked up, pointing at the letter. "There are some personal things to me and Walter. I'll skip ahead." She refocused her eyes on the single sheet. "As you know, we have been very busy here. I can't very well tell you the details of my duty, but you know the entire front has been very active and Number Five Squadron has been very busy. I have been flying two and three patrols a day and training new chaps at the same time. The food is good and I am in excellent health. I now have seven victories. We haven't seen hide or hair of Oswald Boelcke. His Jagdstaffel was last reported over Verdun. Please don't worry about me. I am flying in the best machine in the RFC and I serve with the finest aviators in the world. Give my love to Brenda and kiss my nephews for me. Love, Randolph." The old woman removed her spectacles and rubbed her moist eyes, failing in her attempts to choke back the sobs.

Brenda took her hands. "He's well, Rebecca. He's well."

"Yes," her mother-in-law said. "He was well a week ago. Perhaps by now..." She was unable to finish her sentence.

"He's a fine aviator—a smart and resourceful chap, Rebecca," Reginald said.

"And he loves to fly, Rebecca," Brenda added.

"Yes. He loves to fly." The old woman struggled to her feet. Slowly, she walked back to the house, clutching the letter to her breast.

VI

Armed by two hot coffees each charged with a dram of Scotch by the prescient Sergeant Major York, Major Randolph Higgins walked toward the mess hall in the early morning light. Staring to the east where the sun was breaking free of the horizon in a theatrical display of oranges and reds reflected from the silhouettes of stringy low-hanging clouds, he was gripped with a familiar mystic sense of predestiny, a languid melancholy, a sense of unease and disquiet. Adding to the morbidity was the rumble and bark of artillery firing "morning hate" barrages a few miles to the north. For almost four months, the battle had raged along the Somme on an eighteen-mile front and the promised breakthrough had never materialized, three full divisions of cavalry still waiting impatiently in reserve to pour through the opening that had never come. The casualties had been ghastly; over four hundred thousand British and French had fallen and the battle was not yet finished. Even the use of the new armored machine—code-named *Tank*—had failed to break the stalemate. The battle had proved one thing conclusively: masses of infantry could not overwhelm quick-firing field guns and well-sighted Maxims. And Lloyd was out there somewhere in the mud and slaughter. Feeling a sudden chill, the major jammed his hands down deep in the pockets of his leather flying coat and hunched forward.

Further depressing the major were thoughts of the terrible losses suffered by the RFC. The new Albatross D.1 was a powerful, formidable opponent. Equipped with the new scout, which the press rightfully called a "fighter," the German Air Service had destroyed over four hundred Allied aircraft since the offensive began—the majority British. Rumors had given way to reports that Oswald Boelcke and his Jagdstaffel Two had ceased operations over Verdun and had been loaded on board a train bound for the Somme front. "All the brightly colored aircraft on the cars looked just like a traveling circus," an intelligence officer had reported, giving birth to the sobriquet "flying circus." They could appear over the Somme front at any time.

Goaded into an offensive posture by air marshal Hugh "Boom" Trenchard, the English continued penetrating deep behind the German lines with bombers and reconnaissance aircraft, exacerbating their losses. Flying regular patrols and escorting Bleriots, Caudrons, and Voisin bombers, Number Five Squadron had suffered grievously: three killed, two wounded, and one captured since June. Randolph's stomach grew queasy and his knees weakened when he thought of taking his four new pilots—two had reported only the day before—against the new German scout. As squadron leader Higgins opened the door to the mess hall, he was in a somber mood indeed.

Randolph entered a large canvas and wood frame building with a rear door opening on the back of the farmhouse where the kitchen was located. The room was furnished with two long tables made of boards laid over sawhorses, two stoves, a sideboard stacked with liquor, and four battered easy chairs pushed into the corners. White cloths covered the tables and eleven pilots sat around sipping tea, coffee, and cocoa. Most of them were smoking, the room redolent with the smell of tobacco and liquor. Although two new pilots were in regulation RFC uniforms, the other nine flyers were dressed according to individual taste: artillery and cavalry tunics, *combinaisons*, naval jackets, leather flying coats. Thrown carelessly on the table was their headgear: forage caps, berets, peaks, and leather helmets. But every pilot wore the gold RFC wings embroidered on his breast. They snapped to attention as their squadron commander entered.

"Be seated, gentlemen," he said, moving to the side of the tent where a blackboard was located. Sergeant Major York entered, handed Randolph a cup filled with thick black coffee, and left. The major observed a firm rule: No more than two drams of liquor before flying, and his batman made certain the rule was observed. This time, he sipped pure black coffee.

Higgins moved his eyes slowly over the expectant faces. New faces. New faces replacing new faces. Always so young and growing younger. The reliable, methodical Freddie Southby's number had come up, uselessly dying when his engine quit on takeoff, his Nieuport crashing into the attic of a farmhouse near Bailleul. And the two new subalterns, Armstrong and Cartwright, who had reported the day before his leave, were both dead, replaced by two newer, younger faces belonging to Flight Lieutenant Jarret Barton and Flight Lieutenant Edward Winter. Both were fresh out of the flying school at Oxford. "How old are you?" Randolph had asked the pair the day before as they stood at rigid attention before his desk.

Barton, a tall, muscular athletic type, had stared back unflinchingly into Randolph's eyes and said, "Nineteen, sir."

Winter, also tall but very slender and slightly bent like young sapling exposed to a stiff breeze, stared above the major with moist eyes, answering in a barely audible whisper, "Eighteen, Major."

"Good Lord," Randolph said. "You laddies should be playing cricket and rugby, not war."

"By your leave, sir. We left Cambridge together, volunteered together, we have a right to serve the Crown together," Barton said.

Randolph cut him off. "How many hours do you have?"

Barton said, "Forty-four of solo time in trainers, four in Nieuport Seventeens."

"Forty-two in trainers and six in Nieuport Seventeens," Winter added.

Randolph sagged in his chair hopelessly. "Then you'll die together, unless I can perform a miracle."

Barton continued, almost as a spokesman for the pair. "We knew the risks, sir."

Higgins slapped his desk. "Rot! You don't know the risks, old boy. Do you know the average life of the pursuit pilot is three weeks?" The boys stiffened. "You won't last three hours."

"But, sir," Barton said. "We are a product of the system, not the system."

"Yes. Yes, I know," Randolph said. "Don't tell me about the system. Just listen to me."

"Yes, sir," the boys chorused.

"Barton flies with me and Winter, you're teamed with Captain David A. Reed—my best man."

For the first time, the flight lieutenants brightened. "Yes, sir. Yes, sir."

"And listen to me, watch me, and watch Reed. We'll try to give you a condensed course in aerial warfare. But we don't have time." He had pounded the desk with a clenched fist. "Time! The front has bloody well exploded." Randolph gestured to squadron clerk corporal Longacre who was at his table, listening to every word while pretending to be engrossed in a report. "Corporal Longacre will show you to your quarters," Randolph said. "I'll see you at a meeting of all the pilots in the mess hall tomorrow morning at zero seven hundred. Be in flight kit. You'll make your first patrol tomorrow morning with me and Captain Reed. Carry on."

And now the two new young faces were there with the other nine bright young faces, staring eagerly at the squadron leader. "All of you have met our new chums," he began, nodding at Barton and Winter who were in flying kit. The two new pilots squirmed uneasily. "I know you older pilots have heard this a dozen times, but I want to discuss the new German scout, which Fritz calls a fighter, because it is our most dangerous opponent." Picking up a piece of chalk, he wrote "Albatross D-1" on the board.

The older pilots nodded knowingly. David A. Reed shouted, "Hear! Hear!"

"The Fokker Eindecker was easy meat for us," Higgins said, moving his eyes over the faces. "And a lot of us ran up our kills. But now"—he tapped the board—"this new air-craft has changed things." His eyes moved to Barton and Winter. "The Albatross is a sturdy machine, covered by pre-formed slabs of plywood screwed to a skeleton of hardwood 'O' formers and light wooden stringers. Also, it is powerful with a new one-hundred-sixty-horsepower in-line Mercedes engine and the first Kraut pursuit armed with two Spandaus. It's seven hundred pounds heavier than a Nieuport and can take a tremendous weight of shot before it's disabled."

"Sir," Barton said, waving a hand. "How do you know all this?"

Randolph waved at David A. Reed who now wore cap-tain's patches on his flying jacket. "Captain Reed shot one down at the end of our runway. We went over it from spinner to skid." Reed smiled back with his usual slow grin. "Re-member," Randolph continued, "the D-One is faster and heavier than a Nieuport—can outdive us. But nothing can dogfight the Seventeen. Nothing can turn with us. They'll try to dive through us and only turn to fight if they out-number us."

"Sir," Barton said suddenly. "The D-One must have other weaknesses."

Randolph was pleased by the boy's perceptiveness and deferred to Reed with a nod. As Reed came to his feet, Randolph realized he not only respected the young captain, but also he regarded him with the same affection he reserved for his family. They had flown together since the squadron had been formed a year earlier and were the only survivors of the original twelve. At first, Randolph had mistaken the preoccupied, distant look in Reed's eyes as the conceit of a snobbish aesthete who preferred isolation to the company of inferiors. But common danger, slaughter, terror, and triumph tested both in the eyes of the other and found neither want-ing. Quickly, a bond of comradeship grew, ripening into friendship, which deepened into respect and love that bonded stronger than blood. A deadly shot with skill that was sharpened hunting windblown grouse on his family's estates in Lancashire, David could take deflection instantly like a machine and was the only pilot besides Randolph who could make a full deflection shot good. Both realized neither would be alive without the other. No closer tie could exist.

Half smiling, Reed spoke with his usual precise cultured enunciation. "Our commanding officer has already mentioned the fact we can outmaneuver the D-One." The dreamy blue eyes moved around the room, stopping on Barton. "But, yes, there are other weaknesses or I wouldn't be here." A nervous titter swept the room. "Actually, it has beastly visibility forward. The cabane struts are in the pilot's way and the upper wing is poorly slotted. In fact, the German I scragged bloody well never saw me." Reed nodded at Randolph. "He was diving on the major who led him directly into my sights." He held up his hands simulating two aircraft in the classic manner of the pursuit pilot. "I attacked from here." One hand dove on the other. "From the front where his visibility was poor and his other weakness killed him—his radiator is mounted on the upper wing directly above the cockpit. A half dozen rounds of ball there and a boiled Kraut copped it at the end of the runway—boiled like a cabbage in his own coolant." A hand peeled off and crashed into the tabletop with splayed fingers. More nervous laughter as Reed returned to his chair.

"Thank you, Captain Reed," Randolph said. He moved his eyes over the faces. "Remember the captain's words and remember we worked as a team to make the kill." He turned to the board and began to write as he spoke. "And burn into your minds my rules for remaining alive on the Western Front—no more lone wolf heroics, always remain in your elements of two; keep the sun behind you; always carry through an attack when you've started it; fire only at close range and only when your enemy's wingspan fills both rings of your sights; fire short bursts so that your Vickers will not be held open too long, overheat, and jam; keep your eye on your opponent and never let him deceive you by ruses; attack from behind and preferably from a blind spot, every plane has one; do not dive if your enemy dives on you, instead, fly to meet him; when over enemy lines, never forget your line of retreat and the prevailing westerly winds that work against you; and always, always remember altitude is your most precious commodity. It can always be traded for speed."

He drank from his cup while two batmen circulated, filling cups and glasses. Remembering Southby's useless death, Randolph pressed on. "Inspect your aircraft—every detail—before taking off. We lost one of our best pilots, Lieutenant Freddie Southby, two weeks ago in an accident that might have been prevented by a careful preflight inspection. Load your own ammunition and oil each round. If you're careless about your aircraft, your mechanics might bloody well emulate you." His eyes swept the white, intent faces. "Your life hangs on that prop, not theirs. And remember, each Nieuport Seventeen costs the Crown seven hundred pounds."

Waving a hand and receiving an assenting nod from the squadron commander, Winter said, "Shall we use the 'bird test,' sir?" A rumble of laughter swept the room and Randolph remembered the absurd story of pilots who supposedly released birds in the maze of stays and wires holding the old Vickers gun buses, Voisins, and Caudrons together. If the bird escaped, the pilots knew the airplane was not properly rigged.

"No. No," Randolph said through his chuckles. "I'm pleased with your concern, but a close eyeball inspection for leaks, loose bolts, poorly patched canvas—a tug or two on stays and wires will be sufficient."

"Yes, sir," Winter sputtered, his face the color of the sunrise.

Randolph finished his coffee and his demeanor became serious. "Captain Reed and I will take our new chums on the morning patrol." He looked from one expectant face to another. His gaze stopped on Lieutenant Leefe Hendon, a Canadian who had grown up in the forests of northern British Columbia. Trained with hundreds of other Canadians, he had completed his primary training at Kelly Field in Texas and his advanced training at the famous French aerodrome at Issoudun. He was thoroughly schooled in acrobatics, flying, and gunnery, and could fly almost any type of aircraft. Incongruously baby-faced with a pudgy round visage of vanilla pudding, he had grown up in the forests where he began to hunt as soon as he was big enough to carry a gun. The broad expanse of pudding was placid, usually as expressionless as a Michelangelo statuary. But his eyes—his most striking aspect—flashed with strength, with an edgy nervous watchfulness—a strange hunger that was the look you expected to see in the eyes of a wild animal, a stalking pitiless predator, but never in the eyes of a human. A deadly shot, he was an intelligent fighter and ruthless killer who often fired on his targets from as close as thirty feet. In fact, once he had shredded the rudder of a Halberstadt D-2 with his propeller, sending it crashing into the English reserve trenches while he glided to a dead stick landing in a pasture. He had run up a score of six kills in only five weeks. The Canadian had a brilliant future.

Nodding at the Canadian, Randolph said, "Lieutenant Hendon will lead our noon patrol consisting of himself, Lieutenant Smith, and flight officers Cowdry and Anderson over our usual sector between Mametz and Hamel, one element at fifteen thousand feet, the other at eight thousand. Division is concerned about Kraut artillery spotters and be alert—watch for the Hun in the sun." His gaze moved to a group of four pilots seated together at the far end of one of the tables. "Flight Lieutenants Gaskell, Morris, and Jillings will be under the command of Lieutenant McDonald in the ready alert tent." The four pilots groaned.

"Not again, sir," McDonald said with a strong Scottish accent. He gestured. "Sure an' these clods canna beat a Scotsman at whist, sir." Everyone laughed.

"Well, sure an' they'll get their chance today," Randolph said, mimicking the Scotsman. More chuckles. And then seriously, he said, "You are dismissed to your duties." With sighs and a scraping of chairs on bare wood, the pilots came to brief attention and then filed through the door. Winter, Barton, and Reed remained with Randolph.

"Be seated, gentlemen," Randolph said. The three flyers sat. The subalterns lighted cigarettes. Randolph felt frusrated—there was too much to learn. He punched a palm with a closed fist and stared at the new flyers with hooded eyes. "The Hun loves the sun and if you want to live, remain alert. A good pilot never rests his neck unless he wants to rest in peace. Move your head in short, jerky movements and never concentrate too long on one spot. Look to the side of an object—often, your peripheral vision serves better than a direct stare." He reviewed his system of hand signals, which were mandatory with aircraft incapable of carrying clumsy, eighty-pound wireless. "And watch for a waggle of wings from either Captain Reed or myself. This will mean something's amiss." The subalterns nodded.

"We patrol defensively today. That is, we are not escorting. Instead, you understand, we will stay on our side of the lines and search for Boche reconnaissance aircraft. The Fourth and Eleventh reconnaissance squadrons are opposite us. They fly Rumplers." He gestured to the top display of a series of black silhouettes tacked to the wall behind him. "Understand." The boys nodded.

The squadron commander pinched the bridge of his nose. Strange he should feel tired so early in the morning. He moved on. "If you attack a Rumpler—a diving attack, he will automatically bank to give his gunner a better shot. Otherwise, he might shoot off his own rudder. Don't bank with him." The flight lieutenants raised their eyebrows. "He will expect you to be directly under his tail, which would give you your best killing angle, but you'll be giving him his best killing angle, too. I've lost four pilots this way. So make a maximum bank away from him and then turn back after diving at least two hundred feet below his belly."

Winter spoke up. "He may keep on banking, sir."

"Right-oh. But that's what we want. Nothing can turn with the Nieuport." The new pilots nodded.

"Another thing, you may see no aircraft at all. Even during a big battle like this one we can go for days without sighting another aeroplane. But then, again, the skies can rain Huns and we may sight other RFC aircraft—the Nieuports of Number Twelve Squadron to the north, Sopwith one-and-a-half strutters of Number Sixteen Squadron also to the north, and the FE-two-bs of Number Twenty-six Squadron to the south." Randolph leaned forward on the table, tapped his fingers restlessly. "Questions?"

"Yes, sir," Barton said, fixing his commanding officer with his steady stare. "Anything of Boelcke's Jasta Two?"

"No. Intelligence reports they're moving into our front, but we haven't sighted them."

Winter spoke, his high, raspy voice tight with excitement. "They're the best in the German Air Service, sir?"

"Quite so," Randolph said. "And easy to sight—each aircraft is brightly painted according to the fancy of its pilot." He glanced at his watch. "It's time, chaps. Chop, chop." He turned to the door.

The four pursuits were lined up on the edge of the tarmac with the mechanics and armorers making last-minute checks. Fortunately, the sun had burned away the early morning mist and there was promise of a clear bright sky with the exception of few high-cruising cumulus to the north and a milky scum of cirrus to the south and east. Looking like a green tent in his stained green overalls, chief mechanic Cochran greeted Randolph with the usual elfin grin. "She's ready for you, sir. Like a bride on her wedding night—an' that she truly is." There was pride in his voice.

Randolph chuckled as he began his inspection, the chief mechanic close on his heels. He patted the cowling while staring at the radiation fins on the nine cylinders, looking for loose spark plug wires, petrol or oil leaks, or anything out of sorts; tugged at a drag wire rigged from a landing gear strut to a V strut; kicked both tires and inspected the bungee springs; removed the inspection plate just behind the cowling, which had been unscrewed by Cochran, and checked the petrol and castor oil tanks and lines for leaks; pulled on an aileron, looking for slack in the operating horn and control wire; tested stagger wires connecting the cabane struts to the V struts and grunted with approval at the strong tension; pushed hard on the fragile lower wing inspecting the doped canvas carefully for wrinkles and minute tears; moved to the tail plane running a palm over four black patches covering bullet holes and pushed and pulled on the rudder and elevator and found no slack. "Very good. Very good," Randolph said as he walked toward the cockpit, pulling on his otterskin gauntlets. A signal from Cochran and an assistant screwed the inspection plate back into place.

Carefully, Higgins placed a foot into the stirrup beneath the cockpit and helped by Cochran, stepped up onto the wing. Then he flung a leg stiffened by layered flying clothes over the padded coaming and lowered himself into the tiny cockpit, the wicker seat creaking under his weight. Carefully, he locked his safety harness and palmed his flare gun and oxygen bottle, assuring himself they were both charged and firmly locked in their racks. A quick glance at his five instruments—fuel and oil gauges, altimeter, rev counter, and compass—told him their needles gave correct readings. He pushed hard on the rudder bar and watched the rudder in his rearview mirror answer his commands. Quick movements of the stick told him ailerons and elevators answered precisely.

Cochran took his position in front of the Nieuport while two of his men held the wingtips and two more grasped ropes attached to the chocks. Randolph was ready. And so were Winter and Barton. But something was wrong with Reed's plane. His chief mechanic had removed an inspection plate and was working furiously on some lines.

"Petrol leak!" the captain shouted from his cockpit, shrugging helplessly.

Randolph cursed. Ordinarily, Reed would have been left behind. But with two new chums, it would have been unthinkable to leave the veteran. They would wait.

Throwing his head back in frustration, Randolph's skull struck the padded headrest and suddenly familiar faces swam before his eyes. Brenda was there, enigmatic and distant—almost ethereal in her loss and illness. Would he ever tell her he loved her? Could he ever bring himself to this face-to-face with his brother's memory? And Cynthia Boswell had written him and, surprisingly, the letter had reached him despite the lack of the eleven-digit number that identified the squadron's location. Memories of that fierce night with the stunning widow had chased Nicole from his dreams and fantasies. Cynthia had claimed she loved him and would wait for him. Randolph snorted. War compressed your life—no doubt about that. But love? After one night together? She loved majors. RFC majors. And he was convinced she would continue to haunt the Empire searching for duplicates of her dead husband. There had been a hint of madness in her eyes, a birdlike glint like light reflecting from a hollow crystal. Randolph knew he would soon be out of her mind.

He squirmed uneasily and looked at Reed's plane where a team of mechanics worked furiously on the defective fuel line. Cursing, Randolph punched the instrument panel so hard the needles jumped. In his mind's eye he could see his mother's stricken face. Grief and worry were destroying her. Fortunately, she had Nathan and Rodney. Without them, he was convinced, she would have withered into her grave by now. Walter was another source of anxiety. The old man and Brenda were on a collision course. There would be an explosion. Brenda's strong will would see to it. He could see it in the baleful glances she and Walter threw at each other; the acid exchanges. He had always been convinced the old lecher had been attracted to Brenda. Perhaps that was the seat of it.

There was a shout from Reed's plane and the captain was stabbing a finger skyward and the mechanic replaced the inspection panel and strode clear of the aircraft. Sighing with relief, Randolph circled a single finger over his head and immediately Reed, Winter, and Baron repeated the signal. The major stared down at Cochran who had placed both hands on the propeller and stared back expectantly. Randolph and Cochran had trained together at Pau when the squadron picked up the new Nieuports. Taught by French officers, they still relied on French commands in the starting ritual. In fact, they enjoyed the foreign banter—an inside thing that brought a minute moment of intimacy and pleasure. The major gave the mechanic a brief two-finger salute.

After returning the salute and nodding at the men at the chocks and the men holding the wingtips, the heavyset Irishman grinned up at Randolph and shouted in ruptured French, *"Monsieur Commandant! Coupez—plein gaz!"*

Randolph pushed the throttle forward, put the mixture on full rich, and checked to be certain the ignition switch was turned to "Off." Quickly, he turned the handle of the fuel pump a half turn and pumped it until he felt the pressure build up in the tank. Locking the fuel pump handle down, he repeated the command. The beefy mechanic raised one leg, hesitated a moment to adjust his balance, and then heaved down hard with all of his two hundred pounds. With the ignition off, the engine gasped and wheezed as it rotated a half turn, sucking petrol and air into its carburetor and cylinder heads. Down the line, Randolph could hear shouted commands and gasping engines as the other members of the patrol proceeded through the same ritual. Cochran wiped his hands on his overalls and again stepped to the propeller. *"Monsieur Commandant! Contact—reduisez!"* he shouted, raising his leg.

"Contact—reduisez!" Higgins repeated, turning the ignition switch to "On" and closing the throttle two notches.

Cochran heaved the propeller again and retreated quickly. The Le Rhone barked and coughed asthmatically, backfired twice, jerking the propeller around stiffly and shaking the airframe, belched blue smoke, and began to fire erratically, finally coming to life with a volley of bangs, hard coughs, and sputters. Suddenly, there was a salvo that sent the blades spinning in a blur and Cochran, who had hastily retreated to a position just off the right wing, smiled proudly, shrugged his shoulders, and turned his palms up like a French chef and shouted, "Voilà!" Down the line, three more engines burst into life.

Randolph thinned the mixture three stops and within a minute all nine cylinders began firing and warming, the engine settling down into the familiar uneven roaring sound of the warming Le Rhone. Randolph smiled as a new thought crossed his mind. Like a woman, when cold, the rotary could be capricious and stubborn. But when hot, with lubricants flowing, the versatile fighter would mold herself to him, purring contentedly and ready to obey his every whim.

While the Le Rhone spun in its high-speed idle, Randolph checked his fuel and oil gauges and pulled back slightly on the Vickers's cocking handle, assuring himself of sufficient spring tension. It was very firm and the major nodded at the armorer who smiled back. Randolph cursed and held his breath as a cloud of castor oil fumes filled the cockpit. It would not do to take a powerful physic before a two-hour patrol. Luckily, a sudden gust of wind cleared the fumes and the major was able to breathe again.

Finally, after five minutes of waiting and fretting, Randolph saw his oil gauge climb to one hundred sixty degrees. Then, looking over his shoulder, he gave a thumbs-up salute to the patrol. The pilots answered. A final check. Randolph pushed the throttle forward until the rotary whirled at its maximum rpms—1,200 showing on the rev counter. The roar was deep, even, and unfaltering. Satisfied, the major throttled back and gave the thumbs-up signal to the handlers, who were staring at him expectantly. The squadron commander felt the aircraft vibrate as the chocks were pulled, the wingtips released, and the handlers and Cochran stepped warily away.

The pursuit lurched forward and Randolph taxied out onto the hard earth runway, manipulating the throttle and turning the ignition on and off to fire the rotary in bursts to slow the Nieuport to a crawl. A last glance at the wind vane assured him the breeze, as usual, was southwesterly and he pointed the nose of the Nieuport down the middle of the runway, the three other planes of the patrol close on his tail. Turning the plane into the wind, he took a deep breath and pushed the throttle lever hard open against its stop. The lithe pursuit leapt forward.

Randolph was pressed back into the wicker as the Nieuport gained speed and raced eagerly down the runway. Within seconds, he had accelerated to a dizzying eighty miles per hour and he moved the stick slightly to the left to counteract the enormous torque of rotary and then forward slightly to lift the tail skid and clear his forward vision, sensing more than feeling the plane lighten and begin to reach for the sky. Pulling back on the stick gently, the little scout fairly leapt into the air with the hunger of a grounded hawk. Smiling, Randolph gained altitude, clearing the row of poplars at the end of the runway by thirty feet. He banked counterclockwise, the roofs and spires of Bailleul visible off his right wingtip, green patchwork farms separated by stone walls and hedgerows filling his view in all of the other quadrants. Steepening his bank, he watched as the other members of the patrol took off, one after the other.

From the very beginning when he was first learning to fly with Geoffrey DeHavilland and Tommy Sopwith, Randolph had loved the moment when first airborne—that magic instant when the destiny of the plane was passed from the earth to the sky; its natural habitat. True, since then, he had seen death and war in all its horror and although he was not a religious man, at this moment there was still a near spiritual communion—a merging with God, perhaps—if God dwelled on the Western Front. Certainly, it was a transcendental experience where a man bridged reality, emerging into a kind of intimate sense of being where he existed with his personal rulers; where he was master of his body, yet demanded a bare perception of it. Attuned to the machine, and indeed becoming part of it, just the thought of moving the controls commanded ailerons, rudders, and elevators, maneuvered the Nieuport, which not only blended into one's consciousness, but spiritual self as well. Randolph thought of this moment as a prelude—a tranquil overture to the mortal danger of aerial combat and its frenzied, hysterical excitement.

Gaining altitude and pointing the cowling of the scout plane at the high cumulus to the north, he smiled at his foolishness and shook the philosophical cobwebs from his mind. War was the ultimate reality. It murdered philosophers.

Fourteen and a half minutes later, the flight was at twelve thousand feet and, fortunately, the sky was empty. Leading with Jarret Barton off his right elevator followed by Edward Winter and David Reed in echelon a thousand feet higher, Randolph led the flight over the front, paralleling the British trenches on a northwesterly course. Randolph prayed that they would meet no Germans.

Again, nagging thoughts crept into his mind—the musings that afflict all men at war. Would the youngsters live lone enough to become veterans—bemedaled heroes? Who were the heroes? All of those who flew five miles high strapped into wood and fabric crates as volatile as a Chinese firecracker? Perhaps. Randolph shook his head in frustration. Only war brought such extremes of futility and loneliness and constant fear of death. Then a truth struck home with the brilliance of a Very light: the war's real heroes were the men who screamed into the slipstream to vent terror yet performed at their best; who soiled their flying clothes but never ran; who obeyed orders to the letter while the fingers of fear strangled them like an executioner's garrote; who fought not knowing why they faced the horror day after day, the only compelling imperative the patrol, the comrades off their elevators.

Randolph twisted his head, ran his eyes over the other three machines. For these men he fought because they fought for him, would die for him. He knew he could never bear the shame of being less than Reed, Hendon, the new chums, or any of the others. That was it. King, country, grand strategy, victory, defeat had nothing to do with it. He began to shiver and blamed it on the altitude.

It was cold at twelve thousand feet. He raised his hands and wiggled his fingers, stiffened by the cold despite the heavy gloves. His toes, too, felt the cold and he tried to restore circulation by moving them as much as the heavy boots would permit. And as usual, his back and neck began to ache, the rough wicker pushing through the layered flight clothes. He twisted against the straps in frustration, not allowing his stiff neck to inhibit his constant search.

Time to clear guns. Turning his head, he waved a fist stiffly from right to left and back. His pilots repeated it. Quickly, he charged the Vickers with two quick pulls on the cocking handle, opened the safety lock, and pressed the red button. The airframe shook like the victim of the flu as the Vickers jerked and blazed, spewing a half dozen brass shell casings against the guards and down the chute and into the slipstream. The other pilots emulated their leader. "At least they can clear their guns without shooting me down," Randolph said to himself.

Randolph believed there were four stages in the career of a pursuit pilot: students, beginners, middle-age and old age. Having survived student training, which could be as lethal as combat, Barton and Winter were beginners with still so much to learn they could very easily and fatally be daring at the wrong time and cautious when they should be bold. Combat demanded automatic reactions, but the novice had no reserve of experience upon which to draw. In the stress and terror of combat beginners quite often froze and simply did nothing. They were marvelous targets. This period lasted about three weeks. Most pilots died during this stage. If his new pilots could survive fifteen to twenty aerial encounters, then they would enter the pursuit pilot's middle age. This was the safest stage. The Canadian Leefe Hendon was here and possibly McDonald and Cowdry were also enjoying their middle-age. The intense excitement and terror of combat was still at hand, but the senses were not overwhelmed and the middle-aged pilot was capable of thinking, of reasoning, making weighted rational decisions in the panic of combat, and surviving on the basis of skill and intelligence, not just luck. The last stage was old age. He and Reed were in this stage. It was a dangerous time in a pilot's career. Survival could foster contempt for the odds, bring about overconfidence that gave birth to carelessness. He had seen the veteran aces Alfred Clayson and Roger Venter die this way and most certainly, carelessness killed the redoubtable Freddie Southby. Randolph could never believe that their luck had just run out and that fate had finally turned up their numbers.

Restlessly, the major glanced downward. Although the British push had bent the line northward forming a new salient a few thousand yards past Thiepval Ridge, High Wood, Delville Wood, and the villages of Ginchy and Morval, the front had not changed much since June—four long, bloody months. Millions of shells had churned topsoil, clay, and rock into a quagmire that made landmarks hard to find. Everything—fields, villages, forests—took on a sameness of blasted, dung brown ruins. It was disgusting, as if a blight had erupted on the face of the earth, pockmarking once lush lands with loathsome sores. From the air, it looked as if some great dragon had seared the land with flaming breath and then vomited along the banks of the Somme until the surrounding landscape was drowned in puke. Summer should have brought daisies, buttercups, marguerites, poppies, and laburnum. Flocks of swallows and robins should have been swooping and feeding and new stork nests appearing on the house roofs. But below there was ooze, blood, excrement, and the moldering corpses of hundreds of thousands of men.

Randolph shook his head and studied the Somme River. It was the one constant thing in this shifting hell and he was able to judge his position by the great bend to the north and spires of the comparatively intact Peronne jutting below his right elevator. Moving his eyes south and west he found a heap of smashed timbers that he judged to be the village of Hamel, the northern limit of his patrol. There was a light mist fixed with smoke over the front and the shell bursts appeared to be winking lights in a brownish white veil. He caught a glimpse of Thiepval Ridge beneath his wing and slowly banked to his left, away from the front. As the cowling swung around through one hundred eighty degrees, he sighted something moving far beneath them and to the southeast. A flight of five aircraft headed south at six thousand feet. He waggled his wings and stabbed a finger downward while checking the river and his compass and straightening on a reciprocal course. The new pilots leaned, banked, stared, and shrugged hopelessly. Randolph cursed and studied the intruders. They were old twin-engined Caudron G-4 bombers; tough old airplanes in brown, yellow, and green camouflage headed home after bombing in the German rear. Probably from Number Twenty Squadron based at Demicourt. Neither Barton nor Winter could see them despite the fact that both he and Reed were pointing.

Angrily, Randolph pounded the side of the fuselage and

then choked his agitations down. Keep them alive. Keep them alive, ran through his mind. A few deep breaths calmed him and he studied a new cloud buildup that thickened suddenly to the south and east in the lee of a cold front, big and billowing, forming with magic swiftness as only clouds can form over northern France in the summer air. Majestic protuberances of towering cumulo-nimbus were battlements and ramparts of castles, spires, and cornices of cathedrals. Windsor, Buckingham, and St. Paul's were there, burnished by the sun and splashed with golds and silver. In peacetime, he would have been awed by their beauty. But today he cursed the misty hiding places—concealment for possible ambushers.

But there was no ambush. Nothing but the five Caudrons that passed innocuously beneath them. Finally, after almost two hours, Randolph turned the patrol toward home. Barton and Winter were bitterly disappointed.

There was no rest. After a quick lunch, Randolph led the patrol into the sky again. But they headed south away from the front over peaceful green farmland that had never seen war and here they played at it, taking turns in elements of two, first attacking and then defending, rolling, diving, looping, closing on optimum killing angles. Barton showed some promise, handling his machine with a surprisingly sure hand, a touch that showed an understanding, an appreciation for his Nieuport's strengths and limitations. However, Winter was hesitant, reluctant, or unable to push his machine to the limit. His handling was clumsy and several times he almost mushed into a stall that could have led to a wing-shedding spin.

Gunnery practice was held on two broken wings and a piece of fuselage of a Rumpler and the fuselage of the Albatross Reed had shot down. The wreckage was spread on a field near Douve and the pilots took turns diving and firing. With stationary targets, the critical multidimensional problem of deflection in aerial combat was missing. But any practice was better than no practice at all. Both subalterns were poor shots, but after several days of practice they learned to bore in close and hold their fire until within point-blank range—forty- and fifty-foot ranges where no one could miss.

For three days the foursome flew the same patrol without encountering a single German machine. An observation balloon was reported over Serre, but a pair of one-and-one-half strutters from Number Twelve Squadron shot it down before Randolph could assign a patrol to it. Sham dogfighting improved the new chum's flying, but still, Randolph's stomach turned queasily when he thought of their inevitable baptism of fire. Could he and Reed shepherd them through it? Or would they just be dead meat like so many others?

On the fourth day while approaching Contalmaison on the southern leg of the patrol, Randolph sighted a flash of color between Trones Wood and Morval where German heavies were pulverizing some newly won British trenches. Glancing around quickly, he found Barton's Nieuport just off his tailplane, bouncing up and down on summer turbulence while two thousand feet above. Winter was weaving unsteadily while still above him, Reed providing top cover. Reed was waggling his wings and pointing downward

Waggling his wings, Randolph pushed his goggles up and leaned over the coaming. A Rumpler. Spotting for the heavies. Barton and Winter stared helplessly, unable to pick out the camouflaged observation plane despite the gestures and pointed fingers of their companions. Frustrated, Randolph scanned the sky with the veteran pilot's search—a quick, flitting probe that covered the sky above him, sweeping back and forth and down and under. Nothing. Nothing but scattered blobs of morning clouds, dirty gray blue on one side and glaring Alpine white on the side struck by the sun. Abruptly, he felt an atavistic seethe of unease grip him, cold premonition in his guts again, an instinct for impending disaster he had felt since returning from his leave. He swept the sky again and then leaned over the coaming and stared. Could be bait. A classic trap. But the sky was clear and an enemy aircraft was directing fire. Killing Tommies. There was no option. He must attack.

Turning north, he lost altitude and continued to point. Finally, he saw first Barton and then Winter smile and point, acknowledging the Rumpler. Most squadron commanders would have taken the easy kill themselves. But Randolph knew his fledglings cold learn their craft only in the crucible of fire. He waggled his wings, pointed at the Rumpler, stabbed a fist over his head twice and then three more times. The new pilots acknowledged the command for attack by planes two and three.

With Barton leading, the two Nieuports half rolled sharply and split-essed into near vertical dives. Randolph winced at the reckless maneuver, watching the double wings bend and the fabric of both scout planes wrinkle at the roots. Luckily both machines held together and the Germans were so intent on the barrage below, they remained unaware of the deadly danger above. Barton opened fire at eight hundred yards. Despite a good killing angle and only one-quarter deflection, the novice completely misjudged the Rumpler's speed. Alerted by the stream of wide tracers, the German pilot quickly banked to the north while his gunner got off a quick burst at Winter who bounced in Barton's prop wash and sprayed a long burst that missed the target by fifty feet. Randolph grimaced in exasperation.

Barton had learned something during the past four days. He banked to the south away from the Rumpler and beneath it and then jinked sharply back under the lumbering plane's fuselage. Inadvertently, Winter helped his companion by violating Randolph's rule and banking with the Boche. He gave the gunner an excellent shot. A dozen rounds punched through the Nieuport's wing just as Barton pulled up sharply beneath the observation plane and fired a long burst while hanging on his propeller at a range of only fifty feet. Struck in the buttocks, genitals, and groin by the hail of .303 ball, the pilot and observer fairly leapt against their straps, waving their arms and screaming into the slipstream. Immediately, the big plane dropped off on one wing and began its final spin, its crew flopping loosely in their cockpits as if they were made of gelatin.

Triumphantly, the two subalterns climbed back toward Higgins and Reed. Randolph was pleased. After an initial misjudgment, Barton had shown remarkable recovery and adjustment for a fledgling. He had pressed his second attack coolly and intelligently, precisely as he had been taught, from close range and with the instinct of a killer. He had probably saved Winter's life. With a little luck, he could become an outstanding pursuit pilot.

The attack had carried the formation far north of its patrol and suddenly an ugly brown smear erupted a hundred yards beneath Randolph's wingtip. Then another and another; black and brown octopus with white phosphorescent tentacles trailing earthward. Randolph banked south, away from archie and pulled back on the stick. Altitude. They needed altitude. Again, he was gripped with that nameless dread, an atavistic prescience that turned his blood to ice and sent a million cold needles to stab the flesh of his face and neck. This time he would take them up to sixteen thousand feet— so high no Hun could surprise them upsun.

With the two novices tucked back into formation, Randolph turned the patrol back onto its southern leg, the ruins of Contalmaison sliding past far below. As they gained height, the vast panorama of northern France—even the southern part of Belgium—opened beneath, the green farms quilted geometrically; green for crops, brown for ploughed fields. The actual front faded, the trenches and disputed no-man's-land nothing more than a serpentine of brown, the misery and slaughter there illusory.

The two veteran pilots never relaxed their search, heads turning in rhythmic set patterns, searching every quadrant, every corner of the sky, never resting, eyes never allowed to focus short or become fixed by the sun, a cloud, or the whirling fan of the propeller. But Barton and Winter were exuberant, waving and smiling in the euphoria of victory. Repeatedly, Randolph stabbed a finger at the horizon and gesticulated wildly. The subalterns would search for a moment and then turn back to each other, waving and laughing. Fuming, Randolph pounded the coaming, vowing to chastise the pair unmercifully when they returned to the field. A glance at the altimeter and Randolph leveled off at fifteen thousand feet, just below parallel rolls of white cumulus that stretched to the horizon like cheese cake in a baker's window. Feeling slightly giddy, he pulled the tube from his oxygen bottle and took several long pulls. He saw the other pilots doing the same thing. He knew they were too high for any Jasta to pounce on them from above. The premonition of disaster began to fade.

Abruptly and miraculously he was proved wrong and the sky above them was filled with garishly painted diving aircraft and the chatter of machine guns. Even in stunned astonishment, Randolph reacted with the instincts of the survivor of dozens of air battles, kicking left rudder and horsing back on the stick until the horizon fell away and his cowling and Vickers were pointed at the attackers. Staring at the needle-nosed attackers, astonishment became fear that went beyond fear, a full circle back into courage. He choked back the dread lumped in his throat and stared through his ring sight.

There were six of them, all new Albatrosses and obviously of Oswald Boelcke's circus. The leading German, red and yellow fuselage with a checkerboard upper wing, was the master killer himself and he would have riddled Randolph if the Nieuport had not reacted like a startled cobra and lashed back at its attackers. Nevertheless, Randolph felt a riveter's hammer pounding the plane as shot struck home and a stagger wire parted with a twang like a bowstring. But the major got off a short burst that ripped fabric from the German's upper wing near the spot where the radiator should have been. But it was not there. Boelcke plunged past. To Randolph's horror, he counted the best pilots in the German air service, identified by their gaudy paint jobs known to everyone: Werner Voss, Max Mueller, Manfred von Richthofen, Erwin Boehme, and the coldest butcher of them all, Bruno Hollweg, flying a black machine with a jagged yellow arrow stretching the length of his fuselage.

There was something different about these Albatross scout fighters. The radiator was beneath the upper wing, which had been lowered and the visibility had been improved by enlarging the slot in the upper plane and splaying out the cabane struts in the form of an N. Must be a new model. The

D.2 with a higher service ceiling, flashed through Randolph's mind.

Reed had turned into the attack with a tight chandelle and had fired a burst that had ripped chunks and splinters of plywood from a blood-red Albatross fuselage. Surprisingly, Barton was still off Randolph's tail plane, but Winter was already a dead man. Paralyzed by the first attack, the eighteen-year-old had committed the pursuit pilot's cardinal sin; he had flown straight and level while looking around in confusion. Hollweg's black machine had slashed in on him like a shark smelling blood, ripping his fuel and oil tanks with a score of rounds, sending the volatile mixture into the hot engine where it ignited in a yellow flare like a flame thrower. The doomed Nieuport twisted past Randolph, curving toward the ground, leaving a black epitaph of smoke behind, Winter waving and screaming as he roasted alive. Watching the boy's hideous death, sudden madness possessed Randolph; no fear, no doubts, not even conscious thought—only the urge to kill. He was an animal and the sky was his jungle.

A green Albatross with yellow tiger stripes swooped down on David's tail on an ideal killing angle. With all his strength, Randolph pulled back on the stick and kicked right rudder, snapping into a half roll to the right, taking advantage of the tremendous torque of the rotary. He felt his wings vibrate, wires jerk and screech. The green machine filled both rings. Snarling in released tension and triumph, the major pushed the button, trying for a three-quarter deflection shot. A stream of tracers caught the Albatross just back of the cockpit, punctured the big white Maltese cross, ripping splinters from the fuselage and fabric from the tail plane. The enemy machine dropped away in a screaming dive.

Randolph fell in behind Reed, and following his flight leader, Barton protected Randolph's tail. The outnumbered and outgunned Nieuports began to circle while five Albatrosses roared up around and over the trio, looking for openings. None could be taken without price. The sixth Albatross, the green machine that Randolph had riddled, banked slowly to the north and dropped in a shallow dive toward the German trenches. It trailed smoke. Randolph was sure it was Voss. He waved a fist in the air. "Come on, Kraut buggers! Come on! I still have a tank full of three-oh-three-ball."

Jagdstaffel Two adopted new tactics. Two pairs, Boelcke and Erwin Boehme, Hoehe and Hollweg, flying in very close tandem, continued to circle the Nieuports while Manfred von Richthofen climbed and lurked a thousand feet above the deadly cotillion, waiting for an opening. With Boehme clinging hard on his tail plane, Boelcke half rolled and charged in on David, squeezing off a quick burst while inverted. Showing iron discipline, David continued his turn while Randolph's gun sight came to bear on the checkerboard Albatross. A sharp move of the stick with a matching movement of right rudder for balance, and Randolph had Boelcke centered. Randolph heard a creature growl deep in his throat as he squeezed the tit. A two-second burst. The Vickers bucked, the belt raced up from the tank, brass shell casings streamed from the chute, and a whiff of cordite struck like a sexy woman's perfume. Eighteen rounds and a half dozen strikes on the checkerboard's upper plane and the D.2 trailed puffs of paint dust and ripped fabric. Furiously, Randolph kicked rudder without bank throwing the Nieuport into a spar-bending, flat, skidding turn that hurled him against the side of the cockpit, his Vickers tracking the Albatross like a hunter following grouse.

"I'll jump your king, checkerboard bastard!" Randolph shouted, ignoring the pain he felt in the shoulder bruised by the coaming. But before he could fire again, the checkerboard completed its roll and dropped out of his sights. He cursed bitterly.

There was a blur of red overhead. Richthofen. Diving. Breaking the ring. Barton pulled up sharply. Fired a burst at the diving machine. Richthofen ignored the young pilot, eyes glued on Reed's Nieuport. A short burst from fifty feet and Reed's Le Rhone began to trail smoke. Like a pride of lions singling out an injured wildebeest from the herd, Richthofen pulled up and Boelcke and Boehme banked sharply toward Reed's crippled Nieuport, smelling the kill.

Screaming "No!" Randolph banked toward Reed while Barton rolled toward Boelcke. Instantly, the orderly cotillion collapsed into a disorderly free-for-all. But the sky was too crowded, six aircraft converging on the tiny bit of space holding Reed's scout plane.

Showing unbelievable daring for a novice, Barton slashed into, perhaps, twenty feet of Boelcke, his stream of .303 tracers ripping canvas from the great squadron leader's already damaged upper wing like skin slaking from a molting serpent. Either out of control or surprised by the reckless attack, Boelcke pulled up hard while Boehme, trying to protect his leader, plunged past in a sharp dive after Barton. Too close and intent on the young Englishman, Boehme's left wing slashed through Boelcke's right upper plane, knocking off the aileron horn and severing the control wire. With the aileron flopping loose like a door in a gale and canvas ripping from his wing, the great flyer throttled back and turned gradually into a shallow dive toward his lines. But the dive sharpened quickly as the main spar broke and his top wing ripped free and fluttered behind the fuselage, trailing wires, torn fabric, plywood, and broken struts. Immediately, the lower wings sheered off and the fuselage steepened its dive into a streaking vertical death plunge like a stone dropped from a bluff.

"Die! Die, murdering bastard!" Randolph shouted joyfully.

The Germans were stunned and for a moment, seemingly paralyzed by the loss of their leader and the ferocity and skill of their enemies. Randolph felt hope surge as he pushed his stick forward and dropped after Barton and Reed who had turned off his engine and was gliding for a landing. Boehme and Richthofen, both damaged, suddenly turned for home. But Hollweg, followed by the blue and white bumble bee striped machine of Max Mueller, suddenly half rolled into a dive, streaking for the retreating Nieuports.

Defying his shaky wings and followed by Barton, Randolph pulled back hard on the stick and felt the wicker seat sag, wings vibrate and threaten to buckle. The sharp turn and climb cost him speed and he slowed to a near stall. With little air flowing over his airfoils and control surfaces, he had to fight the vibrating controls with the tired muscles of his arms and legs to bring Hollweg's black machine into his range finder. A head-on attack: that was what he wanted. He gripped the stick with all his strength and pushed hard on the rudder bar, working it back and forth like a child's seesaw to maintain balance. Hanging by its prop, the Nieuport trembled anxiously like a predator poised for its killing leap. He had only an instant, but for that instant the black machine filled the concentric rings.

Both pilots fired simultaneously. A stream of fireflies whipped past Randolph. There were snapping sounds like whips cracking in his ears and suddenly the Albatross filled the whole sky. In a wink it was past him, hard rubber tires of the landing gear almost brushing his head and jarring the tiny scout plane with its backwash like the passing bird of death. Max Mueller and Barton were firing on each other, exchanging bursts that crippled. Engine missing and streaking oil, the German turned for home. Barton, engine riddled and leaking its own life's blood, dropped off in a steep dive. Hollweg, still diving, flattened his dive into a perfect killing angle as he closed the range on the helpless David Reed.

Shouting "No! No!" Randolph dropped out of his stall and split-essed the Nieuport into diving pursuit. But the light scout plane had no chance, the heavier more powerful Albatross diving at a much higher speed. It was over in seconds. Helpless, Reed turned in his cockpit to face his executioner. He was waving a fist when a dozen rounds caught him in the chest, smashing his ribs, lungs, and heart. Immediately, the Nieuport flipped on its back and plummeted to the ground, crashing in a field just back of the British reserve trenches. The Albatross streaked for home.

Randolph eased his throttle and circled the wreck as artillerymen rushed to it. He leaned far over the coaming with his goggles up, the slipstream whipping the tears from his cheeks. The sobs were bitter and anger and grief carved his face into an ugly mask—all hard, deep, down-slashing lines. His brother had died again. "I'll kill you, butcher," he shouted at the Albatross, which had become a speck on the horizon. And then waving his fist, he said, "This isn't war —this is murder. I'll kill you, Hollweg—kill you if it takes my life."

Blinded by tears and keening to himself like an injured animal, he turned for home.

VII

The news of *Oberst* Oswald Boelcke's death was reported joyfully in the British press. But there was no joy in Fenwyck despite the fact that Number Five Squadron was given credit for the great flyer's death. Walter was the exception. Exuberant and slavering over his toasts, the master of Fenwyck crowed and gloated, boasting, "One Englishman was worth a squadron of Huns. Randolph will teach the bloody Boche how John Bull can fight."

Filtering from the overcrowded hospitals, horrifying rumors about the battle in the Somme valley persisted, began to spread through the populace like influenza through the slums of the Isle of Dogs. Late in September, the liberal *Manchester Guardian* reported, "On the first day alone, one of every two men of the entire attacking force of 143 battalions had been a casualty; three of four in the case of officers." Notwithstanding, Field Marshal Sir Douglas Haig insisted on pressing the offensive, arguing, "These losses cannot be considered severe in view of the numbers engaged, and the length of the front attacked." And the meat grinder continued to devour the flower of England's manhood until the populace became numb and sickened by the horror.

Mercifully, rains came with November and the fighting

bogged down. Haig bragged that a strip of land twenty miles long by six miles deep had been wrested from the enemy. But the price had been over 400,000 British casualties and nearly 200,000 French. Brenda found the numbers incomprehensible, like trying to understand distances to the stars.

There were strange doings at the War Office and Ministry of Munitions and rumors were rife of revolutionary new inventions to unlock the deadlock: a calcium arsenide powder to be scattered by shell fire that would be ingested by the enemy as dust, causing arsenic poisoning; coal dust to be fired over the German lines, then ignited to cause the type of explosions that ravaged coal mines; carborundum powder to be scattered over enemy positions to jam the mechanisms of small arms and artillery; smoke bombs fired by four-inch Stokes mortars; huge flame-throwing machines similar to the German *flammenwerfer* but much larger and secretly dug in and assembled close to the German positions. All of the "battle winners" except the smoke bombs and a tracked fighting vehicle called "Tank" were abandoned. There were calls in Parliament by disgruntled MPs for the resignation of Prime Minister Herbert Asquith and his liberal government.

Postcards and letters from Randolph and Lloyd continued to arrive sporadically. Randolph's letters brought joy to Rebecca yet, at the same time, they were disturbing. Consuming hatred and a craving for vengeance permeated his sentences and the style was strangely distant, as if the writer were speaking to himself, pulling aside the drapes that hid his subconscious and baring his secret soul. He was possessed by a German, *Hauptmann* Bruno Hollweg, who had inherited Boelcke's Jasta Two. His whole life force seemed to be directed at killing this man. He was given credit for shooting down the ace Max Mueller and his kills climbed to twenty-two.

Reginald Hargreaves visited often. *Lancer* had been repaired and moved to Portsmouth on the south coast. Although the commander could not admit it, the ship was the leader of a squadron of four destroyers assigned to the Channel fleet to intercept German raiders—usually fast destroyer sweeps aimed at sinking coastal steamers. Occasionally, daring German raiders shelled coastal towns. Fortunately, there had been a lull since Jutland. Brenda looked forward anxiously to his visits.

Early in November Brenda was standing at her french windows when Reginald's Hillman touring phaeton charged up the drive. Nicole mirrored her mistress's excitement and giggled while helping Brenda into a green diaphanous palehued tea gown of softly draped mousseline. *"Magnifique, ma maitresse,"* the Frenchwoman murmured as Brenda left the room.

Walking down the stairs, Brenda wondered about the handsome naval officer. *Why am I so eager to see him? Does it show?*

Reginald was on his way to Chatham for a meeting of destroyer commanders and could remain only for a few hours. He loved the garden and they spent the afternoon under an umbrella shading a table placed at the edge of the lawn and next to lush flower beds that were still blooming despite the late season. Dorset served tea and cakes. Luckily, Walter was in London and would not return until late afternoon and the women gathered around the commander eagerly.

Immediately on seating himself, Reginald found Rodney on his lap. It was obvious to everyone the boy had adopted the young naval officer as his substitute father. Brenda felt her heart wrench as she watched her son crave for his dead father's attention. Somehow, in his child's mind, the boy had come to terms with his father's absence. Although he had never been told his father was dead and had no concept of death, he knew Geoffry was gone and would never return. He rarely spoke of his father; questions about his father visibly upset his mother and grandmother. He understood this.

After Rodney's playtime was over and Nathan had crawled through the garden chasing butterflies and grasshoppers until exhausted, the boys were taken by Bridie and Nicole to the nursery for their afternoon naps. Rebecca, also obviously tired, excused herself and retired for a brief rest. Reginald and Brenda were alone.

"Do you feel you have mourned long enough?" he began,

eyes moving audaciously from her face, to her breasts, to her waist, to her hips and back again.

The man could excite her. There was no doubt about that. "What do you want, Reggie?"

"To see you alone—take you to lunch, dinner—a show."

"You want me in bed."

He started at her boldness, his eyes widening. "You Americans are blunt."

"True or not?"

"Of course I want you in bed—nude, next to me." His eyes probed hers with the intensity of lights searching for Zeppelins. "Don't you want that, too?"

She turned away. "No! I don't want that," she said flatly.

"I can't believe you."

She turned back to him, the blue of her eyes heightened by moisture. "You're attractive, Reggie, and I like you. But I told you before, I'm not ready for that."

"Will you ever be ready?"

"I don't know."

"Did you love Geoffry that much?"

"That isn't it."

"Then what is it?" he asked in exasperation.

She studied her teacup and her voice was unsteady. "I don't know, Reginald. Please . . ."

"I'm sorry," he said huskily. "I've been an unfeeling cad."

"No. No. You're sweet and I love to talk to you."

"Then daresay, that's good enough, Brenda."

She smiled and nodded.

He continued. "Dinner, an innocent soiree. You promised months ago."

She laughed and trapped him with her eyes. "Promised? I don't remember."

"I do—vividly." The blue of his eyes bored into hers. "I've got duty for a fortnight or so. Ring you up when I return?"

"All right," she said, not able to break away. "Please be careful." She touched his rough, hair-stubbled hand and ran her fingers over his knuckles and wrist.

"I'm always careful," he said, grasping her restless fingers and holding them in his own warm palm.

When Reginald left, Brenda watched the Hillman race out the drive from the Tudor porch, a disturbing primeval craving gnawing deep in her soul. She became angry with herself.

Walter returned just before supper in a vile mood. He railed to the women about how mismanagement by a subordinate had cost him a coveted contract to an American competitor, Langhorne Textiles. "Damned bloody Yanks," Brenda overheard him mutter as he retired to his library to begin his evening's drinking. He wanted his solitude. He spent it reading the interminable casualty lists in *The Times*.

By the time Walter sat at the dinner table, his face was flushed and his speech slurred. Before Dorset and Nicole had finished serving the soup, he glared at Brenda and said, "When are you Yanks going to come in and help? Englishmen are tired of dying for you." Rebecca looked up. The servants stepped back to the wall and stared in embarrassment.

Rebecca spoke up. "Walter, Brenda does not formulate American foreign policy."

"Blast it, woman. Don't tell me about American foreign policy." He turned to Brenda, a malevolent glow in his eyes.

Brenda studied the scarlet face, puffed mosaic of veins rimming his nose and spoiling his cheeks. He was drunk and spoiling for a fight. She would accept nothing; not for Langhorne Textiles, not for business, not for the Western Front. Nevertheless, her anger drew her in like a victim of quicksand. "Hundreds of Americans serve voluntarily in France. They drive ambulances—fly for the Lafayette Flying Corps—die just as dead as Englishmen," she fired back.

"Don't get on my wick, Brenda. You're using us. Making money off the flower of our youth."

Brenda felt the hot blade of rage twist deep inside of her and her cheeks warmed suddenly as her anger surfaced. "Do you work for nothing, Walter? Are your contracts nonprofit?

You're just angry because you were underbid and you're not going to take it out on me."

"Go to your room!"

"Walter!" Rebecca cried.

Brenda ignored her mother-in-law. "You told me to go to my room once before. I didn't accept it then and I won't accept it now."

The line of his mouth altered and the rims of his nostrils flared and turned pale as bone china. "Oh, you won't."

"No, I won't."

"This is my house. You're guest here. You've got to obey me or . . ."

"Or what, Walter?" Brenda snapped, interrupting him.

"Or get out straight away."

Horrified, Rebecca said to Walter, "You can't do this."

"Don't tell me what I can't do, woman," he snapped at his wife.

Brenda came to her feet, eyes flashing cold blue light like the glinting of bayonet tips. "I'll do better than that," she retorted. "I'm leaving—going back to the *colonies*."

"This is insane. Both of you . . ." Rebecca managed before Walter interrupted her.

"Good. Good," Walter said, draining his glass and knocking his knuckles against the table with finality.

Rebecca turned her brimming eyes to Brenda. "The submarines, Brenda. You can't."

"Submarines be damned," Brenda hissed, turning toward the door. Then, followed by a white-faced Nicole, she left the room.

It was two days before Brenda left. However, not even her outrage could lead her to risk Rodney and Nathan to the submarines prowling the North Atlantic. A call to Lloyd's wife, Bernice, and a furnished house in London's fashionable Belgravia area was leased. Brenda did not explain her reasons for leaving Fenwyck, but she felt Bernice knew— had even anticipated her departure. There was no trouble with money. Geoffry had left a generous trust and Brenda inherited a thirty percent ownership in Carlisle Mills, Limited. Her accounts at The Bank of England amounted to six figures and were approaching seven.

By noon of the second day the Silver Ghost with Caldwell at the wheel wound its way out of the long drive. Brenda, the boys, and a crestfallen Rebecca, who had insisted on coming, were in the back of the limousine. Bridie cuddled Nathan while Rodney explored his jump seat, climbed to his mother's lap, then to his grandmother's and back to the jump seat to repeat the circuit again and again. Nicole would follow, accompanied by a lorry for the mountain of children's toys, clothes, and a few items of furniture.

Despite the somber news from the front and the depression that gripped the nation, Brenda was in a buoyant mood. She was free of Walter and possessed the most valuable currency in the world: her independence. True she had lost her husband, been ravaged by a terrible disease that had killed the new life within her, and the men she cared for were at terrible risk, but for this one day, this one golden moment in a succession of unending tragic moments, she felt a surge of happiness that approached exhilaration. She was determined to enjoy it to the fullest.

Brenda had been to London on numerous occasions. However, she usually made the trips to see her hairdresser on West Cromwell Road or shop at Knightsbridge: she loved the Edwardian charm of the haute couture shops lining Brompton Road, the fashions and fabrics of Sloane Street, the chic shops of Beauchamp Place, Walton Street, and South Kensington. These were her haunts and she had never seen Belgravia and was not prepared for the opulent enclave. While a morose Rebecca remained silent, Brenda questioned Caldwell who slid back the glass partition and much like a tour guide pointed out landmarks. "Cadogan Square, madame," he said in his resonant baritone. "Your home is on Grosvenor Crescent, just south of here." He pointed to a large building surrounded by carefully tended flower beds. "St. George's Hospital. They have a magnificent flower show in May. Don't miss it."

Just like the British, Brenda thought. They would have their flower shows if the devil, himself, invaded the Empire.

The area reminded Brenda of the gauche ambience of Fifth Avenue: the streets lined with huge Victorian houses that were ornate and pretentious, as if their builders had wanted everyone to know they had arrived. The architecture was a blending of French, neo-Georgian, and Italians styles with a dash of classical flavor thrown in at random. To Brenda, it seemed the men who had ordered these buildings had told their architects any style would do as long as it looked like money. Fortunately, the harsh lines were softened by hundreds of trees and well-tended grounds. Conspicuous consumption and lavish spending, Brenda thought. More Walters—England was full of them.

"Belgrave Square, madame," Caldwell announced. "There's your place, and over there, Buckingham Palace."

"Suitable neighbors," Brenda said softly. For the first time in two days, Brenda saw Rebecca smile. Bridie laughed heartily.

Caldwell waved a hand. "There is a saying amongst the fine old families, madame, 'If God had had his way, this is the way he would have built all of London.'"

Bridie looked up from Nathan who had fallen sound asleep with his head against her breast. "Sure anna God canno' afford it," she said in her thick Irish burr. Everyone chuckled.

Within two days and with the help of Bernice and Rebecca, Brenda and the boys were completely moved in. The house, a two-story with seventeen rooms, was finished with the usual ponderous beams and dark woods the English loved so passionately. Although Brenda considered the exterior of the house crassly vulgar with a senseless variety of crude and undigested details, a half dozen protruding bay windows, two towers, and porches spanning both front and rear, it had a bright, cheery sitting room comfortably furnished and opening to the south and west to catch the afternoon sun. The furnishings were eclectic: Queen Anne, Georgian, Sheraton, and Regency pieces were to be found in most of the rooms, but Louis XVI was favored. She disliked the stiff, uncomfortable furniture, but she was happy to move into the place. Not a small amount of luck was involved.

The owner, Bernice's brother, Commander Timothy Anderson, was a career officer in the Royal Navy and had been stationed in Sydney, Australia since before the war. His wife Francine, two grown sons, and a sixteen-year-old daughter had moved to Sydney just before the outbreak of war. The house on Grosvenor Crescent had stood empty for over two years. Bernice was the custodian of the property and had been instructed by her brother to lease the property "to people of gentle breeding."

The grounds were large and well tended by an old veteran of the wars in northern India, Touhy Brockman. Thin as a reed, the old man was as insubstantial as a phantom, the years and Indian diseases leaving only parchmentlike skin, stringy sinew, and brittle bones. Despite his frail appearance, the old veteran was tough and durable, manicuring the grounds and proudly coaxing reluctant daisies, roses, and marguerites into bloom late into the season. Touhy lived by himself in a small cottage tucked into a corner of the property and hidden by trees and shrubs.

The boys loved the house. Suddenly, Nathan discovered he could walk and he stumbled after the racing Rodney through the shrubs and flower beds on unsteady legs, chortling and laughing. By the second day, the women had arranged the lawn furniture near the flower beds where they could watch the children playing. Bridie's husband, Douglas, was an adequate cook and took command of the kitchen. Servants' quarters were located behind the kitchen and here Bridie, her husband, and baby lived. Nicole, who always considered herself a "downstairs maid," was thrilled to receive the unbelievable bounty of an upstairs bedroom across the hall from her mistress's large sleeping quarters.

Brenda's bedroom was actually the master bedroom. It was huge with a large four-poster of unclear antecedents, two Venetian commodes with delicate serpentine and cabriole legs, gilt-wood Louis XVI pier mirrors on opposite walls that gave infinite reflections, an exquisite carved rosewood Louis Philippe sofa, and blue Chinese carpets with matching watered silk drapes over french doors overlooking the garden. Paintings by Burne-Jones, Lord Leighton, and Ruskin hung from the walls. The closets were enormous. The American was pleased.

Brenda was able to buy a four-year-old Reo town car with a side entrance and complete with hood, lamps, and full equipment and best English coachwork for seven hundred pounds, twice the cost when new. She was lucky to find it and luckier, still, to hire Wendell McHugh, an old Irishman from Bray who worked as a combination butler and chauffeur. The old man, a widower, moved from his miserable lodgings in the slums of Shadwell in the East End into a comfortable downstairs room next to the O'Conners. Shadwell was a dreadful sprawl of tumbledown shacks originally peopled seventy years earlier by refugees from the potato famine. Crowding into the tiny, barren shanties, the newcomers added mean and cold rooms of scrap lumber, trash, and driftwood. There was no plumbing. Typical of denizens of Shadwell and its neighboring slum, the Isle of Dogs, McHugh talked in a strange mixture of Irish argot heavily tainted with cockney. He was grateful, considered himself lucky, and proved to be conscientious and loyal.

Two weeks after Brenda moved into her new house, Bernice burst through the door early one morning to announce joyfully, "The Coldstreams have been pulled from the line. They're in a rest camp near Chantilly. Lloyd will be home soon." She waved a letter.

Brenda led Bernice to the sitting room where they sat side by side while the ecstatic Bernice read and reread the letter, all the while dabbing at her eyes and laughing and crying at the same time. "He'll be home soon?" she asked herself over and over as if the incredibly good news could not possibly be true.

"But he is coming home, Bernice," Brenda assured her sister-in-law, trying to share Bernice's joy, wrap herself in the euphoria wives felt when they knew their men were free of the mortal danger of the front, safe and returning. But it was no good. Geoffry was at the bottom of the North Sea. She would never know what Bernice felt. She had not even viewed his corpse. She thought of her other great loss, her baby, the end of a life yet unlived, the mockery of the gift of life that sprang from her body, and the depression of the early summer began to creep back like a debilitating incurable delirium.

Sensing Brenda's mood, Bernice sobered quickly. "I'm hurting you, Brenda. It's thoughtless of me to . . ."

"No. No," Brenda said, taking the little woman's hand. "I'm happy for you—you know that. I love Lloyd, too."

Bernice sighed gratefully. "Yes. Yes. Of course." She caught her breath and stared at a Zoffany equestrian painting of one of her husband's long-dead ancestors on the far wall. There was a sudden grimness in the timbre of her voice. "Rebecca told me Randolph was eligible for a leave but won't take it."

"Won't take it?" Brenda repeated incredulously.

Bernice nodded. "Yes. It's that Hun—that Hun killer. Ah, Bruno . . ."

"Bruno Hollweg."

"That's right. Bruno Hollweg. Randolph writes rarely and when he does write, his letters are sick. He won't come home. He flies constantly looking for that Hun. It's confirmed that he killed the ace, Max Mueller, but he's not satisfied—it's a vendetta, a bloody crusade. It'll kill him." Her voice trailed off and she shook her head as if she were trying to free herself of the sudden depression that had seeped into the room, filling every corner, smothering the women like a wave of sticky fluid. She tried to break the mood. "That young destroyer captain, Reginald Hargreaves. Have you heard from him?"

Brenda was surprised by the query. How could Bernice know enough about the handsome commander to ask a question that implied Reginald had more than a passing interest in Brenda? Rebecca must be passing along more information than just news about Randolph. Brenda felt her cheeks warm. "I haven't heard from him in a fortnight. Must be at sea."

"Does he ring you often?" Bernice asked with rare boldness.

Brenda managed to shrug casually. "He phones."

Bernice beamed. "Let's go shopping. I'll take you to lunch in Piccadilly."

The exuberant mood was back. "Love it. "I've never been there." The women came to their feet.

Bernice's chauffeur, a burly old retired miner named Henry Merda from Newcastle, drove the women through the hustle and bustle of wartime London—a London Brenda had never seen before. They parked in Piccadilly and the women, in a festive mood, decided to walk. With Merda following at a respectable distance, they began to explore Piccadilly, touring the Berkeley and the Burlington Arcade before lunch. Famished by noon, they ate at the Elysée, a charming downstairs restaurant, while Henry enjoyed a "pint" at a nearby pub.

After lunch their mood carried them, energizing legs that should have been fatigued. In fact, the only thing that slowed them was concern for old Henry, who huffed and puffed and perspired in his black serge uniform and peaked cap. Brenda suspected the old man had had more than one "pint." They walked back out into the sights, sounds, and smells of Piccadilly: the Academy; Solomon's; the fruit and flower shops; the Ritz and Spink's fabulous jewelry; the roar and bustle of streams and taxis, buses, hansom cabs, drays drawn by enormous Clydesdales and Shires; the smell of burning petrol, steaming horseflesh. And every avenue and byway teemed with the tumult and eddy of humanity: swarms of fashionably dressed women; lean, hungry men in khaki and Tommy serge with South Africa, New Zealand, Canada, Australia stitched on shoulder patches everywhere, crowding the women like predators, staring at Brenda as if she were a morsel to be snatched from a gourmet buffet. Red-capped, white-gloved, and belted military police walked in twos and threes, watching the current of humanity with hard looks. Brenda felt she was at the headwaters of the Empire, being carried along by a river—the mainstream through Piccadilly fed by tributaries that gorged the stream, all redolent of war; death and easy sex its harvest.

Finally, tired by the long walk and the excitement of the spectacle, Bernice signaled Henry and the trio walked to a side street where Bernice's Silver Ghost was parked. Brenda had no conception of her weariness until she sagged back in the embrace of the Rolls's upholstery. It was good to be off her feet. But Bernice was still powered by the news of her husband's return. "He'll be home in less than a week," she kept repeating.

"Yes, Bernice, it will wonderful to see him," Brenda answered. But the empty, hollow feeling returned, dimmed the festive mood of the morning.

Three days later, Reginald phoned from Portsmouth and Brenda accepted a dinner invitation. It had been nearly seven months since Geoffry's death and she told herself she had mourned long enough. But deep down she knew being free of Walter and Rebecca's sad eyes had relieved her of a subtle restraint. "Hypocrite," she told herself. But the commander was handsome and she needed the company of a man.

"*En grande toilette*, tonight, *ma maitresse*," Nicole said, helping Brenda into a spectacular embroidered velvet *robe phenicienne* overlaid with panels stitched in beads of blue, mauve, and rose, crossing at the neck and continuing down the sides, clinging to her full, sculpted hips as if glued to her flesh. The young Frenchwoman stepped back, admiring her mistress. The *capitaine* is—" she pursed her lips, kissed her bunched fingers, and then popped her hand open as if she were flinging confetti—"ooh, la, la."

Brenda laughed heartily as Nicole placed a fur around her neck. "Oh yes. I like him," Brenda said.

"We all like him," Nicole said, smiling and baring her perfect white teeth.

Brenda felt a pang. The French maid could make good use of the commander. Probably exhaust him so much he would not be capable of standing on the bridge of his ship in a calm sea.

* * *

They dined at the Savoy because the food was excellent and because Marie Lloyd and the Bing Boys were entertaining. Seated at a table in the enormous dining room, Brenda smiled as she remembered Reginald's face when he first saw her in the entry that evening. He had been nearly speechless as his eyes moved over her body, perfectly delineated by the tight gown. Even the butler, old Wendell McHugh, stood in self-conscious silence until the commander murmured, "You look absolutely smashing." And then he kissed her hand, lingering too long, and tracing her wrist with warm, moist fingers. Brenda had felt a thrilling warmth spread deep within her, capturing her heart and sending it pounding. Disturbed, she tried to ignore it. It was the first sweet response of a woman feeling arousal and there was nothing she could do to help herself.

Reginald ordered for both of them, a lavish meal for wartime London or peacetime, for that matter: hearts of artichoke with pâté de foie gras; *salade de lègumes;* a marvelous *poularde à la vapeur* wrapped in muslin and cooked in a cognac marinate and lemon rind. Seasoned to perfection, it was served with a butter, cream, and mixed egg yolk sauce. Dessert was a delightful fruit *macedoine*. Fawning waiters kept their glasses filled with Louis Roederer. Despite the rich food, Brenda felt the effects of the champagne, which she consumed in unusually generous amounts. In fact, the room began to move as if it were part of a carousel. She pressed her foot to the floor and shook her head, but the unsteadiness remained. Then, after dinner, black coffee and Martell Cordon Bleu. She toyed with the pony, but drank her coffee. The carousel slowed.

The entertainment began; Marie Lloyd singing with the Bing Boys and the hotel orchestra, telling amusing stories spiced with bawdy asides. Bare-legged chorus girls in bright, brief uniforms drilling with sequin-encrusted toy Enfields, astonishing buttocks flouncing and twitching at the audience. Beads, spangles, silk tights, half-bared breasts, and brassy music. Everyone singing war songs; "Mademoiselle From Armentieres" and "Tipperary" were the two favorites. There were choruses of "The Bonny Earl of

Murray" and "Barb'ra Ellen." Finally, the dancing, the moment that Brenda had awaited eagerly. Reginald's arms around her at last.

They made their way to the dance floor, crowded with dozens of couples, every man in uniform. He was a superb dancer, holding her close and commanding her with a strong lead in perfect three-quarter time as the orchestra avoided Strauss waltzes and broke into "Hearts and Flowers." She felt his arm tightening, pulling her body against his. Still heady with champagne, she tried to hold back but slowly yielded, finally pressing her breasts and pelvis against the hard wool of his uniform, his flat stomach, his hard chest. It was indecent, but everyone was doing it. "Queen Victoria be damned," he whispered in her ear. She laughed, a young girl's high, delighted giggle. The effects of the liquor, the music, a strong man's arms around her seemed to transport her somewhere else. For an instant she was no longer in England. Maybe she had defied time—had found a happier time in the past. That was it. The same thrill she had felt at her first college dance. But this was not Troy Richardson; she was in Reginald Hargreaves's arms. A trade was unthinkable. The present was better.

More waltzes. Song after song blended one into the other. She was at home in his arms and it was very right. Maybe the music would never end. His hand was on the small of her back, pushing, and she felt his sun- and salt-roughened cheek against hers, his warm breath caressing her ear, smelled his cologne like fine rum. In spite of herself, she ran her hand over his back, feeling the hard, bunched muscles. Suddenly, contractions of her chest and lungs left her breathless and she felt a remarkable heat on her cheeks and the skin of her throat, tiny cold insects scurrying up the back of her neck, and the same warmth spreading lower in her body. Suddenly they were alone, totally alone with only the music to seep in from some distant place. She wanted to touch him closer, feel his flesh. She found the back of his neck, traced her fingers over the short, bristling hair. His arms tightened and they pressed against each other hungrily. She felt warm lips against her cheek and she allowed her body to go limp, mold itself to his. "I want you. I want you," he said thickly.

She shook her head, broke the dream, pulled away. "Reggie," she said in a hoarse whisper. "Let's sit down."

Unmoving, he stared down at her. "What's wrong?" The other dancers began to stare.

"Nothing. Please. Let's sit down." Slowly, he led her back to the table.

He recharged their glasses with Martell. "Come to my place, Brenda. We can be alone."

Feeling the barrier come erect, she sighed. "I want to, Reginald."

"But you won't," he said bitterly.

"No."

"Then why that show?" He gesticulated at the dance floor. "Why lead me on?"

She said with anguish, "I'm not a tease."

"I didn't say you were. I just want to know why the passion?"

She palmed her hair back and sighed. "I couldn't help myself."

He tapped his forehead with white knuckles. "But you refuse—won't come to my place."

"I'm not ready—I'm sorry. I've told you before."

"Quite. Quite. Shall I take you home?"

"Perhaps you'd better."

"I won't see you for a while, Brenda."

"You're angry. I wouldn't blame you if you never saw me again."

"No. I'm not angry and I want to see you. But the squadron's taking another short training cruise. Be gone for a few days."

Again, she felt the deep acid feeling of dread. "Dangerous, Reginald? Be careful."

He smiled. "An easy slog—rather simple training exercises. We've been hard at it for months. A short run." He smothered her hand in his. "I—I regard you with a lot of affection."

"And I feel the same for you, Reggie. Please phone me when you return."

"Yes. As soon as we dock."

"You're sure you're not angry with me?"

"Impossible, Brenda." He took her hand and helped her to her feet. "And don't worry about me, Brenda. This is a safe one—safer than a stroll through the East End."

She smiled up at him and then turned toward the exit.

VIII

Winter in the English Channel is never pleasant. The November morning Destroyer Squadron Four slipped its moorings, the sky was a low, sullen blanket congealing into a leaden shroud that spilled to every horizon, the sea the color of a halfpenny. Fortunately, there were breaks in the blanket and Commander Reginald Hargreaves standing at the wooden windscreen on the forebridge of destroyer *Lancer* could not only hear the bells of the channel buoys, but also he could see the red markers dropping off to port and the green buoys to starboard. Occasional bright flares of the morning sun broke through and his lookouts shouted sightings and the chief quartermaster was even able to take tangents on Haying Island as it dropped off to port and the Isle of Wight broad on the starboard beam. Astern, destroyers *Unity*, *Victor*, and *Paragon* followed in *Lancer*'s wake.

"Fair in the center of the Channel, sir," the new navigation officer, Lieutenant Desmond Farrar, said, turning from the small chart table and pulling the canvas hood aside.

"Sea buoy bearing red zero-three-five, close aboard, sir," the port lookout shouted in a high voice that was almost a falsetto.

"Very well," Reginald acknowledged, nodding at the lookout, boy first class Basil Goodenough, whose teenage eyes were the sharpest on the ship. Raising his glasses, Reginald brought the tall red and yellow striped buoy into focus.

After a quick clattering movement of parallel rulers and dividers, the navigator said, "Suggest course one-three-zero, sir."

"Very well, pilot." Reginald turned to Lieutenant Pochhammer who stood close to his side. "Make the hoist, Number One. Course one-three-zero, speed twelve."

The tall first officer, who was hunched over as if he were trying to make himself a smaller target for the cold, repeated the order. Then he turned to the flag locker at the back of the bridge where yeoman of signals Leslie Henshaw, a grizzled twenty-year veteran of the pre-dreadnought navy, was standing with his assistant—young ordinary signalman Byron Heathstone, a sallow seventeen-year-old whose youth and clean fuzzy cheeks like a fresh peach contrasted sharply with the yeoman's. Commands were shouted and pennants and flags raced upward on their halyards to the yardarm, whipping and snapping in the freshening northern breeze, which felt like it had been frozen on the polar cap. The first officer, both signalmen, and the navigator all trained their glasses astern. "All vessels have acknowledged, sir," the yeoman of signals shouted, his breath white banners ripped from his lips by the wind.

"Very well." Reginald turned to Pochhammer. "Let me know when the last vessel has cleared the sea buoy."

"Aye, aye, sir."

For a long moment the first officer leaned into his glasses. "Last ship has cleared," he finally shouted.

"Very well. Execute!" Reginald heard the hoists whipped down and back into the locker.

"All answer," Henshaw shouted.

"Very well." Reginald turned to the front, leaned against the teakwood rail, and wrapped his hands around a clutch of voice pipes that connected him to the engine room, gun stations, director, W-T, and pilot house directly beneath his feet. Steel chilled like ice, the cold penetrated the leather of his gloves, stinging the flesh of his palms. "Pilot house."

"Pilot house, aye," came back through a pipe.

"Port ten."

"Port ten, sir," the voice answered. "Ten of port wheel on, sir."

"Midships."

"Wheel amidships." A pause. "She's steady, sir."

"Very well. Course one-three-zero and watch your head, quartermaster."

Another pause. Finally, the tinny voice came back. "Steady on one-three-zero, Captain."

"Very well. One-half ahead together."

"One-half ahead together," came from another voice tube. Reginald could hear the jangle of engine room telegraphs and the vibrations beneath his boots quickened. "Speed twelve, one hundred ten revolutions, Captain."

"Very well." Hargreaves tightened his knotted silk scarf, thrust his hands deep into the pockets of his duffel coat, and stamped his heavy sea boots on the grating. The cold was penetrating—an insidious cold that grated the marrow of a man's bones and froze his soul. Glancing astern through the rapidly thinning mist, he nodded to himself; *Unity, Victor,* and *Paragon* were in his spreading wake precisely where they should have been.

There were the sounds of a new presence on the forebridge. Senior steward Smith spoke. "Cocoa, sir." He was carrying a tray filled with seven white porcelain mugs.

"Jolly good idea," Hargreaves said, reaching for a cup with *Lancer*'s shield and *Captain* stenciled in gold paint. It was the only one laced with rum. Gratefully, the other members of the bridge crew accepted their cups and began to gulp the steaming hot liquid. Reginald drank his slowly, savoring the rich flavor of the cocoa and liquor and the warmth creeping from his stomach.

Raising his glasses, he scanned the horizon to the southeast where the rising sun had burned off the early mists, inflaming the sky with virulent reds, oranges, and purples. To the north, the improving visibility showed the entire horizon cluttered with high thunderheads and low-line squalls that obscured the sea with solid blocks of rain like pearl dust. The morning sun played games with the clouds, capriciously painting some with gold and silver; others showed pink, rose, and misty mauve while the undersides were all dark bruises of purple and gray and here and there black showed through. Reginald knew there was a storm to the north, its harbingers endless rows of swells arranged in neat ranks and advancing diagonally like infantry on the Western Front. The first skirmishers began the assault, comber after comber quartering *Lancer* on the port side, the narrow ship reacting with deep rolls that sent every man's hands to rails and stanchions.

Reginald turned to Pochhammer. "You can fall out the special sea duty men, starboard watch to defense stations, if you please, Number One."

The lieutenant shouted down the voice tubes, there was a trill of pipes, and Reginald heard boots on ladders, the slam of doors as off-duty men scurried below to the warmth of the mess decks. Pochhammer disappeared down the ladder. Stiffly, Hargreaves lowered himself into the captain's padded chair that was high and on the right side of the forebridge, affording an unobstructed view of all four quadrants. The new pilot, Desmond Farrar, eased himself alongside, taking the position of the OD and raising his glasses.

Reginald was not enthused about his new navigator. A thirtyish career officer, Desmond Farrar had sharp, aristocratic features and narrow gray eyes that were as unreadable as gunmetal. Years at sea had sun-darkened and tanned his skin like leather with deep creases at the corners of his mouth and outlining those strange eyes. He seldom smiled or showed any emotion, for that matter, except pride and arrogance. He was immensely proud of his rich, fox-hunting family and when drinking he would quickly bore anyone within earshot with tales of the good life on his father's estates on the moors of South Devon. His record was suspect. At sea by the age of thirteen, he was commissioned in 1906 and served on the old armored cruiser, *Cornwall*. He was assistant navigator in battle cruiser *Inflexible* off the Falkland Islands when Sir Frederick Doveton Sturdee's force destroyed Admiral von Spee's cruiser squadron, sinking *Scharnhorst, Gneisenau, Leipzig,* and *Nürnberg* in 1914. This great victory should have accelerated Farrar's career; instead, his records showed frequent clashes with his superiors over a variety of matters from tactics to the recovery of German survivors—Farrar argued abandoning enemy swimmers to freeze in the cold waters off the Falklands. His conduct at Jutland had been workmanlike but undistinguished. Overall, his ratings had been poor, causing Farrar to be passed over several times. Now he was suffering the indignity of serving under a captain at least six years his junior.

"Starboard watch closed up at defense stations, sir," Farrar said in his soft, raspish voice. "As per your orders, course one-three-zero, speed twelve, Captain." He focused his glasses over the bow.

"Very well, Lieutenant," Reginald said. "At ten hundred hours come to zero-four-zero."

Farrar lowered his glasses. "Put us in the center of the Channel, sir."

"Just as you shaped it, pilot."

"Think we'll stuff the Jerries this time, Captain?"

"We have a plan and we'll give it a go, Mister Farrar." Reginald felt his stomach churn with an amalgam of anger and despair, bitter thoughts flashing through his mind. A plan—Watts with his bloody stupid plan.

He grasped the arms of the chair as a large comber caught the destroyer full on the beam, green-gray water breaking over the quarterdeck. The ship took a vicious roll to starboard, then righted herself with the short, snapping rollback typical of narrow-beamed ships with low freeboard. Reginald heard the crash of crockery in the pilot house followed by curses.

"Things will be better when we come about and put our bows into this lot," the navigator said, grasping the teakwood rail with both hands.

Reginald nodded, his mind on the sweep and the details of the plan that had been outlined at Whitehall three days before. Every detail of that turbulent meeting in Operations Room Four had been burned into his memory.

Located in the basement of Whitehall, Operations Room Four was a large room with a long, highly polished walnut table and walls covered with charts. Twelve destroyer captains representing three full squadrons had been seated around the table, eyes fixed on Vice Admiral Sir Rosslyn Watts. Watts was the fattest man Reginald had ever seen. Positioned at the head of the table, Watts had stood with his legs set apart and his body braced much like a heavily pregnant woman hard put to counterbalance her monstrous womb. The blue expanse of his tunic required to cover the bulge of his stomach and chest was so vast, it reminded Reginald of the curtain at the Palladium. His chins hung down in rows like a soft chop at sea, white and sickly in color like rancid vanilla pudding. Always open, his mouth was a purple gash, laboring for breath. The son of a wealthy barrister, Watts had attended the best schools and in his youth, had served in Africa without distinction. However, in 1898 he happened to be the commanding officer of a gunboat during the relief of Omdurman where the the Twenty-first Lancers were trapped. The relief force fought its way up the Nile and the siege was lifted. One of the rescued lancers was Winston Churchill who was eternally grateful and, it was said, became his patron. Watts's star rose from that moment on and had not declined with Churchill's after the Gallipoli fiasco. His only level of communication was a hoarse, whiskey-addled rasp that showed no feelings and, to Reginald, little intelligence.

His opening gambit had been a casual, almost careless reference to the top-secret British decoders who had been reading German wireless transmissions for over a year. "According to the chaps in Room Forty, a German force of six new B-class destroyers under *Korvettenkapitän* Max Schultz has reinforced the German flotilla at Zeebrugge." An excited rumble filled the room. "Added to the Sixth Flotilla at Ostend and the Tenth at Zeebrugge, the Hun has at least eighteen vessels ready for sea and Schultz has taken command of the whole lot. Obviously, this force increases the threat to the Dover Patrol and Channel shipping in general."

Commander Norman Griffith, the commanding officer of Destroyer Squadron Eight, said, "The B-boat, sir. I understand they mount ten-point-five-centimeter guns."

Watts nodded to a yeoman of letters seated at a small desk to his left. The yeoman handed the vice admiral a document. He read: "Length two hundred eighty feet, eighteen hundred forty-three tons, speed thirty-two, three funnels, three deck level fifty-centimeter torpedo tubes, two ten-point-five-centimeter guns." There were groans. The vice admiral raised his hands. "Your K-boats have three, quick-firing four-inch guns mounted on better platforms with superior sea-keeping qualities and manned by the best gun crews on earth." The captains exchanged skeptical looks. Watts surveyed his audience with beady eyes, purple lips slashed downward in a scowl that was lost in the fat.

He continued, irritation obvious in the timbre of his voice. "I have a plan to lure them out, engage them, and dispose of the lot." He tapped the desktop with a single finger. "As you know, the Dover patrol has been hard put to contain destroyer raids. Squadrons from Zeebrugge and Ostend have raised bloody hob of late and now Schultz's flotilla makes the threat even more grave to say nothing of the U-boats operating out of the Channel ports." He glanced at the yeoman who handed him more documents. He spoke with a new solemn tone in his voice. "Last night German destroyers shelled Dover and Margate and sank two steamers off the Downs anchorage. Two enemy ships were spotted as close in as the Maàs lightship and light buoy Eleven-A." The captains exchanged looks of dismay and anger. "Whitehall is screaming for action and, as you well know, the papers will be crying for blood in a day or two." He thumped the table. "You know these attacks cannot be kept secret."

Reginald waved a hand. The vice admiral nodded in his direction. "Sir," Hargreaves said. "What happened to the plan to attack the ports of Zeebrugge and Ostend with monitors?"

Watts smiled respectfully. "You were in planning in fifteen, Commander Hargreaves?"

"Yes, Admiral."

Watts spoke directly to Reginald. "The War Office was hoping the Somme offensive would put a quick end to this whole bloody business—put the Ostend-Zeebrugge plan on the shelf. But now"—he shrugged—"I believe we'll be dusting it off." Reginald nodded. The vice admiral continued. "*Korvettenkapitän* Schultz is known as a daring commander—a hothead who can be reckless in the stress of battle." Watts placed both hands on the table and supported his weight by leaning forward. "We intend to lure him out and hope the other flotillas will follow." He moved to a chart attached to the wall under a picture of King George V and picked up a pointer. "A slow convoy—eight merchantmen, three colliers, and an oiler with a weak escort of two patrol craft and a minesweeper—will leave South Shields tonight and head south through the Channel at eight knots. Their wireless discipline will be sloppy and German direction finders should pick them up as they stand out. Anyway, German U-boats and small craft patrols are sure to pick them up and I am convinced Schultz will not be able to resist the bait." A smile creased the broad face and his beady eyes moved over the assemblage.

Norman Griffith asked, "Not even in daylight, sir?"

"Not even in daylight," Watts said, his smile exuding confidence. He struck the chart. "Commodore Tyrwhitt's Harwich cruiser force of six cruisers and eight destroyers will steam north and circle back of the convoy." He struck a long arc from south to north and south again. He turned to the captains and indicated two of the older officers sitting close together at the end of the table. "Commanders Griffith and Gladden will take Destroyer Squadrons Eight and Eleven on a northerly course to intercept the convoy here"—he struck the chart with the rubber pointer—"off Skegness." He turned to Hargreaves. "At the same time, Commander Hargreaves, you will strike out across the Channel with Destroyer Squadron Four and place your ships between the German destroyers and their home ports." He tapped his open palm with the pointer. "That's my plan," he added proudly. "We'll have them on an anvil."

Reginald felt the acid of anger and dread seethe deep within and icy prickles began to chill the back of his neck. "Admiral Watts," he said, not bothering to wave. "It is possible my squadron may be forced to engage eighteen enemy ships, six armed with ten-point-five-centimeter guns, and two knots faster than we are."

Anger boiled through the fat. "There's little chance that can happen, Commander—not with Commodore Tyrwhitt's cruiser force hot on their sterns and"—he gesticulated at Gladden and Griffith—"not to mention Destroyer Squadrons Eight and Eleven."

Reginald felt control begin to slip away. "On their sterns, sir—on their sterns. Destroyer Squadron Four will be hot on their bows with hostile shore guns behind us. We'll be on the anvil. We'll need cruiser support."

The layered fat began to purple. "Commander Hargreaves, the ships aren't available and if you're afraid . . ."

Reginald shot to his feet, discretion and years of training forgotten, cold rage bursting from his lips. "No one challenges my courage, Admiral." There was a shocked silence, every eye focused on Reginald. "Steam with me, Admiral. Fly your pendant from my masthead. Die with my chaps." There was undisguised sarcasm in his voice.

The eyes moved back to Watts whose face was a book of rage. Surprisingly, he managed to control his voice, speaking with only a slight tremor. "Because of the pressing exigencies of the moment, Commander Hargreaves, I will not remove you from your command." Watts thumped the table with a hand like a sack of jelly. "You will carry out my orders precisely as I have outlined." He gestured to the yeoman. "My writer will give each of you a detailed description of your duties and responsibilities, departure times, ETAs, courses, speeds, codes, recognition signals, and dispositions. And keep in mind, there is nothing I would enjoy more than to personally lead you. But the admiralty forbids it—requires me to remain here." He looked around silently, smoking eyes finally coming to rest on Hargreaves. His voice was cracking ice. "You and I will discuss this matter —your conduct—when the operation is concluded. You are dismissed."

Reginald was the first to leave the room.

The next day in a conference room in Portsmouth Reginald met with his own captains: Commanders Liddel Wolcott of *Unity,* Nathanial Blankenship of *Victor,* and Dewey Woolridge of *Paragon.* With memories of the previous day's scene in Operations Room Four still fresh in every man's mind, the meeting was somber. There was the usual distribution of orders, charts, the discussion of departure times, readiness statutes, steaming formations, signals, radio silence, and the multitude of details facing a squadron preparing for sea and battle. "And regardless of what you heard in Operations Room Four," Reginald concluded, "we have our orders and I need not tell you we will execute them to the letter." Then Reginald had taken a last look around the bright, intense faces staring up at him: Wolcott and Blankenship both fathers of two, Woolridge newly married. Was he about to create a new clutch of widows and orphans? One thing was a certainty: these brave, loyal men would follow him through the gates of hell. Suddenly he felt anger and resentment, a thickening and closing of the throat. "You are dismissed," he said hoarsely. The captains filed silently out of the room.

Now he was leading four ships, over six hundred men, on a run north that would place them just a few miles off the coast of German Belgium. He had tried to hide his misgivings when presenting the plan to *Lancer*'s officers in a wardroom meeting. But the senior officers, Pochhammer, Farrar, and the new gunnery officer Horace Gibbs, saw through it immediately, yet, as the disciplined professionals they were and taking their cue from their captain, they accepted the orders and possibly their death warrants stoically with only a few questions about execution and tactics, not overall strategy. But there had been resentment and anger smoldering in Farrar's strange eyes.

Farrar's soft voice in his ear and an unusually vicious roll brought Reginald back to the present. He spoke boldly, using expressions from the mess decks. "By your leave, Captain, the plan is a load of pusser's duff—a sure ticket to blighty."

Reginald's first impulse was to rebuff the pilot. However, the voice was soft, confidential, and, despite the crude level of expression, the sentiments were his own. "The Frenchies would say, '*C'est la guerre*,' pilot," Reginald said.

"Even the Frogs would do better than this, Captain. We need a big-gunned ship. We can run into ships that can out-gun us and outrun us. We need a big-gunned ship—a cruiser division."

It was time to bring the conversation to a halt. "They aren't available and we have our orders."

Farrar would not let go. "And orders are sacred."

"Of course. For what other reason do we exist?" Reginald waved his hand in a gesture of irritation and finality. Piqued, Farrar moved to the other side of the bridge and sullenly raised his glasses.

A break in the clouds and a bolt of sunlight struck a low ridge of clouds rouging a large sector to the southeast in spectacular shades of vermilion and cinnabar, banishing thoughts of Watts and his plan, bringing back Brenda's hair and the way she looked when he held her on the dance floor of the Savoy. Like all men who had spent long months at sea, Reginald's memories came back with vivid, real images, a presence that struck with a physical impact, and he could feel the American's firm, tiny waist under his hand, her hard stomach and groin pressing against his, inflaming him. The maddening heat and arousal of the moment rushed back and the young commander twisted in his chair uncomfortably like a tortured spirit. She was an enigma. Passionate, no doubt. She found him attractive; there was no doubt about that, either. But she would not accept him as her lover. There was a barrier. Did she have a secret lover? Randolph? He shrugged the idea away. No. There was something terribly wrong with Brenda. She loved men, but could accept none. Certainly, it was not Geoffrey. Her husband's death had been a blow—everyone knew that. But he felt she had never really loved Geoffry romantically—passionately.

Maybe it was guilt. Maybe it was guilt over all of the dead young men. But how could that be? He loved Brenda but could not tell her. What was wrong with this world? Was there so much hate love ceased to exist? Certainly there was sex—that was what everyone sought. Everyone except Brenda. He sighed and rubbed his head in frustration.

A lookout's call jarred him. "Ship! Fine on the port bow!"

"Very well," Desmond Farrar said, raising his glasses.

Reginald came erect, glasses hard against his face. A small unarmed drifter, wallowing in the swells. Probably trying out the new hydrophones that were supposed to detect U-boats miles away. Reginald dropped his glasses in frustration. If the small, helpless vessel ever encountered a U-boat, all it could do was cry a warning on its wireless and hope destroyers from the Dover patrol arrived before it died. Bloody terrible way to fight a war. Throwing away good brave men—like his own.

The sun was high in the eastern sky, but it was still very cold. He glanced at his watch. The convoy had left South Shields four hours before Destroyer Squadron Four had put to sea. By now the bait was off Flamborough Head with the Harwich Cruiser Force eight miles astern and Destroyer Squadrons Eight and Eleven were poised in Dover with steam up. They would put to sea in another thirty minutes. There was a sharp whistle and Reginald leaned forward and opened one of the voice pipes. "This is the captain," he said into the steel tube.

He recognized the voice of his young signals officer, Sub-lieutenant Ian Carpenter. "This is the W-T, sir. Just received a signal on fleet channel B, Captain. 'German destroyers putting to sea from Ostend and Zeebrugge.'"

"Very well. Do not acknowledge."

Carpenter's voice came back. "We are maintaining silence, sir."

"It's started, sir," Farrar said in a hard voice.

Reginald felt the same pang of helplessness all men feel when committed to battle by the minds, hopes, and ambitions of other men. He was a totally expendable pawn who had very little to say about whether he would live or die in the next twenty-four hours. He could only follow his orders, pray, and trust to luck. "Yes," he said simply. "The plan is working."

"Like a clockwork mouse," Farrar said laconically, turning away and raising his glasses.

As the force worked its way slowly northeastward, frequently changing course to mislead curious eyes that could be watching at the end of a periscope below or staring down through binoculars from the clouds above, several ships were sighted. Six merchantmen with two small escorts passed to the southwest, hugging the coast of Folkestone, and headed for the Atlantic, coal black funnel smoke smearing the sea in rolls in the heavy air. Then, a half hour later, two minesweepers, both converted trawlers, passed in line abreast with gear deployed. They passed within four miles sweeping the Channel landward of the force. Recognition signals were exchanged while the ready gun, X-gun, tracked. The crew was not called to action stations. Reginald had his lunch brought to the bridge.

By 1400 hours, the squadron passed through the narrowest part of the Channel with the *Pas de Calais* visible off the starboard side, Dover and its high white cliffs like a long row of hulking spirits to port. The wind had died and the sea had calmed with just a deep swell like the heavy breathing of a dying man to change the hues from dark gray to black. The sky had changed, too, from grays and black to solid pewter with streaks of ostrich feather cirrus smeared across it. The air itself seemed charged—heavy with static that made Reginald's skin tingle, the cold still oppressive and insidious.

By 1530 hours, Dunkerque was off the starboard quarter and the first attack signals were broadcast from the convoy. Ostend was thirty miles away. They could run into enemy patrols. Reginald turned to Farrar. "Your clockwork mouse is moving, Mister Farrar. Action stations," he said matter-of-factly.

Farrar shouted down the voice pipes and in a moment boatswain mates' pipes shrieked and buzzers sounded in every compartment in the ship. Instantly, there was a pounding of running boots on decks and ladders, the shouts of officers and petty officers, the clang of water-tight doors being slammed, the hard sound of steel on brass as breeches received four-inch shells, the declining whir of fans as deck-hands were turned off. Farrar moved to the chart table and Pochhammer took his place next to the captain. Reports echoed up the voice pipes: "A-gun manned and ready"; Y-gun manned and ready"; "W-T manned and ready." On and on they went, Pochhammer relaying the reports, Hargreaves acknowledging with "Very well." Finally, *Lancer* was ready, alert, claws bared, holding her breath.

Reginald glanced at the Belgian coast looming through the gathering gloom off the starboard side. He needed more sea room. "Port one point," he said into the pipe.

He felt the ship heel as the helmsman put the wheel over exactly eleven degrees fifteen minutes. "One point of port wheel on, sir," came back through the pipe.

"Very well. Midships. Steer zero-one-zero."

"Wheel amidships. Steady on zero-one-zero, sir."

"Very well." He spoke into another tube. "W-T, any more messages from the convoy?"

Carpenter's voice came back. "Nothing since the original contact report."

Hargreaves turned to Pochhammer. "Have the lookouts be especially alert for small craft." Reginald knew the order was redundant. By this time, enemy eyes on shore and probably in submarines had doubtless spotted the destroyers. Now their survival depended on timing, skill, courage, and no small measure of luck. To foil lurking U-boats, Geoffry increased speed to sixteen knots and led the squadron on a zigzagging patrol only six miles off the coast, first north-eastward and then reversing with his bows pointed to the southwest.

At 1600 hours, Carpenter reported more wireless transmissions: the convoy had lost two cargo ships, a collier, and an oiler. They were crying for help.

Pochhammer struck the windscreen. "Where's the bloody cruisers?"

Reginald was jarred by the starboard lookout's shrill cry. "Flames! Rockets!" The voice belonged to a new eighteen-year-old midshipman, Orville Tucker, and it grated on the captain's nerves like the screech of a taut, erratically played violin string.

Reginald knew the sighting had to be to starboard and swung his glasses. But the panicky youngster needed a lesson. "Bearing? Range, old man. Chop, chop!"

The boy shrieked back, "Flames and alarm rockets broad on the starboard beam—over the horizon."

"Very well." Reginald had already brought his glasses to the western horizon where two suns were setting. No doubt about it. Fifteen to twenty miles away, an uncertain blood red glow spreading over the horizon, lighting up the low clouds like the pulsing electric signs in Piccadilly. Balls of light soared high above it, silver and red spheres that exploded and rained down red, white, and green stars. "Must be the oiler—poor bloody bastards," Pochhammer muttered, staring through his binoculars.

There were huge flashes to the northwest and Reginald saw groups of lights arc lazily above the mist and plunge into the sea to the south where they disappeared in wavering red and salmon glows. "Gunfire!" came down from the director, which was mounted on the mainmast above the forebridge. The voice belonged to Lieutenant Horace Gibbs, the new gunner. "Big guns."

"Must be the Harwich cruisers," Pochhammer said.

"Right," Reginald agreed. "But they're firing at long range. They're too far north."

"Bloody foulup."

Carpenter's voice from the W-T: "More transmissions, Captain. Radio silence has gone bally west. The convoy is scattering and Squadrons Eight and Eleven are engaging. But apparently they're having trouble with the cruisers' fire and U-boats. The cruisers are firing on everyone. There's a fog and recognition signals can't be read and it's turning into a shambles, Captain."

Reginald heard Farrar's voice. "The clockwork mouse has broken a spring."

"Very well," Reginald said. He turned to Pochhammer. "Alert all stations—we may be engaging German destroyers within the hour and watch for periscopes. The convoy is no more than twenty miles away and under heavy attack and the Germans bloody well know we're here." He glanced at the shore. They were too far south. "Bring the ship to her reciprocal course—zero-zero-zero." Pochhammer shouted into the voice pipes.

Reginald discovered his estimate was off by almost thirty minutes when a half hour later a masthead lookout's voice rang out, "Ships! Many ships fine on the port bow, range five to six thousand yards!"

Holding his breath, Reginald leapt from his chair, binoculars pressed so hard against his eyes they watered with pain. At first he saw nothing. Then, in the gloom of sunset and racing through the swirling mist and gathering fog, he saw them: one, two, three, and more gray shapes charging toward him; two columns of steel monsters slashing the slate gray ocean with white tatters of the sea in their teeth, flinging spray recklessly, spewing black smoke. Either the Germans did not see them or were being pursued by heavy ships and had no choice. In any event, the enemy vessels were already in range and appeared not to have seen the British.

Reginald felt the usual wild surge of excitement that always charged his veins just before battle. There was terror there, too, and a hard, frigid spasm raced through his bones and muscles, his heart a mallet against his chest. But his mind was clear and he knew he must engage the enemy to port with both guns and torpedoes and in a single column. At the moment he was in the best possible tactical situation —by luck he had intercepted in position to cross the Germans' T. His voice was calm. "Number one, if you please, hoist pendants three and four and the B flag, course zero-one-zero, speed full."

While Pochhammer shouted at the signalmen, Hargreaves spoke into the voice tubes to the gunnery officer. "'Guns,' target bearing red ten, range five thousand, fire when ready."

Pochhammer's voice: "All ships acknowledge, Captain."

"Very well. Execute!" Back to the pipes. "All ahead full

together, course is zero-one-zero and hold her steady—engineering, give me every knot you can squeeze out of her."

Orders were repeated and acknowledgments made. Reginald clung to the windscreen as *Lancer*'s screws flurried to maximum revs, the ship digging her stern into the sea and lunging ahead, speed climbing to thirty knots. Crashing her bows into the seas, she flung spray and slate gray water over her forecastle like an angry tiger rushing through heavy undergrowth. For the moment, he had done everyting a captain could do. Now he had to depend on his gunnery officer who was perched twenty feet over his head peering through his new split-image range finder. Perhaps, later, their lives would be in the hands of nineteen-year-old Sublieutenant Trevor Grenfell who was standing by the torpedo director on the quarterdeck. He brought up his binoculars and refocused them.

Gibbs's voice came through a pipe. "Range four-five-zero-zero."

Reginald shouted, "Open fire!" He heard the tinny sound like sleigh bells of the firing gong at A mount and gunlayers chanting, "Layer on! Layer on!" All three guns fired simultaneously, lashing the mist with eight-foot yellow tongues, jarring the windscreen and sending a loose screw flying into the binnacle with a high, pinging sound. The grating bounced up and down and bits of paint dropped off metal and woodwork. The crack was like a great whip that overwhelmed the ears' ability to hear, stabbing the brain with pain instead of sound. Reginald choked back a groan. The other ships were firing, and staring through his binoculars Reginald saw a forest of white spouts leap into the sky in front of the enemy destroyers.

Gibbs was shouting into his intercom, "Short! Up one hundred. Deflection eight right." There was a jumble of voices in the pipes then Gibbs again: "Shoot!" More concussions. "On target. Rapid fire!" All three mounts fired a continuous stream of shells, loaders working like madmen and shouting excitedly, brass casings clattering to the decks and rollling to the scuppers. The pungent smell of cordite filled

Reginald's nostrils and afterimages of muzzle-blasts flashed from his retinas like ghosts of welders' torches.

The enemy was reacting. Reginald saw fearsome flashes on the forecastles of the two leading destroyers and they were changing formation, too, at least nine ships appearing to both left and right, coming to line abreast. But they did not change course. The reckless head-on attack continued. Pochhammer seemed to read his mind. "The cruisers must be hard on their arses, Captain," he said casually.

There was a roar and shriek overhead like a huge sheet of canvas being ripped and something fearsome passed over the mainmast and exploded in the sea a hundred yards away, a gray white waterspout sixty feet tall leaping into the sky, the flash of exploding lyddite snuffed out immediately by the water. More enemy destroyers were firing: high-velocity eight-point-eight-centimeter shrieking, piping, hissing; ten-point-five-centimeter rumbling and roaring. More waterspouts and spreading rings and spray, shrapnel kicking up water in little white tufts. They were creeping closer.

At that instant, Reginald envied the infantryman. The Tommy could hurl himself to the ground, press himself into the earth; his mother, his friend, bury his fragile flesh deep within her safe from the whining steel hell. And she protected him, muffled his cries in the shelter and warmth of her bosom, lavishing another few seconds of life upon him. But the sailor knows none of this luxury. He must firm up against the instinct to go to ground, repulsed by the steel deck beneath his feet. He must stand tall behind tissue-paper-thin bulkheads and wooden windscreens and not allow a trace of his terror to alter even one line of his face. Discipline—discipline himself beyond the bounds of human intelligence, human reason.

"We've hit the bloody sods," came from the masthead. There were flashes and dull red glows on the bridges and forecastles of two of the ships like open fireboxes. Suddenly, the vessel to the far right staggered and fairly leapt from the sea, her forecastle and most of her bridge leaping hundreds of feet in the air on the tip of a giant yellow white shaft of flame. The light was like high noon, illuminating the sea for miles with an eruption of flames and swirling smoke, chunks of twisted steel raining into the sea in a huge arc.

The crew cheered wildly, but Reginald could see at least eight destroyers charging toward Destroyer Squadron Four in a loose formation that approximated a ragged line abreast. Far to the south, Reginald found another group of three enemy ships skirting his formation and heading for Ostend or perhaps his rear. "The anvil," he said to himself.

The captain heard Gibbs's voice. "Cease firing! Shift target! Red four-zero, range three-five-zero-zero." Again the chant of the gun layers; again, "Shoot!"; again the concussions.

Another German was hit, a leading vessel staggering, slowly, and veering wildly to the side, flames leaping from its bridge and quarterdeck. There were explosions and debris and men rained into the sea. The stricken vessel began to settle fast by the bow and heel over. More cheers.

A flare arced high in the sky from a leading destroyer and the German line turned abruptly to port, bringing themselves into a parallel course with the English. All of the enemy's armament would bear. Reginald choked back his sour, burning gorge. "Enemy vessels broad on the starboard beam!" came from the captain of Y gun. A quick glance through his binoculars and Reginald knew the enemy force of three vessels had skirted behind him and turned to attack.

There was only one chance for survival. He shouted at Pochhammer, "Number One, nine turn, engage with torpedoes!"

While Pochhammer relayed the order to the signalmen, the captain bellowed down the voice pipes. Within seconds all four English destroyers veered about hard, heeling into their full power turns toward the German line like drunks teetering on curbstones, sluicing up huge waves with their knifelike bows that broke over their quarterdecks and streamed off their sterns and quarters. They completed their turns in perfect alignment in a line abreast. But *Victor*, with new, powerful Brown-Curtis turbines and the flamboyant Nathanial Blankenship on the bridge, immediately pulled away from the British line.

Reginald turned to yeoman of signals Henshaw. "By flashing light, squadron commander to *Victor*—reduce speed—maintain station—expedite!"

The signalman scampered up onto the light platform and there was a clatter of shutters. "He doesn't answer, sir," Henshaw shouted.

Reginald cursed. Either Blankenship did not see the signal or he was deliberately ignoring *Lancer*'s flashing light. In any event, Blankenship would have his way. "Very well. Return to the flag locker."

"Break the enemy line—like Nelson at Trafalgar, Captain." Farrar giggled watching *Victor* pull away, an insane glint in the strange eyes. Hargreaves heard the pilot's mocking voice in the din. "England expects every man to do his duty." The pilot's laughter sprayed spittle.

If the navigator was mad, he would have to deal with it later. Reginald shouted into the voice pipes, "Midships. Steady as she goes."

"Steady as she goes—two-eight-five, sir."

"Very well. Keep your bows on the enemy line." Into another tube: "Torpedo gunner stand by."

He heard Trevor Grenfell's high, frightened voice acknowledge, "Torpedoes ready, sir."

Hargreaves glanced at the enemy line, which was turning toward him. "Mister Grenfell, stand by to engage to starboard." The sublieutenant acknowledged. Reginald had picked the leader—probably Schultz's vessel, a new B-class with black smoke boiling from her three funnels, bow gun firing. The surprise was over. The Germans were too efficient, too good at their work to continue missing. Guns blazing and flashing like a forest fire, Reginald was looking into the mouth of hell itself. The hits came.

"*Paragon*'s bought it!" came from Basil Goodenough in an anguished voice. *Paragon*, which was the outside vessel on the left, suddenly staggered and fell off on her port side, bridge demolished and tilted dangerously over the side. A flurry of explosions sheered off both funnels and flames burst up from her engine rooms through the exposed holes in her decks. Two of her guns were still firing, but she quickly increased her list to port and rolled over on her beams' ends. Then, in a few horrifying seconds, she completely turned turtle, rolling, rocking, and settling in her own stew of bursting bubbles, escaping steam, and burning oil. Survivors scampered into her red-leaded bottom and clung precariously to her rolling keel or tore their hands on clusters of barnacles. Others flailed and screamed in the burning sea, breathing flames, roasting their lungs. As the wreck dropped off astern, Reginald felt the blade of horror slash through him like a shark's fin through water and his bowels seemed to drop out of his body.

Swallowing hard, he shouted hoarsely into a voice pipe, "Guns! Shift to target bearing green ten!" Gibbs acknowledged and A-gun blasted shell after shell at Schultz's ship, which fired back. A great flare and blast turned Reginald's head to port. *Unity* had exploded, an eruption of metal plates, guns, and debris that reached high for the clouds on a solid column of water and flame. What had been a proud ship a moment before was now junk and corpses raining into the sea. "Just break the news gently to Mother—Mother, for I'm not coming home . . ." Farrar was singing, arms waving, drool running off his chin.

"Shut him up," Reginald shouted at Pochhammer. But Farrar continued to sing the old war song.

The sky hailed annihilation, two plate-bending blasts close alongside rocked the ship and the hull echoing from the near-misses like the explosion of mines, booming in hollow agony that sent nervous strokers scurrying for ladders. The next two shells did not miss. X-mount and the ship's boat were wrenched and rent by two, three quick hits, the boat disappearing in a cloud of splinters, the gun crew dismembered and blown over the side and onto the quarterdeck, mangled bundles of bloody rags and broken bones. Blood like red molasses ran to the scuppers and stained the sides.

Lancer was hit by two more 10.5-centimeter shells almost simultaneously, the first nicking the forward funnel and detonating a few feet off the port side, the air burst riddling the director and the crow's nest and carrying away the wireless antenna. Immediately, blood showered down on the bridge and main deck and shattered recognition lights hailed red, green, and yellow chunks of glass like gay New Year's Eve confetti. Severed signal halyards snapped and whipped overhead like a sack full of snakes. The second shell struck the bow just forward of A-mount, penetrating to the second deck and exploding in the paint locker, reverberating in the hull like a great temple gong. Plate and splinters shrieked and howled over the forecastle and bridge, the anchor clattering into the depths with its severed chain following. The gun crew was protected by their shield, the pilot house by steel plate, the forebridge by plywood.

Staggered by the two concussions, Reginald clutched the chair, vision starring with afterimages of the explosions, gagging on the stink of nitric acid explosives. Wood splinters flew into his face, something plucked at his chest and sleeve, and screams dinned in his ears. Farrar's singing stopped and turned into a shriek followed by gurgles. A soft, pulpy rain fell all over Reginald and his lenses were suddenly fogged by fragments of brain and shattered bones.

Stunned, the captain stumbled back from the chair and turned. The bridge was a charnel house. Orville Tucker, the top of his head neatly severed as if by a giant scalpel, had tumbled from his platform and flopped loosely on the deck, arms and legs jerking spasmodically, the gray red contents of his skull spilling on the grating, eyes blown from their sockets and rolling on the deck. Farrar had been destroyed. Torso, chest, and throat ripped by steel, the navigator lay on his back, clutching his throat and abdomen. His lower jaw had been blown away and part of his tongue severed and lay on the deck with his jaw and broken teeth. The sounds he made were strange and animallike. Red bubbles swelled from his shattered mouth and holes in his trachea, his intestines slithered to the deck in a gray heap like live snakes. Behind him, blood and gore were splattered on the windscreen as if it had been painted by a lunatic.

Both signalmen were down in a writhing heap of spreading blood and twisted limbs. The director continued to leak blood and Lieutenant Gibbs was silent. Pochhammer and Goodenough were untouched.

Reginald shook the horror from his head and shouted into the voice pipes, "Surgeon and SBA to the bridge!"

Pochhammer was yelling and pointing overhead at the director. "Lieutenant Gibbs and his chaps have copped it, Captain! X- and Y-guns don't answer."

Blindly, Hargreaves reached under his chair and grabbed a megaphone. "Local control! Local control!" he shouted at the crew of A-gun, leaning over the windscreen.

More hits amidships and the ship staggered and lurched but plowed on. The aft funnel was blown over the side by another big shell and oily black smoke swirled over the forebridge, choking and gagging the survivors.

Victor, almost a cable's length ahead of *Lancer,* scored, her shells killing a German's bridge crew and opening her bows at the waterline. At thirty-three knots and out of control, the German ship scooped up water and crushed her own bulkheads like a snowplow devouring drifts, her great engines fairly driving her beneath the waves like a crash-diving submarine before they could be stopped.

Then it was *Victor*'s turn, two German destroyers veering off to starboard and firing torpedoes, three others "taping her" with their guns. Caught just abaft her funnels by two torpedoes, her keel was broken and she was blown from the sea, settling back in a welter of spray and debris in two distinct parts, no longer a racing greyhound—just sinking wreckage, burning oil, and dying men.

"Blankenship! Blankenship! You fool!" Reginald screamed with helplessness and anguish. He punched the windscreen until his knuckles bled.

Suddenly, the sky to the northwest blossomed with red and orange gun flashes and swarms of bright fireflies climbed lazily into the sky in long arcs that accelerated as they raced toward *Lancer.* Then a forest of thick towers of water rose majestically among the German destroyers, spaced precisely between the enemy ships. More glows. More towers of water.

"Eight-inch, Captain," Pochhammer shouted. "The Harwich cruisers! They have the range."

A German was hit by two eight-inch shells, blowing off his stern. Another, hit at the waterline by a full salvo, heeled hard into a starboard list and stopped dead in the water. Reginald could see the cruisers—great hulking gray shapes, hulled down on the horizon, flames rippling and flashing the length of the column, tearing the mist and lighting up the low clouds.

The enemy formation, already disorganized by *Victor*'s attack and death, veered in disorder, Schultz's vessel swerving to port, bearing away from Reginald's starboard side. A-gun continued tracking and firing. X-gun and Y-gun were both silent. But only the German's stern gun was firing—and erratically.

Reginald grasped a voice pipe, supported himself, his mind surprisingly clear. He shouted into the voice tubes, "Mister Grenfell—engage with torpedoes vessel at green ten."

"Target at green ten, standing by with both tubes, sir," came back, voice tight with shock but controlled.

Reginald felt the ship swerve. Again, down the voice pipe: "Mind your helm—keep her steady on two-nine-zero." A frightened voice answered the command.

The captain felt a new terror. They would pass through their own friendly fire. He had no choice. He moved his glasses to the German destroyer. It had been badly hit. Only one funnel remained, the pilot house and bridge were torn and blackened, wireless room wrecked, and there was no trace of the mainmast and director. White-clad crewmen could be seen working frantically on A-mount and a half dozen more were on the fantail unlimbering a machine gun and studying *Lancer* through binoculars. Others were inert bundles huddled on the deck. She was listing and her speed was no more than twelve knots. He could see B-23 in large white letters on the side of her hull.

It was time. "Torpedoes away!" came from the voice pipe. With a hiss of compressed air, two twenty-one-inch torpedoes leapt from their tubes and plunged into the sea, leaving long trails like white daggers in the sea. At a range of six hundred yards, it was hard to miss. But B-23 was not finished, a single torpedo splashing into the water and heading for *Lancer*.

"Starboard full!" Reginald shouted into the pipe.

"Starboard full rudder on, sir," the voice came back. *Lancer* heeled and rolled as full right rudder was put on at thirty knots. The German, too, was turning, but slowly like an injured man negotiating a difficult stair.

As Reginald shouted more commands and *Lancer* picked her way past the trail of white bubbles, B-23 was struck by both torpedoes. The result was instantaneous and cataclysmic: two great holes flooded her starboard side, abruptly rolling her over and at the same instant her aft magazine exploded, disintegrating her stern. Within seconds nothing was left on the sea except planks, wreckage, and the heads of a few survivors and the usual burning oil.

Now there was a huge gap in the German line and Reginald took it. More flashes on the horizon, more waterspouts and the sky rained bellowing death. Chasing the salvos, Reginald evaded the friendly fire and wove his way into the Channel. The surviving German destroyers—Reginald counted three under way, two wallowing helplessly in the burning sea and three more that had never been engaged racing from Ostend and Zeebrugge—fell off quickly far astern and the cruisers' fire ripped far overhead. Reginald reduced speed.

He raised his glasses and looked astern at the vast killing ground: towering explosions still spreading rings of tortured water and spray; acres of burning oil and palls of thick black smoke carrying all the way to the Belgian coast; the stern of one sunken German destroyer pointing at the sky; casks, broken furniture, brass powder casings bobbing up and down like stubby yellow fingers; huge bubbles of air and oil vomiting up from sunken ships; bodies everywhere, caught in the oil like flies on fly paper, stretched on wreckage or just drifting in clusters with arms and legs extended the way dead men always float. He had led Wolcott, Woodridge, and Blankenship and their crews into the jaws of hell and they had been devoured.

A strange air of unreality permeated everything. A dream. A nightmare. An asylum. A zoo peopled by savage animals. He had fallen into a whirlpool of insanity that had sucked him into its vortex. The young commander felt as if his entire being had just been carried off by the fury of the storm and now, slowly, he was seeping back into himself. Where else can men do these things to each other? Where else can you rip throats, mangle, obliterate, and be called hero for it? Farrar knew. Maybe the insane pilot had been the wisest one of all—the only one who truly belonged in this place.

There was a new presence on the bridge; the leading sick bay attendant and an assistant were hunched over ordinary signalman Heathstone and yeoman of signals Leslie Henshaw. Both were moaning and writhing. Tucker was an inert bloody heap in the middle of the platform, Farrar sat propped up against the windscreen, stilled by the cold hand of death. His eyes were open and to Reginald, they seemed to mock him still.

A cold stab of air shocked the commander erect and cleared the strange thoughts. Pochhammer was at his side, but the captain ignored him. Reginald cursed. He knuckled his temple and for the first time noticed the blood running over his hand and the torn sleeve. His chest burned and so did his forearm. "Ticket to blighty." He snickered to himself crazily. Then there was rage—blind, white-hot rage that twisted in his viscera like a hot snake and caused his hands to tremble and perspiration to bead even in the cold air. Watts. The incompetent, fatuous swine. All his dead men— the fine young men, the new widows, the new orphans.

"You're hit, sir," Pochhammer said. The first officer's eyes were glassy with shock and his voice dead.

"Nothing. Nothing at all in this show," Reginald said. He licked the blood from his hand like a small child. But his chest was sticky and warm and there was a throbbing there. Pochhammer remained silent.

Goodenough's voice interrupted him. The youngster was sobbing, but he managed to blurt, "Ships—ships, sir. Fine on the starboard bow."

Reginald raised his glasses with one hand. They were very heavy. English destroyers charging over the horizon. But late. Too late. He dropped his binoculars to his waist and rubbed his heavy eyes, leaving traces of blood on his cheeks.

There was a terrible pain in his chest and suddenly his knees were rubber and he began to sink. But Pochhammer's strong arm caught him. "I'm quite all right—really, Number One."

Brenda was there for a fleeting instant, white face distinct as if backlighted in the growing twilight. Then the black curtain of night fell.

IX

Brenda's face was back, framed by a penumbra of light diffused by curtains like clouds behind her. A new vision, the face of an angel, soft, white like ivory, eyes colored with the depths of the Mediterranean searching his anxiously. He would lose himself in this vision, wipe out the sight of Farrar, Goodenough, Henshaw, Heathstone, and the others. The destroyed Destroyer Squadron Four and his dead captains; Liddel Wolcott, Nathanial Blankenship, and Dewey Woolridge and their crews. And the burning sea. The burning sea with the dust of battle on it.

And the pitching and rolling had stopped as if *Lancer* had

been set in concrete. The whole front of his body burned and there was pain in his arm and there were bandages on his face. She leaned close and her lips were on his forehead; cool, soft like satin.

He said to the vision, "I love you, Brenda."

The apparition moved her lips to his ear. "You've lost a lot of blood, Reggie."

"You're real! I thought I was dead."

She smiled. "A slight miscalculation."

He started a chuckle, but it was cut short by rippling pain in his chest and abdomen. "Someone used me for a dart board," he managed, grimacing.

Brenda looked around. For the first time Reginald noticed a woman in white at the foot of his bed. Brenda gestured. "This is your QA."

A tall, heavyset middle-aged woman with her hair pulled back in an iron gray chignon stepped forward. "Carolyn Vertigan, Queen Alexandra's Royal Navy Nursing Corps, Commander," she said with a voice strident enough to shame a chief boatswain's mate. "You've lost a lot of blood and you should have pain. It took one hundred seventy-two sutures to put you back together again."

"My ship?"

The timbre of the nurse's voice softened. "Your first officer was just here."

"Pochhammer?"

"Yes, Commander. He said your ship's at Chatham."

"She's bought it?"

"He didn't say. Just that she needs some work."

"Needs some work?" He rolled his eyes back. "Dear God above," he said laconically. Then, in a firm voice, "Am I in Canterbury?"

"Yes," Vertigan answered. "The Royal Navy Hospital for Officers."

"Not again. Do you have a room to let? How long have I been here?

"They brought you in last night, Commander."

"I want a report from my first officer." He turned his lips under and his eyes were suddenly very moist. His voice came from deep in his throat. "Casualty lists—I've got to write; write a lot of letters."

"In due time, sir," the nurse said gently.

"And there's a vice admiral I've got to kill."

The women looked at each other and Vertigan hooked a clipboard to the foot of the bed. "Got to continue my rounds. The doctor will be in shortly."

Reginald stopped her. "When do I get out?"

She smiled. "You have no broken bones. It's a question of your lacerations healing and picking splinters out of your face and chest. Eat, regain your strength, and be a good boy and don't threaten admirals." She turned and left.

Reginald said, "A few minutes ago I told you I love you. You didn't answer." Brenda took a breath and leaned close as if to answer. He stopped her gently with a finger to her lips. "I say, that wasn't fair. The wounded warrior and all that rot." He moved his hand to her cheek and held her eyes with his. Gently, she touched his lips with hers.

"I am very fond of you, Reggie."

"Love?"

Her forehead creased and she pursed her lips. "I don't know if I love you. I'm not sure I even know what it is."

"You're no hypocrite, Brenda." She leaned back, but he smothered her tiny hand in his. "Dinner, Brenda, when they turn me loose? Right?"

"Of course, Reggie. Of course. I want to be with you so very much and if that's love, then I feel it for you." He pulled her back and she kissed him again with an open, warm mouth and he held her with a hand to the back of the head as if he were afraid she would flee him. But she did not try to pull away. Instead, she kissed his cheek, his temple, the cord in his neck while carefully avoiding the bandages.

"Hard to kiss me without getting a mouthful of gauze, iodine, and tape," he said.

"I'll manage." She kissed him again.

Carolyn Vertigan's voice boomed from the door. "It's time, madam."

"No!" Reginald shouted, feeling unbelievable new strength.

"Be a good boy or I'll chain you to your bed," came back from the door.

"I'll be back," Brenda said, pulling away from his grasp.

"Promise?"

"Yes," she said.

"Say yes again."

"Yes, Reggie. Yes," she whispered.

Smiling, he sank back into his pillow.

She paused with her hand on the doorknob. "Reggie."

"Yes."

She smiled wryly. "No more *safe* training cruises. Stroll through the East End instead."

He chuckled despite the pain.

Lloyd, Bernice, Rebecca, and Walter were seated on battered sofas and chairs in a small alcove off the hall, which was a bedlam of hurrying doctors and nurses, attendants pushing wheeled stretchers loaded with mangled young men. Lloyd was smoking a Woodbine cigarette: one of the most evil smokes ever made—a stench that attacked Brenda's nostrils like a gaseous acid. Walter was puffing on a pipe, adding to the unbearable atmosphere.

Walter complained, "Dash it all, they won't let us see him."

"One visitor," Rebecca said.

"I know—I know," Walter grumbled. "The nurse with the big mouth told us." He glared at his daughter-in-law. "And Reginald only wanted to see you."

Ignoring Walter, Brenda turned to Rebecca and Lloyd and described Reginald's condition. "And he's lost a lot of blood and he's heavily sedated," she concluded.

"Nasty business in the Channel," Lloyd said. "Rumors of a U-boat ambush. We lost a cruiser—the admiralty admits that and Reginald's squadron was mauled."

"Mauled?" Walter said. "The whole lot was sunk except *Lancer*. *The Times* reported that." He pulled a silver flask from an inside pocket, took a deep drink, and handed it to Lloyd. Lloyd drank. Coughing and clearing his throat gutturally, Walter wiped his mouth with the back of his hand. "Sank eight Kraut destroyers, though," he said proudly.

"Someone made a muck of it," Lloyd said. "They should've expected the U-boats." He pulled the flask from Walter's hand and drank again.

Walter scratched a new red blotch on his nostril. "The Jerries will think again before raiding our Channel ports. Eight sunk and most of the rest were damaged. Reginald's squadron saw to that."

There was a scream from the hall and a young man with no nose or eyes was carried past.

"Hundreds of our boys are dead and wounded," Bernice said. Her voice was anguished and she was verging on tears.

Brenda felt anger and frustration swell beyond containment. "Terrible trade—terrible trade," she said angrily.

"See here, Yank," Walter said. "You have no right..."

"No! I won't *see here*," Brenda said, bristling.

"Yes, you will!" Walter shouted, rising.

The memory of Reginald's torn body, the knowledge that most of the young men she had met on *Lancer* were dead, the gnawing fear for Randolph, which had eaten at her like a cancer for over a year, and the lingering bitterness over her husband's death exploded from her lips. "You bloody hypocrite," she screamed, bolting from her chair.

Rebecca cried out, "Not here, you two. Have you no respect?"

Walter stepped toward her. Brenda did not give an inch. But Lloyd was there, placing himself between the pair. "Enough," he said.

"No. Never enough," Brenda hissed, turning toward the exit.

The next week the Reo town car left Brenda's home on Grosvenor Crescent daily for the long drive to the naval hospital at Canterbury. Reginald's recovery was slow, his wounds far more serious than at first believed, requiring surgery to stop internal bleeding, which began on the second day. The muscles of his left arm had been ripped and his entire torso scarred by shrapnel like a crazy quilt, and there was danger of blood poisoning and gangrene. Frequent injections of morphia dulled his senses and slurred his speech and often he slept throughout Brenda's visits.

One afternoon Bernice was waiting for Brenda when she returned form a particularly depressing visit to the hospital. Seated in the sitting room sipping tea, Bernice showed new enthusiasm through her usual anxiety. "Lloyd George has been appointed PM," she said as if the statement were a reprieve for her husband.

Brenda had read of the appointment. Battered by disasters on the Somme, the Dardanelles, in Mesopotamia, and in Rumania as well as by rebellion in Ireland and crippling losses to U-boats, the Asquith government had collapsed and the liberal war minister, Lloyd George, had been asked to form a new government.

"He's Rebecca's favorite cousin and Lloyd's godfather, you know. In fact, my husband is named after David Lloyd George."

"I didn't know," Brenda said with surprise. "I never heard him mentioned at Fenwyck."

"Ha!" Bernice snorted. "Fell out with Walter right after the christening. Politics, of course. Walter's to the right of Henry the Eighth and couldn't stand David Lloyd George's liberalness." She shrugged and turned her palms up. "And Lloyd George is from a poor Welsh family and, of course, Walter has no patience for poverty, either." Brenda smiled and nodded her agreement. Bernice continued. "But he'll lead us out of this, Brenda," she enthused. "You'll see."

Brenda stared at Bernice, moved by a feverish glint in her sister-in-law's eyes. She knew Bernice lived in a perpetual state of dread while Lloyd was gone. Now that he was home, Brenda sensed Bernice verged on hysteria at just the thought of her husband leaving again. And Lloyd had suffered—the changes in his character deepening. His countenance had become a relief map of horror and pain as if a fiend had hurled acid in his face, scarring him with deep new lines that belonged to a very old man. And he drank too much and when his tongue was oiled with liquor he spoke of dead comrades in the idiom of the trenches—an endless parade of names and personalities who existed no more.

Bernice ran on. "There'll be a reception for the new PM at Ten Downing Street next Saturday and Lloyd George wants you to come."

"Wants me to come? He doesn't even know me."

Her demeanor easing suddenly, Bernice giggled nervously. "He's heard of you. Saw you once at a party before the war." She toyed with her cup. "He has an eye for attractive women."

Brenda laughed. "I hear he'll mount any woman who'll stand still for thirty seconds."

Bernice recoiled in mock horror. "Please, sister-in-law. That wasn't very nice."

Brenda laughed for the first time in a week. She held up her cup. "Here's to Lloyd George." Smiling, Bernice touched the lip of her cup to Brenda's. "Stay out of his bedroom," Brenda added.

"Hear! Hear!" Bernice laughed. She drank and changed direction again in her disconcerting mercurial fashion. "You've been seeing Reginald?"

"Every day."

"He's better?"

"Yes, but it's slow. The first officer told me he refused attention when first wounded—so many of the crew were injured. He lost a lot of blood, has some internal injuries, and he'll be terribly scarred. The ship's surgeon and first officer saved him or he would've bled to death."

Bernice tapped the bone china with a single manicured nail. "Do you love him?"

Brenda knew Bernice too well to be surprised by the forwardness of the question. "I've only known him for six or seven months."

"You can learn all you need to know about a man in six or seven minutes." She placed her cup on the table and challenged Brenda's eyes with a hard stare. "You never loved Geoffry, did you, Brenda?"

Brenda was taken aback by the bold, incisive remark. She felt her cheeks flush. "Bernice, you've gone too far."

"I'm sorry, Brenda. But you can't live in a world of guilt —cloister yourself, become a nun without a convent. You're too young—beautiful, and," she sighed resignedly, "and before you can tell me, I know this is none of my business."

Brenda could feel no anger toward Bernice. She knew her sister-in-law loved her, respected her, and shared her antipathy toward Walter. The American studied her cup. "I know what you're trying to do, Bernice. But I'm not ready for another man—marriage, to love fully and become part of a man's life—part of him."

"Did you ever feel that way about Geoffry?"

Brenda fingered her cup. "After his death," she said bitterly.

"Is that it, then? Geoffry?"

"I don't know." She looked up, eyes deep with moisture. "Maybe it's all of them."

Bernice nodded and there was understanding in her eyes. "Yes, I know." She sighed and brightened. "But the party— you'll come."

"Can't disappoint the PM," Brenda said, smiling.

The women touched cups and finished their tea.

The affair was not held at Ten Downing Street. Instead, to avoid criticism of a luxurious party held in the prime minister's residence while English boys died miserably on the Western Front, it was held in a magnificent old mansion on Trevor Place off Knightsbridge. The host was not actually David Lloyd George but a minor functionary of the exchequer named Ramsey Kavanaugh. Kavanaugh, scion of a Sheffield steel fortune, had smoothly transferred his allegiance from the conservative government of Herbert Asquith to that of the liberal David Lloyd George. It was common knowledge that Lloyd George favored duties on tobacco, gasoline, beer, and spirits, and pushed for land taxes. Not only had he antagonized the old landed gentry in his early years, but also now he feuded with the generals, publicly criticizing the conduct of the war and the waste of manpower. "British troops should never be buried in the holocaust of French trenches," he had been quoted as saying. He had even enlisted the support of the conservative Winston Churchill who had resumed his seat in the House of Commons after being sacked from the admiralty.

But ambitious men gravitate to power and in December of 1916 David Lloyd George, son of a Welsh schoolteacher, husband to a farmer's daughter, a plebeian who had been accused of "socialist plundering," and "unscrupulous demagoguery," sat in the ultimate chair of power—an unsteady chair with weak legs true, but, nevertheless, still the consummate seat of power. And dutifully the aspiring came to pay homage when the strong man beckoned.

Brenda regarded her invitation—a formal engraved invitation had been hand delivered—with mixed feelings. Although she had lost her fascination with fashion, she still enjoyed the knowledge that male eyes turned and female lips tightened whenever she entered a room. She had not bought a new gown in over a year and approached her preparations for the party with indifference. However, Nicole would have none of it. Eagerly, the maid chose a gown by Lucile; an evening dress of gentle blue chiffon with gossamer batiste under-sleeves and a tight bodice laced up the front with gold thread. Transparent at oblique angles even in weak light, the gown was worn over a beaded mauve silk chemise with embroidered birds and flowers that imparted a youthful, ingenue quality to the American's beauty. Hastily, Nicole took in a stitch here, a tuck there until the gown fit every curve and undulation of Brenda's body as if brushed on.

"*Magnifique, madame,*" the maid said, admiring her mistress. She waved a thimble. "Lucile is *très élégante.*"

"I think she knows what she's doing, Nicole," Brenda said, surveying her reflection in the pier mirror from upswept auburn hair to her highest-heeled evening shoes. "After all, she does dress the Dolly Sisters, Lily Elsie, and even Irene Castle."

The maid looked puzzled. "The actresses, *ma matresse?*"

"Yes, Nicole. The actresses."

But Brenda was not acting when, following Bernice and a slightly drunk Lloyd, she entered the entry hall of the Kavanaugh mansion. She was surprised and pleased by the opulence and beauty of the Kavanaugh home. A huge rotunda-like room with a glass-domed ceiling, the entry had an exquisite marble floor, paneled walls hung with Gainsboroughs and Monets, and a spectacular cut rock crystal chandelier that reminded Brenda of the Garnier monstrosity hanging in the Grand Opera House in Paris. Four people were in the receiving line: the portly Ramsey Kavanaugh splendid in a perfectly tailored tuxedo, his wife Denise, and Lloyd George and his wife Margaret.

Kavanaugh, fiftyish with a round, beefy face and stomach to match and a bald pate that glared in the light as if it had been polished with paste wax, grasped the American's hand and held it too long. "Welcome, Mrs. Higgins," he said. "You will add considerable beauty to our gathering. Please save a dance for me." His wife overheard him.

When Brenda accepted Denise Kavanaugh's hand, she felt she was holding a glove filled with cold jelly. The narrow eyes were gray glaciers. A bulky, lined woman, she had obviously had herself cut, scraped, patched, and colored countless times in fruitless attempts to retain a once-famous beauty. Denise Kavanaugh had spent most of her prewar summers in the South of France where she became a Francophile whose affectations and enormous bosom had earned her the sobriquet, *The Grand Tetons*. Her gown was a gorgeous black brocade and her coiffure sprinkled with diamonds. but no attempts by couturiers, hairdressers, or jewelers could eliminate the ravages of years of overeating and dissipation. "Welcome to our house," she said coldly through layered chins and turned to the next guest.

Brenda heard David Lloyd George and Lloyd Higgins greet each other with an exchange of "Cousin" and "Godfather." There were concerned questions about the front and low, almost unintelligible answers. She heard the PM and the colonel promise to talk later, Lloyd George speaking with an unmistakable Welsh lilt.

Now Brenda faced the Welshman. The prime minister was impressive. With a brown, neatly trimmed mustache, dark hair blemished by only a few strands of gray, and an unlined face, Lloyd George appeared youthful for a man well into his fifties. The jaw was square and strong, eyes inquisitive and bold as they wandered over Brenda's body with a disrobing look the American had felt many times. Smiling, he held Brenda's hand and surprised her by mumbling condolences over the loss of her husband. "A fine patriot and gentleman to the end," he said, refusing to release her hand.

"Thank you, Mister Prime Minister," she said, finally managing to disengage herself and follow Bernice and Lloyd into the adjoining ballroom.

The ballroom was enormous. Two stories high and decorated in golds and white, it was elliptical in shape with an orchestra playing on a dais at the far end in front of a wall of renaissance mirrors. It was filled with high-ranking officers in fine uniforms, glistening with polished leather, brass buttons, and decorations worn on proud chests. The women were in fine silks, velvets, and glistening jewels. The orchestra was playing and the dancers swirled and glided. One wall was lined with tables laden with hors d'oeuvres, canapés, meats, exotic fruits, and elaborate salads served by liveried servants. Ypres, Vimy ridge, the Dardanelles, Jutland, the Somme, and the rest of the bloody horror were far, far away.

Glancing around the room, Brenda knew she was seeing the heart and soul and brains of the British war effort. Dozens of generals and admirals danced with stately women or stood in groups or sat together, smoking, talking seriously and animatedly. The timbre of their voices, the measured stance, drinks held high, arms carelessly akimbo, the tilt of aristocratic heads, soft, confident laughs, and the hungry glitter in their eyes filled the room with an arcane aura—a palpable force exuded by men on the brink of history about to quench their boundless thirst for celebrity. And Brenda sensed it would be done without counting the cost.

Lloyd grabbed a Scotch from a passing tray and handed the women champagne. Leading them to a pair of plump velvet sofas tucked in a corner, he was obviously upset, downed his drink in two gulps, and commanded another one. Bernice drank slowly and eyed her husband anxiously. He waved his glass at a cluster of blue uniforms and glistening gold braid clustered around a pair of nearby tables. "The Royal Navy's here. All the big admirals—Jackson, Jellicoe, Beatty, and their tiffies. They got their noses bloodied in the Dardanelles, at Jutland, and now they've got to kiss the new PM's shoes if they want new dreadnoughts to play with."

Brenda remained silent, but Bernice gasped, "Lloyd, please . . ."

Lloyd ignored his wife and gestured at a group of army officers standing nearby. "And over there, see those peacocks," he said in a loud voice. "Commander-in-Chief General Douglas Haig and his lackey, General Henry Rawlinson." He waved carelessly. "They're talking to Chief of the Imperial General Staff Sir William Robertson." He emptied his glass, spoke in slurred sarcasm, "These are the geniuses who plan the grand strategy, populate the grand cemeteries—none of them—not a single bloody one of those blokes has ever been to the front, knows anything about trench warfare, or gives two stuffs for the poor sods in the trenches." He took a generous drink from a recharged glass. Leering, he continued, "If a zeppelin dropped a bomb on this place England could win the war in two months."

"Please, Lloyd," Bernice insisted. "People can hear you —heads are turning."

"Better a few heads turned here than heads blown off on the Western Front."

Bernice drank nervously and continued, "But if they're incompetent, the new PM will sack the lot."

Lloyd laughed bitterly. "As much chance as the kaiser playing cricket at Eaton." He pulled another drink from a passing tray. "David Lloyd George is weak—doesn't even have the support of the liberals. Most of them still follow Asquith. He can only stay in office with a coalition—with the support of Winston Churchill and the conservatives."

There was desperation in Bernice's voice. "Certainly, the new PM can do something."

Lloyd drank thoughtfully. "Yes. He'll probably cut down on manpower—give the generals less cannon fodder." He ran a finger thoughtfully over his glass. "Maybe put them under the Frogs." He nodded at a French general surrounded by his own suite of magnificently uniformed underlings in horizon blue who had joined Haig's group. "That's General Robert Nivelle. He just replaced Joffre as commander-in-chief."

"Oh yes," Brenda said. "I've heard of him. 'The hero of Verdun.'"

Lloyd snorted. "That hero lost three hundred thousand Frenchmen." He drank. "Another butcher and the whole lot of them is planning a new offensive. See the happy smiles on their faces?"

Shock broke Brenda's silence. "A new offensive? And you—they can talk about it casually."

"It should be a secret," Bernice said.

"They don't do the dying."

Suddenly the crowded room was oppressive; stuffy and heavy with tobacco smoke. "Excuse me," Brenda said. "I need some air." Quickly, she rose and walked to the far end of the room to a pair of open french doors. She stopped on the sill, filling her lungs with sweet, fresh air.

"Close in here, madam," a soft, friendly voice said in a strange accent.

Brenda turned to face a small Japanese naval officer wearing the three stripes of a commander. In his early thirties with jet black hair and fine olive skin, his black eyes like newly mined coal chips were fixed on Brenda's surprised stare. He had the look of a man who was quickwitted, tenacious, and resourceful. "I surprise you, madam?" he asked.

"Why no," Brenda said, captured by the eyes and the rare experience of looking down when talking to a man.

"I am Commander Isoroku Yamamoto of the Imperial Japanese Navy. We are allies?"

Brenda smiled. "I'm an American." She introduced herself.

He bowed but did not proffer his hand. Brenda took it anyway. Two fingers were missing.

"Russian shrapnel—Tsushima," he said.

"I'm sorry."

"Do not feel sorry, Mrs. Higgins. The way of the samurai is to offer up his life gladly for Emperor Meiji. The loss of fingers was an honor." He smiled up at her. "Soon, perhaps, Mrs. Higgins, we will be allies."

Brenda sighed and answered with a noncommittal "Perhaps."

Isoroku continued. "I, too, craved fresh air. Arrived with you." He gestured at the doors. "And you are so lovely. Japanese women are beautiful, too. But western women"—the black eyes roamed her breasts, her hips—"are different in many ways." He blushed like a schoolboy. "I am sorry. I have been far too bold—impolite."

Brenda laughed, remembering the few Japanese women she had seen in California in her youth and the remarks the other girls had made. "Flat-chested," "Bow-legged," and "No butts," were just a few of the unkind remarks that came to mind. "No," the American protested. "You're not impolite. I find you quite charming, Commander."

"A dance, perhaps, Mrs. Higgins? Would your husband object? He must be very much in love with you and any man would be jealous of one so beautiful."

Brenda explained that she was a widow. Yamamoto was properly sympathetic and then led her to the dance floor. He was a superb dancer and although he was at least two inches shorter than Brenda, his physique was solid, shoulders broad and muscled.

After the dance, General Douglas Haig caught Yamamoto's eye and Isoroku led Brenda to the group of officers. There were bows, handshakes, and Brenda had her hand shook by the Englishmen and kissed by Nivelle and an Italian general named Pietro Badoglio who had joined the group. The Italian slobbered and Brenda found him distasteful. All were drinking, all were in boisterous spirits, and all eyed the American from head to toe and made her promise dances. The fact that she was a widow had apparently circulated quickly.

Haig was the most impressive officer of the group. Of medium height with splendid military bearing, he personified the general officer with perfectly groomed gray hair, tanned skin, and neatly trimmed mustache. Although his features were not large, the bones of his jaw and cheeks and forehead seemed weighty and firm as stone. His nose was straight and patrician, brow beetling, and his mouth unsmiling and immobile. Slender of build, his uniform was beautifully tailored and his leather polished as if it had been stropped with Kiwi polish. His eyes never left Brenda. "A dance—you promise, Mrs. Higgins?" he said. Brenda smiled and nodded.

Delicately, Isoroku excused himself and led Brenda back to the french doors where a handsome young Japanese lieutenant was waiting. "My aide, Lieutenant Yoshikazue Nakamura," Yamamoto said, introducing the young officer. "We are both attachés at the Japanese Embassy," Yamamoto explained.

The young officer bowed and shyly asked for a dance. Brenda soon found Nakamura to be a fine dancer, too; lithe, graceful, and a strong leader like Yamamoto. When they were finished, she gestured to Lloyd and Bernice. Nakamura took her to the sofas, bowed when introduced, and excused himself.

"My, those Orientals are so polite," Bernice said, watching the young officer disappear into the crowd.

"Someday, we'll be fighting those polite bastards," Lloyd growled.

"They're our allies," Brenda protested.

Lloyd snorted. "Allies? Ha! Long enough to grab off Tsingtao and every German island in the Pacific—that's all they've done."

A deep, cultured voice interrupted. It was General Haig. "Mrs. Higgins. You promised a dance. Will you honor me?" He turned to Bernice and Lloyd, who had come to his feet slowly. "Good to see both of you again."

Before Lloyd could answer, the orchestra launched itself into a waltz. Quickly, Haig circled Brenda's waist and swept her away to three-quarter time.

"You're an American," he said, holding her close.

"Yes."

"Live on Grosvenor Crescent?"

"Why yes."

"Have you ever had lunch with a general?"

"Is this an offensive, General Haig?"

He chuckled. "Perhaps."

"Sorry. I don't lunch with married generals or married privates, for that matter."

"You take no prisoners, Mrs. Higgins."

She laughed. "I'm not a tactician, General Haig, but sometimes there are less casualties if an advancing army knows precisely what the defenses are."

"Formidable—formidable," he said unsmiling. "Ludendorff and Hindenburg could not have said it better." He was obviously disappointed.

Brenda opened the space between them and finally, when the music ended, Haig led her back to the sofas where Lloyd still stood unsteadily.

After thanking Brenda, Haig turned to leave and then hesitated and spoke to Lloyd. "You and the Coldstreams have done splendid work at Thiepval Ridge, Colonel Higgins."

Lloyd glared back. "Most of my chaps enjoyed the duty, General. In fact, they liked it so much, they're still there— buried."

Bernice gasped and Brenda felt an involuntary smile curl her lips. But the general appeared unruffled. "We must expect losses, Colonel," he said evenly.

"When will you visit my sector, General?" Lloyd shot back.

Haig's square jaw jutted like a stone. "As soon as I return to France. Will you be there?"

"Of course. It's the only place you can find an honest man."

Haig wheeled and left, heels clicking on the polished wood floor like closing rifle bolts.

Brenda heard a chuckle. David Lloyd George was standing behind her. "The general is retreating in disorder, godson," the prime minister said, obviously enjoying Haig's discomfort and drunk enough to be indiscreet.

Lloyd pulled another drink from a passing waiter and sank

back on the couch. "Rule Britannia, godfather," he said, smirking at the glass.

"Don't talk that way, Lloyd," Bernice said.

The prime minister said to Brenda, "Our dance, Mrs. Higgins?"

"Of course," Brenda said. Lloyd George put an arm around Brenda's waist and they circled into the swirl of dancers. Immediately, he held her too close and Brenda stiffened.

"You're one of the most beautiful women I have ever seen," he said huskily, breathing heavily into her ear and relentlessly pulling Brenda's body to his. "Perhaps I can show you around Ten Downing Street."

"Thank you. I'm not politically minded, unless you can do something to stop the insanity in France." She pushed against his chest and opened a gap.

He sighed and eased his grip slightly. "I know, Mrs. Higgins, the conduct of the generals"—he nodded toward Haig's group—"has been ah—unimaginative. My attitude is no secret. I've been quoted in the papers."

"Their conduct has been stupid, Mister Prime Minister. Men like my brother-in-law are the true experts."

"I am committed to the prosecution of the war, but I can assure you, Mrs. Higgins, I have plans to control the generals—plans which cannot be discussed here and now, but if you care to visit me in my private conference room . . ." He tightened his grip.

She pushed against his chest and, strangely, felt more amused than angry. "No!" she said into his face, baring her perfect white teeth in a rictus of determination. "Take me back, *now*, Mister Prime Minister, or I'll make a scene." He smiled into her eyes, but his grip was unrelenting. "It'll cost you votes," she said loudly in a sarcastic voice. The grip eased and he led her back to Bernice and Lloyd.

"She's the Hindenburg Line," Lloyd scoffed and then laughed raucously. Even Bernice giggled. David Lloyd George whirled and lost himself in the crowd.

"Colonel Higgins," resounded in a cultured, dulcet voice that sounded as if it belonged on the stage of the Royal

Shakespeare Company. "Good to see you again." Brenda saw a smiling, handsome man approaching, hand extended to her brother-in-law who grasped it eagerly and smiled for the first time that evening.

Lloyd turned to Brenda. "Brenda Higgins, I would like to present Winston Churchill to you—an old friend, comrade-in-arms, and member of Parliament." He nodded at Bernice. "You know my wife, Bernice."

"Good to see you again, Mrs. Higgins." Forty-two years of age, Winston Churchill appeared much younger. His hair was chestnut, skin clear, his strong features molded to the classic line of his Anglo-Saxon lineage with thick heavy brows almost meeting over a straight nose. But Brenda was most impressed by his voice and the strength evident in the set of his bulldog jaw and penetrating eyes—a look that hinted at a gift of prescience. He reminded her of Teddy Roosevelt, but Churchill was much more handsome. "You are Geoffry's widow, Mrs. Higgins," Churchill said, picking his words carefully like a man selecting ripe plums.

Brenda acknowledged the statement with an affirmative nod.

"He was a fine officer." Churchill raised a snifter of cognac, Lloyd followed suit with his glass, and the women saluted with champagne. Everyone found a chair.

"You're an American," Churchill said, sinking back into velvet brocade and fixing Brenda with his amazing eyes.

"Yes, Mister Churchill. I grew up in New York City."

The MP smiled. "My mother was American, you know, Mrs. Higgins. She was born in Brooklyn." He turned to Lloyd. "Terrible business on the Somme."

"It's got to be stopped, Winston." Lloyd said to Brenda, "Winston knows—he served on the Western Front with the Second Grenadier Guards and the Sixth Royal Scots Fusiliers." There was respect in the voice Brenda had not heard for the entire evening. "In fact, we attended Sandhurst together, served together in India in the Thirty-first Punjab Infantry, and in Africa in the Twenty-first Lancers. Daresay, got into a bit of a bind together in Omdurman and Khartoum—right, Winnie?" Their laughter was that of old comrades.

Churchill said to Brenda, "I served on the front after that business in the Dardanelles. The whole nasty lot was my idea."

Lloyd leaned forward with an intensity that belied the amount of liquor he had consumed. "Not your fault, Winston. It was a good idea. The bloody navy loaded the ships backwards—everyone knows that."

"Backwards?" Brenda asked.

"Yes," Lloyd said. "What was needed first on the beaches was put aboard first—in the bottoms of the holds." He took another drink. "Stupid! Stupid! And the admiralty cut short the bombardment of the Turkish forts just as the bloody Turks were running out of ammunition, were ready to capitulate."

"I appreciate your defense," Churchill said. "But it was my idea and regardless of the reason, the failure was mine."

"It was grand strategy these idiots"—the colonel waved a glass, spilling a few drops—"were incapable of understanding. And they'll waste tanks, too."

"They already have," Churchill said bitterly. He nodded to a group of women seated across the dance floor. "I'd better be leaving. I'm afraid I've been neglecting my wife, Clementine."

He rose, shook hands all around, and left.

"A brilliant mind," Brenda said.

"Too good for this bunch of stupid sods," Lloyd growled. "The only capable leader we have and now he's out of it because of the bloody navy."

"Maybe he'll get another chance," Brenda said.

"Not in this century," Lloyd answered bitterly.

Brenda felt the large quantity of champagne she had consumed begin to lurch and bubble on the floor of her stomach and the warm atmosphere and hanging clouds of smoke suddenly became unbearable. And there were thoughts of the great men she had met and the fools most of them had been. The thought that her husband and hundreds of thousands of others had been sacrificed by these vainglorious men brought a wrenching anger and despair to add to the upset caused by the liquor. "Let's leave," she said huskily.

Lloyd smiled. "Yes. We'll leave. Maybe none of us belong here." He came to his feet and Bernice took his arm.

Brenda's words came from a growing anger and her voice was heard by a wide circle as she addressed her brother-in-law. "If these are England's leaders, Lloyd, God help us, because we're due for one disaster after another."

Lloyd laughed raucously and rocked on his heel. More curious faces turned. "You're very perceptive, sister-in-law. We need you in politics—the general staff." There was true admiration in his voice.

Bernice took Lloyd's arm and led him toward the door. Brenda followed, her mind whirling. *They killed Geoffry, wounded Reginald, and they've broken Lloyd. What have they done to Randolph? Dear Randolph, don't let them kill you, too.*

She caught her breath and followed Bernice and Lloyd out into the cool evening air.

A week later, Brenda felt better about Reginald's condition. The operation to stop the internal bleeding had been successful and the commander was recovering. But recuperation was slow and his confinement would be long. Each day she held him, kissed him, or, if he were asleep, sat and looked at his dear, sweet face—so boyish and innocent despite new lines etched there by suffering. She felt joy in knowing he was alive and when awake, he smiled with love in his eyes. When he held her she felt the warmth she had known when they had danced pressed against each other in their last night together at the Savoy. Away from him, she felt that terrible void, the incompleteness all women without men suffer. *Did she love him? Or did she just need a man—the same hunger she knew when she first entered womanhood? And what was love? What was this undefinable, elusive stranger everyone sought so frantically and when finally within grasp, slipped through one's fingers like wisps of London fog?*

The daily visits were trying, but she found respite in her garden with her children and in the company of her servants and friends. December was drawing to a close after a dismal Christmas when on an unusually sunny afternoon she joined Bernice and Lloyd in her garden, sipping afternoon tea and watching Rodney and Nathan playing with Bernice and Lloyd's children, fourteen-year-old Trevor and nine-year-old Bonnie.

Tall and gangling and as yet unable to adapt to his rapid growth, Trevor was a fair duplicate of his father. Already, the straight back and square shoulders gave the youngster a military bearing and his voice had dropped to a brittle baritone reminiscent of his father's. Although Bonnie was on the tall side like her father, her yellow hair and green eyes and exquisite features spoke of her mother. And she loved to play the mother—as all little girls do—chasing Rodney and cuddling Nathan like a live doll. She was even allowed to feed the baby his sieved vegetables under the watchful eyes of the women. Trevor disdained the childish games, preferring to sit next to his father and listen to the adult conversation.

His father was irritable; his mother elated. Informed that he was temporarily posted to a training command at Chigwell—a small town eleven miles north of London—Lloyd was obviously upset and Brenda suspected he felt his place was with the Coldstreams who were due to leave the rest camp at Chantilly and return to the front at the end of January. Everyone knew—presumably the Germans, too—that Nivelle was planning a last great spring offensive that would end the war. Was it possible Lloyd could not tolerate the thought of missing this "show"? Even after the bloodbath on the Somme? While Lloyd sulked and drank his Scotch, Bernice sat quietly wrapped in her own veil of euphoria.

In the middle of the afternoon, Wendell McHugh, the only cockney butler in the city of London serving the haut monde, approached his mistress. The old Irishman never looked comfortable in his livery and he was perspiring as he spoke. "There's a brace o' orf'cers to see missus." He gestured to the porch where two American officers were descending the stair. One was a captain and the other a lieutenant. The captain was Brenda's brother, Hugh.

Brenda was out of her chair and in her brother's arms in seconds. Sobbing, she managed, "I didn't know! I didn't know. Why didn't you write—let me know you were coming?"

She looked up into the smiling face. Now twenty-nine years old, Hugh Ashcroft had matured into a ruggedly handsome soldier. His eyes were bluer, hair darker, shoulders broader, and his waist looked smaller, pulled in severely by his Sam Browne belt. "I did write—I did write, sister," he said, over and over. "Maybe the U-boats . . ."

She stepped back. "Or my father-in-law. None of my mail has been forwarded."

Hugh gestured at the young lieutenant standing behind him. "Lieutenant Barry Cooper, my aide."

Of average height, Cooper had thick black hair that poked out in tufts from under his rakishly angled cap. His youthful grin seemed to veneer the face of a much older man—a reckless man waiting for the chance to burst out. Gray-green and narrow, his eyes had the hawkish tilt and the hungry look of an experienced hunter. He was obviously a man who attracted women with little effort.

Brenda made introductions all around and Hugh explained that he and Barry were officially attachés to the American Embassy. However, their unofficial duty was to observe the Western Front and write detailed reports for the army general staff.

Brenda shuddered. "The Western Front?"

"Of course, sister, that's our business."

"Perhaps I can be of some assistance," Lloyd offered.

"You wouldn't go into the front lines," Brenda asked before Hugh could respond to Lloyd.

The officers laughed. Hugh answered, "Of course not, sister. We would be neutrals, probably attached to some divisional staff."

Lloyd's eyes sparkled and his grin was friendly. "That's safe, Brenda. I can assure you."

Nicole and Wendell McHugh, responding to a wave from

Brenda, interrupted, placing tea, coffee, and liquor on the large round table. "'Ere's your drinks, your lordships," McHugh said, serving drinks to the men while Nicole poured tea for the women. Hugh and Barry eyed the butler curiously while Brenda and Bernice hid their smiles with their palms.

Brenda questioned her brother about home. Sipping his bourbon, Hugh assured his sister that their father and mother, John and Ellen, were in good health and business was prospering. Their sister, Betty, was engaged to an Italian barber named Alfredo Carpelli and John and Ellen were horrified. Nevertheless, the strong-headed Betty insisted on the match. John had threatened to disown her.

"But if they love each other, what else can matter, Hugh?" Brenda said. "This world needs love more than anything else."

The captain eyed his sister with narrowed lips as if he were seeing her in a new light. He appeared puzzled but spoke firmly. "Our parents consider him far below our station."

"Do you?" There was an embarrassed silence, all eyes moving to the American captain.

"Yes. I've met him. She can do better." Tactfully, Hugh changed the subject to more news—grim news. An old friend and business associate of their father's, Troy Richardson, had drowned on the *Lusitania* along with over 1,100 other innocent people. He had been making a business trip to England when the ship was sunk by a U-boat. Brenda remembered the handsome, courtly man who had been such a passionate companion when she was a young girl. Now he was just another cadaver, a product of the madness gripping the entire world.

Lloyd interrupted, adroitly moving the conversation further away from the Italian, asking Hugh for an opinion on the newly reelected president, Woodrow Wilson. Hugh thought for a moment and offered diplomatically, "He's a good man, trying to do his best."

"But he's not as neutral now as he was in 'fourteen," Lloyd said. He surprised everyone by quoting the American president's words in a recent speech. "'We are holding off, not because we do not feel concerned, but because when we exert the force of this nation we want to know what we are exerting it for...'" Lloyd lighted a Woodbine and offered them around. Brenda was thankful when Hugh and Barry refused.

Hugh said to Lloyd, "You do know the man. I'm sure he's considering intervention. After all, Lloyd, that's why I'm here."

"No!" Brenda cried, feeling panic rise. "That can't be true. He's tried to mediate—has talked to the Germans and the Allies. He has even proposed a number of points to be observed by all belligerents who are to stop fighting with no victors and no losers. There are thirteen or fourteen of these points—and they're reasonable. It's been reported in *The Times*—all the major papers."

Lloyd exhaled a huge cloud of smoke. "Never work," he said. "Too much pride—too much hate and there are still some Englishmen who haven't been killed yet." He took another puff. "Nivelle may take care of that minor item with his grand new offensive."

Hugh and Barry exchanged a quizzical look. Barry said, "We've heard of rumors of the offensive, too."

Lloyd laughed bitterly. "Who hasn't? Nivelle has publicly stated he is going to crush Boches like a mallet cracking walnuts. Next, he'll send a telegram to the kaiser."

Barry Cooper tossed off his whiskey and an alert McHugh recharged the lieutenant's glass with a smiling, "Your drink, guv'nor."

Cooper spoke thoughtfully to Lloyd. "There's one thing that would end American neutrality, Colonel."

"The U-boats," Lloyd answered promptly.

Both American officers nodded agreement. "Yes," Barry Cooper said with unusual confidence for one so young and in the company of superior officers. "I'm convinced unrestricted submarine warfare would pull America in. Wilson is pledged to defend the freedom of the seas."

Brenda felt her heart sink. "But the U-boats are restricted —respect neutral shipping," she pleaded.

"The Hun respects nothing," Lloyd growled. He emptied his glass and McHugh swooped over it with a full decanter. "I'll lay my bit on unrestricted warfare within two months." There was a solemn silence.

Hugh broke the silence. "Your brother, Captain Randolph Higgins, he's made quite a name for himself, Colonel."

Lloyd straightened, and there was pride in his voice. "Squadron commander—twenty-nine kills. He's third behind Albert Ball and Billy Bishop."

"Love to meet him," Hugh said.

"Little chance, brother. He refuses his leaves," Brenda said. Hugh turned to his sister in surprise. Brenda answered his unspoken question. "He has some kind of vendetta going with a German squadron commander . . ."

Lloyd said to Hugh, "The butcher Bruno Hollweg. He took over Boelcke's Jagdstaffel Two."

"A personal duel?" Barry Cooper said. "Like something out of the Middle Ages."

Lloyd nodded agreement. "Randolph's that way. But it's a big sky. Chances are they'll never meet."

Brenda felt a sudden chill prickle her neck and run to her fingertips. "Oh, I hope you're right, Lloyd. Hollweg's Germany's greatest flyer. He's killed so many. Over fifty, they say." She swallowed some hot tea, which suddenly felt very warm and comforting. It was time to change the subject. She looked at her brother. "Hugh, can you and Barry stay with me? I have seventeen rooms and we're only using eight of them." Brenda saw Nicole stiffen and throw a familiar sidelong glance at Barry Cooper. The lieutenant glanced back and the French girl fumbled a teacup as if it were charged with electricity.

Hugh looked inquisitively at Barry who smiled his acquiescence. "We'd be delighted, sister," Hugh said. Brenda smiled. Barry smiled. And Nicole licked her lips.

A week later, on the fourth day of 1917, Brenda was filled with joy when Reginald was discharged from the hospital. His strength had returned with amazing speed, but he was badly scarred over his entire torso and the upper thigh of his right leg. His left arm was weak and he carried it at a slightly bent angle with the thumb and first two fingers turned in clawlike. He assured everyone exercises would restore the arm and hand and he would be ready for sea shortly.

However, his psyche was injured, too. Brenda noticed a subtle attitude change. Although he still eyed the American with love and desire, there was a reluctance—almost a barrier that caused a stiffening, a withdrawal when Brenda took his hand, kissed him, or offered any other form of close contact. In fact, after a prolonged kiss at the end of her last visit to the hospital, Brenda was convinced she had seen fear glimmering in the distant, midnight blue eyes. The American was disturbed and depressed as McHugh drove her home.

To celebrate Reginald's release and anxious to have him meet her brother, Brenda arranged a dinner party at her home, including Lloyd and Bernice. Douglas O'Conner prepared a meal of roast beef, potatoes, Brussels sprouts, and Yorkshire pudding. French cuisine was beyond the Scotsman and Brenda had learned to prefer his plain but wholesome fare to the highly spiced dishes from the Continent. Nicole and Wendell McHugh served, Nicole hovering about Barry Cooper.

Brenda smiled inwardly. On the third night of Hugh and Barry's stay, she had been awakened by what she thought were mice scurrying around in her closet or in the attic. But the sounds were coming from across the hall and they were rhythmic—a pulse as old as mankind. Then she realized her maid was entertaining a visitor. Restlessly, the young widow tossed and turned, warm thoughts of Reginald causing sleep to elude her until the early morning hours. From that night on, Barry wore a tired but happy smile on his face while Nicole walked with a new spring and relaxed air Brenda had not seen for over a year.

Slicing his beef, Reginald spoke of his ship as if she were an injured mistress. "Knocked about a bit," he said. "But she should be ready for a go by spring."

"And you, Commander?" Hugh asked, washing down a morsel with red wine.

Reginald smiled. "Not ready for the scrap yard yet," he said. There were guarded chuckles from the men. "They want to relieve me of command of *Lancer* and give me a desk job at the admiralty, but I'm not ready for that lot." He held up his hand, flexed his fingers, and gripped a wineglass. "See?" he said, raising the glass.

"Bravo," Lloyd said. Everyone nodded encouragingly. There was a common spirit, an unspoken communion between the two men who had grappled personally with death that excluded everyone else in the room. Brenda had felt it on *Lancer* when Reginald had introduced her to his officers and she was convinced she saw envy on her brother's face. A troubling memory came to mind.

"Reginald, you had a problem—a problem with a vice admiral. I hope you haven't done anything—ah . . ."

The commander smiled. "Rash, Brenda? Is that what you mean?" He chuckled. "The vice admiral was Sir Rosslyn Watts. He planned the insane action that wiped out my squadron and put a cruiser down. He got the DSO and they shipped him out to the Falklands."

Lloyd Higgins said, "If he'd lost the whole force, they'd have given him the Victoria Cross and made him first sea lord." There was humorless laughter.

"Like a scene from *HMS Pinafore*," Brenda offered.

The officers raised their glasses to the American. "Quite so, sister-in-law," Lloyd said, grinning. "Gilbert and Sullivan knew the Royal Navy." He turned to Hugh Ashcroft. They had become very close friends in a very short time. It was a trait Lloyd had learned in wartime where friends came and went in a blur. "I'm going to Chigwell tomorrow for three or four days. Would you and Lieutenant Cooper like to accompany me? We can provide billets for you. The food is terrible, but I can show you some of the latest in trench tactics. Can you take leave from your duties at the embassy?"

"Delighted," Hugh said. "We're an independent team—just inform the ambassador of our plans. Our orders are to observe and report at my discretion. As long as we write our monthly reports, Washington is happy." Barry Cooper nodded agreement.

Lloyd finished his drink and held up his empty glass for Wendell McHugh who rushed over with a decanter. "You won't see anything on the Western Front new to Americans." He smiled, a cruel, frightening look. "The same tactics used in your Civil War. The firepower has changed, but the stupidity of the generals remains." Everyone squirmed uncomfortably. He drank deeply and eyed Hugh over his glass. "Would you like to know what it was like on the Somme?"

Bernice broke her silence. "Lloyd, not now. It's too..." She turned away.

The colonel answered, "Sorry, love, he must know. It's his job and the Americans may be in it soon."

Silence, a thing of weight and substance that made Brenda's spirits quail, filled the room. She felt a cold shudder race up her spine and she shook her head vehemently but remained silent, staring at three of the four men she cherished the most in this world: dear Reginald and his torn body; Lloyd, with his torn mind; Hugh, her only brother, sitting with an eager expression on his face, waiting for his chance to toy with the fates, test his manhood, or find whatever drove men to the crucible. Only Randolph was missing, and his face came back suddenly. Now she cherished him, too—dear Randolph driven by his search for his own white whale.

The Englishman pulled another Woodbine from his pack and put a match to it, focusing his eyes above Hugh and staring into a dim past that could never be past. Brenda's thoughts moved to that evening long ago when, at the dinner table at Fenwyck, a drunken Lloyd had talked of the front. The horror of his words had been burned into her memory, but there was a fascination about the front that gripped everyone—a curiosity about mankind's greatest lunacy that cast a hypnotic spell over all of the millions who would never see it, know it, ever chance dying in it. Even the servants stood quietly and waited as Lloyd exhaled a huge cloud of blue smoke.

The colonel was not drunk this time. His eyes were red-rimmed and watery, but not from liquor. He appeared to be under tremendous pressure like a boiler with a clogged safety valve. Brenda sensed his burden could only be relieved by drinking himself senseless or by an explosion of words—a torrent that could only temporarily wash the poisonous remembrances from his mind—but never his soul. She had never seen him so thin and in the shadows of the dining room's weak light his sunken cheeks were dark hollows in old parchment. His eyes were as dark as tar pits and burned from deep sockets under huge, bony brows, thinning hair brittle and unkempt, and his white teeth seemed large, flashing ivory through thin lips so pale they were hardly visible. Brenda shuddered. Suddenly, she was looking at a cadaverous death's head and she steeled herself as if she were about to hear words from the Prince of Darkness himself.

His speech was slow, methodical, as if his lips were scissors and he were clipping his words from an endless tape. "First, you must realize," Lloyd began, "that most battles on the Western Front are races for the parapet." He looked around at the curious stares. "It's simple. You bombard your enemy and drive him deep into his dugouts, then you stop your guns and rush your infantry across no-man's-land to his trenches and hope to reach his parapets before he does. Whoever reaches that parapet first lives, the others die. I had been briefed on Haig's great plan in detail. We were to demolish the enemy with a seven-day bombardment that would deliver twenty-one thousand tons of high explosive on the Hun—one million five hundred thousand rounds." He took another pull on the Woodbine. "Sounds like a jug full, doesn't it." He ignored the rhetorical question. "Haig said the bombardment would kill all of the defenders and all that we would be required to do was occupy the Jerries' trenches and bury the dead." He chuckled to himself. "But he wasn't bagging Fuzzy Wuzzies this time. The Krauts are good soldiers—dig their dugouts deep and reinforce them with giant timbers. Only heavy guns can reach them, and we . . ." The next thought gagged him. "We fired a million of the shells from our eighteen-pounders." He looked at the women. "Light, very light. Just a field piece that couldn't even cut the Kraut wire."

"You must have had bigger guns," Hugh insisted.

"Of course. Four-point-five-inch howitzers, a few batteries of nine-point-two divisional artillery, and a few fifteen-inch howitzers firing fourteen-hundred-pound shells. We needed hundreds of these fifteen-inchers. We had six for the whole bloody front. One was assigned to my corps." He took a big swallow of cognac. "Daresay, it was spectacular, flame, smoke dust, and fountains of earth. That gave the game away."

"What do you mean, Colonel?" Harry Cooper asked.

"I mean the small shells waste their power upward, flinging dirt and metal to the sky and not downwards where the Hun and rats hide. And the omniscient generals plotting brilliantly in their châteaus decided we would carry seventy pounds of equipment."

"Good Lord," Hugh whispered.

"Two hundred rounds of ammunition, two days' rations, empty sandbags, rolls of wire, wiring stakes, Mills bombs, shovels, rockets, and even pigeon baskets and the like. Finally, the day of the attack came. It was seven-thirty. The bombardment ended. I blew my whistle and the Coldstreams went over the top."

He emptied his glass, signaled Wendell McHugh who recharged it. He drank deeply as if he were gathering strength for what was about to come. "We had about five hundred yards of no-man's-land to cross." He drank again and snickered. "A stroll in the morning sun." The voice dropped and came from deep in his being—from the stygian depths where a man hides his most virulent, intolerable memories. "We were the first wave. We moved forward in long lines, stumbling in the shell holes and our own wire. No shouting, no fuss, no running; just solid English lads doing what they had been trained to do, dressing their lines the best that they could, arms ported, doing their bit for jolly old England.

And it was all wrong. Immediately, I could see the Germans unlimbering their machine guns on top of Thiepval Ridge and their artillery began to come in and by the time we had cleared our own wire the Maxims began."

He shuddered. "You should hear them. They sounded like a thousand mad blacksmiths pounding on sheets of metal. Popping, banging. From the front and from enfilade they cut us down. My battalion lost five hundred men and all of its officers in four minutes. Shot down in neat rows by sheets of bullets like scythes harvesting wheat. It happened along the whole bloody front. And the wire wasn't cut, my lads had to rush back and forth trying to find a way through until they were shot down, too. Some places the dead were so thick a man couldn't walk without stepping on dead Tommies. They choked shell holes, piled up on the German wire. In the sector next to mine, hundreds of the First East Yorkshire never even reached their own wire—were shot off their own parapets and stacked in their trenches like cord wood. And the brilliant generals had rear battalions leave our reserve trenches and advance in the open to give quick support. They were shot down before they could even reach our first line and our communications trenches were heaped with bodies, too. We had to throw them out like trash or die, too."

Brenda had never felt so empty, helpless, defeated as she watched Lloyd. He rocked back, eyes half-closed, stubbed out his cigarette and lighted another one, and raised an eyebrow in Hugh's direction. "But the British Tommy is the finest soldier on earth. Most of the following waves were shot down, but a few survivors kept on coming. A few of us found our way through the wire and bombed and bayoneted the Jerries out. Took their trenches and held them. We had sixty thousand casualties that first day—twenty thousand dead. But Haig had his great victory." He drank and put the cigarette to his lips. "You should've heard the screams of the wounded. Many were gut-shot. Horrible. They screamed like maddened banshees and we had to ignore them—move on. There were so many the orderlies couldn't reach them all. Some were out there for days, died slowly. They gurgled near the end—cried for their mothers. It tore a man's guts . . ." His voice thickened to the point where the words would not come and he punched the table with a gnarled fist, breathing deeply.

"Lloyd, darling—please," Bernice beseeched him. "Enough."

"No, love. I must. They've got to know—everyone's got to know," he managed. He moved his rheumy gray eyes to the American officers, drank, and brought control back to his voice with a deep sigh. "And it went on for days, for weeks, for over three months, attack and counterattack and the dead piled up by the hundreds of thousands and the great generals chortled about their victories but never got their breakthrough." He looked around the room slowly. "Do you know they actually had three cavalry divisions waiting to pour through holes in the German lines?" He laughed bitterly. "There were plenty of holes, all right—in Tommy serge."

He sagged in his chair, gripping his glass with one hand, his cigarette with the other. "So you see," he said to no one in particular. "We have a lot to learn."

Hugh spoke softly. "What would you suggest?"

The colonel looked up and there was new strength in his voice. "The tracked armored vehicle code named *tank*. Winston Churchill has been advocating them for over a year and ordered hundreds built."

"But they've been used," Barry Cooper said.

"Misused in small numbers—only thirty or forty and their breakthrough went for nothing. Haig had his chance at Flers and Courcelette and botched it. Churchill wanted to wait— attack with hundreds. End the bloody business with them once and for all in one stroke. All Haig did was alert the Krauts, allowed them to prepare defenses."

"Infantry tactics?" Hugh said.

"Rushes by small groups—teams. Probe for weak spots along with tanks. Support each other. This is what I'll advocate at Chigwell. Fighting in small teams is not new. Your American Indians fought this way. Those illiterate savages knew more about tactics than our general staff. Stand-up, walking attacks by massed battalions is suicidal. Didn't work at Gettysburg and doesn't work on the Western Front."

A watery-eyed Bernice spoke to her husband. "But you're posted to a training unit, Lloyd. You're out of it."

"I know, love. I know."

"But you'd go back," she insisted. There was a sudden tension between the couple and all eyes followed the exchange.

"I didn't say that. I've never said I didn't want blighty."

"But you want to go back—I know it. I can see it in your eyes."

He took her hand and held it on his lap. "These things are best discussed at home," he said with new gentleness.

Her voice caught. "Of course, Lloyd. Of course. Let's leave, Lloyd. I'm very tired."

"Yes, love."

Brenda glanced at the pedestal clock in the corner. She was amazed. It was nearly midnight. Numbed by Lloyd's words, she saw her guests to the door while Hugh and Barry climbed the stairs silently. Reginald was the last to leave.

Standing at the door, they held each other and he kissed her with the strange restraint she had sensed in the hospital. "You've done the same—been through it, too," she said. "How can men suffer this? What's driving Randolph on his bloody crusade? How can you remain in those terrible battles like brainless machines waiting for destruction?"

"I have often wondered this, too, Brenda."

"Lloyd would return to the Coldstreams. I'm sure of it. Bernice knows. And you to *Lancer*. And Randolph won't come home. But why? Why?" Her voice trembled and she felt herself slipping to the edge of hysteria.

He pursed his lips and squinted thoughtfully. "I can't say it's duty. That's too simple—too trite."

"Then what is it?"

"The others—the fear of letting down the others—my crew, I'd say."

Brenda stared into the unblinking blue eyes. "It's more than that, Reggie."

"More?"

"Yes. It's a fascination with death. You're gamblers. It's born into all of you. It's the ultimate roll of the dice, isn't it, Reggie?"

He turned his eyes away from her stare. "I don't know. I've never thought of it that way." He shrugged helplessly. "It's possible. It's as good an explanation as any other for this bloody lot." He turned toward the door.

She could not allow him to leave like this. Her hand on his arm stopped him and he turned back to her. She looked up at him and spoke softly. "You promised me a dinner, Reggie."

"I know, darling. As soon as possible. Just the two of us."

She traced a finger over his cheek. "I've never been to a cinema, Reggie. Everyone's talking about *Birth of a Nation, Intolerance, Tillie's Punctured Romance.*"

He chuckled. "*Tillie's Punctured Romance*—Charlie Chaplin was funny in that one. He started in a music hall, you know."

"I've never been to a music hall, Reggie, either."

He smiled warmly. "Variety theater, they call them. Loud and noisy, but not as bad as the cinema."

"Take me."

"You're sure?"

"Dinner and then a music hall."

He pulled her close and kissed her with a hint of his old fervor. "Dinner and then the Palace. I hear they have thirteen new acts. They can sometimes be vulgar," he warned, running his hands over her back. "Actually, music halls are cockney in origin and much of the humor comes straight from Lambeth—the gutters of Lambeth."

"I know. But even the Prince of Wales and the king himself have been to them."

"All right. But, daresay, I warned you."

"Saturday night, Reginald?"

"Yes. Saturday night."

She tightened her arms around his neck and pushed her body hard against his. For a moment the restraint was gone and they held each other hungrily; mouths open, tongues darting, thrusting and exploring. A deep atavistic heat spread from deep within her, and she pressed herself against him, moving her pelvis in a grinding motion against his arousal, feeling a drive to pull him down with her on the sofa behind them here and now, servants and guests be damned.

A cough behind her broke the spell and they parted. It was McHugh. "Sorry, missus. But it's the nipper."

"The nipper?"

"Yes, missus. Bridie says Nath'n 'as colic. 'E's bawlin' 'is 'ead off for ye. Bit o' a temp', she says."

"Tell her I'm on my way."

McHugh left with a "Yessum."

She turned back to Reginald. "Saturday night, Reggie—if Nathan's all right."

"Quite right. Let me know about the lad." He turned and left.

Like so many mysterious children's illnesses, Nathan's colic came on suddenly with a high fever and vanished just as quickly. By Friday he was enjoying his rousing games in the garden with his brother and the servants. Even Wendell McHugh and the old grounds man, Touhy Brockman, enjoyed playing with the two "nippers." Brenda was happy; her boys were healthy and she would see Reginald Saturday night.

Because Reginald had closed his place on Wellington Road and had dismissed all of his servants except a grounds keeper, he was at the wheel of his Stevens-Duryea touring phaeton when he picked Brenda up. "The Ritz," he said, helping her up onto the running board. "Have you ever been there?"

"Why yes. With Bernice once. It's beautiful."

"Marvelous cuisine," he said.

"Well, let's shove off, Captain," she said blithely.

"Anchor's aweigh." He laughed, putting the big machine into gear.

The dining room was magnificent with fine linens, expensive silverware, and tuxedoed waiters. Brenda noticed that all of the waiters were elderly and the service was somewhat slow. However, the meal was excellent despite a menu bare of exotic seafood dishes and a wine list missing many of the old glamorous wines Brenda had expected to find in all of the better restaurants. The U-boat blockade was beginning to take its toll.

After a remarkable dessert of orange *Cote d'azur*, they were both sipping their second Grand Marnier when Reginald said with tight lips and a hard jaw, "I've been posted at the admiralty. Planning—dash it all."

"Oh, wonderful," Brenda said, feeling a sudden happiness despite his obvious frustration.

He snorted and drank. "Perhaps." He tried to drum the table with the injured fingers of his left hand, gave up in frustration, and pounded his knuckles instead. "Pochhammer has taken command of *Lancer* at my recommendation. He's a good man. I saw to his third stripe."

"Of course. I remember him. A fine, intelligent gentleman," she said. "Then you'll open your place on Wellington Road?"

"Quite right. It's only a short drive to Whitehall."

"Your duties, Reggie. Can you speak of them?"

He toyed with his glass. "Hush, hush and all that bit, of course. But I can tell you this, I'm working on a pet project of mine I proposed in 'fifteen." He rubbed his head as if in sudden pain and spoke bitterly. "If that ass Watts and his lackeys had listened to me then, Destroyer Squadron Four would still be afloat and those chaps of mine . . ."

"Please, Reggie." She reached across the table and took his hand. It was thin, but the grip was strong.

He smiled into her eyes. "Of course, darling. No shop talk." He glanced at his watch. "We'd better hurry. Curtain's going up on your great adventure at the Palace Music Hall."

"Right-oh, your nibs," she said, imitating a cockney.

He laughed heartily as he came to his feet. "This way, ham shank."

"Ham shank?"

"Why yes, ducks. That's cockney for Yank."

Hand in hand they left the dining room.

* * *

The Palace was located only a short drive from the Ritz at Charing Cross Road and Shaftsbury Avenue. Seating themselves in a private box to the left of the stage with the largest proscenium arch Brenda had ever seen, the young American looked over an enormous rectangular auditorium, jammed with nearly two thousand noisy, boisterous fans. Most of the men were in uniform and liquor was being served and drunk in large quantities.

The program began with the blare of a brassy band playing a familiar beat to the wild cheers of the crowd. "Ragtime," Reginald said into Brenda's ear. "Imported from the States, you know. It's popular in the music halls."

The great curtains parted and the show began. First came the Canadian Maud Allan with her sensual "Dance of Salome." As the petite woman swayed sinuously across the stage, the crowd cheered itself hoarse. Then Albert Chevalier sang his uproarious street-monger songs, the crowd joining in with "Ta-ra-ra-boom-de-ay" during the refrain of his final number.

Then in quick succession came Little Tech, a deformed dwarf who played the clown and the buffoon—pathetically to Brenda, uproariously funny to the crowd; Marie Lloyd singing her risqué song "Johnnie Jones" and delighting the crowd with her blue humor that made Brenda blush; George Robey who mastered the audience with his jokes, pantomime, and feigned tantrums at misplaced laughter; Harry Lauder with his sophisticated humor, sentimental songs, and sketches.

There were many more, the best in music hall, ending with the famous Vesta Tilley dressed in her immaculate Edwardian man's suit, imitating a man to perfection with her walk, voice, mannerisms, gestures, and singing her songs to rapturous cheers and often to the accompaniment of the audience. The effect was continuous noise from the stage, orchestra pit, and auditorium.

Finally the curtain rang down and the enormous crowd—a mob to Brenda—stood as one and cheered until all of the performers trooped back on stage to bow to the audience, to the orchestra, and to each other. Brenda felt Reginald's hand on hers. "Time to leave, my dear, or we'll get caught in the crowd." Brenda grasped his hand as she rose.

"A nightcap?" he asked, leading her to the door. "There's a delightful lounge nearby at the Ritz."

Brenda looked at his tired, thin face and the new lines racked there by pain. The control had eroded three nights ago in the entry of her home and her desire was stronger than ever. She could not understand her feelings but could not deny them. "Your place, Reggie," she said, locking his eyes with hers.

He swallowed hard and his lips twisted into a line Brenda had never seen before. "You're sure?"

"I'm sure."

Reginald's house was typically Victorian: a large, dark three-story with crowded downstairs kitchen, workrooms, and servants' quarters; billiards room, study, and drawing room on the second floor; bedrooms, bath, study, and a combination smoking and gun room on the third floor. Without a staff, the house was deserted and most of the furniture was covered. Reginald ushered Brenda into his study, a large room lined with bookcases and comfortably furnished with two luxurious sofas, a huge walnut desk, and several chairs. All were uncovered and Reginald obviously favored this room. The American sighed and sank into the red velvet of one of the sofas. She realized she was very tired.

"Benedictine?" he asked, moving to a sideboard. She nodded. In a moment he sank down beside her and handed her the liqueur.

She touched his pony with hers. "To your new posting."

His smile was noncommittal. "Right-oh. May the Admiralty listen to Commander Reginald Hargreaves's limitless wisdom," he joked, touching her glass.

They sipped the sweet, fiery liquid and tabled their drinks. Then she found her way into his arms as if they had been made to embrace her. She felt her passion flow as his open mouth covered hers and she felt herself pushed back onto the cushions of the sofa. He was above her and it was right. His hands moved over her body and his weight pushed her deep into the sofa. The heat was back and she sighed and whispered his name into his ear, into his kisses. She felt him pull her dress up and her knees began to part.

Suddenly he stopped, sat up, and pounded his temple with a clenched fist. "What's wrong, Reggie? What is it?" She came erect.

He stared at his glass. "There are some things about me —some terrible things you don't know."

The American was stunned. "Terrible? Are you married?"

He laughed. "No, it's not that."

"Then what?"

He refilled his glass and spat out the words as if he had bitten rotten fruit. "My wounds."

Brenda stared at the anguished face silently, her mind filled with thoughts of the horrifying wounds she had heard about. Was it his manhood? But it could not be that. She had felt his arousal pressed against her in the entry of her own home. Perhaps he was sterile. Shrapnel could do that easily enough. She could not bring herself to ask the question. He answered it for her.

He stared at the table with a grim look setting the muscles of his jaw in tight bunches. "When I was hit, I was standing on the bridge." He drank and seemed to be talking to the Persian rug under his feet. "Two shells hit us almost simultaneously. Shrapnel—a blizzard of shrapnel tore through the windscreen, ripped me open from neck to here." He struck his thigh. "Went right past me, caught my poor pilot full in the face and neck. Killed my lookout, wounded my signalmen. Left me ripped and bleeding. I didn't know how bad it was; anyway, *Lancer* was in mortal danger. I had to refuse attention." He lifted his wide, moist eyes to her. "We had so many wounded—injured far more seriously than I. But I lost blood. Finally passed out. The ship's surgeon and Pochhammer saved my life. The surgeon had to sew me up to stop the bleeding and then at Canterbury they had to rip it all out—infections and some internal injuries and all that." He emptied the glass but did not refill it. "Then they sewed me up again."

"I know, Reggie. I know about the wounds."

"But you don't know about the scars," he said thickly. "I'm a hideous crazy quilt of rough welts and crevices like the Western Front had been fought and charted on my body."

She kissed his cheek, his neck. "Is that it? Is that what has been holding you back from me?"

"Yes." He grasped her hand. "I want you, Brenda, more than anything I have ever wanted in my life. I've wanted you from the first moment I saw you and you know it." He turned away. "But the thought—the vision of seeing you turn away from me in revulsion—in disgust . . ."

She silenced him with her lips. He kissed her back and held her very close. She began to unbutton his tunic. He pulled away. "Please," she pleaded. She felt him sag and tremble like a disciplined child. She helped him pull the jacket from his shoulders and arms and then dropped it on a chair.

"All right," he said, standing. In a moment his chest was bare. In the dim light the scars were jagged and rough red welts, most in horizontal lines that showed the path of the shrapnel as it had ripped through him. The stitching was still visible. But there were other lines, too, running haphazardly as if Jack the Ripper had made one of his insane attacks. He moved closer to the light and it was clear the impact of red-hot jagged metal and the closing and reopening of the wounds had caused thick scars to form in red ridges and purple hollows, rough like twisted cords, and in some places, still showing small scabs.

She stood. Ran her hands over the muscles of his neck, shoulders, arms, and then she caressed his chest. "You are one of the most attractive men I have ever met, Reggie."

"You feel sorry for me."

"No!" she retorted sharply. "No." She kissed his neck, his shoulder, then his chest, and the wounds. She felt strangely aroused by the scars and she suddenly had the notion the touch of her lips could heal—not only heal his body, but also wash his mind clean of the pain. If this be love, then so be it, ran through her mind.

She felt him shaking and his breath was hot and short as passion overwhelmed restraint, his hands suddenly pulling the straps of her dress and teddy down over her shoulders and caressing her swollen breasts, toying with her nipples. Then his mouth clamped over her breast and he tongued the nipple and areola frantically, tingling sensations like electric current racing low and deep, causing her to twist and gasp. Trembling hands fumbled with her dress, pushing it down as she moved her hips from side to side and it slid to the floor. Then in a quick movement, she pulled her teddy loose and let the garment fall to the floor with the forgotten dress. She was nude except for her stockings and shoes. He stepped back, eyeing her from head to toe. "My God. You're magnificent."

"And so are you," she said, pressing her pointed breasts against his chest and rubbing them against the scars. He led her to the bedroom.

Dawn's light softened by heavy curtains brought her to wakefulness. Resting on his outflung arm, her forehead was against his cheek. His breath was slow and heavy as he slept off the fatiguing effects of their frenzied lovemaking. She could feel the stubble of new growth on his cheek and she rubbed against it gently. Tenderly, her hand explored the scars on his chest, grooves and ridges where hair would never grow again. Pressing her body against his, she was filled with an ineffable joy and she wanted to make love to him again.

She had never known a night like this. Unlike Geoffry, Reginald knew her body and its special needs thoroughly and he ministered to them with skill and loving patience, taking her again and again, but only after he had brought her with caresses and kisses to the verge of crying out "Now! Now!" The first time he lowered himself between her knees and she took him in her hand and guided him. It had been so long for her, the stretching and filling brought her a slight discomfort, but it was immediately washed away by waves of sensations that left her mindless and whimpering and she rode his thrusts like the branch of a tree whipped back and forth by a storm, their suppressions exploding quickly, leaving them both weak.

The last time had been early in the morning when they were both tired yet still hungry. It had been the best. Slow. Deliberate. And she held him trapped deep within her with her arms and legs for a very long time, bending her knees and meeting his onslaught with her upthrusting hips, gasping into his mouth, which was clamped over hers, dueling his tongue, feeling his heart pound with hers, blending with him as she engulfed him until even their thoughts seemed to merge and they cried together at the last ecstatic second, "I love you. I love you." And then, even after the shuddering and spasms had ended, she would not release him and they fell into deep sleep still locked together.

He stirred and yawned. He turned toward her and pushed her onto her back, his hand moving down over her abdomen. "Please, Reggie," she said, turning. "I've got to go home. My brother and Barry are in Chigwell, but I must be there when the children awake. I always have breakfast with them."

"All right," he said, sighing. "But I love you, Brenda." He kissed her. "And you love me?"

She sighed. "Yes, Reggie. After last night I want to be with you forever. Yes. Yes."

"We'll marry."

She bit her lip then kissed his eyes, his nose, his lips. "I don't know. It hasn't been a year, darling."

He pushed himself up on an elbow. "Appearances?"

"No, Reggie, you know me better than that. I owe it to Geoffry."

He ran a hand over her breast, then downward, dipping it at her small waist and then to a trim hip and buttock. "We can marry in June. It'll be a year."

She nodded. "Yes. Let me think about it—I need time, Reggie."

He rolled to his back and cradled his head in his hands, disturbed by a new thought. "No. No. It's not cricket."

"Not cricket? Not fair?"

"Yes, Brenda. You're a widow once," he said grimly. "I could make you a widow twice over." He turned toward her. "It's not fair to you."

She kissed him. "We'll both think about it, dear Reginald."

He kissed her gently and turned toward the window. "It's dawn," he said with a new, hard tone. He sat up and stared at the light, which had become harsh as the sun began to creep up over the horizon. "This is the worst moment for the Dover patrol. They're at morning action stations. The U-boats and torpedo boats like to attack out of the sun. It's almost impossible to see torpedo tracks in the glare of the sun off the sea." He came to his feet and pulled the drapes open a crack. The light slashed in like the blade of a sword. "And on the Western Front the morning hate barrages are starting." She stood next to him and stared at the light. He continued, "And the dawn patrols are taking off." He turned to her, eyes gleaming strangely. "Randolph is up there somewhere." He waved to the east. "Up there somewhere on his bloody hunt."

She shuddered and reached for her clothes.

X

The raucous voices carried through the canvas walls of Number Five Squadron's mess hall all the way to Major Randolph Higgins's small office in the farmhouse. Uncomfortable and warm in his flight kit, he sipped his coffee and thumbed through sheaves of reports, listening to the words he knew by heart:

When you soar into the air on a Nieuport scout,
And you're scrapping with a Hun and your gun cuts out,
Well, you stuff down your nose 'til your plugs fall out
'Cos you haven't got a hope in the morning.

For a batman woke me from my bed;
I'd had a thick night and a very sore head,
And I said to myself, to myself I said,
Oh, we haven't got a hope in the morning!

Despite the mournful lyrics, Randolph did not wonder at the boisterousness of the voices of the eleven pilots waiting for him for the morning briefing. Today, they would take to the air in their new fighter, the S.E.5. They were enthused and eager to scrap with the Albatross D.2. And perhaps the celebrants had consumed more liquor than coffee despite standing orders and the early hour.

Every man had liquor stored in his billet, none more than he. In fact, he had found it necessary to brace up with a few extra nips now and again. And at night, sleep would no longer come without first downing a half dozen toddies. God knows, losses had been heavy and the Albatross D.2 was a devilish fighter that was faster and far more durable than the Nieuport 17. But Number Five Squadron finally had its new equipment, too; the third RFC squadron equipped with the new S.E.5 scout plane. Number 109 Squadron and Number Ninety-seven Squadron had gone into action with the new machine three weeks earlier.

The pride of the Royal Aircraft Factory, the S.E.5 was a superb fighting machine. Square and squat with very little streamlining, it was strongly built and durable with a single Lewis gun on a Foster mount above its top wing. Small like the Nieuport 17, it weighed seven hundred pounds more, had forty more horsepower, and was the easiest plane Randolph had ever flown and the steadiest gun platform. At two thousand pounds, it was as heavy as the Albatross D.2; however, its wingspan was three feet shorter. With its short span and light wing loading, it was very maneuverable and could turn inside the German fighter. Powered with the new 150-horsepower Hispano-Suiza V-8 engine, it had a top speed of 110 miles an hour and a fraction of the torque of a rotary-powered fighter. Nevertheless, when Randolph first flew the new airplane, he was not satisfied, convinced it was under-powered. He wanted more speed and a ceiling higher than the S.E.5's seventeen thousand feet—a greater altitude that would take his squadron above the Albatross D.2.'s service ceiling of eighteen thousand feet.

After studying blueprints of the new engine and carefully examining the airframe, Randolph drew on his early experience in design with Tommy Sopwith and Geoffrey de Havilland, made his sketches, mulled over his calculations, and then gave his orders. Under the direction of chief mechanic William Cochran, who shouted an uninterrupted stream of epithets for sixteen straight hours without repetition, engines were pulled from the fourteen scout planes and, working night and day with pilots alongside mechanics, new, special high-compression pistons were installed, heads ground down, valves and cams ground and polished to jewellike luster, and the horsepower raised to two hundred. Randolph was not satisfied. He had the windscreens removed and replaced with smaller screens and the pilot's seat lowered six inches. The upper wing tanks were removed and the dihedral angle of the wings was increased by screwing up the tension on the rigging wires, adding another two or three miles an hour.

Randolph disliked the wing-mounted Lewis gun perched high above the propeller tip on its Foster mount. Fed by a ninety-seven-round drum, it could deliver two pounds of fire in an eight-second burst and then had to be reloaded. The pilot was forced to put the stick between his legs, pull the gun down on its track, reach up, release the empty drum, and replace it. In a hot dogfight, reloading could be fatal. In addition, the high mounting above the propeller tip was another wind drag. The guns were removed and a recessed Vickers was mounted in front of the pilot. Bolted to the engine housing, the machine gun was synchronized with the new Constantinesco gear. Hydraulically driven, it had nearly double the rate of fire of the old Vickers-Challenger gear, eliminated much maintenance, and easily adapted to the Hispano-Suiza.

Within two days, the modifications were completed, adding another fifteen miles an hour to the top speed and raising the aircraft's ceiling to 22,000 feet. Now they had a fighter, a true fighter, and Randolph ordered the squadron's old Nieuports turned over to the newly formed Number 112 Squadron.

Randolph accepted his second cup of coffee spiked with rum from his batman, Sergeant Major Johnathan York, who handed it to him with his usual raspy, "Your coffee, Major."

Randolph sipped the hot liquid, savoring the heat of the coffee and the strong flavor of the dram of rum. His eyes ran over the reports on his desk. It had been a bad winter for the RFC. As it has for centuries, rain and mud had mired the European enemies on the ground and the slaughter had abated, the two armies recoiling from each other like two stags who had locked horns, bloodying each other without either emerging victorious. Licking their wounds, they had pulled back into their lairs to wait for spring and to prepare for more carnage.

Nevertheless, there had been no respite in the air. General Hugh Montague "Boom" Trenchard's latest bulletin in bold-faced type stared up at Higgins mockingly. He gulped down the coffee as his eyes found the most galling passage: "The sky is too large to defend. Carry the war into enemy territory and keep it there. Squadron commanders must keep in mind the airplane is not designed for defense and relentless and incessant offensive pressure must be put on the enemy."

"You bloody killer. You're nothing but a flying Haig," Randolph said to himself. He emptied his cup and York re-filled it with straight coffee.

The squadron commander picked up the latest report on losses. The taste of sour rum and coffee rose in his throat. British D.H.2s, R.E.8s, and B.E.2s had been easy meat for the new Albatross fighters. Only the Sopwith Pup and the new S.E.5 could stand up to the Albatross scourge and they were too few in number. And Trenchard's insistence on aggressive, offensive spirit with British scouts and observation planes still penetrating far behind the enemy lines even in the most miserable weather had led to frightening slaughter. In late December seven R.E.8s were attacked by Bruno Hollweg and his Jasta 2 and every one of the British machines was shot out of the air without loss to the Germans.

Then in early January, Richthofen's new Jasta 11 shot five Sopwith one-and-one-half strutters out of the sky still without loss. A week later a flight of eight F.E.2bs vanished without a trace. In the months of November and December the RFC had lost 211 machines to thirty-nine for the Germans. It was all in front of Randolph in cold, heartless statistics, yet Trenchard commanded and harangued and bragged.

Richthofen was emerging as one of Germany's leading aces. With twenty-four kills, including one of Britain's finest flyers, Major Lanoe Hawker, commander of Number Twenty-four Squadron and holder of the Victoria Cross, the baron's blood red Albatross had become a scourge and the French assigned the sobriquet *Diable Rouge*, the Red Devil, to it. But Richthofen was still second to Hollweg, who was the greatest killer, boasting an incredible fifty kills.

Number Five Squadron had been lucky. The heavy action had moved to the sectors to the north, toward Arras and Vimy Ridge. This was where Jasta 2—the Germans now called it Jasta Boelcke—and Richthofen's new Jasta 11 were operating. It also meant Randolph had little chance of meeting Hollweg. He sipped his coffee again and he felt hate boil. Night after night he had lain awake, his mind's eye seeing Reed standing helplessly in his cockpit, beating at the flames as Hollweg murdered him.

Higgins had a small measure of revenge when he killed Hollweg's wingman and rumored best friend, the ace Max Mueller. Mueller, too, was helpless when he died, engine shot dead by Randolph's full deflection shot from an incredible four hundred yards. Randolph smiled, remembering how casually he had come within twenty feet of the Hun before squeezing the tit. Mueller had turned to the Englishman just as eight rounds hit him in the face, shattering his skull, blowing off his goggles and helmet, and filling the slipstream with gore. Randolph had laughed and pounded the coaming with delight. Mueller had been his twenty-first. Now his score had reached thirty.

There were rumors the great defensive line, which the Germans called Siegfried and the allies Hindenburg, was almost ready. A system of interconnecting dugouts and concrete blockhouses, it was considered impregnable by Ludendorff and its creator, Hindenburg. Already, there were reports that German divisions were beginning to pull back into the line out of the Somme salient. "They'll pull back," his new adjutant Captain Hartley Carter had said. "Pull back and let Nivelle and Haig waste our chaps on their bloody line until they deal with the Russians. Then they'll bring their whole bloody army to the Western Front. Then we'll catch it."

Randolph looked across the room past a small table where squadron clerk Corporal Harvey Longacre was drawing up lists of the day's patrols on his typing machine to Hartley Carter, who sat at a desk next to the room's rock fireplace where a fire roared. With a full head of gray hair and bushy sideburns and drooping mustaches, the man had a formidable leonine mien to him and appeared much older than his forty-five years. In fact, when the burly captain walked he had the look of a stalking lion—especially when angered by the stupidity of a new pilot. A graduate of Harrow and Sandhurst Military Academy, Carter had fought in India and in the Boer War. Shot through the hip while defending an armored train outside of Natal, he was imprisoned at Pretoria where his wound festered and poor treatment left him with a slight limp, which he disguised by hunching and stalking. Like Sergeant Major York, duty with a front line regiment was out of the question for Captain Carter.

The new adjutant had been an enormous help to Randolph, relieving the squadron commander of the innumerable administrative duties that interfered with his function as squadron leader and as Carter had put it so succinctly, "chief Boche killer." But no one could relieve the major of the letters—the unending stream of letters to next of kin.

Tossing off the last of his coffee and rum, Randolph nodded at Carter, rose, took the lists from Longacre, picked up his helmet and goggles from a nearby table, and walked to the door. Carter opened it for him and the cold hit Randolph like a frozen fist and he was suddenly happy he was wearing his flight clothes. To the north there was the usual pulsating salmon and rose glow of the front, and the rumble and bark of the morning "hate barrage" could be heard like thunder. This morning heavier pieces had added their roll and drumming rumble to the bark and snap of the seventy-sevens and eighteen-pounders. "Heavy weights exercising before breakfast," Carter said in his usual sardonic tone. "Nine-point-twos and 'Jack Johnsons.' Chap can't get a decent night's sleep these days, sir."

Despite his somber mood, Randolph chuckled at Hartley's use of "Jack Johnson," Tommy argot for German heavy artillery and its terrific punch—like the American heavyweight boxer. Higgins quipped back, "Bloody inconsiderate, old boy. Morning hate barrages should be fired at noon."

"Right, sir," the adjutant said with a straight face, opening the door to the mess hall and standing aside.

As Randolph entered the smoke-filled room, the pilots came to their feet. "Be seated, gentlemen," he said, gesturing and walking to a small table that served as a podium. Hartley Carter took his station next to a blackboard behind the squadron leader. As usual, Randolph felt a mixture of confidence and dread when he looked at the faces of his men. The athletic nineteen-year-old Jarret Barton stared up at him, the blue of his eyes hardened by scores of patrols and six kills. Puffing on the foul Egyptian tobacco of an Abdullah, the baby-faced, cold-eyed Canadian Leefe Hendon, with thirteen kills and wearing new captain's patches, lounged back in his chair. The amiable, reliable Scotsman Angus McDonald sipped his Scotch whiskey flavored with a dash of coffee and yawned grandly. McDonald was second to Randolph with nineteen kills and had also been promoted to captain. Lieutenant Gaskell, with three kills, fidgeted nervously as he smoked, while flight Lieutenants Cowdry and Anderson, both with two kills, sat side by side, toying with their cups and staring at Randolph with eyes that appeared more tired and bloodshot each morning.

Randolph felt his guts wrench as he thought of the missing faces: Lieutenant Anthony Smith who had been Hollweg's forty-seventh kill over Contalmaison, flight Lieutenant Freddie Morris, smashed to strawberry jelly when his wings were shot off at twelve thousand feet; Flight Lieutenant Irwin Jillings, shot through the lungs but still able to land back of friendly lines. Now young Jillings was back in blighty trying to survive on one lung.

And the ever eager, expectant new faces were there: Flight Lieutenants Hollingsworth, Dunlap, Hemmings, and Baldwin. None had more than twelve hours at the controls of an S.E.5 when he reported and not one had reached his nineteenth birthday. Fortunately, the sector had been quiet and the new men had survived almost three weeks of flying, building their hours in the cockpit and their chances for survival. *There's hope*, Randolph thought. *If I can just keep them alive for another three weeks.*

In desperate efforts to protect his new men, Randolph had experimented with a variety of formations. He had tried line abreast, but it forced constant surveillance of the flight leader by all eyes, leaving the end men to be picked off like ripe plums by any experienced attacker. Line astern was just as taxing, each trailing pilot forced to keep his eyes on the machine ahead, neglecting the usual life-preserving search all around. The end man was cold meat in this formation. The full squadron inverted V, preferred by the Germans, had the same weaknesses, the end men being vulnerable. Pairs worked well if both pilots were experienced, or in the event two pairs flew one above the other. But too many of his best men had been lost trying to protect clumsy wingmen. He still preferred pairs when flying with one of his better flyers.

Now he was experimenting with the three. The three simply put an inexperienced man at the leading point of an inverted V while two experienced men trailed off his elevators. This formation put experienced eyes behind the novices where none of them ever seemed to see anything, anyway, and required only that the new chum keep his eyes on the patrol leader and ahead. However, in an attack, the most inexperienced pilot lead and the three depended on his gun more than any other for its kill. Most new pilots were terrible shots. Consequently, after an initial attack and first pass, the three was allowed to break up and it was every man for himself. It tore the major's heart to see his fledg-

lings on their own, but his experienced pilots were too valuable and he had sacrificed too many in fruitless attempts to
protect the new men.

"This morning," he began, eyes moving over the faces,
"we will make a full squadron patrol between Mametz and
Gommecourt." There were raised eyebrows. "Yes," he explained. "Division has moved our patrol north and they want
us up in full strength to support Number Twenty-four Squadron. Number Twenty-four Squadron not only lost Hawker,
but *Diable Rouge* and his Jasta Eleven have inflicted heavy
losses on them. They can only put up five D.H. twos."
Everyone seemed to suck in on cigarettes and drink at the
same time.

McDonald spoke up. "Sure an' we'll show Fritzie with
our new machines, we will, laddies."

There were shouts of "Hear! Hear!"

Nodding, Randolph turned to Hartley Carter who was
busy scribbling the information on the board. Carter handed
Randolph another document. "The Hun is up to some new
tricks. French intelligence reports the German flying service
is organizing huge hunting groups—they call them *Jagd-
geschwaders*. A Jagdgeschwader will be made up of four
Jagdstraffels—forty-eight planes. Already, there are reports
the first will be under Manfred von Richthofen." He looked
around at the solemn faces. "Hunter groups. The sky could
rain Albatrosses. Numerical superiority at the time and place
of their choosing."

Leefe Hendon waved a hand. "And with our esteemed
Trenchard sending our observation planes deep behind their
lines, it'll be more easy kills."

Randolph knew he should squelch the Canadian, but the
man's sentiments too closely reflected his own and even the
new men knew the truth of the words. He continued. "The
new Albatross D.3 has appeared to the north. It has a one-
hundred-sixty-horsepower Mercedes, can do at least one
hundred twenty, service ceiling is estimated at nineteen
thousand. Of course, it's durable and can outdive the S.E.5
But we can fly higher and outmaneuver it. We'll take our

patrol to twenty-one thousand feet." There were shouts of approval.

He stared around at the eleven flyers and the intent eyes focused on his face. Despite the enthusiasm he found, he was gripped by an awful emptiness. The effects of the rum were beginning to wear off and the frightful depression that had haunted him since David A. Reed's death began to return. The thought of losing another pilot was unbearable. Death was part of war—part of life. But young death was so unnatural. And he was a purveyor of death and the writer of crushing letters home. Again, he felt a hunger to be alone. To hunt for Hollweg in his new fighter and think of nothing else. But the young faces looked to him for leadership. For life. They were his cross and he had nailed himself to it. He yearned for another drink.

His tongue became thick and he was afraid to talk—afraid he would look foolish stumbling over words. After several deep breaths he tried to continue but was unable to form the words. A heavy silence fell on the room like a wet blanket and he noticed curious, concerned looks; especially on the faces of Barton, Hendon, and McDonald.

Captain Hartley Carter saved him. "Here it is, Major," the adjutant said, casually handing him flight orders. "Four threes flying in a diamond with your three leading and your aircraft the point."

"Why, quite right," Randolph said, suddenly regaining composure. "The trailing three of the diamond will fly five hundred feet higher than the other elements." Feeling suddenly fatigued, he placed both hands on the table and put his weight on his arms. "Division is sending two B.E. Two artillery spotters over the German lines all the way to Bapaume. They'll be escorted by Number Twenty-four Squadron. But I already told you Number Twenty-four can only put up five D.H. twos and all of you know the D.H. two can't fly above sixteen thousand feet and is cold meat for the Albatross."

"Sir," the adjutant said gently, "the other threes."

Randolph felt his face flush. He spoke sarcastically. "Thank you, Captain. I am quite capable of conducting this meeting." Carter returned to the board while Randolph read off the assignments. Then he concluded, "Check your aircraft carefully, and if you want to survive this lot, check your oxygen bottles. There won't be much up there and you know it. And keep your eyes open for Rumplers and L.V.G.s. They've been crossing the lines at seventeen thousand feet." Then a quick review of Very pistol and hand signals and the caution to watch for wing waggling, which would indicate the sighting of unknown aircraft and the pilots were dismissed. Quietly they filed through the door and walked toward the flight line.

Followed by chief mechanic Cochran, Randolph inspected the S.E.5. Slowly, he walked around the fighter giving it his usual thorough inspection despite his strange weakness. Just the appearance of the fighter raised his morale: the long nose over the huge engine gave the impression of great power; the large control surfaces, which gave the fighter its agility and control; the raked wings and deep dihedral, which helped give the plane its speed and maneuverability; and the single synchronized Vickers, which made the beauty a killer. He grunted his approval and moved slowly to the front of the aircraft. Stroking the beautifully laminated wood of the propeller, he looked up in surprise. An orange spinner was attached to the propeller hub.

"My idea, sir. Add a little more streamlining and maybe two, three miles per hour."

"Where did you get it?"

"We only had one, Major." The Irishman gestured to the north. "I took it from that LVG you shot down last week."

"I'll be damned," Randolph said, chuckling, remembering the audacious German observation plane he had shot down back of British heavy artillery positions and only five miles from the field. Curious and an insatiable scavenger, Cochran had been one of the first men on the scene with his toolbox and a borrowed lorry. Still chuckling, the squadron commander walked slowly around the aircraft toward the cockpit. He was very, very tired. The elusive sleep that escaped him night after night was taking its toll.

As Randolph reached up for the hand grip and placed his foot on the wing of his fighter, he felt the big hand of the chief mechanic on his arm. "You all right, sir?" he asked in his soft Irish brogue.

"Yes. Quite all right," the major answered. However, he welcomed the help in climbing up onto the lower wing and then the slight push up as he threw a leg over the coaming of the cockpit. As he settled into the cockpit he was impressed, again, by the improved view of the S.E.5 and he remembered how hard it had been to peer over the huge rotary engine of the Nieuport. But the plane rocked far too much and the horizon seemed to be turning. While Randolph scanned his instruments and made the usual checks, he felt Cochran tugging at the safety harness locks. After grunting his approval, the mechanic slid to the ground and took his station at the propeller.

Then pilot and mechanic went through their French starting ritual and the big Hispano-Suiza burst into life with a volley of reports like a ragged firing squad, exhausts belching clouds of blue smoke. Within seconds, the warming V-8 engine settled down into its distinctive full-throated roar. Pretending to check his oxygen bottle, Randolph put the tube into his mouth, opened the valve, and sucked some gas into his lungs. His throat felt seared but immediately there was a clearing in his head, the horizon stabilized, and he felt stronger. After securing the tube, more deep breaths helped clear his head further. Strange how the two drams of rum had affected him this morning. He felt stronger. He was ready.

The cold air at twelve thousand feet helped. Head clear, Randolph continued to climb, pointing the formation north toward Bapaume. They would have trouble finding anything in today's cloudy sky and he mumbled thanks for the S.E.5's new instrument, the lateral bubble, which told him if he was on an even keel when blinded by clouds. Looking down, he saw thick clouds stretching to the horizon in layers. The lowest level at two thousand feet was streaking horse's-tail cirrus. Above this deck ranged dense cumulus still heavy with moisture from yesterday's rain. Randolph was leading Number Five Squadron up through the last lingering milky white remnants of the thick layer and he was wiping the condensation from his windshield and goggles with the back of his glove when the mist wraiths drew back with breathtaking suddenness, the sky above opening into an arena of brilliant sunshine domed by a perfect eggshell blue. Dazzling, the light came from every direction, from the heavens, the clouds, from every atom of air.

The slaughter and heartbreak had never inured Randolph Higgins to the stunning beauty to be found in the heavens. To the north and east thunderheads tossed their monstrous heads to twenty thousand feet like a range of majestic mountains, the morning sun rouging the tops of the billowing masses with fleshy tones of vermillion and rose while canyons and valleys were the color of burned antimony, gold, and tarnished silver. Below, as far as he could see, a flat plain of radiant whiteness reached to all four horizons, sparkling in the sun like a tray of diamond chips. Brilliant, thrilling, the province of the gods and those few mortals who dared thresh into the skies in their flimsy machines—tenuous contraptions that seemed to hang motionlessly like butterflies dangling from a collector's ceiling.

He looked at his wingtips only thirteen feet away. There was nothing between him and oblivion except a pair of fragile linen-covered wings, wooden airframe, skinny wires, struts, and a two-hundred-horsepower engine. He looked up. The fabric on the top wing was actually bellying up into the suction above the airfoil—the vacuum that pulled the machine into the sky as he continued his climb. A rip in this fabric and he was a dead man. How insignificant was man in these limitless dimensions where he hung motionless and time and distance had no meaning. An intruder. A gnat. A speck of dust blown on the wind. Transient and gone in a blink.

The wires thrummed, relaxed, and sprang taut as the wing structures reacted to the invisible forces rushing past, rising and falling as the Hispano-Suiza roared and the wooden propeller clubbed the air, pulling the scout relentlessly higher and higher. He scorned parachutes. All RFC pilots considered the use of parachutes cowardly. Anyway, a man should stick with his aeroplane. He who chooses to challenge the skies with his machine should stay with his machine regardless of the consequences.

His head began to feel light. A glance at his altimeter told him he was approaching sixteen thousand feet. Carefully, he adjusted the spring-loaded nose clip over his nostrils and slipped the oxygen tube into his mouth. Checking the canister, the pressure gauge indicated the tank was still nearly full of liquid oxygen and the bladder pulsated as it should with his breath. The nose clip was uncomfortable and the gas always left his throat raw. But they would soon be at twenty-one thousand feet. No man could survive long above sixteen thousand feet without his oxygen canister.

He pounded his head in frustration. It was past time to clear guns. After pumping his fist skyward like a man ringing for a servant, he fired a half dozen rounds from his Vickers. Within seconds, the other eleven pilots cleared their own weapons. Randolph snapped the safety lock back on.

The effects of the oxygen were like a tonic and Randolph looked around with new alertness in his usual search pattern. But the gales sweeping the cockpit made him shiver. He instinctively hunched down, trying to hide from the icy slipstream, and he was glad he had lowered his seat. They had been in the air less than thirty-five minutes and already his neck was beginning to ache. Every day the muscles became stiffer, turned to wood that he rubbed and sometimes pounded with his open fist. Was it fear? Cumulative fatigue? Tension? He had flown over three hundred combat sorties. He firmed his resolve by remembering Hollweg and the way he had murdered Reed.

Wheeling slowly to the west, he estimated they had crossed the lines. Although his visibility directly below was still obscured by cloud cover, far to the south the layers had broken and he could see the ribbons of the Somme and the Oise. Too high to be seen by the naked eye and obscured by clouds, there was no German archie reaching for the patrol. He glanced back at the eleven S.E.5s rising and falling on the invisible waves of air like migrating geese he had seen so often when hunting game birds in the Kentish downs. They too flew in formations, rising and falling in V patterns behind their leader. They, too, were fast, elusive targets. But they could not shoot back. His geese each mounted a Vickers Mark 1 machine gun capable of firing six hundred rounds a minute with a weight of fire of two pounds in a six-second burst; the fastest, most deadly serial weapon on the Western Front.

Finally, they were at twenty-one thousand feet and he felt new confidence despite the bitter cold. The S.E.5 was a marvel. He had expected the controls to go mushy in this rarefied atmosphere, but they were still firm. He rejoiced in the knowledge that no German fighter could be above them. At last he had a machine that eliminated the dread of "the Hun in the sun." Now he and his chaps had the advantage of the fighting scout's greatest asset—altitude—and they were eager to give some Germans a very unpleasant surprise. Checking the rivers to the south, which could be seen quite clearly now, he wheeled the flight over where Bapaume should have been. The cloud layers were thinning and he could catch glimpses of the ground, but there was no sign of other aircraft and from this altitude, he could not even distinguish the front lines. He looked for the characteristic salvo firing of German archie; saw nothing.

His eyes kept moving, but his mind was suddenly on Cynthia Boswell. She continued to write. He answered with an occasional field postcard. She professed love and still promised to wait for him. He laughed out loud. Then he saw Brenda. The auburn hair, the blue eyes, the fine white skin. He loved her. Could never have her. Between the lines of her letters he saw clearly she was involved with Reginald Hargreaves—possibly in love with him. Maybe he was her lover. The idea churned his stomach and left him feeling sick. His mind moved to his mother's letters, which had been heartbreaking. She could not understand why he refused his leaves. He chuckled humorlessly. Well, she did not see Reed die. She did not know his new chaps and how helpless they were.

Warmed by the sun's rays, the cloud cover below broke

suddenly and Randolph had a clear view of thousands of square miles of northern France. Then the salvo firing began, to the north and far below. German antiaircraft. He saw Hendon and Barton waggle their wings and both were pointing. Randolph waggled his in return. Leaning over his coaming, he saw them. At perhaps ten thousand feet, two B.E. 2 observation planes circling to the north of Bapaume and at least seven miles behind the German lines. Flying in pairs behind and above the observation planes was the escort; four ungainly D.H.2 pusher fighters. Ugly black and brown puffs of exploding shells pockmarked the sky all around the lumbering observation planes.

The twelve gaily painted Albatrosses appeared suddenly, diving in pairs out of a layer of clouds to the north at about seventeen thousand feet. "Tally-ho!" Randolph screamed, pulling the Very pistol from its rack and firing a red star shell. Punching the throttle to the fire wall, he jammed the stick to the left, balancing with rudder until the horizon rotated ninety degrees and all lift was lost, nose dropping. Then with the stick horsed forward, the S.E.5 screamed downward into a near vertical dive with the remaining members of the patrol bunched close behind.

Carefully, Randolph worked his controls until the nose of his fighter was pointed toward the Albatrosses. The powerful engine pulled the little plane downward at a speed that exceeded the most optimistic estimates of its designers. But the Hispano-Suiza was smooth, the howling wires and bracing firm, and the wing spars strong. This airplane would keep its wings in a dive. Anyway, there was no time for concern—for caution. The Germans would arrive at their targets before Number Five Squadron could intercept. Randolph pounded the coaming, pushed the safety lock off, and impatiently caressed the firing tit with his thumb.

A black machine with a jagged yellow arrow stretching the length of its fuselage was leading the German attack. Randolph felt his hate flare. Hollweg. The swine. The killer. The leader of Jasta *Boelcke*. And he was not hanging about high above the fight as he usually did, hoping to pick off a helpless cripple and build up his score. Not today. Then

Randolph noticed only seven of the Albatrosses were bizarrely painted; the remaining five wore the standard camouflage of the German air service. New men. Hollweg was breaking in new men. But Randolph knew they would be picked. Top flyers. It made no difference. Teeth bared, neck muscles tight like steel, he stared through his ring sight, the usual early fear that gripped him when first sighting the enemy overwhelmed and washed away by the hatred he felt for Hollweg. The only thought on his mind was to bring the black and yellow Albatross into his sights. Randolph laughed wildly and spittle sprayed into the slipstream. The Huns would never expect an attack from above and as far as he could tell, the Germans were not as yet aware of the death hurtling down on their tails.

The D.H.2s turned bravely to meet their attackers and the B.E.s banked and dived toward the British lines. Suddenly, brown smoke trailed the leading German machines as twin Spandaus came to life. Immediately, one of the British scout planes dropped off on one wing and fell into a tight spin, dead pilot flopping in his cockpit. Another burst into flames and turned downward, leaving a black smear across the sky. A third lost its propeller and shedding fabric from its top wing, turned toward its own lines. But the fourth D.H. scored, putting a dozen rounds into the engine of a camouflaged Albatross. The German, with a dead Mercedes, began a glide northward.

The sacrifice of the D.H.2s had turned the Germans north and west away from the fleeing observation planes and flattened their dives, causing a loss in speed. The pilot of the lone surviving D.H.2 was unbelievable, charging into the middle of the Jasta and forcing the Germans to break their formation and to take evasive action so that they would not collide with each other and die the way Boelcke died. Another burst from the D.H.2 caught an Albatross in the fuselage, but the entire German formation swirled around the gallant pusher in a twisting, snarling box. Then the Germans saw the S.E.5s.

There was a frantic waggle of wings and the D.H.2 was forgotten as the shark-nosed fighters turned upward to meet these strange S.E.5s plunging from an impossible height. Randolph laughed out loud as he brought a camouflaged enemy plane into the center of his ring sight. At a hundred yards, screaming, "You never met an S.E.5 like this, you murdering bastard," he thumbed the tit. He had a perfect zero deflection killing angle. The Vickers bucked, spent cartridges flew from the breech, and the machine gun spewed ball and tracers that smashed first into the Albatross's upper wing and then squarely into the cockpit. The pilot, riddled by a dozen rounds of .303 ball, died instantly, throwing up his hands and sagging against his safety harness. The plane fell into a flat spin.

As Randolph plunged through the German formation, guns were chattering all around him and tracers etched the sky like insane spiders' webs. He felt a familiar reaction possess him; a fighting madness, a near frenzy to kill more, a heightening of senses and vision to abnormal luminous clarity, and a complete disregard for injury and death itself. He shouted with joy as Leefe Hendon scored, his bullets smashing a German's fuel and oil tanks. Immediately, a green and yellow striped Albatross fell off on one wing and began its flaming plunge.

Calming himself, Randolph glanced at his altimeter. He was down to ten thousand feet already. A sharp turn costs a plane a lot of speed and a dogfight tends to degenerate into speed-killing turns and near stalls with each pilot diving to regain speed, losing altitude, and repeating the cycle.

Pulling the stick back hard into his stomach, Randolph saw the dihedral increase in his wings and the wires, spars, and bracing creaked and snapped under the enormous forces as the dive flattened and the horizon dropped below the hood. His seat sagged under his increased weight and he felt the skin stretched tight against the bones of his face and the blood draining from his head.

Looking upward, Randolph screamed with horror and anger as Hollweg, climbing and making a perfect three-quarter deflection shot, caught the left hand S.E.5 of the last three in the wing root and the fighter's lower left wing ripped away like a postage stamp in a gale. Losing its shape, its balance, and no longer presenting a precise line with its airfoils, the S.E.5 ceased functioning as a winged machine; instead its great speed destroyed it in the rushing gale just as if it had run into a stand of poplars. Weakened by the pull of wires and struts of the shot-away wing, the upper wing cracked, bent up, and then ripped away completely. Randolph saw Flight Lieutenant Cowdry's terrified face turned toward him as the bare fuselage of the scout plane plunged past him like an arrow pointed toward the earth. The young flyer would die the same way Boelcke died, trapped in the coffin of his fuselage. Luckily, Randolph could not hear Cowdry's screams. But that white, contorted face would remain with him for the rest of his life.

Higgins turned toward Hollweg, but McDonald's S.E.5 flashed by with a red and yellow checked Albatross on its tail. Kicking rudder and correcting with his stick, Randolph tried for a flat, offhand turning shot that he had used so successfully with the Nieuport. The S.E.5 reacted like a thoroughbred, skidding on its tail as its nose yawed with the target, but slowing. Showing his experience, the German kicked rudder, and rolled away at the last instant, most of Randolph's rounds taking the Albatross in the sturdy plywood fuselage behind the cockpit. Cursing, Randolph dove for speed and pulled back hard on the stick, climbing up behind the Albatross which had settled again behind McDonald's S.E.5.

The three planes formed a murderous daisy chain. McDonald, taking advantage of the S.E.5's power, pulled back on his stick and scissored back and forth from side to side while gaining altitude. And the German, too, tried to emulate the maneuver, keeping an eye on Randolph, who was four hundred yards behind and sweeping from side to side in his own sine curve, gaining and trying to intersect the German's curling path.

The German fired. McDonald jinked and half rolled away as if he had read the German's mind. But another burst hit the S.E.5's lower wing and engine and Randolph saw coolant or petrol begin to spray into McDonald's slipstream. Gently, the major eased his controls, finally intersecting the intent German's path. The German had completely underestimated the S.E.5's speed and the Albatross quickly filled all three rings of Randolph's sights. Laughing gleefully, he pressed the tit.

His tracers chewed into the Hun's upper wing and smashed into the engine. Although surprised, the German showed he was a master flyer, kicking rudder and snapping into a half roll to the left and then all the way over on his back, dropping his nose down into a graceful curving dive. He was trailing smoke. Then flame and he began to sideslip.

Randolph took a quick look around. The dog fight had deteriorated into a series of individual combats that sprawled over miles of sky. Four funeral pyres rose in thinning black columns, but it was impossible to tell who had died. The doughty D.H.2 was still in the thick of it, its brave pilot fighting with a single camouflaged Albatross. He saw Hollweg's plane far to the west and south engaged with two S.E.5s. But Randolph's obligation was to McDonald and he wanted to kill the German who was sideslipping slowly away.

McDonald circled a fist over his head to show he was well and Randolph returned the signal with the cut throat sign to indicate damage and pointed first at the mist of vapor trailing the S.E.5 and then at the British lines. Nodding understanding and throttling back, the Scotsman turned his plane toward home. Licking his lips and smiling, Randolph plunged after the Boche, following the trail of smoke like a predator trailing the spore of an injured quarry.

Randolph was surprised by how low the dogfight had drifted, his altimeter showing only seven thousand feet as he began his dive. The red and yellow checked Albatross was far below, trailing black smoke, but the flames had actually diminished. Must have been the oil tank that flared for a moment and the clever pilot had managed to keep the flames away from the wing fabric. The pilot? Free of the mad swirl of the dogfight, Randolph had time to think. He racked his brain. He had heard of the color scheme and knew it belonged to someone important. Some prominent killer. Landenberg came to mind—an aristocrat like von Richthofen.

August von Landenberg, the Prussian butcher. Second in command to Hollweg and Max Mueller's replacement. He had seventeen kills.

Randolph laughed out loud and pounded his padded coaming. He wanted Hollweg but would be delighted to kill Landenberg. The German was far below and was flattening his dive into a glide, obviously looking for a landing place. The smoke trailing the Albatross had thinned to a brown haze and Landenberg glided south and east toward the lines. The man was thinking. He was approaching the lines where he knew there would be batteries of German antiaircraft guns and machine gun emplacements to give him cover as he made his dead stick landing.

In a near vertical dive with engine roaring and wires whining and humming, the S.E.5 knifed through the stringy cloud cover, which had been nearly burned away, and the terrain was clear, the ground rising at a frightening speed. White and green lines turned into stone fences and hedgerows and the land became creased and irregular instead of flat and featureless as it appeared from great heights. The patchwork green quilt, tiny specks and clusters of trees became stands of poplars and oak, wrecked buildings, and groups of shell holes, water-filled and reflecting light like dirty brown mirrors. There was a clear meadow just to the east of the Albatross and Landenberg banked gracefully toward it.

Randolph pulled the stick back. His cheeks sagged, his guts felt heavy and low, his increased weight drove him deep into the wicker seat. Bouncing and vibrating and with the wires screaming their objections, the fighter flattened its dive. With the horizon below his cowling again and with the needle of his speed indicator all the way to the red line, he rocketed over a battery of heavy artillery and then a sunken road leading to a communication trench, coal-scuttle helmets of Boche infantrymen bobbing up and down like bubbles in a stream. Some startled white faces turned upward and a rifle or two was fired, but the fighter was too low and its speed too great. The shots went wild.

Landenberg was to his left and not more than three

WAVES OF GLORY / 249

hundred feet high. Rándolph kicked hard left rudder, cutting across the German's course like a chord cutting the arc of a circle. Landenberg would drift directly into an ideal killing angle and with a dead engine, there was nothing Landenberg could do but make his peace with his *Gott*. Randolph laughed again and spittle sprayed. He pulled back on the stick, gaining altitude to position himself above the Albatross. He backed the throttle off. He had made a mistake.

There was a great flash to the south and west as an entire battery of seventy-seven-millimeter antiaircraft guns fired. Immediately, four ugly bursts smeared the sky a thousand feet above the S.E.5 with silver balls and brown and black smoke, white-hot bits of shrapnel raining and leaving white trails like the phosphorus of incendiary bullets. "Cut your fuses, you bloody bastards," Randolph shouted, pounding the side of the fuselage. And they did, the next salvo from another battery to the south exploding close enough to rock the little fighter like a cork in a gale. Anxiously, the major looked at his altimeter, which indicated a thousand feet and eased the stick forward and the S.E.5 dropped its nose. Soon the 77s would not be able to depress low enough to track him. However, he would be within range of small bore. He shrugged.

Another great flash from a stand of brush southwest of the meadow turned his head. The little fighter rocked as shells screamed past and exploded hard on its tail. More flashes and explosions, probably 3.7 centimeter. Hunched behind the windscreen and peering ahead of the Albatross, the major saw something that caught his breath and chilled the pit of his belly. At the far end of the meadow, tethered down and carefully camouflaged, was an observation balloon. The balloon was one of the most feared and hated observation posts the Germans had. Floating fifteen hundred to two thousand feet above its winch, observers in wicker baskets had a clear view of the English rear that gave heavies easy targets. Even ammunition dumps had been destroyed by guns directed by balloonists.

But the hydrogen-filled silk bags were highly flammable and could be easily ignited by phosphorus incendiary bullets. Early in December, Randolph had shot one down over Transloy and had almost been killed himself in the great whooshing ignition of hydrogen gas as it mixed with oxygen above the balloon. Because it was a stationary, explosive target, the concentration of archie around a balloon emplacement was far more dense than that protecting any other target. When Randolph returned from the attack, Cochran counted twenty-seven bullet holes and six shrapnel punctures in the Nieuport. "We'll send your machine to blighty after your next one," the mechanic had said, shaking his head.

Now Landenberg was leading him into another inferno. Biting his lip and setting his jaw, Randolph never changed his course as the Albatross approached the meadow at a very low altitude. Now Randolph could see dozens of mounds of earth like rabbit burrows breaking the surface. Barrels were pointed at him like thickets of young saplings. The Englishman punched the throttle to the last stop and placed his thumb on the tit. The Albatross filled the first ring, but it was over the first emplacements and the first line of machine gunners had a clear shot.

Tracers stormed past and Higgins felt the controls jerk and the plane shudder as ball tore through the little fighter. He could see Landenberg looking over his shoulder. He was grinning. *Grinning!* Cursing, the major crossed his controls and then reversed, skidding from side to side and throwing off the aim of the machine gunners. But he lost speed and Landenberg was out of his range finder. Then he ruddered back to the Albatross and from one-quarter deflection he thumbed the tit and saw his tracers pound the enemy airplane with macelike blows that sent plywood and fabric flying. Risking a stall, Landenberg banked hard to his left toward a stand of poplars and a grassy meadow to the east. There were at least twenty emplacements dug in in front of the trees. It would be point-blank and zero deflection. Randolph had no choice; it was kick right rudder and turn away from Landenberg or die.

Banking to the north and curving away from the guns, Randolph was followed by a hail of tracers until he had climbed above one thousand feet. Then the 77s started again, dozens of bursts following, rocking him, and now and again the thump of shrapnel striking. Hate was boiling in the major's veins and suddenly all reason, all caution was blown away, replaced by a wild animal's frenzied thirst for blood, hunger for the jugular.

Landenberg had landed in the field, his wheel catching on a mound of soft earth and the Albatross ground looped, shedding its wings and flipping on its side like a dead vulture. The Englishman could see three or four gray-clad infantrymen rushing to the wreck from nearby tents. Renewed puffs of black smoke were rising and flames began to lick at the wreckage. The pilot was struggling to free himself and he appeared to be weak and perhaps injured. As Randolph curved toward the meadow, the first two infantrymen had already freed the pilot and had pulled him clear and placed him on a stretcher. The Englishman began his dive.

Carefully, two of the soldiers picked up the stretcher and began to walk toward the balloon installation. Far to the north and temporarily free of antiaircraft fire, Randolph throttled back and then curved back toward the group, bringing them into his ring sight. Within seconds he had bored in so close, he could see the red crosses on the arm bands of the stretcher bearers and the blood on Landenberg's leg and flying jacket. His helmet was off and his blond hair was blowing in the wind. The German pilot turned toward the approaching S.E.5. He was very young, like so many of Randolph's dead pilots. The madics, too, turned their faces to the approaching fighter and Randolph could see that they, too, were just teenage boys. There was no fear there, the boys apparently convinced their red crosses protected them from attack.

Machine guns began to fire and more tracers raced to meet the S.E.5. The major could feel the fighter tremble from the strike of shot and a half dozen slugs shattered his instrument panel and his compass exploded, splattering his left leg with alcohol and stinging his cheek with bits of glass. But nothing could stop Randolph. Eyes wide, lips skinned back into a grin that collapsed into roaring laughter, he thumbed the tit at the long range of four hundred yards. He could not miss.

Dirt spurted from the field in tall brown clouds of dust, shattered rocks, and clods, and marched toward the stretcher. The surprised bearers dropped Landenberg, hurled themselves to the ground, and began clawing at the earth frantically, trying to escape the death roaring toward them with their fingernails. Randolph wanted the stretcher, but approaching from the rear of the group, all three men were lined up perfectly. The Vickers stitched a stream of ball through first one bearer, then Landenberg, and finally the last medic. Randolph felt an amalgam of intense excitement and joy, deep warmth, and his mouth was suddenly filled with saliva. Throttling back two notches, he flattened his dive and worked his rudder bar back and forth, the Vickers spraying the group with a long burst, the hammer blows jerking the trio spasmodically like victims of epilepsy; blood, dirt, brains, and gore flying. Finally, the end of the belt jerked up from the tank and the firing pin clicked on an empty chamber.

Jamming the throttle full forward and roaring over the corpses, Randolph leaned over the coaming and waved a fist back over his elevator. He shrieked with laughter. "Three letters home, you bloody bastards!" he screamed. Then, leveling off at no more than twenty feet, he hopped over a copse of trees and raced to the south and the safety of the British lines.

Randolph was the last pilot to return from the patrol. Cutting his switch as he taxied to the end of the flight line, his fighter became the tenth S.E.5 in the row. The engine had not yet gasped its last when chief mechanic William Cochran, followed by his four-man crew, raced up. While the mechanics stared in amazement at the torn and ripped wings and fuselage, Cochran helped the major down from the cockpit. "Flight Lieutenant Cowdry bought it," Randolph muttered. "Who else? Who else, Sergeant?"

"Flight Lieutenant Baldwin, sir." The old sergeant sighed and avoided Randolph's eyes. "A flamer, sir."

A cold hand closed on the major's throat and he turned toward the farmhouse. The mechanic's voice stopped him.

"By your leave, sir," Cochran said, waving at the S.E.5. Randolph stopped, turned, and walked back to the plane. "Upon my word, Major, did you fly through a threshing machine?" the mechanic asked, peering through a one-foot rip in the fabric midway between the cockpit and the tail. "Two broken ribs, a severed stay." He gestured at the perforated wings. "I can see a broken wing rib from here, two shot-out compression braces, and your main upper wing spar was nicked and splintered and Lord knows what else, sir. There must be a hundred holes in her."

"Do what you can," Randolph said, impatient for his first Scotch. "If she's too badly chewed up, scrap her and I'll fly a reserve."

"Right, sir." And then to the four wide-eyed mechanics staring at the torn fighter, he said, "Step lively, men. Into the hangar with her." Quickly the mechanics gripped the aircraft and began pushing it into the hangar. Randolph turned and walked to the farmhouse.

Captain Hartley Carter questioned Major Randolph Higgins and wrote the major's report. It was nearly noon and Randolph had stripped off his heavy flying kit and was on his second Johnnie Walker before Carter sat across the desk from him. His body ached and his head was a stone and he sank down with his chin almost touching his chest, his face limned with a gray patina of fatigue. He could hear the pilots' celebrating voices coming from the mess tent. They had shot down eight Albatross D.2s to a loss of two S.E.5s. But Randolph's mind was on his losses—Cowdry's face looming through the effects of the Scotch; a book of horror, white, strangling on his own screams, beginning a death ride that would take over a minute to complete. Interminable. A long, long time to think about it. And Baldwin. Another young, bright-faced lad immolated slowly in his burning fighter. But the squadron had a victory and the party was on. But not for Randolph. His drinking would be solitary over two letters.

"You had a kill?" Hartley Carter began.

Randolph looked up. "Two," he answered, lighting a Havana cigar from a box Walter had sent him. He did not particularly enjoy the harsh, biting tobacco, but it was a form of celebration after a kill. Today he would smoke two.

"Southeast of Bapaume?"

"Quite right. The first at about eleven thousand feet, a dozen rounds into the cockpit. He was a dead man long before he hit." The memory brought a smile to Randolph's face and he drew on the Havana.

Hartley Carter nodded. "Captain McDonald and Lieutenant Leefe Hendon witnessed the kill." He turned his lips under and drummed his temple with the pencil. "But we have no witnesses to the second kill," the adjutant added.

"I don't give a tinker's dam. That Kraut is still dead." The squadron leader laughed wildly and tossed off the rest of his drink. Sergeant Major York recharged his glass.

"Where, Major?"

Randolph sipped his drink thoughtfully. "It began south of Bapaume. It was *Oberleutnant* August von Landenberg. I recognized his paint scheme. I put a burst into him—he was on McDonald's tail." He stared hard at Carter. "McDonald has got to have seen us."

"Yes, sir. He saw the Kraut hit and dive out of the dogfight with you in pursuit. But no one saw the kill."

Randolph tapped his desk. "I boffed him to the south about a mile from the lines on a straight line between Bapaume and Bailleul."

"Altitude?"

Randolph's smile had the dust of death on it. "Zero." He broke into maniacal laughter. Carter chewed his lower lip, Longacre stopped typing and looked up from his machine, Sergeant Major York stared at his major.

"Zero, sir. Are you sure, sir?"

It took Randolph a few moments to regain his composure. Then he gasped between chuckles, "As sure as von Landenberg is a corpse. As sure as Hollweg is writing a letter home to Landenberg's Prussian parents." The convulsive laughter returned, the major bending at the waist and holding his stomach.

* * *

Two hours later, Randolph was still at his desk, sipping his fourth Scotch and studying his pilots' reports. He had just lit his second cigar when the two officers arrived. One, a captain, was the effeminate Wilfrid Freeman from division. The other was a major who Randolph had never seen before. Longacre, Carter, and York all came to their feet while Randolph remained seated, chewing on his cigar and staring up expectantly at the newcomers who stood rigidly, almost at attention in front of his desk, swagger sticks smartly tucked under their right arms. Both were in tailored uniforms that glowed with spit and polish.

The major was a fat, middle-aged man with a confident, haughty look of a career officer on the rise. "I'm Major Liam Townshend from Corps," he said uneasily, like a man about to plunge into icy water.

Randolph did not offer a chair or a drink. Instead, he blew a cloud of smoke into the air and sank back into the battered cushions of his chair, contempt burning in his eyes. Townshend wrinkled his nose disdainfully at the pungent fumes and continued. "It has been reported through Swiss channels that this morning an S.E.5 from Number Five Squadron killed three Germans on the ground."

Randolph took another puff of smoke into his mouth and then blew it toward the major. Anger flickered in the officer's eyes as he continued. "The men were helpless. Two stretcher bearers and a wounded pilot—August von Landenberg. The stretcher bearers were wearing Red Cross arm bands."

Chuckling, Randolph held the Havana before his eyes and turned it, examining it as if it were a valuable heirloom. "I flew that fighter—I killed them. What took you so long? It's been almost eight hours," he said, grinning. He put the cigar back in his mouth. Longacre, York, and Carter stirred uneasily.

Freeman spoke in his high-pitched voice. "Good Lord, sir. Not medics—not helpless men?"

Before Randolph could answer, the major said, "Dash it all, Major Higgins. Corps doesn't approve—the government doesn't approve of the murder of helpless men. There's the small matter of the Geneva Conventions the Crown signed over fifty years ago."

Randolph felt the liquor boiling in his stomach and the fire spread through his veins to every vestige of his being. "Murder! The Geneva Conventions!" he shouted, straightening and leaning forward, stabbing the cigar at the major.

"Yes," Townshend said grimly. "We fight like gentlemen. There are certain rules of warfare we must—"

Randolph bolted out of his chair. "Gentlemen?" He rocked on his heels with uncontrolled laughter. Longacre, Carter, and York looked at each other anxiously. The staff officers stood impassively. "Gentlemen!" he repeated incredulously. "Tell Cowdry and Baldwin about the gentle art of killing. Tell them about the Geneva Conventions. Tell all my dead boys."

"Please, Major Higgins," Townshend said. "There is no need for rudeness."

"How polite is a Spandau? A Parabellum? How polite is it to kill my boys?" Randolph gestured overhead. "That bloody bastard Landenberg had seventeen kills." He leaned forward, eyes narrow, jaw jutting. "He was a butcher and I made sure he wouldn't give me any more letters to write home." He stabbed the cigar at the major as if it were a weapon and growled, "Tell that to Corps, you bloody spit and polish popinjay."

There was a long silence and every eye focused on the officer from Corps. Townshend spoke, his face a red mask of rage, his voice trembling. "I'm afraid, Major, this matter will go all the way to Whitehall—to a military court."

"Let it go to Buckingham," Randolph spat. "The Crown is paying us to kill and by Jove, there're getting their money's worth."

The two officers whirled and pounded through the door.

An hour before sunset, the black Albatross with the yellow arrow on its fuselage hedge-hopped the poplars and roared over the field, twin Spandaus blazing. Two mechanics and an armorer were killed and three other men wounded. A bundle with a red banner tied around it fluttered to the ground as the enemy plane banked sharply and disappeared to the west. Only one antiaircraft crew at the west end of the field managed to fire a burst from a Lewis gun. The plane escaped undamaged.

An hour later after sending up Hendon, McDonald, Gaskell, and Barton on a sweep around the field, Randolph stood in the mess hall with all of the remaining pilots and all of the off-duty men gathered around. Anger was on the faces of the silent men, a tangible force that filled the room. He opened the package. It was a cardboard container weighted with a half dozen bullets. It contained a letter. Randolph read it silently to himself and then—answering the curious stares—he read it to the squadron: "Major Randolph Higgins, This morning an S.E.5 with an orange propeller spinner murdered August von Landenberg and two stretcher bearers clearly marked with Red Cross arm bands. It is believed the aircraft was flown by you. You are also the man who killed *Hauptmann* Max Mueller when he was helpless to defend himself. These are acts of barbarism and savagery outlawed by the Geneva Conventions."

Randolph threw his head back and laughed uproariously while confused and anxious looks were exchanged by the men. The major continued reading: "I would like to settle this matter between us. This would be done privately, like gentlemen; if the word has any meaning to you. I will be at fourteen thousand feet over Longueval tomorrow morning at oh-eight hundred. Longueval is midway between our lines. I will be alone. Meet me, if you have the courage. *Gott strafe* England! Major Bruno Hollweg, Commander, Jasta Boelcke

"Sir," flight Lieutenant Anderson pleaded. "You won't do it."

"It's a trap, Major," Dunlap shouted.

"Hear! Hear!" resounded in the room.

Randolph held up both hands, silencing the shouts. "It's worth a go." There were groans. "I want that Kraut."

Clutching the letter and smiling happily, Randolph left the room.

* * *

The next morning at 0715 Randolph took off in a new S.E.5 with the orange spinner attached to the propeller hub. It was a fine aircraft and he had put it through its paces the previous afternoon. Its left rudder was a little heavy, but otherwise it performed beautifully. As he climbed and pointed the nose of the fighter toward Longueval, he smiled, remembering how his pilots had pleaded with him to allow a patrol to accompany him. But Randolph refused, afraid the appearance of other S.E.5s might drive Bruno Hollweg off.

There was cloud cover similar to that of the previous day, but much lighter. In fact, as he approached Longueval at fourteen thousand feet, he broke into a clear bright sky surrounded on every quarter by towering ramparts of clouds that rose in rows and terraces like boxes and balconies. Soaring full to the heavens, he was in a vast coliseum. It was the Palladium, the Empire, the Hippodrome, the Palace combined and he a featured performer. He looked around for the telltale speck on the horizon but saw nothing. The clouds rolled and boiled, flashing lightning as if they were impatient for the drama to begin.

Banking, he scanned every horizon. Still nothing. He pounded his instrument panel. Then his eye caught a glint to the north. Airfoils leaving trails of mist behind as an airplane emerged from some high-flying clouds. A black Albatross. Bruno Hollweg. Randolph screamed with joy as he kicked rudder and banked toward the enemy. He jammed the throttle to full military power.

Closing at a combined speed of over two hundred fifty miles an hour, the two fighters closed the range quickly. In his mind's eye Randolph could see David A. Reed burning and jerking as Hollweg's bullets tore into him. *The Geneva Conventions*. He laughed and then licked his lips. There was a total lack of fear. Only a driving passion to kill—to kill even if it meant his own life. A compulsion to not only kill but also to wipe away the memory of Reed's death that had tortured him day and night for months. And there were all the other dead young boys.

One way or another, the German would never leave the arena alive. He would riddle him. Ram him. He would drive his propeller shaft down the throat of the Mercedes. The black vulturelike wings grew in his range finder. He held his fire as his target grew, his bull's eye the huge yellow propeller boss in the center of the whirling fan of the propeller. Struts, wires, the exhaust mounted on the right side and top of the Mercedes became clear, the radiator under the low top wing, and the pilot hunched down behind his guns and range finder. There was something strange about this machine—the configuration was not the same; did not fit precisely with the memory of the other Albatrosses he had fought.

The nose of the Albatross blossomed with bright sparks of fire as the twin Spandaus were triggered to life. Randolph thumbed the tit and his Vickers jumped and stuttered, his stick and rudder bar pulsing as the gun shook the aircraft. Tracers smoked past, snapping and whispering in his ears. Several thudded into his upper wing and he saw his smash into the German's nose and wings. He thought he saw splinters fly from Hollweg's propeller and he held his controls steady, the enemy plane filling his ring sights. Then the whole horizon. They were very close—under a hundred yards.

Grinning, Randolph made no attempt to change his course. Just before the point of impact, the German pulled back his stick and hopped over the S.E.5 like a runner clearing a hurdle, his undercarriage grazing the Englishman's top wing. Immediately taking advantage of the S.E.5's turning ability, the Englishman kicked left rudder and horsed the stick to the left and back. He came around expecting to find the Albatross swinging into his ring sight. It was not there. Instead, Hollweg had curved away and up, gaining altitude and making his turn far out of range.

Randolph's stomach churned with anger and frustration. The rugged fighter appeared undamaged and it was much faster than any Albatross D.2 he had ever seen. Maybe it was powered with the new Mercedes D.IIIa engine—a new power plant rumored to have close to two hundred horsepower. Like a Nieuport, the outer chord of the upper wing appeared longer and the chord of the lower shorter, and a new strut had been added from the leading interplane strut to the leading edge—no doubt to improve visibility and prevent flutter in high-speed dives. In any event, it was a radically modified D.2 or an advanced type—stronger, faster, with better visibility and a better acrobat. Randolph felt his guts tighten and a familiar sour taste filled his mouth.

Grimly, the Englishman pulled the stick back and made a wide sweeping turn toward Hollweg. The German avoided the head-on pass, perhaps suspecting his enemy would ram him if given the chance. Bearing to this right away from Randolph, the two aircraft passed each other and then both pilots banked, forming a circular pattern with each aircraft on the ends of a diameter. Circling hard and trying desperately to close on each other's tails, the diameter shrank rapidly and Randolph found his bank steepening and speed bleeding away. Closer and closer the planes whirled in their murderous carousel, the pilots staring across the shrinking distance between them. Neither man dared break the pattern.

Randolph was so close he could see Hollweg's black jacket, white silk scarf. He wore the usual brown helmet of the German flying service and his goggles were up. Although his face had been darkened by exhaust and gun smoke, he appeared to be fair and young. In fact, the countenance appeared far more cherubic than lethal. His eyes were blue and glinted with hatred.

Horrified, Randolph felt his controls go mushy as the S.E.5, banking almost vertically, began to lose lift and threatened a high-speed stall. Hollweg, too, was in trouble, but he managed to flatten his turn and his great engine pulled him up and out of the circle and above Randolph. He began his turn toward the British plane. In a moment, Hollweg would have his killing angle.

Randolph had no choice. Kicking right rudder, he jammed the stick forward and split-essed out of the near stall into a power dive, the Albatross trailing. The major could see Hollweg in his rear-vision mirror, two hundred yards behind and gaining. The twin machine guns danced with red muzzle flashes and tracers smoked past, the stick jerking in his hands as the rudder took a blow.

Randolph kicked rudder and pulled the stick back, then

rolled to his right in two quick, snapping barrel rolls. Sawing the rudder bar back and forth, he rolled, dipped, and weaved, throwing off the German's aim and pointing the nose of the fighter toward a nearby cloud bank. The German was firing again as Randolph plunged into the milky white cover. Watching his lateral bubble, compass, and altimeter, the major pulled back hard on his stick and climbed, clawing for life-saving attitude. Then a half roll and he headed back toward Longueval. Within seconds, he burst into the brilliance of the clear sky over the village.

Like a hyena deprived of its meal, the black Albatross was below and ahead of him and sniffing at the clouds where the English airplane had disappeared. The Englishman laughed. Hollweg still did not appreciate the S.E.5's great climbing ability. He had the advantage now. He jerked the S.E.5 over onto its back and in a single smooth motion brought the stick back hard again, tramping on the rudder bar and whipping the inverted fighter into a split-ess that accelerated it downward into a screaming dive, earth, sky, and the entire arena whirling around him. He brought the nose of the S.E.5 to the black Albatross's tail.

Showing his experience, Hollweg turned the Albatross brutally to meet his attacker, but the slower turning speed of the German fighter took its toll. The Vickers yammered and tracers smashed into Hollweg's upper wing and fuselage, a cabane strut disintegrating into a stream of splinters. Then the German was firing and in a wink the planes passed each other. Randolph cried happily. Fabric was ripping from Hollweg's upper wing and he was losing coolant. The Hun whipped his damaged machine into a tight turn, heading toward the clouds where there was a slight division between towering, dangerous thunderheads. With the S.E.5 close on his tail, Hollweg dove desperately for a dense mass of cirrus just to the right of the cleft in the clouds, which now had taken on the appearance of a great canyon between white Alpine towers.

Two specks were high in the canyon between the thunderheads. "Swine!" Randolph screamed. "A trap! A gentleman. You bloody bastards."

He was so close to the Albatross he could feel the S.E.5 bounce in his enemy's prop wash. Ignoring the two specks that had enlarged into a pair of Albatross D.2s, the major punched the tit. The Vickers spit out Randolph's hatred and the smoke and cordite that blew back into his face hit him like a double charge of Johnnie Walker. He saw his bullet strikes on his enemy's radiator and engine. Pushing the stick forward gently, he brought the stream of tracers down, trying for a killing shot into the cockpit. Randolph screamed with joy as motes of fire burst from the Albatross's engine and then red flame streamed back and black smoke struck the Englishman in the face. Releasing the tit, he reveled in the smell of burning oil, petrol, fabric, and wood. The Albatross dropped off on one wing and began its last plunge, Hollweg standing, screaming, and beating at his burning flying clothes.

A quick glance told Randolph the two Albatrosses were screaming down in power dives and would be in range within seconds. He knew he was almost out of ammunition and his only chance was the clouds—wing-breaking winds and lightning be damned. He rolled into a dive and pointed the nose of the fighter toward the base of a thunderhead where rain fell in a gray mass and lightning flashed. But the Albatross could outdive the S.E.5 and the pair of enemy fighters gained slowly. "Come on! Come on, old bird!" Randolph shouted, glancing into his rear-vision mirror.

The two enemy planes had separated slightly, one back of his right elevator and the other his left. They would catch him in a cross fire. Tracers smoked and then more white trails whipped past and Randolph could hear the roar and clatter of the four Spandaus. Dropping below two thousand feet, the clouds were very close and he was entering the first filmy wisps. More strikes and fabric ripped from his top wing. Horrified, he felt the stick jerk and the controls grow sloppy with slack. Looking at his left wing, he saw the aileron shot from its hinges and tear loose, followed by huge patches of fabric, exposing ribs, spares, and control wires. With its trim lost, and bouncing and vibrating, the S.E.5 dropped its left wing and tried to roll to the left. Randolph corrected by horsing the stick to the right and gripping the stick with all his strength.

Instinctively, he hunched forward trying to make himself a smaller target when his instrument panel disintegrated and a red-hot poker struck his left leg. The pain was excruciating and he could feel warm liquid in his boot. Suddenly the Hispano-Suiza began to vibrate and oil squirted like black geysers through bullet holes in the top and side of the cowling. The engine shrieked and clattered and a loose connecting rod beat itself to fragments. He felt heat. He smelled burning petrol as thick black smoke filled the cockpit, but he dared not cut the ignition. He would never make the cloud and his left leg felt paralyzed. But there was a small foothill, a precursor of the thunderstorm directly ahead. He plunged into the white vapor and finally cut his ignition. The Spandaus stopped. He pulled the stick back into his stomach.

The cloud was much larger than he had at first thought. He was at a thousand feet, almost level, but flames were creeping back from the engine. Reducing the stick to three-quarters right, he tramped the rudder bar despite the pain, nursing the airplane carefully, allowing the damaged left wing to drop and pull the S.E.5 to the left toward the beginnings of a left-hand spin. He had to take the chance. Then, as the fighter began to turn, he kicked hard right rudder and forced the nebulous spin into a sideslip, blowing the flames away from the cockpit. Watching his compass and groaning with pain, he nursed the falling plane south. He broke out of the cloud.

He was two hundred feet above no-man's-land and the Albatrosses were gone. Flames had broken through the fire wall, bursting through the shattered instrument panel and began leaping up through the floorboards. Blood had filled his boot and spread across the floorboards. He could smell burning leather and blood as his boots caught fire and there was a pop like a gunshot as the alcohol in his compass came to a boil and the instrument exploded. He screamed and beat at the flames with a single glove.

No longer answering to the controls, the airplane dropped in a flat turn toward a jungle of barbed wire. A wheel caught on a concertina and the S.E.5 moving at at least eighty miles an hour spun around like a child's top, shedding its top wing, and crashing into a shell hole. Randolph felt the nose plunge into the soft, wet soil. Then the fighter gyrated wildly, bouncing out of one hole and into another, spars, braces, and ribs parting like gunshots, finally coming to rest with its belly to the sky.

Randolph, thrown from side to side and feeling his head crack against the coaming time and again, was knocked into blackness. But the darkness could not blot out the heat—a pitiless, searing inferno that burned layer after layer of clothes from his body. He was hanging from the cockpit, burning alive and too weak to release his safety lock. Never had he felt pain like this. He was screaming and continued to scream when the strong hands reached him.

"Cut the bloody straps a'fore we burn our bollocks off, you lead-swingin' arse hole," a strident, hoarse voice commanded.

"Right, Sergeant."

There was a tugging and sawing and suddenly he fell headfirst into two pairs of strong arms and then with mingled curses he felt himself crash into the bottom of the hole in a heap with his rescuers. His nose was in mud and it stank of cordite and rotten flesh. He heard the deliberate pounding of a Maxim firing in the distance.

"Grab 'im by the 'and. I've got t'uther," the hoarse voice said. "And keep your arse down 'til we're through our wire. Fritzie will bugger you with seven-nine-two ball."

"Right, Sergeant."

Randolph felt his hands and wrists grabbed and then he was being pulled across the muddy ground. The Maxim fired again and he heard zinging and pinging sounds as bullets struck the wire above his head, particles of rust falling on his face and into his eyes. He screamed with pain as his wounded leg scraped over a rock and then a strand of barbed wire dug into his side and he felt burned skin peeling off his side and thigh. A new level of pain had been invented for him and him alone. Darkness blotted out the horror.

The pain jarred him back into consciousness. He was

lying in the open with hundreds of others on a stretcher with a blanket over him. There was a wrecked farmhouse nearby with a large white banner emblazoned with a red cross hanging from it. He was in a casualty clearing station. There were groans, shouts, screams all around. A white-hot pain added Randolph's voice. It was an hour before someone came to him. He was given water and then he was injected with morphia. Pain fading, he dozed off into cool darkness.

The rocking and the clatter of steel wheels on rails awakened him. The pain rushed back. He was in a hospital train jammed into a carriage with dozens of others. He was assaulted with the stench of wounds that had rotted, vomit, stale urine, unwashed bodies, and excrement. There was a dressing on his leg wound and his flying clothes had been cut away from most of his torso. A greasy dressing had been smeared on his burns and he was covered with gauze. The pain returned and an exhausted orderly injected him. As he drifted off, he heard voices. "Bloody crime—a scandal. All of them left out too long. We'll lose half of them to gangrene, sister."

A woman spoke. "This one, Colonel, the flyer?"

"First-, second-, and third-degree burns and a gunshot wound, poor chap. And he's lost blood. I'm afraid he's bought it, nurse."

They're talking about me, Randolph thought. *About me!* He drifted off again.

XI

The room was large, white, and there were other men with him. Randolph could hear them groaning. He could smell alcohol and ointments, and strangely, his feet were too high and someone had built a framework over his bed—a latticework that kept the blankets from touching his body. "Where am I?" he said, turning his head from side to side. "Where am I?"

"The Queen Victoria Hospital for Officers at Hyde Park, Major," a soft but firm voice answered from behind him. He turned his head and immediately a white-clad beauty was leaning over him. The face was diffused; perhaps by the light, perhaps by his drugged state, but without a doubt, it was lovely, white, and delicate like a doll. Her dark hair of burnt umber was swept up beneath the white cap and her forehead was smooth and intelligent. Sad eyes were a mysterious blend of blue and green, cheekbones high and vaulted in a classic way, her full lips chiseled in graceful sweeps like the wings of a gull. "I'm Kimberly Piper, your QA," she said, leaning close to his face. He could smell a unique jasmine and hyacinth perfume that struck like a spring breeze after the foul stench of burned flesh and rotting wounds.

"How long have I been in London?"

"Three days, Major."

"This is the burn ward."

"Quite right, Major."

He felt pain in his left leg and then his entire right side. He gasped, "I've bought it. I heard the nurse and doctor on the train. They said . . ."

Her cool hand on his forehead interrupted him. "You didn't buy the farm, Major. Just a ticket to blighty."

Running his hand down and up onto the cradle, he said ruefully, "Those Krauts fried me."

She nodded and he saw a sad glint in the remarkable eyes. "You have first- , second- , and third-degree burns over most of the right side of your body and chest from your neck to your knee and a gunshot wound in the upper thigh of your left leg."

"My mouth feels like the Kraut army marched through it."

"You bit yourself when you crashed and you probably won't have any hair growing on the right side of your chest, but with time and care you will recover."

"I'll be scarred."

"Yes, I'm afraid so, Major."

He was suddenly possessed by a new horrifying thought. "Did anything else burn off?" He ran a hand down the cradle to a point over his groin.

A mischievous smile twisted the perfect lips. "No, Major, your, ah—social life remains intact."

A new shot of pain made him writhe and groan. He heard another man two beds away shout incoherently. Kimberly turned her head and then quickly reached for a hypodermic needle.

"For me? Lotus land again?"

"Yes, Major."

He felt the needle puncture his arm. "My mother, my father," he anguished. "I want to see them."

"They've been here and they've seen you," she said, straightening and returning the hypodermic to its alcohol bath.

"My mother. She's so . . ."

"Your mother was happy to see you. The first reports were that you were dead." She smiled wryly. "Your present condition is an improvement over that."

"I crashed in no-man's-land."

She nodded. "Quite right. No-man's-land."

Randolph was seized by a great sadness. "Those Tommies. Those poor bloody blokes risked their lives for me. I'll never even know their names . . ."

Brenda, Rebecca, and Bernice were at the hospital every day, sitting in the waiting room, waiting for a chance to see Randolph. Walter, Reginald, Hugh, and Lloyd were in and out, whenever their schedules permitted. It was hideous. Even Randolph's neck was burned and he was always drugged. And the entire third floor of the huge building was filled with burned young men. Many were aviators, others officers from the new tank corps, and still others had been burned by *flammenwerfers*. The staff was overwhelmed. Not until the fourth day did the women talk to a doctor.

Doctor Oliver Henniker was a tall, thin, middle-aged man with a tired, harried look. He directed his words at Rebecca while Bernice and Brenda stood at her sides. "He came in

with first-, second-, and third-degree burns over forty percent of his body, with a gunshot wound in his left leg, and
suffering from shock. The gunshot wound had been well
served at the field hospital and on the ship, but burns are
hard to treat and he was suffering from shock. Shock must
be treated first. We use the latest medications—morphia,
atropine, strychnine, camphorated oil, and caffeine and at
first we surrounded him with hot water bottles."

"Hot water bottles?" Rebecca said.

"Of course."

"But his burns?"

Henniker sighed. "He's out of shock and I ordered bicarbonate of soda baths three times daily beginning yesterday.
And, of course, the burned areas are left undressed and daily
I cut away all necrotic and sloughing material. Then we
bathe him in a peroxide solution and dust with stearate of
zinc and thymol iodide and soon we will expose him to the
direct rays of the sun . . ."

"Please, Doctor," Rebecca interrupted him. "Will my boy
recover? That's what I want to know."

Henniker recoiled with the pique of a college professor
whose lecture had been interrupted by an unruly student.
"Why yes, madam. It's a matter of how complete."

"How complete?"

Henniker cleared his throat. "Quite. There will be heavy
scarring and a loss of mobility in his right leg, which suffered most of the third-degree burns."

Rebecca's eyes narrowed and her face twisted strangely.
"He won't return to the front?"

"No, madam. Not unless there's a miracle."

Slowly, a smile spread across Rebecca's face.

When not at the hospital or caring for Rodney and
Nathan, Brenda sought time to be with Reginald. Despite a
left arm that was weak and slightly bent, he was up for a
fourth stripe. Something was afoot at Whitehall and the
commander often worked long hours into the night. "My pet
project may go," he said, laughing one evening over dinner

at the Savoy. "But we keep our secrets. We don't have big mouths like Nivelle."

"But you can't see active duty," Brenda said hesitantly. "You haven't recovered."

Brenda saw a rare glimpse of Reginald's temper. "Me! A bloody C-three. Never!"

"C-three?"

"The lowest grade of malingerer—a wounded hero looking for a cushy post."

Brenda felt her patience thinning. "My God, Reginald. Everyone knows you were wounded—severely wounded." She nodded at his arm and his hand, which still showed a thumb and first finger that were bent and stiff.

"I'm as good as the next man," he said deep in his throat.

"Of course you are," she agreed, conciliation in her voice. She reached across the table and took his hand. "I can't bear the thought of losing you, Reggie. And if you're not one hundred percent fit, you could endanger others."

"I know. I know," he said, his brow wrinkling in long lines of frustration. Then he raised his arm and flexed the thumb and fingers of his injured hand. "It'll be ship-shape soon—you'll see."

"Of course." She felt her dinner churn in her stomach and she averted her eyes.

Once or twice a week, the impatient lovers would drive to Reginald's house—a sanctum that became an island in the storm. Here for a few frantic moments they were in another world of their own, isolated from the horror and losing themselves in each other.

Brenda wondered at the change in herself. After Geoffry's death she had been seized by an inexplicable aversion to love—especially the thought of physical love. She remembered how she had put off Reginald, not really understanding the strange confusion of emotions and forces dueling within her. Not until he was wounded and she sensed he had feelings that he was less of a man than he had been, had Brenda been able to accept him. Certainly, there was a drive to love him because he was a man and she needed him, but there had been something else—a strange feeling she had known when Rodney or Nathan had been ill. It was the compulsion every mother knows to hold her sick baby close —to even hope, somehow, the closeness would transfer the fevers and pain from the baby to herself. To see the baby healthy and smiling and bright. Did she feel this with Reginald? Doubtless, she had brought him joy and restored confidence in himself. And, strangely, she began to find solace in his wounds. They kept him off the bridge of a ship where she was sure he would return if he could, wounds be damned.

Reginald was the ultimate lover, worshiping at Brenda's body. Always careful to caress and manipulate those secret places that pushed her to the brink of hysteria, he insisted that the young American always disrobe in front of him and then he would stare at her body, his eyes moving over her with so much hunger she felt a tingling wherever they fell. One evening, pushed beyond the limits, she tumbled him backward onto the bed and clawed at his buttons. Laughing, he disrobed and then Brenda said, "Now, it's my turn." She pointed to the foot of the bed. "You perform."

Scars and injured arm forgotten, a laughing Reginald stood and then posed and pirouetted in a parody of a music hall entertainer. Finally, Brenda shouted, "Enough!" and Reginald leapt into her arms.

The days passed slowly for Randolph and he grew well acquainted with burns and their painful treatment. Kimberly Piper was in constant attendance and Doctor Oliver Henniker made daily visits. Randolph soon discovered most of the other men in the room were even more badly burned than he. In fact, the patient next to him, a South African captain of the Tank Corps, had third-degree burns over most of his torso, chest, and face. It seemed impossible that he could still be alive. His lips, nose, eyebrows, eyelids, ears, and most of the flesh of his chin and one cheek had been burned off and he lay motionless on his back day after day staring at the ceiling sightlessly through eyes with pupils and corneas burned away. Even through thick layers of salves his flesh appeared black and rough like charcoal forgotten in a dirty fireplace. With no lips and his skin charred away, most of the blackened teeth on one side were visible almost to the back of his jaw and he seemed to have a perpetual grin on his face like an exhumed body of one long dead. His breathing, clogged by mucus, popped and bubbled like a thick stew boiling on a stove top.

He was kept heavily sedated; however, each afternoon it was allowed to wear off and liquids were forced down his throat by Nurse Piper and two orderlies. This was done until the tanker began to gag and vomit. As his senses returned the man began to scream in a high falsetto shriek like the Royal Scot approaching a crossing. Then he was given morphia and more liquids were forced into him subcutaneously and by a rectal tube.

One night Randolph was awakened by rustling sounds like dry leaves blown by the wind. They were coming from the South African's bed. At first the major thought he was suffering more drug-induced hallucinations. Then he decided the sounds were definitely coming from the burned tanker, but they were incoherent. Turning as much as his painful burns and leg wound would allow, Randolph could see minute movements of the charred mouth in the dim glow of the night lights. Listening carefully and straining toward the captain, he heard words hissed through the ruined mouth and burned-through cheeks. "Mate. Mate. Kill me. Please kill me. Kill me, mate . . ." The voice trailed off and Randolph remained awake for a long time despite the effects of the morphia.

The next morning Randolph gestured at the inert captain and said to Kimberly Piper, "He wants to die."

"How do you know?"

"He told me."

"Impossible. He can't speak."

Randolph felt anger. "Do him a favor, nurse. Be a human being!"

"Why do you think I'm here, Major," she said sharply. Carrying a tray loaded with empty vials and medication bottles, she turned and left.

That night Doctor Henniker instead of Kimberly administered morphia to the captain. It was an unusually large injection. Within an hour, the captain stopped breathing and by midnight his body had been wheeled away. Randolph felt the same hollow feeling of loss he had known when one of his men had been shot down, yet there was a deep sense of relief in knowing the South African would suffer no more. His suspicion that Henniker had killed the captain grew, especially in the following days when both the doctor and Kimberly seemed preoccupied and never mentioned the death of the captain.

Randolph learned much about medical treatment and terminology. At the end of the second week at a rare moment when his head felt fully cleared, Doctor Henniker entered with Kimberly and stood staring down at the aviator. The doctor gestured at a hypodermic.

"No, Doctor. Please. Not this time," Randolph pleaded. "I've been adrift since I came in here."

"But I'm going to examine you. It may be very painful."

"Please, Doctor, let me try." He nodded at the needle in Nurse Piper's hand. "I'm becoming dependent."

Henniker grimaced. "Very well, Major." He pulled the bed covers back off the cradle and leaned over the aviator's body with a torch in one hand and an instrument in the other. Kimberly Piper stood by with a clipboard and pencil. Randolph felt the instrument probing but choked back the pain.

"Heavy eschars, granulations, and bebs on the right leg." He glanced up at Randolph. "Your leg suffered the most—third-degree burns. When third-degree burns heal, they heal with a degree of scar tissue which is greater than any other healing process in the body."

"I won't lose it?"

"No, Major Higgins. But you will lose mobility."

"Work a rudder bar?"

The doctor snorted. "I wouldn't lay my bit on it. We will splint it to avoid contracture."

"If that doesn't work?"

"Skin grafts, but I'm afraid you'll have a stiff leg for the rest of your life." Henniker turned to the nurse. "There will be heavy scarring of the neck, chest, and torso, but not as severe as the leg. Now we should be able to dress his chest, torso, and upper leg with sterile gauze soaked in picric acid. Change daily and moisten with a saline solution when you remove the dressings."

"Continue with the sodium bicarbonate baths, Doctor?"

"Yes. Once daily." Randolph felt the instrument probe his abdomen and hip. "Heavy granulation here, nurse."

"Yes, Doctor."

"Apply nitrate of silver solution as strong as the patient can tolerate."

"Balsam of Peru?"

"No, nurse. And I don't believe in scarlet salve. You know that." The timbre of the voice was curt.

"Yes, Doctor."

"He's showing heavy vesication. Have you been puncturing the blebs?"

"Yes, Doctor Henniker. But they reappear."

Randolph interrupted. "What are you talking about?"

"Blisters, my good man," Henniker said impatiently. He turned back to Kimberly. "Of course they reappear. Continue puncturing the vesicles with a sterile needle and allow the serum to flow out, but don't remove the pellicles and apply a five percent solution of picric acid ointment after puncturing. This should relieve some of his pain, prevent suppuration, and perhaps we can cut down on the frequency of the dressings."

Randolph heard the nurse writing furiously and finally she said, "I have it, Doctor."

Henniker stood erect and fingered his chin. "His urine? Any signs of nephritis?"

"No, Doctor. It's clear."

"Good. Good." He spoke to Randolph. "Your kidneys are holding up." Back to the nurse, he said, "Continue with the potassium citrate, twenty grains, with spirit of nitrous ether in plenty of water. Administer four liters of normal saline solution daily subcutaneously."

"Good Lord," Randolph said. "I can't take that much."

The doctor's smile was evil. "Then we have ways to see to it."

"What do you mean?"

"We insert a tube up the rectum and . . ."

"I can take the lot, Doctor," Randolph assured the doctor hastily.

Henniker turned back to Kimberly. "His bowels must be kept free and open. Nephritis is always a threat and he must eliminate actively."

Nurse Piper continued writing and finally Doctor Henniker asked, "You have my instructions?"

"I do, sir. Do you wish me to read them back?"

"Not necessary. I'm overdue in the next ward." Henniker whirled and was gone.

For the first time in nearly two weeks, Randolph had been clearheaded when examined. The medical jargon had been confusing but at the same time sobering. He had a stiff leg and would probably never fly again. He pushed back the depression philosophically and stared at Kimberly Piper's lovely face and trim body. The view raised his spirits. He felt a sudden flush of embarrassment. "Ah—" he began. "You know me pretty well."

Looking up from her notes, the nurse smiled slyly and pulled the blankets back up to his chin. "As well as your mother." She put a cool hand on his forehead and leaned close.

Her flesh was as clear and perfect as satin and he could smell the perfume again. He realized it had been a long time since he had bedded a woman. Not since Cynthia Boswell. Suddenly, without warning, he felt an intense arousal and a stiffening. The major was happy there was a cradle to hold up the bed clothes.

By the end of the fourth week, Randolph was able to refuse morphia except at night. He could not sleep without it. But his mind was fully alert and he was able to examine himself under the cradle. The scarring was horrifying, long, liverlike tissue, hardened in layers on his flesh like loathsome parasitic creatures that had climbed out of a bog and attached themselves to his body. His gunshot wound was almost completely recovered, but his right leg was seared and appeared withered like the branch of a tree caught by a forest fire. The splints were uncomfortable, but he knew the thick scars would contract his leg permanently without them. He had to walk—must walk—but he was not even capable of standing.

His mother, Brenda, and Bernice were at the hospital every day. Walter stopped in frequently and smuggled in occasional bottles of Johnnie Walker. One afternoon Brenda and Reginald Hargreaves, who was wearing captain's stripes, spent nearly an hour with him. Brenda was radiantly beautiful that afternoon and when Kimberly Piper entered the room, for the first time the nurse's beauty seemed second-rate and Randolph realized *all* women suffered when Brenda was nearby. The major sensed there was something between Reginald and Brenda. He felt a terrible loss of something he had never possessed and was depressed for two days.

Then Lloyd stopped in with Brenda's brother Hugh Ashcroft, whom he had not seen since Brenda and Geoffry's wedding. Lloyd appeared very thin and old. He was also bitter over the army's refusal to even watch a demonstration of some new infiltration tactics he was advocating and defense in depths that he considered essential. "Bull-headed sods. Bunch of bloody Haigs still fighting the Indian wars," he had grumbled, standing over the bed. He smiled in his sudden, unexpected manner. "You killed the butcher Bruno Hollweg. You can add the DSO to your Military Cross, and you may be up for the Victoria Cross."

"And a court-martial."

"Court-martial?"

"Yes. I killed some Krauts in a most ungentlemanly fashion—had the Geneva Conventions thrown in my teeth by some 'dugout king' named Liam Townshend."

Lloyd snorted. "Hah! I've heard that nonsense, too. Kill them any way you can before they kill our chaps—that's what I tell my lads."

Randolph punched the rim of the cradle. "I beat him, Lloyd. Man to man. It was a personal thing. And they ambushed me."

"The bloody swine," Lloyd growled. "I heard. Hartley Carter wrote Mother."

There was a long silence. Randolph decided to turn the conversation away from the painful memories. Self-consciously, he turned to Hugh. "Good to see you, Hugh. It's been a long time."

"Five years," the American answered. "It was at Brenda and Geoffry's wedding."

"You're an attaché?"

"Yes, but Lloyd has been kind enough to find me a billet at Chigwell. I've been studying training techniques." He fingered his chin. "You know, the American army has never employed such large masses of troops as the Western Front requires."

"You talk as if you expect to be there."

Hugh and Lloyd exchanged a look. Hugh continued. "You know about unrestricted submarine warfare?"

Randolph shook his head.

Hugh said, "Germany declared unrestricted submarine warfare two months ago. They've sunk hundreds of ships including neutrals."

"What month is this?"

"March. The end of March. Just last week, three American ships were sunk. There have been war parades in Philadelphia and Chicago."

Lloyd interrupted. "You've heard of the Zimmermann telegram, Randolph?" Randolph shook his head again. "Been round the bend, brother."

Lloyd continued. "Zimmermann is Germany's foreign secretary. Zimmermann sent a telegram to Heinrich von Eckhardt, the German ambassador in Mexico City, instructing the ambassador to assure the Mexicans that in the event of a war between Germany and the United States, Germany would assist Mexico in reconquering lost territory."

Hugh broke in. "Only Texas, New Mexico, and Arizona, is all. The proposal was not received with enthusiasm in Washington. Congress is in an evil mood and has severed diplomatic relations with Germany. It looks like the U.S. will be in this soon."

"Less than a month," Lloyd hazarded.

Randolph said to his brother, "Your trailing billet—do you like it?"

Lloyd and Hugh exchanged a knowing look. "I've requested transfer back to the Coldstreams. Something's brewing at Arras."

With new clarity in his head, Randolph remembered something he had heard in December. "I thought Nivelle was going to end this whole bloody lot."

Lloyd laughed and Hugh smiled. Lloyd suddenly became grim. "That buffoon will kill another million Frenchmen and a fair lot of our lads."

"I heard about different tactics—his 'method.' He did well at Verdun?"

"Did well? Do you know what this so-called method of his is all about?" Randolph shook his head and looked at his brother expectantly. "Well, I assure you the Heinies know. Twice, with small forces on small fronts he made limited attacks using no more than nine divisions. The attacks were successful only because the Frogs had superior artillery on those narrow fronts and their rolling barrages worked. Now he's convinced the politicians, including Lloyd George, he can make it work on a grand scale—seize the gun line with a renewed spirit of élan."

"Two to three thousand yards behind the German lines," Randolph said.

"Quite right, brother. And to make things worse, the Krauts have pulled back into their Hindenburg line."

"I heard of it. Saw aerial photographs of some of the blockhouses."

"Tough fortifications on the reverse slopes where they belong. They've pulled their whole army out of the Somme salient and retreated some places twenty miles. The Western Front has never seen fortifications like these. Nivelle is exactly what they want. His method can't work against superior artillery and the Germans have it. He was lucky at Verdun. Another bloody massacre."

"Why do the politicians keep picking these incompetents?" Hugh asked.

The Englishmen exchanged a glance and Lloyd answered. "Nivelle is half English, has a nice smile, and he's Protestant."

Hugh blurted in astonishment, "Protestant! What in the world can religion have to do with picking your commander-in-chief?"

Both Englishmen snorted humorlessly. Lloyd said to the American, "Everything. Republican politicians don't trust Catholics—won't allow a Catholic general to take command, and they have some officers who aren't as incompetent as Nivelle—Fayolle, de Castelnau, and d'Esperey are all Catholics and the Republicans have turned thumbs down on the lot."

"My God," Hugh breathed. "Sounds like the Middle Ages."

"You don't know the French mind," Randolph said. "Most of them are still back in the nineteenth century wallowing in Napoleon's glory." He moved his eyes to Lloyd. "You don't want to miss the show, brother?"

"I want to be with my lads. You can understand that, Randolph. Haig is jealous and has plans to upstage Nivelle at Arras—that's the latrine rumor." Lloyd shuffled his feet restlessly and spoke to the floor. "I say, brother, when you see Bernice I would appreciate discretion on your part. She doesn't know about my request for a change in posting."

Randolph smiled knowingly. "Of course, Lloyd. I'm always the model of discretion, you know that." And then his demeanor changed and he cried out angrily, punching the cradle, "Dash it all, I'm chained to this bloody bed."

"It's time, gentlemen," Nurse Piper said from the door.

There was a shaking of hands and promises to return and the officers left.

A few days later Brenda visited the hospital and for the first time she was able to spend some time with Randolph alone. He had been moved to a private room. It was tiny but had two large windows where burn patients could take the sun. Although scarring was visible on his neck and she knew that most of the rest of his body was badly marked, he was vastly improved and in high spirits. "Brenda," he announced proudly, "I can walk." He gestured at a pair of crutches leaning against the wall. "My splints are off and I went to the bathroom all by myself just like a big boy."

She leaned over him and kissed him on the forehead. She felt his hand on her arm and he pulled her closer. Gently, she pulled away. "What's wrong, Brenda? Afraid I'll ravish you here and now?"

The American laughed. "I can see you're feeling much better, Randolph."

"You're serious about Reginald?" he said suddenly with new seriousness.

"Yes."

"You'll marry him?"

"Yes."

"When?"

"We haven't set a date. But it will be after June." Feeling uncomfortable, she changed the subject, telling him of her new place in Belgravia, her new servants, her cockney butler McHugh. She glowed when she described Nathan and Rodney's latest antics.

"And Nicole?" he asked shyly. "How is she?"

Brenda averted her eyes. "Fine. Fine. But she received word her uncle vanished at Verdun."

"Vanished?"

"His whole regiment disappeared during a bombardment last November. Not a trace."

There was a rustle behind her and Brenda caught the scent of jasmine and hyacinth. Without a word to Brenda, Kimberly Piper moved to Randolph's far side and beamed down at him. "Taking your liquids like a good lad," she said, smiling. "We have the tube, you know."

"Quite right—gallons, nurse." Eyes on the nurse's face, he gulped down a full glass of water.

Brenda chuckled inwardly. When a man was injured and helpless, he inevitably reverted back to some of the attitudes of childhood when as a sick child he was ministered to by his mother. Perhaps it was because the wounded were usually tended by women. Flat on his back and dependent on others for his most basic physical needs, he accepted orders and admonishments that he would have rejected as unthinkable if he were well and on his feet. Commands to "eat it all" and to "drink it all" were heard constantly and the vocabulary was that of childhood: "good boy"; "good lad"; "big boy" were heard most often.

Brenda turned her attention to the nurse. She had not even acknowledged Brenda's presence and was usually gruff and brief when she did speak. And when the QA looked at Randolph it was with a warm glow that far exceeded professionalism—a look that women reserve for men who attract them. Although she was attractive in her own right, she was unmarried and with most of the eligible men in uniform, probably very lonely. And Brenda had seen hostility glimmer in Kimberly's eyes whenever she looked her way.

The nurse raised the blanket and peered under the cradle. "Much better," she said. She applied some salve and Randolph squirmed uncomfortably. "Soon, we'll go out in the garden. Would you like that?" The timbre of the voice struck Brenda as odd indeed. Soft and warm like a lover arranging a tryst.

"It's a date," Randolph said. "And then dancing at the Savoy."

Kimberly laughed like a schoolgirl. "But none of that new American jazz. It's too hard on me."

"Just waltzes," Randolph assured her. The nurse made a few notes on a clipboard hanging at the foot of the bed and left. As she walked through the door, she almost bumped into an RFC captain.

"Leefe! Leefe Hendon," Randolph cried as the officer walked to his bedside. They grasped hands. "You made captain."

"Right, sir, and it's good to see you," the captain said with an inflection that Brenda guessed hinted of the western United States or Canada.

Randolph gestured at Brenda and introduced the Canadian. Brenda looked into a unique face—the visage of a young, innocent boy on a man. His black eyes were nervous, edgy, and disturbing. She guessed he could be a ruthless killer or a violent lover. Randolph confirmed his talents as a killer.

"I heard you have nineteen kills."

"Twenty-two, Major."

The two men stared at each other with the same intimate bond she had sensed on *Lancer* when Reginald introduced her to his officers. Again, she had the feelings of an outsider looking in on a man's private world she could never know. She felt pangs of anger and frustration and oddly, envy.

"They ambushed me, Leefe," Randolph said grimly. "Two of the bloody *gentlemen* chivalrously tried to murder me after I scragged Hollweg."

"I know, sir. I was there."

"You were there?"

Hendon's smile had the look of a schoolboy confessing a transgression. "McDonald and I were above you—above everyone. Just to be sure Hollweg remembered to be a gentleman."

"You chased off the two Albatrosses?"

Hendon chuckled. "One of the sods became my sixteenth kill. McDonald cashed in the other for his twentieth."

"Well, I'll be damned."

"Why do you think they didn't jump you when you sideslipped out of that cloud? You were still at least two hundred feet above the ground and you were cold meat. But by then both of the Krauts were on their way to Valhalla."

"I was a stupid sod. Stupid," Randolph spat bitterly.

"We thought you'd gone west for sure, Major," Hendon said. There was a silence and then the men spoke of Number Five Squadron, of kills and casualties. Their voices were soft and warm as if they were talking of family. Brenda learned that two flyers named Hollingsworth and Hemmings had been killed and that the Scotsman named Angus McDonald commanded. McDonald had killed twenty-seven Germans. The Jastas were still superior with their new Albatross D.3s, but new Allied fighters were appearing in greater numbers and beginning to turn the tide: the French with their new Spad 7s and 13s; Sopwith with its new triplane and great new F.1 humpback fighter dubbed the *Camel;* and, of course, the S.E.5a. "With these new fighters, we'll give the Boche a real go, Major," the Canadian said.

"Who took command of Jasta Boelcke?"

"*Hauptmann* Stephan Kirmaier," Hendon said.

"Yes, I've heard of him. Hartley Carter mentioned him in one of his letters." And then with anxiety, he said, "Have you been mixing it with them?"

"No, Major. Not Richthofen either. Both Jastas are operating to the north of us."

The major nodded and Brenda saw his face relax. "You're on leave?" Randolph asked.

"Not really, Major. I'm testing the new S.E.5a."

A confused look crossed Randolph's face. "Why you—a front line pilot?"

"Because it's nothing but a copy of the S.E.5 you modified." Both men laughed. "They've upped the horsepower to two twenty-five and added a Lewis gun on a Foster mount."

"Kept the Vickers?"

"Yes, sir. Two guns and every improvement you made. It's a great machine—an Albatross killer."

Randolph nodded his approval and twisted restlessly, his face a mask of frustration. He wanted to return. Brenda was sure of it.

Hendon's voice became solemn. "You're looking well, sir. But I hear you're out of it."

"A few burns—stiff leg and all that rot. Should be fit shortly."

"Chop, chop," the Canadian said, imitating Randolph's voice. They both laughed raucously.

Brenda spoke with disbelief. "Randolph, you can't plan on returning. My God, you can't even walk. How can you fly?"

The major came up off his pillow, moist eyes blazing. "I will, by God. I will." He sank back and an embarrassed silence filled the tiny room.

Brenda was confused. So many men tried desperately to shirk military service. She had heard of malingering "lead swingers," C3s, SIWs (self-inflicted wounds), conscientious objectors, château generals, and even "dugout kings" who

Lloyd said were high-ranking officers who never showed their heads aboveground from the moment they entered a position until relieved and it was time to leave. Yet Lloyd, with what appeared to be shell shock, and Reginald and Randolph, with terrible wounds, seemed determined to return to the carnage. It was in their eyes—she had seen it many times, a faraway look that spoke of another land few could ever visit, that was horrible beyond description but irresistible. She had even seen a hint of it in her brother. *Why are the men I love so anxious to get themselves killed?* she thought in bewilderment.

Randolph's voice broke the silence and her thoughts. He asked Brenda calmly, "You didn't bring Reginald?"

Brenda welcomed the turn in conversation. "He's at the admiralty."

"He's in planning—right?"

"Yes," she said, looking down on the face that suddenly appeared dear and precious to her. The big, strong, handsome man was so thin and drawn. She had an impulse to take him in her arms and hold him close as she would Rodney or Nathan. Instead, she leaned over and kissed him on the cheek. She felt his hand on the back of her head. "I've got to leave," she said.

"Be back tomorrow?"

"I'll try. Maybe with Bernice and your mother."

"Give my best to Reginald," he said softly. "He must be very busy."

"Yes," she acknowledged. "He's very busy." She brushed her lips gently across his warm forehead, took her leave of Leefe Hendon, and left.

Operations Room Two was filled with a score of uniforms and the deep sounds of men in earnest conversation. Most of the uniforms were the blue of the Royal Navy. However, seated on the podium with an admiral and two commodores, Reginald recognized Brigadier General Humphrey Covington—a staff officer and old friend who had been promoted from colonel the previous year. The admiral was Sir Alexander Middleton, a planner and liaison officer, who spent as much time with the army's general staff as he did at the admiralty. Reginald had seen the commodores at the admiralty and had attended meetings with them but was not personally acquainted with either. He knew that Middleton and the two commodores were all veterans of the colonial wars and the war in South Africa. They were Victorian men over sixty years of age and all were proud of service on sailing vessels in their youths. All were too old for sea duty and Reginald was convinced none of them appreciated the killing power and efficiency of the war machines of the new industrial age.

Most of the other faces of the men seated around the long oak table belonged to younger men and longtime friends and acquaintances. The lowest rank in the room belonged to the three stripes on the cuffs of Stephen Pochhammer, who sat next to Reginald, and one other commander who sat at the far end of the table. Most of the men were smoking and a dense cloud of blue smoke hung in the middle of the room.

After exhaling a huge puff of smoke and stubbing out his cigarette, Middleton stood and eyed the group silently and the conversations came to an abrupt halt. A large, stout, sixtyish man, his once-powerful physique had softened and grown flaccid with time and overeating. The son of a vicar, his voice was deep, stentorian, and punctuated with the practiced pauses of an experienced preacher. "Gentlemen," he rumbled. "We are here to discuss our projected operations against Bruges and its exit ports, Ostend and Zeebrugge." He glanced at Reginald and smiled amiably. "Most of you have heard of these plans—plans to bombard with monitors and lay mine fields. However, in the last month, top-secret revisions have been made and none of you has heard a whisper about them." He looked around at the intent faces. "I can tell you now operations against the ports were planned first for June of last year, and then postponed because of the prospect of ending the war with the Somme offensives. Of course that was dashed and the operation was rescheduled for next month. All of you command units that are scheduled to participate in this operation." There was a rumble of voices. Middleton continued, "Here to tell you of the details of the new plan is Captain Reginald Hargreaves, who you all know and who led Destroyer Squadron Four so gallantly in its action against Schultz's flotilla off the coast of Belgium."

Quickly, Reginald walked to a huge wall chart and picked up a pointer. Stabbing at the coast of Belgium, he began, "The port of Bruges is eight miles inland—an ideal haven. According to latest intelligence, it has the facilities to service over thirty destroyers and about thirty U-boats. Our operatives have spotted on the average two U-boats putting to sea daily." There was a murmur. He moved the pointer. "They sortie from Zeebrugge, or if of shallow draught, here"—he moved the pointer—"they can move through these canals and use Ostend twelve miles to the south." The pointer traced a long arc northeastward past Holland and into the Baltic. "Their nearest German ports are over three hundred miles to the northeast at Wilhelmshaven and Bremerhaven." He turned back to the officers. "Bruges adds at least six hundred miles to their range." He glanced at some notes. "In February U-boats sank over half a million tons of shipping, in March almost six hundred thousand, and the rate is increasing." Shouts of anger. "Our new plan will use block ships to block the ports of Ostend and Zeebrugge."

There was a grim silence as Reginald allowed the implication of his words to sink in. "The admiralty has tentatively assigned six outdated light cruisers to the operation—*Vindictive, Thetis, Intrepid, Iphigenia, Brilliant,* and *Sirius*. At this moment they are being converted at Chatham. I intend to block Ostend with *Sirius* and *Brilliant* and Zeebrugge with *Intrepid, Thetis,* and *Iphigenia*."

A slender, middle-aged captain with alert brown eyes raised a hand. Reginald nodded. Coming to his feet, the captain said, "Edgar Mansfield, Destroyer Squadron Eleven here, Captain." Mansfield gestured at the chart. "In peacetime I made those ports many times on merchant vessels and, daresay, Zeebrugge would be a tough nut, indeed. It's seventy-four miles from Dover, has shifting sandbanks and treacherous tides. There are two piers and a mole a half mile west of the canal mouth." He stabbed a single finger at the chart. "That mole is nearly two miles long, maybe a hundred yards wide, with a sixteen-foot-high wall ten feet thick on its seaward side and no doubt the Jerries have fortified it. One battery on that mole could make a bloody slog of the whole lot of us."

"Quite right," Reginald agreed. "So we'll take it."

"Take it?"

"Yes, Captain Mansfield. *Vindictive* will be converted into an assault ship." Hargreaves waited until an excited babble subsided. "*Vindictive* will carry a storming party to the mole. Infantry will silence the German guns."

Mansfield's face twisted sardonically. "You mean *Vindictive* sails right up to the mole, moors, and disembarks her storming party without the Krauts even noticing." A silence like a cold wall descended on the room.

Reginald felt anger flare but controlled his voice. "The RNAS has developed new smoke generators. *Vindictive* will make her approach under the cover of smoke."

Shaking his head and obviously unconvinced, Mansfield returned to his chair. Reginald felt a disquieting new emotion. He remembered the scene when Admiral Rosslyn Watts had presented his plan to intercept *Korvettenkapitan* Max Schultz's flotilla. Then, Reginald was the skeptic. Then Reginald was sarcastic and caustic. The wheel had made a full turn and the captain felt disquiet and unease at the ironic shift in roles. But the ports had to be blocked. Destroyer Squadron Four would still be afloat and Wolcott, Blankenship, and Woolridge and their gallant crews would still be alive if it had not been for the nest of German destroyers that swarmed out of their evil lair. And Hun ships and U-boats were using the ports in increasing numbers, attacking and killing in the Channel and the Atlantic.

Another hand was raised and another officer came to his feet. "Commander Willard Wisdom here, Captain Hargreaves. First officer in destroyer *Llewellyn*." Reginald nodded recognition. "Sir, why not proceed with the original plan—bombardment by monitors and the laying of mine fields. Fifteen-inch shells would make a hash of the lot and mine fields would make good corks for those narrow channels."

"Quite so," Reginald agreed. "Big-gun shelling would disable the ports and, as you point out, mine fields do 'make good corks.' However, at best, shelling and mines provide only a temporary solution. All of you know Fritz is a genius at repairing damaged equipment, and mines can be swept." He tapped the table with the rubber tip of the pointer. "No, Commander Wisdom, we need a permanent solution—a solution that will deny the Krauts the channels. The only way to do that is to block those channels."

"Could be expensive, sir."

"Quite right, Commander, but Destroyer Squadron Four has already made part of that payment."

Silence filled the room. Wisdom fidgeted nervously. He pointed at the base of the mole. "They'll rush reinforcements to the mole, sir. Directly the attack begins."

Reginald placed the pointer on the spot where the mole joined the land. "There is a viaduct here about three hundred yards long joining the mole to the shore. We've been assigned two C-class submarines. We'll pack the bows of the submarines with explosives and ram them into the viaduct. This should do the trick neatly." Again silence and an exchange of glances. Wisdom returned to his chair.

"May I speak?" Brigadier General Humphrey Covington inquired politely, coming to his feet. The request was academic, superior rank taking precedence under any circumstances. Reginald appreciated the courtesy and found his chair.

Covington moved to a large map of the Western Front attached to the opposite wall. "Gentlemen," he began. "Your plans are very impressive and appear to be well thought out and one of the reasons I was sent here was to learn of the details." He shifted his weight uneasily and Reginald felt a stab of apprehension. "However, the other reason why I was sent here was to inform you of the general staff's plans for the Western Front. General Haig and General Nivelle have planned great offensives that will explode across the Western Front shortly." He pointed at the chart of the coast of Belgium on the opposite wall. "Your plans for Zeebrugge and Ostend may be premature—may cost casualties needlessly."

Reginald felt a familiar rush of frustration and anger while Covington tapped the table with his knuckles and then faced the chart and picked up a pointer. "Here, on sixteen April" —he struck the chart—"in Champagne along the Chemin des Dames the French will strike with over a million men and five thousand guns." He moved the pointer north. "On nine April, the BEF will make a diversionary attack around Arras, striking at Vimy Ridge and Cambrai. General Haig will attack with twenty-one divisions, three thousand guns, and seventy new Mark Four tanks. General Nivelle predicts a breakthrough within forty-eight hours and complete victory by, perhaps, the end of the summer."

"But, sir," Captain Mansfield said. "The Krauts have pulled back into their *Siegfriedstellung*. A shorter line with concrete emplacements."

Covington nodded appreciatively and adopted the demeanor of a lecturing schoolteacher. "Quite right. Pulled back into the Hindenburg line. Shortened the front by twenty-five miles and allowed the withdrawal of ten divisions."

Reginald wondered at Mansfield's persistence as the captain pressed on. "And we've all read reports of their new defense in depths, heavy barbed wire entanglements. We never really destroyed their wire at the Somme."

Covington was obviously impressed by Mansfield's knowledge. "Bully, Captain. You've most certainly been well informed." He stabbed the chart again. "But this time" —he thudded the rubber tip against the chart for emphasis —"this time, we have more heavies and a new fuse." He looked around at the expectant faces. "Yes, a new fuse—the one-oh-six, which will detonate on grazing the ground. A real 'daisy cutter' with increased antipersonnel range and capable of cutting wire more effectively and it actually does less damage to the ground. Also we have new gas projectors that are highly efficient."

Reginald stood. He spoke evenly despite strong suspicions that churned inside him. "Sir. We were planning our attack for next month—to put an end to that vicious nest of killers once and for all."

Covington nodded solemnly. "I know." He nodded at Admiral Sir Alexander Middleton. "I have been informed and that is why the C-in-C sent me." He gestured at the chart. "After our breakthrough at Arras, the BEF will sweep north and west in behind Zeebrugge and Ostend and capture the entire Belgium coast." He turned both hands up in a gesture of futility. "So why involve the Royal Navy? Why sustain more casualties when we're going to take the ports by assault, anyway?"

Despite the difference in ranks and years of friendship, Reginald's anger boiled through. "We heard that before, General. We're losing ships and men now because of—"

"Captain Hargreaves!" Covington said severely. "At this moment, Admirals Jackson and Jellicoe are meeting with David Lloyd George. The PM is in full support of General Nivelle's plans. The order to postpone your attack comes from Ten Downing Street."

"Until when, sir?" Reginald asked with a tight jaw.

The voice softened. "The end of summer. By then the war should be over." He smiled benignly and then shrugged. "And if it isn't won, then you can proceed." The general sat and Admiral Middleton came to his feet.

Middleton spoke. "Are there any more questions?" Silence. "Then this meeting is closed."

Staring straight ahead, Reginald remained in his seat. Pochhammer lit a cigarette and leaned back in his chair, smoking solemnly. "Stephen," Reginald said. "They told us that in 'sixteen."

"I've never been in planning, Captain."

"I know. You're fortunate. I spent an entire year in it before taking command of *Lancer*—can drive a man 'round the bend."

Admiral Middleton reentered the room and claimed a forgotten bundle of reports. Reginald addressed him. "Admiral Middleton, I would like to return to sea—destroyer duty, preferably."

Middleton narrowed his eyes. "Tired of sailing a desk, Captain?"

"Quite right, sir."

Middleton sighed. "I can understand, Captain." He tapped

his temple with a single finger. "You know it isn't in my hands—you must convince the medical staff that you have fully recovered from your wounds."

"And if the medics approve?"

"Why then you can have a seagoing command."

"A destroyer squadron?"

The admiral smiled warmly like a father beaming down on his ambitious son. "A division, if I can arrange it."

Reginald rubbed his arm. "Thank you, Admiral. A few more weeks of exercise and it should be right."

"I hope so, Captain." The admiral left the room.

XII

On April 6, 1917, three days before Haig's scheduled offensive and ten days before Nivelle's attack, the United States declared war on Germany. There was joy in the Allied camp, but it was quickly tempered by news of the outbreak of revolution in Czarist Russia two weeks earlier. The news was slow in arriving, but reports began to appear in the papers of great food riots in Petrograd. Huge mobs of hungry people carrying red flags had stormed through the streets and the garrison of 190,000 men, even units of the Imperial Guard, joined the angry crowds. The mobs stormed the Winter Palace, burned public buildings, murdered officials, and released political prisoners from the Russian "Tower," the Fortress of St. Peter. Then news sifted out that rocked the world: Nicholas II had returned to Petrograd but had been unable to control the insurgents, his own troops joining the mobs as fast as he dispatched them. He abdicated in favor of his brother Michael. Still, authority was uncertain, the

Duma electing a provisional government under Prince Lvov, which ran into bitter opposition from a group of Marxist revolutionaries calling themselves the Petrograd Soviet.

The provisional government under Alexander Kerensky declared its determination to continue the war. "... to carry the war to a victorious conclusion."

But the Allies were unconvinced and depressed despite Lloyd George's statement: "We believe that the revolution is the greatest service the Russian people have yet made to the cause for which the Allied peoples have been fighting."

But the Germans and Austrians were rejoicing, too, and with better cause because the Russian army refused to attack, remaining quietly in the trenches, nailing officers' epaulets to their shoulders, then murdering them and electing soldiers' governing committees. Certainly, most Englishmen were not convinced that Russia's agony would bode nothing but good for their cause despite statements to the contrary by their politicians. Quite simply, the enemy of Germany and Austria on the Eastern Front was paralyzed and everyone knew if Russia collapsed, the entire weight of the German war machine would be brought to bear on the Western Front. All hopes rode with the coming Allied offensives.

Brenda was devastated by the American declaration of war. Hugh actually seemed happy at the news of U.S. involvement. On April 9, the Haig offensive exploded at Arras. There were the usual early glowing reports of rapid advances and victories. Then, on April 16, Nivelle hurled his troops against the German defenses on the Chemin des Dames between Soissons and Rheims. More optimistic communiqués crowded the front pages of the newspapers. But the breakthroughs did not materialize and the interminable casualty lists began to appear. As April drew to a close, there were rumors that British casualties exceeded one hundred thousand and French losses were almost two hundred thousand. Then came whispers of open rebellion in several French divisions. Nivelle's dismissal and replacement by Pétain confirmed the stories.

Early in May, Brenda, Reginald, and Hugh attended a

solemn dinner at the home of Lloyd and Bernice Higgins. The large old house just north of Regent's Park was dark and forbidding that evening. Lloyd was in a grim mood. Puffing on a Woodbine after a drab dinner, Lloyd looked down the long Sheraton dinner table and said, "Another Somme. Haig and that whole lot is incapable of learning—not one bloody change. Same stupid stand-up charge. And Nivelle had destroyed the morale of the Frog army. *Élan—cran*, don't work against shrapnel and bullets." He glanced down the table at Brenda. "Spirit—bravery," he explained.

"I know, brother-in-law," she said.

"And the Ivans have had it—worse than the Frogs. They're finished," Lloyd added.

Bernice spoke up. "But Kerensky claims Russia's in the war to the end."

Lloyd snorted bitterly. "A lot of rot—eyewash. Mark me, the Russian army's finished." He took a long drink of cognac and stared at Hugh. "With the Ivans out of it, we'll need you chaps more than ever. Do you know General John Pershing, the C-in-C of the AEF?" he asked.

Hugh brightened. "Black Jack? Of course. I served with him in Mexico when we chased Pancho Villa."

Lloyd smiled. "Never did catch him, did you?"

Hugh sipped at his drink. "He was elusive."

"This Pershing—he's a good man?"

The American officer nodded. "Yes, Lloyd. A fine man —intelligent, a complete professional."

"Can he learn?"

"I'm sure he can and will," Hugh said. He turned to Brenda. "I've applied for a transfer to the Forty-second Division—Rainbow Division, sister." He moved his eyes to Reginald and then Lloyd. *"Rainbow* because it will draw men from all the states," he explained.

Brenda's face showed her surprise. "I didn't know there was an American division in Europe. Why, General Pershing isn't here yet."

Hugh smiled. "You're right, sister. Pershing will arrive with his staff within two weeks and American divisions will follow and the Rainbow Division will be the first. The chief of staff is a colonel I've known for years—Douglas MacArthur. I've written him and he's promised me a company."

"Bully for you," Lloyd said with a genuine congratulatory tone in his voice. "Better than Chigwell. Anything's better than Chigwell."

"When are you leaving, Lloyd?" Bernice asked matter-of-factly. Everyone shifted uneasily.

"What do you mean, love?"

"I mean you've applied for a transfer back to the front—haven't you?" Lloyd's eyes moved to Reginald and then to Hugh. "Oh, no one had to tell me. It's written all over you, Lloyd. You turned down a promotion to brigadier general, didn't you? You turned it down because it would take you back from the lines to safe billets."

The colonel studied his glass. "A man must do what he believes is right and it's not right that those inept *château* generals should be murdering my chaps."

"Is it right for a man to make a widow of his wife and leave two children fatherless?"

Lloyd's face flushed and his lips thinned into a flat slash. "You'd better become accustomed to the idea, Bernice. I'll be gone in a fortnight."

"No! No!" She stood, hand covering her mouth, and ran from the room.

Silently, the guests came to their feet and left.

An hour later, Brenda was snuggled against Reginald on a plump sofa in his study. Besides passion, there was warmth and security to be found in his arms. Sipping her Benedictine, her mind was filled with images of Bernice's anguished face. "He's going back," she said. "I can't understand him."

Reginald drank and said, "I can."

Brenda felt a cold shudder of fear. "You can? You want to return, too?"

He flexed the fingers of his impaired hand and stared at the table. "The doctors will decide that, Brenda."

Her voice was flat and dead. "But you do want to return?"

He pondered his pony for a brief moment. "No one—absolutely no one wants to risk his neck, love. But"—he shrugged—"but, on the other hand, a man can't let the other chaps down."

"That's what fuels it, Reggie—keeps it going," she said in a hard voice.

"Perhaps, Brenda. You've very perceptive and we both saw that in Lloyd." He toyed with his drink, sloshing the thick liquid back and forth in the tiny glass. There was tension in his voice. "There's something about your other brother-in-law—Randolph."

She drained her glass. "What about Randolph?"

"You still see him every day."

"Yes. Without fail."

"He loves you, you know."

Shocked by the statement, she was wordless for a moment. Then she sighed deeply and said, "He's never expressed it to me, Reggie."

"He has to me—every time he looks at you." He recharged her glass.

"Perhaps you're right, darling, and perhaps you're misreading him. I just don't know." Drinking, she stared at him over her glass and felt a twinge of anger. Could he be jealous? Jealousy, the foulest, basest human emotion? The timbre of her voice hardened. "I love Randolph and he's important to me. I'll continue to see him as long as he needs me, so don't ask me to stop seeing him."

He looked up, obviously startled by the tone and the words. "Good Lord, I wouldn't ask that. I know the poor chap needs you—your company, attention, I mean. Remember, I've known him longer than you and I love him, too." He chuckled. "I'm not jealous, Brenda—really."

Sighing and soothed by his words, she finished her drink and tabled it. Quickly, she circled his neck with her arms. "I love you, Reggie— love you. There's no one else—could never be." The kiss was wet and passionate. She pulled him down on the couch. "Let's marry," she breathed into his lips.

He pulled back. "When, darling? When?"

"Two weeks. The middle of June. We'll find a nice chapel—a quiet ceremony."

"The day after tomorrow I've got to make a trip to Scapa

Flow for a fortnight or more. I've got to see Admiral Beatty about some changes in plans." He pursed his lips. "End of June, darling."

"Can't the war wait?"

He laughed. "After Scapa Flow we'll make the whole world wait." He kissed the pulse in her neck and whispered in her ear, "Can you drop me at Victoria Thursday morning —you're the only family I've got."

"Yes. Yes," she whispered. "Of course I will."

"I love the way you say yes."

Sighing happily, she pulled him down and clamped her mouth over his.

The next day just before noon McHugh pulled the Reo town car up to the curbstone in front of the Queen Victoria Hospital. Brenda walked quickly to Randolph's room but found it empty. "'E's in the garden, mum," a young, white-clad orderly volunteered from the door. After thanking the young man, Brenda walked out of the back of the hospital onto the vast grounds of Hyde Park.

Once a hunting preserve for Henry VIII and later a fashionable resort for Charles I, the vast sylvan grounds interspersed with lakes and stands of trees reminded the American of New York's Central Park and the grounds of some of the old antebellum plantations she had seen in the Deep South. The British love of flowers was everywhere; beds of azaleas, roses, and a dozen other varieties showing their early spring colors. And white-clad wounded men were as abundant as the flowers. Some were in wheelchairs, others hobbled about on crutches—many on one leg—and others stood erect and walked unaided. All were tended by nurses, orderlies, or friends and relatives.

Walking down the dozen stairs of the enormous porch that ran the width of the huge building, Brenda began her search. She walked through groups and clusters, searched the faces of passing patients to no avail. About to give up in frustration, she finally found Randolph. Actually, she saw Kimberly Piper's shock of brown hair with its precariously perched white hat first and then Randolph's tall, thin figure.

With the nurse's hand on the flyer's elbow, the couple was walking along the shore of a long, crescent-shaped lake. Brenda wove through the crowd.

Up close the wounded were even more heartbreaking. Most were very young. Some were missing limbs, others hobbled on canes, and still others stared straight ahead with dead eyes as they were wheeled about in chairs. Most wore bandages. Some, blinded, had white gauze wrapped around their sightless eyes. Brenda shuddered when she thought of the terrible wounds that must be concealed under the layers of gauze.

"Randolph! Randolph!" she shouted, overtaking the couple.

"Brenda," he said, turning with surprising ease and smiling. Although his leg was still heavily bandaged and his neck deeply scarred, Brenda was pleased to see the broad shoulders square and proud again, the smile showing hints of the old confidence.

"Oh, Mrs. Higgins," Kimberly Piper said, her voice a sheet of ice, eyeing the American from head to toe. "Nice to see you. You don't miss a day, do you?" she added. She turned to Randolph. "If Mrs. Higgins can look after you, I'll return to the ward. We have some new patients and I have reports to do on my typing machine."

"Thank you," Brenda said coldly. "I'm sure I'm capable of looking after the major."

"I'm sure you are," the nurse said, whirling on her heel and disappearing into the crowd.

Brenda took Randolph's arm and they began to walk along the shores of the lake. He gestured at the water. "The Serpentine. Shelley's wife drowned herself here." He chuckled, obviously in high spirits. "We British love our traditions." He waved to a small rise where a huge statue was visible. "Over there in the center of the park, a twenty-foot statue of Achilles, cast from melted guns captured in some of Wellington's greatest victories. A tribute to him put there at the expense of the women of Britain." He laughed uproariously. She looked at him quizzically. "Well, dear Brenda, the statue is a nude—a gigantic nude and, daresay, the assembled ladies were shocked, indeed, at the unveiling." He laughed again and quickened his pace. She noticed he walked with only a slight limp. Now she could account for his high spirits. His recovery had been almost miraculous.

"You're doing very well, Randolph," she said, genuinely impressed.

"Do you think so, Brenda?" he said like a little boy looking for approval.

"Well, you'll be riding to the hounds in a fortnight," she said in her best imitation of an English accent.

He laughed again.

A voice behind them stopped the pair. "Major Higgins!" They turned and faced Doctor Henniker. "Better return to the ward. Time for lunch and I don't want you to exhaust yourself. You've been out here for over an hour."

"I feel fine, Doctor." Randolph nodded at Brenda. "My sister-in-law just arrived and I'd like to visit and all that."

"Therapy after lunch. You know that. Your new schedule."

Randolph's face fell and then brightened. "Then can I leave the grounds tomorrow?" He turned to Brenda. "Take me to lunch—at Scott's."

Brenda glanced at Henniker and spoke hesitantly. "Why yes, if it's all right with the doctor."

Henniker tapped his temple thoughtfully, then said to Brenda, "You can motor him there?"

Brenda glanced at Randolph and the expression on his face reminded her of Rodney's expression when he begged for another sweetmeat. "Yes. I have an automobile."

Henniker beamed at Randolph. "Very well, Major. If you're a good boy and return by fourteen hundred hours."

Randolph turned to Brenda in an exuberant mood. "Sound your horn at noon and the walls will come tumbling down." Everyone laughed.

The next morning, Brenda saw Reginald off at Victoria Station. The huge, dark barnlike structure was a bedlam. A half dozen trains lined up, hissing their steam like old dragons, filling the air with the smell of burning coal and oil. Uniformed men and their women everywhere, wives, mothers, sons, fathers, lovers. Men and women clinging together, the men boarding the trains, the women turning their backs and walking away alone, shoulders shaking, handkerchiefs clutched to their faces. And men were crying too. Young privates, grizzled NCOs. And those returning on leave were dirty, unshaved, and exhausted. Most had rifles slung across their shoulders, puttees and field shoes caked with mud, service caps crumpled and askew, all marked with regimental badges—ravens, horses, stars, lions, triangles, and circles with red numbers—the King's Own Leicestershires, the Black Watch, the Humberside Fusiliers, and a dozen others. Mingling, milling, striding in bewildering swirls of Tommy serge and khaki, streaming to the Red Cross canteen for tea and coffee and sweet cakes. Many clutched their women furiously in happiness as they clung to them and those women losing their men stared at them enviously. It was a terrible, depressing scene and Brenda wished she could turn her eyes away from it. But there was no refuge except in Reginald's arms.

And she found herself there, holding him close when they reached the door of his carriage in the press of sobbing, laughing, shouting humanity. With his arms around her, she felt a great sense of relief—almost a smug confidence in the knowledge her man was safe; at least temporarily. He spoke softly into her ear. "End of June. You have an appointment, darling."

"One I'll never miss." She was interrupted by the high-pitched shriek of the engine whistle and Reginald broke away and entered the compartment jammed with officers.

"I'll write you." The train gave a violent jerk and he staggered. "A fortnight, darling." The train began to move.

"I love you, Reggie."

"I love you."

She stood on the platform and waved, suddenly terribly alone as the train roared and chugged its way out of the station and the carriages clattered past. As the engine puffed and shrieked and the last carriage left the station, she slowly worked her way through the crowd until she reached a newspaper kiosk at the entrance where groups of people were standing and talking in excited voices. She bought a copy of *The Times* from a stack that was delivered just as she arrived at the kiosk. With the paper under her arm, she walked to the curb where McHugh waited with a hand on the door of the Reo town car.

"The hospital, Wendell," she said as he closed the door behind her. As McHugh pulled from the curb, Brenda opened the paper. One glance sufficed to explain the excitement back at the kiosk. The paper was filled with news of devastating Hun air raids on the east coast towns of Shorncliffe and Folkestone. Shocked, Brenda read the horrifying news. Squadrons of new bombers called "Gotha" had killed and injured hundreds of people. Brenda shuddered, then looked up from the paper as McHugh wheeled the big Reo town car to the curb in front of the hospital.

Randolph was waiting on the broad walk in front of the building. He was dressed splendidly in his RFC uniform: brown shirt, black tie, brown tunic, Sam Browne belt, fine gray wool trousers, and brown boots. Even the gold embroidered cloth wings, RFC emblem, and crown on his left breast glistened in the noon sun. In fact, when he stepped into the passengers' compartment, Brenda could smell Brasso, Kiwi Polish, and Soldier's Friend. He was very thin, his skin was pasty white, and a brilliant red scar extended up the right side of his neck all the way to his lower jaw like a layer of liver. He was still in high spirits.

"Scott's," Brenda said to McHugh, pulling the partition aside as Randolph slammed the door.

"Yes, mum," the chauffeur answered. "Mayfair."

"Right," Randolph said. "Twenty Mount Street." Brenda closed the partition and sat back. She showed him the paper.

"Bloody butchers," he growled, scanning the headlines. "Gothas. Deadly machines. I've heard of them. A much better weapon than the zeppelin. Twin-engined, three-man crews, a thousand pounds of bombs." He pounded his fist into an open palm. "London's next."

"But there are guns and airplanes to protect London."

"I know, Brenda. But I heard the Gotha has a ceiling of

over twenty thousand feet. If that's true, the interceptors will have a deuce of a time attacking them."

Brenda sighed and sagged back, her mind filled with thoughts of her boys. She could only say, "Oh, Lord."

Randolph took her hand. "Come, sister-in-law. Let's not let those nasty Jerries ruin this day—my first day of freedom."

Brenda came erect and she smiled brightly despite an empty, sick feeling deep inside. "Of course, Randolph. This is a special day."

Randolph continued. "Tomorrow, Mother is taking me to Piccadilly and, perhaps, the day after, I'll be discharged from the hospital."

"Oh, wonderful, Randolph."

Driving east on Oxford Street, they left Hyde Park behind and then turned south on Bond Street. Randolph stared out of his window hungrily like a young boy on an outing. There were few cars and only occasional small groups of uniformed men were clustered on the walks—especially around the fashionable shops and clubs—but not nearly the numbers to be found in Piccadilly and the Burlington Arcade. He waved at a group of fine buildings. "The Temple," he announced. He answered the confused look on Brenda's face. "Since the Middle Ages solicitors and barristers have congregated here."

"You mean lawyers?"

"Of course." He waved at a luxurious building. "Lincoln's Inn and down the street, Gray's Inn—havens for the purveyors of the law." He gestured again, "And their homes."

"Yes. I've been here with Bernice. It's lovely." Brenda stared up at terraces where huge elegant houses of brown and gray brick with white trim were built in rows. To Brenda, they seemed to glower down on the outsider like haughty old dowagers.

Staring down Bond Street, Randolph noted, "Not many automobiles."

"Petrol shortage."

"The blasted U-boats."

Brenda nodded. "Yes. I've heard there's only a six-week supply of food in the country and less of petrol."

"And you Yanks expect to transport your army through that lot."

Brenda shuddered. "Yes. There's talk of giant convoys escorted by warships."

"Long overdue," he muttered. He changed the subject abruptly. "You're in love with Reginald?"

"Yes. I told you already," she said uneasily.

"You'll marry him?"

"Next month. I want you to come."

He sighed. "I'll try." For a long moment only the chug-chug of the engine and the sounds of tires on flagstone pavement could be heard. "He'll return to sea?"

Brenda felt an anxious tightening of her stomach. "That's what he wants. He's at Scapa Flow now meeting with Admiral Beatty. I took him to Victoria Station this morning."

"Beatty, that flamboyant ass. What's Reginald doing up there?"

"It's all very hush-hush, Randolph. Some secret project Reginald's working on."

"And he hopes to get a seagoing command out of it."

"I think they're tied together," she conceded grimly. "But he must get a medical okay."

They pulled to the curb suddenly and McHugh pulled the glass partition aside. "'Ere we are, mum," he said out of the side of his mouth.

Randolph opened the door and helped Brenda from the town car.

There were very few uniforms in Scott's. The opulent decor exuded luxury; red velvet drapes, watered silk wallpaper, gold filigree, plush chairs, fine linen and china, sparkling silver service. Most of the patrons were prosperous-looking middle-aged men who talked in loud voices and smoked expensive cigars. Many were accompanied by young women richly dressed in furs, silks, high heels—painted and perfumed. Their laughter was loud and shrill and could grate on one's nerves. Brenda saw anger gleam in Randolph's eyes whenever he glanced at the other patrons.

Brenda soon found that even the fashionable Scott's was suffering from shortages. In fact, lunch was a plain meal of roast beef, potatoes, and a sparse green salad. Fortunately, Graves was in abundant supply and after a few glasses, Brenda found the plain food much more palatable and Randolph's happy mood returned. After dessert of petits fours with a dash of anemic vanilla ice cream, Brenda sank back, toying with her drink, rolling her cognac around the bottom of a huge crystal snifter. Gothas were on her mind, but she avoided them. "You want to fly again," she said.

"Quite right. It's my life," he answered simply.

She remembered troubling statements she had heard from both Lloyd and Reginald. "You feel that Number Five Squadron needs you?"

He squirmed uncomfortably. "Academic, dear Brenda."

"What do you mean?"

He snorted with frustration and patted his right leg. "Got to convince the medics. Henniker told me this war's got to stagger along without me."

"But you don't believe him."

"Doctors make mistakes."

"And you'll prove him wrong." Tension raised her voice and she felt inexplicable anger swell.

"What's wrong, Brenda?"

She answered with a sardonic timbre edging her voice. "Oh, nothing much. Only, it seems, the men who mean the most to me—the men I love—are all so anxious to get themselves killed."

He looked up from his drink and caught her eyes with his. "You love me?"

"Of course."

"Like Hugh or Reginald?"

She laughed. "Both, dear Randolph. Both."

"Like Rodney and Nathan?"

She laughed again. "Most certainly, Randolph." She took his hand in hers, spoke boldly. "Randolph, you attract women. Kimberly Piper, for one, seems very close to you, and there have been others." She felt her cheeks redden as she thought of Nicole. "You have had many attractive women interested in you."

He sighed. "Please, Brenda. Don't try to build my confidence." He rubbed his chest. "I have a few problems, you know." He glanced at his watch. "Zero hour. Time to return to the dungeon or the ogre will lock me up."

They rose together and walked out of the restaurant hand in hand.

Two days later, Randolph was discharged from the hospital. Despite his mother's pleas, he refused to return to Fenwyck, preferring to live alone in his small apartment in Kensington. Bernice claimed Randolph could not tolerate his own father. Brenda smiled understanding. Bernice had been to Randolph's place and found Kimberly Piper there. "She was hanging over him like a mother hen. I actually think the snip was jealous of me." Bernice was in high spirits. Lloyd's orders had been changed and he was to remain in the training command for at least another month. She chuckled. "My dear husband's fit for an asylum."

For several days Brenda was unable to visit Randolph because both Rodney and Nathan had come down with fevers and coughs. Rebecca rushed from Fenwyck and Bridie, Nicole, and Brenda fussed over the youngsters while McHugh and old Touhy Brockman hung about outside the nursery door. Everyone was worried about "trench fever," which had been sweeping through the population since 1916. But the hearty little boys began to recover by the fourth day and by the fifth were cavorting in the garden. That afternoon the Gothas visited London.

Happy as only a mother can be after nursing her children through an illness to finally see them playing and laughing again, Brenda was seated with Bernice in a lawn chair when she was startled by the roar of artillery. At first there were desultory detonations, but soon the explosions blended into a solid roar like thunder and the ground shook. It was a fearful sound. "Bridie!" Brenda shouted. "Take the boys to the basement!"

Quickly the governess herded her charges into the house. "The basement, Brenda?" Bernice asked.

At first Brenda had the compulsion to hide, but the sounds were far to the south and there was an overwhelming urge to watch—to see this war that had finally found London. She remembered feeling the same emotion that night long ago when she had watched the Zeppelin fall burning from the sky near Fenwyck. She led Bernice upstairs to her room. The women stared out the french windows toward the Thames and the Liverpool railway station where smoke was rising.

"There they are!" Bernice shouted, pointing a finger.

Squinting and shading her eyes, Brenda stared high in the eggshell blue sky. First she saw scores of white and brown puffs and then something glinted. Propellers, wires, the sun off of painted surfaces. Soaring in the heavens she could see them. Great gray moths moving ever so slowly through a blooming garden of shell bursts. "One, two, three . . ." She counted them. Over a dozen.

The drumbeat sounds of the antiaircraft guns rose in ferocity. Then their clatter was punctuated with the booming, thudding sounds of bass drums as bombs went off. One after the other great explosions ripped through an area of the city that appeared to be among the docks and warehouses. Soon flames were visible and smoke drifted across the southern horizon. Brenda felt relief that not one bomb had fallen within a mile of fashionable Belgravia. Strangely, she felt guilt, too.

"Why aren't our chaps up there shooting them?" Bernice asked, a catch in her voice.

"They are," Brenda said, pointing at a score of climbing airplanes far below the bombers. "At least they're trying."

"They're a mile below the Jerries," Bernice said in disgust.

"Randolph told me the Gothas can fly very high—that

our airplanes would have a devilish time ever reaching them."

"Damn you!" Bernice shouted, waving her fist at the Gothas. "Damn you, you filthy butchers." There were tears of frustration on her cheeks.

Exactly one week after having lunch with Randolph at Scott's, the town car headed for Kensington. Randolph had no telephone so Brenda took her brother-in-law by surprise. As he opened the door, Brenda could see he was not in the same high spirits she had found the last time she had seen him. "What are you doing here?" he asked, ushering her in. "I didn't know you even knew where this place was."

"Bernice gave me the address." She seated herself on one of the room's two large couches.

"Something to drink?" he asked, standing in front of her.

"Bordeaux?"

He smiled and limped to a sideboard pushed against the wall and returned with two glasses of wine. He sat beside her and touched her glass with his. "A happy marriage for you and a quick recovery for me." She smiled at him over her glass and they both drank. He raised his glass again. "The Gothas."

"You're toasting them?"

He drank and smacked his lips. "Why not? Remember that lot of fat sods, stuffing themselves at Scott's?" Brenda nodded. "I'd bet my bit that every one of the lot has grown fat off this bloody war."

"You can't say that."

"Yes, I can say that. Profiteers. The city's full of them. They need a taste of it. Bully for the Gothas."

"A lot of innocent people were killed, Randolph."

"I don't give a stuff." He gesticulated to a corner desk where letters lay spread on the desktop. "See those letters. They're from my adjutant and the chaps at the squadron." Brenda nodded. "Two more of my chaps are dead—another wounded. He rubbed a clenched fist against his temple. "My adjutant told me the lads call May 'Bloody May'—over three hundred fifty of our planes shot down in that month alone, and that butcher Richthofen claims twenty-one for himself."

Brenda shared his agony. "But what can you do? Haven't you done enough?"

"No! And do you wonder why I'd like to skewer profiteers?"

She put her hand on his arm. "Of course, I understand. But you can't sit here in this little flat and let yourself be consumed by hate and bitterness." She tried to find his eyes, but he stared at the far wall mutely. Appalled by his attitude and eager to change the subject, her eyes were caught by what appeared to be a small gym in the far corner of the room: weights, pulleys, and dumbbells on a thick mat. "Your own gymnasium?"

"Yes," he said, welcoming the turn in conversation, rubbing his leg and side. "Henniker prescribed a therapy program for me."

Brenda studied a strange contraption in the corner next to the gymnasium. It consisted of a wicker chair bolted to a one-inch-thick sheet of plywood, a hinged bar of wood attached to a two-by-four nailed to the plywood in front of the chair, and what appeared to be a broom handle on a pivoting base attached to the plywood. "Controls," she said with disbelief. "You've actually built your own controls."

"Yes. My S.E.5," he said.

She felt frustration gnawing deep. "Lord, you're anxious to return."

He stabbed a finger at the letters. "There are honest men up there. And there's no hypocrisy at the front."

"It's more than that, Randolph. It isn't just the other men—'Bloody May,' is it?"

"What difference does it make? The war exists, doesn't it? Like a disease—a religion. It's here and I'm here and I'm part of it." And then bitterly, he said, "Or I *was* part of it."

Brenda sensed the same barriers she had known with Lloyd and Reginald when they talked of the war. She knew it was beyond her and she would never understand them. Instead of arguing, she pointed out simply, "You still limp."

"I know and that blasted Henniker says I'll never fly again." He drank. And then with a rising voice, he said, "But he's wrong." He turned to Brenda. "Do you understand—he's off his bloody wick." The brown of his eyes was heightened with moisture and there was a plaintive look on his face that reminded her of Rodney pleading for another dessert or the chance to play in a forbidden part of the house. Randolph was shattered.

Brenda was gripped by a confusion of emotions. *Why am I here?* she asked herself. *Why?* She loved Randolph—not romantically, but certainly she had a feeling of family for him. A responsibility like she felt for her boys and the agony and frustration he felt seemed to penetrate her mind, grip her soul until she cried out for some way to help him—to see him again the strong man with the confident smile on his face. Involuntarily, she took his hand. "You're attracted to Kimberly Piper," she said.

"You think I need a woman."

"Of course."

He shook his head. "That's ended for me. I have the body of a lizard."

The conversation seemed familiar to Brenda. She had covered the same ground with Reginald. "It would take more than a few scars to make you repulsive, Randolph."

"Don't patronize me, Brenda."

"I'm not patronizing you, Randolph," Brenda said in exasperation. And then emphatically, she said, "You are an attractive man."

He ran his hand over his neck and then unbuttoned his shirt and exposed his chest. The white flesh and hair were gone, replaced by a hardened crust of livid scars arranged in overlapping layers. "It's worse on my legs," he said. Suddenly, the curl of his lips was cold and enigmatic and the voice came from deep in his throat. "Would you go to bed with this, Brenda?" He gestured at his body with open fingers like a broom sweeping.

Oddly, Brenda was not shocked—not even surprised. The question seemed logical; appropriate. There was no hesitation. "Yes. I'd go to bed with you."

He brought her hand to his lips and kissed her palm. "I love you, Brenda. I have for years. I used to lie awake at night and envy my brother." And then ruefully, he said, "Sometimes, I cursed him."

Brenda could not believe her own words. "Take me to bed, Randolph. You've wanted me for years."

He kissed her wrist, her forearm, and then looked up. There was a peculiar gleam in his eyes. "Once I met a woman at the Empire," he said grimly. "A woman named Cynthia Boswell. Her husband had been an RFC major. He was killed. She tried to sanctify his memory by bedding every RFC major she met." He dropped her hand and moved his face very close to hers. "I love you. I won't make a prostitute of someone I love."

"Then you *will* sleep with a woman?"

He shrugged. "Perhaps. I'm a normal man. I have the same desires all men have." His smile was twisted. "Maybe, someone I don't know." His voice hardened. "It can't be love—can't be romance."

"Not that, Randolph. Not a whore."

He shook his head and looked away. She heard him mumble, "It would take money—a lot of money."

"Don't say that, Randolph."

She stood slowly. He rose and took both of her hands. She kissed him full on the mouth and he held her for a long moment. "Reginald is a very lucky man," he said softly. He led her to the door.

"I'll be back, Randolph."

He pulled the door open. His eyes glistened like polished onyx and his jaw worked. "No. Please. I love you too much."

"But I want to help . . ."

"You can help me by staying away."

She sighed. "You're sure?"

"Positive."

She turned and left.

XIII

As June wore on more rumors spread about the plight of the French army. Lloyd claimed there had been open rebellion in a dozen divisions, court-martials, and executions. "The lot'll be on us—mark me," he said. "The BEF's got to go on the offensive to save the Frogs' duffs. And Kerensky's finished —the Ivan army's bought it. This'll be a BEF show from now on."

It began one morning with the explosion of a million pounds of ammonal packed into nineteen mines under a ridge in Flanders called Messines. Brenda was at breakfast in the dining room when the mines went off. The house shook and the chandelier swayed. Then a long, awesome rumble rolled through the city. Everyone rushed outside and stared to the east in confusion. Slowly, Brenda realized that they had actually heard and felt the Western Front. That afternoon the papers reported the mines had wiped out the defenders and that British infantry had occupied the ridge. But as the days passed, there were the usual reports of German counterattacks and the same dreary stalemate returned.

Again, British casualties were heavy and on June 20, Lloyd received his orders to return to the Coldstreams. Brenda accompanied Bernice, Lloyd, Trevor, and Bonnie to Victoria Station. Walter, Rebecca, and Randolph arrived a few minutes before departure time. Bernice and Rebecca clung to the colonel's arms talking into his ears simultaneously while the remainder of the family stood in a close semicircle.

Nothing had changed since Brenda had been to the station

to see Reginald off: the smell of locomotives; uniforms everywhere; joyous greetings, tearful farewells; the cacophonous sounds of voices, locomotives, hissing safety valves, and rumbling steel-wheeled carts bouncing off the high-vaulted ceiling and the stone walls, reverberating, drowning out conversation. A trainman shouted through a megaphone and Bernice stepped aside, Bonnie wrapping her arms around Lloyd's waist while young Trevor stood to the side ramrod straight with only a slight tremble in his jaw to betray his emotions. Then he shook hands gravely with his father.

Rebecca returned to his arms, crying and talking fitfully into his ear. Walter grabbed his hand and pumped it vigorously. There were tears on his cheeks and for the first time in years, Brenda was aware of a streak of humanity in her father-in-law. Slightly bent, he appeared shorter and very old. Brenda felt no sympathy for him.

Randolph stepped up and grabbed Lloyd's shoulders. Lloyd in turn clasped his brother's arms. For a long moment the brothers stared into each other's eyes and Brenda watched the men speak. "Take care of yourself," Randolph said.

"I know how and I'll be with the best chaps in the world," Lloyd answered.

Randolph nodded understanding and said, "I know. I know."

Finally, the colonel turned to Brenda and embraced her. Kissing his cheek, it felt rough against her lips. "For God's sake, take care of yourself," she said in his ear through a tight throat.

"I'm a survivor, Brenda. We have a saying in the trenches —'Old soldiers never die' . . ."

"Well, just don't fade away, Lloyd."

He chuckled. "I don't intend to." And then seriously, he said, "Look out for Bernice."

"Of course. She's my best friend."

"Hate to miss the wedding," he said. "When will it be?"

"In a week, Lloyd," she said, stepping back. "Got a telegram from Reginald this morning. He said he'd be back by

Monday. We'll marry on Wednesday. He's already made the arrangements."

"Where?"

"All Saints Church. Fulham."

"Oh, yes. Outer London—magnificent old place."

"But it's to be small—informal. Only a few guests."

The shrill scream of an engine's whistle and the shouting trainman interrupted them. This time Brenda could distinguish his words. "'Board! 'Board. Dover train! 'Board! 'Board."

Lloyd turned toward his carriage, but Bernice flung her arms around him and began to sob uncontrollably, refusing to let her husband go. "I'll never see you again, my love. Never! Never!"

"Please, darling. Please," he implored softly, stroking her head and kissing her cheek. The whistle shrieked again and he looked up at Randolph and Walter helplessly. Gently, Randolph and Walter took Bernice's arms and pulled her away from her husband. The train began to move and Lloyd swung into his compartment with surprising agility and slammed the door. Brenda had the weird feeling that he was suddenly younger, stronger, and far more confident than she had seen him in months.

Slowly, the train gained speed and puffed its way out of the station. Silently, the family walked toward the entrance. Rebecca had a hard grip on Randolph's arm. "You've got to come home to Fenwyck. Now! Now! You're all I have."

"Straight away, Mother. Got to pick up my things at my digs and I'll be at Fenwyck this afternoon."

Rebecca was sobbing and Randolph had his arm around her shoulders as they left the station.

Nicole and Bernice selected the dress. It was a form-fitting Lanvin *robe de style* of periwinkle blue tulle with a sheer silk taffeta appliqué. Delicate and ingenuously attached in the unique Lanvin style, the appliqué appeared to float in thin air while at the neck and hip free-flowing ribbons and petals undulated and flowed with the movements of her body like wisps of vapor. Black high-heeled shoes, an unobtrusive hat, and white kid gloves completed Brenda's trousseau. Standing in front of the pier mirror in the afternoon light streaming through the french windows of her quarters, Brenda turned and pirouetted while Bernice and Nicole stood to one side and admired.

"*Fastueux*," Nicole muttered. "*Magnifique*." A solemn Bernice nodded her approval.

The All Saints Church was located in a magnificent green area in a sharp loop of Thames, just north of Putney Bridge. Built in the fourteenth century, in the British tradition, it contained a collection of monuments and brasses to long-dead warriors and churchmen. Most impressive were a pair of ornate tombstones cemented into the chancel floor commemorating the deeds of William Rumbold, standard-bearer to Charles I in the Civil War, and Thomas Carlos who fought gallantly at the side of Charles II at the Battle of Worcester. And, in addition, when Brenda first entered on her way to the bride's chamber, she saw at least a dozen tombs of bishops of London. Along the walls the funereal atmosphere was strengthened by brightly colored effigies of long-dead parishioners. With a macabre sense of reality, some were kneeling in prayer, others had their heads up and arms outflung, and still others were huddled with their wives and families. Brenda shuddered as the words, a wedding in a mausoleum, ran through her mind. But Reginald loved the place, had attended services here regularly with his father.

At the first notes of the Lohengrin wedding march, Brenda entered with Bernice from a side door instead of making a full sweep of the nave, de rigueur for a large, formal wedding. The enormous nearly empty stone basilica resounded with the sounds of the organ and Brenda smiled back at the small group of guests gathered in the front pews: Brigadier General Humphrey Covington and his wife Helen, Winston and Clementine Churchill, and Ramsey and Denise Kavanaugh.

There was a large group of uniformed men present. Clustered to one side was a group of Royal Navy officers and ratings. *Lancer* was well represented: Sublieutenant Ian Car-enter, Sublieutenant Trevor Grenfell, chief boatswain's mate Withers, chief steward Fuller, young boy first class Goodenough, and two new officers Brenda did not recognize. A lieutenant and a commander from Reginald's new planning section sat to one side.

Reginald's uncle, Dexter Hargreaves, his wife Jacqueline, and their teenage children, Orville and Nancy, sat in a front pew. Living in Coventry where Dexter owned and operated a foundry, they were the only family Reginald had in England.

On the other side of the nave, Barry Cooper was seated with a frumpish-looking young woman who looked as if she had just stepped out of an East End pub. In the same pew were Trevor, Bonnie, and Rebecca. Walter was not present. Rodney and Nathan, dressed in immaculate formal suits, were held in check by Bridie O'Conner and Nicole. Douglas O'Conner, Wendell McHugh, and Touhy Brockman all looked uncomfortable in high starched collars and tight-fitting coats. Randolph claimed he was "out of sorts with a bit of colic," and did not attend.

Hugh led Brenda to the altar, where a beaming Reginald waited. His best man, a grinning Stephen Pochhammer, stood at his side. The vicar was young, inexperienced, and stumbled a few times. But fortunately the ceremony was short, the kiss long and hard, and the guests delighted. The couple exited to Mendelssohn's triumphant recessional and the happy, excited murmurs of the guests.

Reginald had reserved the bridal suite at the Savoy. It was magnificent with a large living room, dining room, bedroom, dressing room, and bath. The furnishings were rich and luxurious, the bed done in satin sheets and crowned with a silk canopy. Seated on a sofa side by side, the couple sipped their second glass of Veuve Clicquot, 1898. In this time of shortages, it was unusual to find such fine champagne in such abundance. In fact, the entire reception in a private room in the hotel had been surprising. There had been caviar, prawns, lobster, and other exotic seafoods; an abundance of green salads and now-rare lettuce. There was no hint of a shortage of food or liquor.

Reginald must have spent a fortune, but he was euphoric; throughout the reception his arm had been around his bride constantly, toasting her with their guests. And she kissed him, held him, never wanted to be out of physical touch with him. It was unreal, like a fitful dream just before awakening, but it had happened, he was there—she could touch him, feel the muscle and sinew under his coat.

He sank back into the soft cushions and raised his Veuve Clicquot. "To us, darling," he said, saluting her glass with his.

"To us, Reginald."

They emptied their glasses. He stood slowly and pulled her to her feet. The kiss was hot and demanding. "You're mine—completely and forever."

"Yes, darling. I'm yours."

He led her to the bedroom.

The lovemaking had been long and ecstatic and Reginald had brought her to exquisite exhaustion with his usual skill. Sleepily, Brenda snuggled her head against his chest. She kissed the hair, the scars, and abruptly she was struck with thoughts of Bernice, home, alone, her bed empty. She shuddered.

"What is it, Brenda?"

"I just thought of Bernice—how miserable she must be. She told me Lloyd was scheduled to return to the lines today. She's alone and wretched while we . . ."

"Please, darling, put it out of your mind. This is our night."

She sighed. "Of course. We own this night." She was struck with a sudden thought. "You know, Reggie," she said, raising her head and looking up. "I belong here."

He laughed. "Of course you belong here, you're my wife."

"No. That's not what I meant. It's stronger than that." She groped for words. "It's as if I was destined to be with you from the beginning."

He smiled and kissed her forehead. "Of course, darling. You're home."

"Yes, Reggie. That's it. I'm home."
He pushed her onto her back.

Engine roaring, the lorry bumped and lurched over the pockmarked road much like a small ship in a rough sea. Lloyd could hear the twelve enlisted men crammed into the vehicle with their haversacks, bandoliers of ammunition, iron rations, field dressings, and rifles curse and complain about the "bloody pavé." Lloyd, too, was burdened; battle bowler (helmet), field glasses slung over one shoulder, and a small haversack and map case over the other, prismatic compass, pistol, torch, ammunition boxes hanging from his belt. Everyone was smoking and the lorry was filled with cigarette and pipe smoke. The men began to sing one of the many songs that came from the trenches. Lloyd had never heard of it before.

> When this bloody war is over,
> O, how happy I shall be!
> When I get my civvy clothes on,
> No more soldiering for me.
> No more church parades on Sunday,
> No more asking for a pass,
> I shall tell the bloody army
> To stick the passes up its arse.

Smiling, Lloyd shielded his torch and looked at his watch. "Twenty-two hundred hours," he said to himself. Then a sudden remembrance brought a soft laugh to his lips.

"All right there, Colonel?" a grizzled platoon sergeant seated next to him queried as the singing died away.

"Quite all right, Sergeant Abercrombie," Lloyd said. "I just missed a wedding."

"I don't give a fig for weddin's, sir, but receptions can be a bit of all right if a man can find 'is fill o' toddies and wenchin'."

Lloyd laughed again. Sergeant David Abercrombie was the only man in the lorry whom he knew. A professional and a survivor of the "old contemptibles," he was one of the handful of "old soldiers" left in the Coldstreams. Lloyd had met him at the railroad transport office in the railroad depot at Popereinghe where the sergeant was sent to meet Lloyd and a draft of eleven Tommies; four returning wounded, two furloughed soldiers, and five replacements. Lloyd and the sergeant had fought through the Somme battles of '16 and had survived the carnage of Thiepval Ridge together. Hundreds of faces had come and gone, but Abercrombie's square-jawed visage had been a constant. He was reliable and thoroughly professional. There was an old maxim in the BEF: "Officers lead, NCOs drive." Abercrombie knew how to drive.

"Colonel Wade'll be 'appy to see you," the sergeant said. "We bet our Dixie pots you were gone to blighty for the rest o' this bloody lot."

Lloyd chuckled. "Does the colonel still keep battalion headquarters in the forward line?"

"Quite right, sir. Only battalion CO in this bloody army who's up front with 'is chaps. Learned it from you, sir—'e's no dugout king back in the reserve line."

They both laughed and began to reminisce about battles, old comrades, home, and loved ones.

"Be at crucifix corners in a jiff, Colonel," Abercrombie said, breaking the stream of reminiscences.

"Crucifix corners, Sergeant Abercrombie?" Lloyd said.

"Right, Colonel. Where the roads from Nieppe and Eglise meet. We've got to dismount there, Colonel. 'Oof it the rest of the way, sir. The Jerries have the corner taped—can be a bit o' nasty with Lazy Elizas, Dust Bins and the like. Once and a while a Wipers Express."

Lloyd shuddered with thoughts of the great German howitzer that fired a one-ton sixteen-inch shell that could do unimaginable things to a man's body with its blast alone. The lorry jarred to a stop. "'Ere we are, sir," Abercrombie said, grinding his cigarette out under his boot. He picked up his kit and rifle and leapt to the ground.

"Fags and pipes out," Lloyd shouted, stubbing out his Woodbine. "No smoking until I give the word." He leapt to

e ground and the other men began to follow. Heavily bur-
ened, they were maddeningly slow in dismounting.

The sky was clear and moonlit. He cursed. Anxiously, he
oked to the north where he could see the blood red glow of
e front, pulsing like a live thing with the flash of battery
re. He could hear the dull thudding roar of gunfire that
hook the ground and came up through a man's legs to tingle
is genitals and turn his guts to water. Glowing balls of light
se like luminous balloons, silver and scarlet spheres that
xploded above the horizon and rained down green, red,
ellow, and white burning stars. Rockets were visible, arc-
ng high in the sky, unfolding silk parachutes and then drift-
ng slowly down, flaring brilliantly like hovering stars. They
ung in their glory for a minute or two and then faded away
be replaced immediately by another and another.

A column of troops rushed past—a compact body of
en, black in the night and hurrying. Limbers rattled
rough the intersection with the clink of trace chains and
ammering of hooves, caissons lurching from side to side,
rivers hunched over the horses' necks, gunners clinging for
eir lives, helmets glistening in the moonlight. A general
tores wagon loomed huge and black and blocked the road
r a moment. "'Urry it up, you sidey bastard," a frantically
aving sergeant with the red cap of the military police
houted. They were very close to the front; too close to be
tanding on an exposed crossroad.

Lloyd decided to clear the air with Abercrombie. "You're
command of these men, Sergeant Abercrombie. Take
em up."

"Yes, sir." Abercrombie turned to the men as the last
ommy dropped from the lorry. "Fall in! Stand easy!" he
houted impatiently. Then hastily as the last man fell into
ne, he shouted, "Attention! Slope arms! Form twos! Left
rn, quick march." With the sergeant leading and Lloyd at
is side, the draft moved quickly off the crossroads. Imme-
iately, the road narrowed and they passed a pair of smashed
mbers and a stores wagon that had been pushed to the side
f the road. Lloyd could smell them before he saw them—
e sickly sweet smell of death. Two dead gunners lay on

stretchers, abandoned next to a blasted eighteen-pounder. These were the first dead men for the replacements and they stared in wide-eyed curiosity and horror.

The road narrowed to a broken path and Abercrombie turned his head, shouting, "Single file! Five paces between men, march!" Hastily, the two columns vanished and a single file formed. They passed a battery of 5.9-inch howitzers firing from no more than a hundred yards to their left. Blinded by the flashes, the men grabbed their ears and groaned as concussions whipped their eardrums mercilessly. Clouds of smoke drifted down on them and the air was acrid with the smell of gunpowder, the pungent aroma bitter on Lloyd's tongue and in his throat. Mist and smoke lay chest high over the fields. Then two great flashes lit a wide sector of the northern horizon and the sky rumbled with a terrifying presence.

"Woolly bears!" Abercrombie screamed. "Down!" He flung himself to the ground. Everyone followed the sergeant.

Lloyd hurled himself down and dug his fingers into the soft, damp earth. A familiar sensation returned. Clinging to the soil, his being rushed back to a primeval time, an awakening of an animal instinct within him that sought refuge in the earth. The earth; his only shelter, his mother, sister, savior, sheltering him and protecting him on her bosom from the fury of the storm. He buried his face and tried to dig himself into her with his fingernails as the great shell droned closer. Descending, the pitch of their passage dropped and took on the rushing sounds of approaching locomotives. He stifled his terror by praying into the loose soil.

Two explosions ripped the earth, the road heaving under Lloyd, and he clamped his hands over his ears as a thunderclap followed by typhoonlike concussions rushed over him. The crossroads. The shells had landed at the crossroads. Slowly, he raised his head. He heard two rumbling thuds. The sounds of the German guns arriving long after the shells. There was a bellowing, howling cry of pain followed by another—powerful sounds like great horns of an orchestra played at their maximum and far too loud to be coming from the lungs of men.

"'Orses. 'Orses. The bastards 'ave 'it some 'orses," a Tommy cried. More screams—frightful sounds that penetrated a man's heart like a hot blade. Lloyd could see large black shapes staggering about, falling, rising, galloping, bellowing with all the pain of gutted creation. He grabbed his ears and tried to shake the agony out of his senses. But the cries drove through his hands, his eardrums, his soul. There was the clatter of hooves. A maddened horse, eyes wide and whites showing in large milky rings, galloped by only a few feet away, trailing its traces, spraying blood from its nostrils and tangling on its own intestines. It screamed in Lloyd's face as he rolled away and the colonel felt blood spray on his flesh.

"Shoot it, Sergeant!" Lloyd shouted, leaping to his feet.

Abercrombie already had his Enfield to his shoulders. Three shots rang out so fast, the reports sounded like a short burst from a Lewis gun. The great black shape tumbled to the ground, legs jerking, breath wheezing. Two more rounds and the beast lay still. A flurry of shots from the crossroads and the other cries died away.

"On your feet!" Lloyd shouted. The men rose. One man, a young replacement, still clung to the earth. At first Lloyd thought the boy was wounded, but then the smell told him differently. "Up, man," Lloyd commanded.

The boy patted his buttocks and looked at Lloyd pathetically. "I'm sorry, sir."

"It's all right, old man," Lloyd said. "Can happen to the best of us. Throw away your underpants and fall in."

"Yes, sir." The young man slunk to a shell hole off the path and dropped his trousers.

Lloyd turned to Abercrombie. "Carry on, Sergeant. This is your terrain—your show."

"Yes, sir," Abercrombie said. He turned to the men. "Keep you blinkin' 'eads down and follow me. Quick march! Chop! Chop!" Bending and taking quick, short steps, he led the column farther along the path that quickly sank into the ground and became a zigzagging communications trench. With the protective earth heaped up on both sides, Lloyd felt his muscles relax and his breath come easier. From a shallow part of the trench, he caught a glimpse of a battery of eighteen-pounder field guns camouflaged with branches and he knew they were within a thousand yards of the front lines. The branches would have seemed gay and cheerful if a battery had not been hidden under the leaves. More flashes on the horizon and a battery of German 77s salvo-fired into a sector just to the south. "Jerry's restless tonight, Colonel," Abercrombie said.

"Must know I'm back, Sergeant," Lloyd said. The sergeant laughed.

They passed the reserve trench and it appeared deserted except for a lone sentry posted at the intersection with the communications trench. As the draft trudged forward, the trench deepened and sandbags began to appear, reinforcing the parapet. They entered the support line and jogged to their right in traverse, passing a Stokes mortar crew firing flares and a Vickers gun in a sandbagged emplacement. They reentered the communications trench and began their last leg to the front line. The light from flares was continuous, casting eerie shadows and coloring the faces of the men in blue and yellow hues.

There was the dry rattle of a machine gun and suddenly the horizons flashed with renewed battery and counter-battery fire. The thunder of the guns swelled and everyone instinctively hunched farther over like men in a gale and steps were quickened. Above, the air teemed with swift movements—hissing bullets like angry snakes, shells of all calibers howling, piping, the heavies bellowing like rutting beasts. Both sides were firing long, searching for reserves, batteries, supply dumps. Lloyd breathed easier. The trench was deep and only a direct hit from artillery could kill a man here.

Suddenly, the communications trench ended and they entered the front line and Sergeant Abercrombie turned sharply to his left. They passed two machine gun posts and a half dozen sentries, peering out through their own wire into no-man's-land.

"This way, lads. Just a few more steps and you'll pinch the kaiser's arse," Abercrombie shouted over the noise.

"Not a good year for tourists," a corporal said, stumbling on a knot of telephone lines and falling heavily on the firing step. Everyone laughed.

Abercrombie gestured to a curtained dugout with a timber roof and sandbagged entrance. "'Eres battalion, Colonel 'Iggins."

"Thank you, Sergeant. Carry on."

"Yes, sir," the sergeant said, saluting casually and smiling. He led the draft down the trench, disappearing behind a traverse.

Pulling the curtain aside, Colonel Lloyd Higgins descended a dozen stairs to a large, smoke-filled dugout. Lit by hurricane lanterns hung from beams, the dugout was furnished with a dozen bunks and two battered trestle tables surrounded by chairs. Field telephones manned by two privates lined a bench against one wall and a wireless was on a stand in a corner with a sleepy operator with earphones clamped to his head slumped in front of it. Maps were tacked to the timbered walls and a stale blue haze of tobacco smoke hung in the air. Rifles were stacked in the corners and gas masks, haversacks, small arms, map cases, binoculars, and sacks filled with Mills bombs hung from nails driven into the great timbers. Perhaps a dozen men were in the room, four seated on a bunk eating bully-beef stew while another group played whist at one of the tables. A pair of clerks hunched over reports at the other. Lloyd recognized no one.

"Colonel Higgins. Colonel Lloyd Higgins," came from a corner. A tall, thin lieutenant colonel came to his feet and walked toward Lloyd. It was Tobin Wade. A rugged, athletic man from Blenheim and a graduate of Sandhurst, Wade was perhaps forty. However, he was at least twenty pounds lighter and appeared ten years older since Lloyd had seen him last. Curious eyes looked up at the newcomer.

Wade grabbed Lloyd's hand with a firm grip and then clasped his wrist with his other hand. "We've been expecting you, sir," he said warmly. "But why, sir? You had a good 'bivvy' back in blighty."

"Musketry, bayonet-fighting, and the lot is bugger all to do," Lloyd said. "Let the shirkers do it. And daresay, Tobin, you can't win this bloody war without me."

Laughing, Wade dropped the colonel's hand. "Daresay, you're quite right, Colonel. It's been a beastly muck without you, sir." He gestured to a corner bunk. "I've saved that one for you, sir, if you want it. Our most expensive accommodations—better than the Savoy." He smiled slyly. "As you can see, it has an unobstructed view of the ceiling."

Laughing, the pair walked to the corner and Lloyd dropped his kit on the bunk. Wade spoke in his ear in soft tones. "Introduce you to the staff in a moment, sir." He clasped Lloyd's shoulder in a big hand. His voice dropped to a whisper. "There aren't many like you, Lloyd," he said. "We need you."

"Thank you, Tobin." Lloyd looked around. "I belong here," he said. And then into Wade's ear, he said, "I'm home."

He's the last hope for justice and freedom in a lawless and battered land. He's Martin Stone—*the Last Ranger*—and he'll fight with everything he has to crush evil at its most diabolic roots.

☐ **THE LAST RANGER**
(C20-235, $2.95, U.S.A.) (C20-236, $3.95, Canada)

☐ **THE LAST RANGER #2: The Savage Stronghold**
(C20-237, $2.95, U.S.A.) (C20-238, $3.95, Canada)

☐ **THE LAST RANGER #3: The Madman's Mansion**
(C20-239, $3.50, U.S.A.) (C20-240, $4.50, Canada)

☐ **THE LAST RANGER #4: The Rabid Brigadier**
(C20-433, $3.50, U.S.A.) (C20-432, $4.50, Canada)

☐ **THE LAST RANGER #5: The War Weapons**
(C20-434, $2.95, U.S.A.) (C20-435, $3.95, Canada)

☐ **THE LAST RANGER #6: The Warlord's Revenge**
(C20-436, $2.95, U.S.A.) (C20-437, $3.95, Canada)

☐ **THE LAST RANGER #7: The Vile Village**
(C20-609, $2.95, U.S.A.) (C20-608, $3.95, Canada)

**Warner Books P.O. Box 690
New York, NY 10019**

POPULAR LIBRARY

Please send me the books I have checked. I enclose a check or money order (not cash), plus 95¢ per order and 95¢ per copy to cover postage and handling.* (Allow 4-6 weeks for delivery.)

___Please send me your free mail order catalog. (If ordering only the catalog, include a large self-addressed, stamped envelope.)

Name _____

Address _____

City _____ State _____ Zip _____

*New York and California residents add applicable sales tax.

325

WARNER TAKES YOU TO THE FRONT LINES.

☐ **SOME SURVIVED** by Manny Lawton
(H34-934, $3.95, USA) (H34-935, $4.95, Canada)
A World War II veteran and prisoner of war recounts the true story of the Bataan Death March—a harrowing journey through dust, agony and death at the hands of the Japanese.

☐ **BIRD** by S. L. A. Marshall
(H35-314, $3.95, USA) (H35-315, $4.95, Canada)
The brilliant account of the First Air Cavalry's heroic defense of the strategic Vietnam landing zone called "Bird."

☐ **FOX TWO** by Randy Cunningham
with Jeff Ethell
(H35-458, $3.95, USA) (H35-459, $4.95, Canada)
A fighter pilot's birds-eye view of air combat in Vietnam, written by a decorated Navy jet commander.

**Warner Books P.O. Box 690
New York, NY 10019**

Please send me the books I have checked. I enclose a check or money order (not cash), plus 95¢ per order and 95¢ per copy to cover postage and handling.* (Allow 4-6 weeks for delivery.)

___Please send me your free mail order catalog. (If ordering only the catalog, include a large self-addressed, stamped envelope.)

Name _____

Address _____

City _____ State _____ Zip _____

*New York and California residents add applicable sales tax.

389